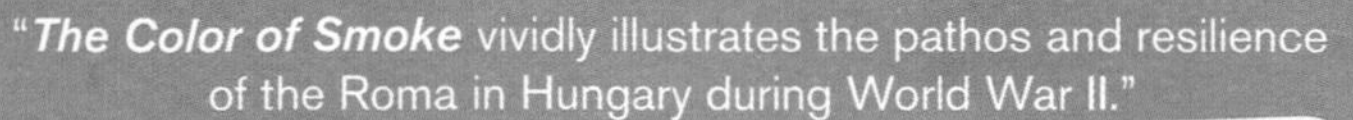

"*The Color of Smoke* vividly illustrates the pathos and resilience of the Roma in Hungary during World War II."

– Ronald Lee, LLD, Romani C… t

"Written by an insider, this long overdue and realistically harsh book opens a window into Romani life during World War II—when Romani people were being herded into labor camps, some destined for Auschwitz."

– Ian Hancock, Director of the Romani Archives and Documentation Center, University of Texas, and author of *Danger! Educated Gypsy*

NEW EUROPE BOOKS

The Color of Smoke

An Epic Novel of the Roma

The Color of Smoke

An Epic Novel of the Roma

Menyhért Lakatos

Translated from the Hungarian
by Ann Major

New Europe Books

Williamstown, Massachusetts.

Published by New Europe Books, 2015
www.NewEuropeBooks.com

Interior design by Knowledge Publishing Services, 2015

First published, in Hungarian, in 1975 by Magvető Könyvkiadó.

The Lantos Foundation for Human Rights & Justice contributed to the publication of this book, whose translation was funded partly by the Hungarian Books & Translations Office of the Petőfi Literary Museum, Budapest.

HUNGARIAN BOOKS AND TRANSLATIONS OFFICE

PIM

Ethel Brooks, Ian Hancock, and Ronald Lee provided much-appreciated advice and encouragement.

This book is a work of fiction and, except in the case of historical fact, any resemblance to actual persons, living or dead, is purely coincidental.

ISBN: 978-0-9850623-4-7

Cataloging-in-Publication data is available from the Library of Congress.

First English-language edition
10 9 8 7 6 5 4 3 2 1

The Color of Smoke

An Epic Novel of the Roma

I

One more barely noticeable sigh, then his eyes became fixed into an eternal gaze. Time froze on his stone-brown face, and Tsino Petro[1] became but a memory—a lasting memory of which Tsino Petro's daughter, Old Liza, or *Grandma,* to me, told stories during seemingly endless nights. Her stories conjured up old memories when time was measured not in months and days, but in the flowers that blossomed and the leaves that fell a hundred and one times under and over her father, as she used to say.

We were the people in whose blood life had lit a fire; neither the winds nor the winters—be they ever so fierce—could extinguish its flame. I knew Grandma as a small, wizened old woman, who sat only on the floor. When talking, she rested her chin on her knees, her stemless pipe clasped between her palms. She was a perfect custodian of bygone centuries. The world we lived in was alien to her; being confined to one place was, to her, servitude. Grandma was just too old to change her ways; the twelve years she had spent among us could not dislodge those earlier times. She felt cold even on the hottest of days. With her long outer skirt thrown upward over her shoulders, and squatting with her feet tucked under her, she smoked relentlessly. In the winter she often slept on the porch, since she couldn't bear the hut's stifling air.

[1] Little Peter

This embarrassed Papa, her son, but if he complained about it, she just waved her hand dismissively.

"Don't take any notice son, let those *Romungros*[2] talk all they like, they've gotten used to this *robiya*[3] but I get coughing fits indoors, and the children can't sleep properly on account of me."

We never once heard Grandma coughing outside.

Sometimes she would crouch in front of the wood-fired cob oven, which, in the kitchen adjoining the main room, was topped off by an old tin can that served as the chimney. There she would feed green acacia twigs through the large opening and stare as they frothed and whistled and curled up amid the flames. The wind often blew its thick, acrid smoke right at us, stinging our eyes.

Grandma could hardly wait for spring. She swept our tiny yard each evening, picking up anything that would burn, like rags and dried horse dung. For a while we thought she did so to keep it clean.

When Papa settled down by the oven and stared into the flames, especially when the air was thick with wood smoke, his face became transfigured as if in prayer.

This feeling wasn't the same for me; all the smoke did was to make my tears mingle with my dripping nose, which Grandma kept wiping with the hem of her skirt.

Later I got used to it and, after cavorting all day, I would rest in front of the oven. Grumpy-looking old folks also gathered round, their skin shiny and dark, like May beetles, and they chased away children who disturbed their thoughts or conversations. They were always telling stories, it seemed. They conjured up their memories from such a distant past that only they could make sense of them. Their deep roots were nourished from a world that to others was by now only history.

Like yellowed sheets of parchment, they bore witness to the history of centuries past. Time did not rush past them; the youthful stories

[2] Hungarian Romani man

[3] prison, slavery

of their fathers and grandfathers lived on in them, faithfully preserving the traditions of ages long gone.

Their mute, wrinkled mouths spoke of the past as their eyes stared at the small leaping flames, flames that perhaps reminded them of the stomping of their long-gone wild horses. Their eyes, akin to the moonlight, at times became swathed in a cloud or else lit up with happy, wonderful purity when they reached a cherished memory along the muddy, dusty highways of time. Scents of forests and mountains emanated from their thoughts, blood bubbled up in their veins, and they could hear the sound of the brisk rivulets on whose banks they had rested long ago.

We went from big water to big water. Grandma didn't use the word "sea," perhaps because she didn't even know it; all she said was *bari pani.*[4] I never did find out whether that passage she spoke of was from the Black Sea to the Adriatic or from the Black Sea to the Mediterranean.

Grandma burnished even the foggiest youthful memory to a luster. She reminisced about her ancestors as if they had been the personification of courage and brains. *Chache Roma,*[5] she used to say about them. To her the later generations of Gypsies were too yellow-bellied, too soft, to endure danger and hardship.

"The road was hazardous in winter but our carts never broke down; the horses we used were of the best. Sure, anyone lagging behind perished. Life in *Ungriko Them*[6] was like being in robiya, but that's where we found the best horses and light carts with iron axles.

"Had a hundred dragons guarded them," Grandma continued, "we still would have taken them. Tsino Petro was molded where fear was unknown. He didn't let anyone into his space, and any person doing so had to pay with his life. All could do as they pleased, but anyone trespassing on another was put on *kris.*[7] Tsino Petro got his nickname,

[4] big water

[5] true Roma

[6] Hungary

[7] (Romani) trial (elsewhere Romani law, Romani court)

Little Peter, for his build, but he certainly wasn't a scaredy-cat, why, he'd spit right into a snake's mouth.

"Once, long ago," she said as she always did when starting one of her stories, "in late fall, we were in Serbia when a group of red-capped Gypsies showed up at our camp. Real steeds were prancing about in front of their rickety carts, but there was no sign of women and children. They helped a gray-bearded old man off one of the carts. He looked awfully sick. They asked us politely to let him sit next to our fire. 'Sit down, old man,' our people said. 'Tell us, what brought you here?' These strangers all wore dappled kerchiefs under their caps. We wondered who they were, these people who spoke our language so well.

"Well, the old man then took off his cap and his kerchief, ever so slowly. First he bent one side of his face toward the fire, and then the other. In place of both his ears were gaping wounds, and his eyes were watery, like black grapes. The others then also removed their kerchiefs; not a single one of them had ears. They couldn't get a word out for all their sobbing. Our women burned mushroom veils and spread the ashes on their wounds. It took the newcomers quite a while to tell their story.

"'A bunch of soldiers surrounded us,' the old man began. 'What could we do? We couldn't try to run off, not with the women and kids still there. The soldiers then beat the men into a group and drove them into the woods. Their commander spoke, but we didn't understand. What he was saying was that they would cut off our ears, kill the women and children, and let us go.

"'That was when God took our good sense away.' The old man tried to swallow his tears, but his lips trembled with silent sobs nonetheless. 'We thought he was saying that if we let them cut our ears off, we could leave. That if we didn't, they'd kill the children and women. What else could we do? We endured it without letting out a peep. Bloodied and ashamed we headed back toward camp. The soldiers were still there, but we found ourselves wading knee-deep in the blood of our women, children, and horses.

"'They hadn't left a single creature alive, only us without ears for everyone to see what befalls those who dare trespass on their territory. When we saw the bodies, we attacked the soldiers with our bare hands, our bare teeth—they killed many of us, but in the end it was them who had to flee. These here are army horses, but what good are they to us? We'd rather be dead ourselves. They destroyed our *dulmuta,*[8] leaving us doomed to be the Gypsies' outcasts. No one will believe that it wasn't our own people who did this to us for some treachery.'

"Tsino Petro now spoke," Grandma said. "'Unhitch your horses,' he said, 'and sit closer to the fire. Tomorrow is another day.' By next morning the old man was dead from grief. They didn't give him a big funeral. They just broke his cart shaft in two, then peacefully smoothed down his grave. The rest of them stayed behind, orphaned, waiting for our father to invite them into his dulmuta.

"That same afternoon," she recounted, "he gave them the widows and marriageable girls and sent them on their way."

Tsino Petro's dulmuta changed its direction, gradually moving across Hungary and Romania up toward Russia, but the harsh weather, shaggy little horses, and wretched villages they found in Russia held out little hope. It was there that Grandma first got married, and as a souvenir, she brought back-for back they came—a little boy named Ivan. He was her first child.

Only around 1870, in southern Hungary, did they again cross paths with the earless folk, who having gone on to multiply greatly, now called themselves "Petro's People" after Tsino Petro, from whose dulmuta they had been reborn.

The old folks in our settlement would sometimes refer to the *phiripe*[9] in telling their tales, and for a long time I wasn't sure just what they were talking about. What I did know was that most Gypsies in Europe

[8] old tribe, as used metaphorically in this novel

[9] place traveled, as used metaphorically by the protagonist's community in this novel; more commonly occurs in Romani as "walking," "traveling"

had migrated north, from the Balkans; of those that had split into two branches in Bulgaria—one moving north along eastern Romania, the other across Serbia-both passed through Hungary.

The tribes had then split into smaller units, each of which called itself a dulmuta. Not that they had broken up, exactly; no, it was like in the army, where a company is made up of platoons and the platoons of squadrons. True, the term *dulmuta* had previously signified a tribe, whereas each of these small groups was but a fragment of the whole that once existed.

You might think all these small groups would nonetheless have still belonged to something larger, something that bound them, kept order, and provided guidance. Each dulmuta was, after all, bound by a set of tribal values. But did these values end where the dulmuta did? Was an overarching "tribal law"—whose details were indeed lost on so many people, if they recognized them at all—no longer binding on each separate group? In fact it was! Everyone was obliged to uphold every unwritten law that regulated their lives regardless of which dulmuta they happened to belong to. This is shown, among other things, by the fact that no dulmuta could use the place another dulmuta traveled in—namely, its phiripe.

On several occasions I quizzed Papa about matters concerning the phiripe even though he was reluctant to let me in on Gypsy secrets I couldn't figure out on my own. All too often his only answer was that I'd find out once I got older. His silence only made me more curious.

As for Grandma, she pretended not to understand me to begin with, and it was obvious that not even she wanted to talk about the phiripe. It seemed that this word, too, was secret. And so I kept pestering Papa about it, and he bawled me out more than once for being nosy. But, in the end, he tired of resisting sooner than I did of persisting.

The dulmutas, he at last explained, had divvied up among themselves the phiripes in the countries they passed through. But just how they went about it, no one could say exactly. Not by conquering those lands, that much was certain. No, insisted Papa, they never had territorial disputes. No matter how tiny a dulmuta was—even if nothing more than a family on a single horse-drawn cart-not even the oldest folks among us could recall a case in which a bigger, mightier dulmuta had stolen the territory of a smaller, weaker one. But as the generations came and went, and as the past gave way to the present day, the desire for material wealth—and for the possession of territory that held its promise-stirred ever more in Gypsies, too.

"The phiripe had to be respected by all," Papa said, meaning that if some Gypsies violated it, other dulmutas came swiftly together to take collective action against them.The phiripes were, in short, "hunting grounds" in both the good and bad sense of the term—ensuring that the Gypsies who passed through them could continue their nomadic ways.

All this was a bit beyond me. Wandering like nomads still required something to get by on, did it not? As for tools and other possessions, well, once they wore out, they had to be replaced. If wandering was the main aim in life, then the phiripes must indeed simply have been hunting grounds. But if wandering wasn't so much a matter of instinct, but more a means of acquiring goods illicitly, then why hadn't the dulmutas sought to take away one anothers' territories?

Papa only cast me an impatient stare when I pressed him with such questions, and he didn't say another word. At times like that, I got back at him by not taking his horses to pasture for days.

"Why don't you ask Grandma instead?" he said, fuming. "I will tell you one thing, though, and get it through your head: if you go prattling on a lot, the Gypsies will cut out your tongue." Maybe this is what helped me figure out the meaning of words that seemed to be a secret. I didn't say anything more about the phiripe.

Cutting out tongues had a lot to do with the real essence of that word, I suspected. In giving me that warning, Papa hadn't simply brushed me off; behind his silence was genuine worry. Although it had been a long time since settled Gypsies had meted out such cruel and wild punishments, it wasn't easy for Papa to get beyond his conditioned responses to these ancient traditions, for he himself had left the world of the dulmutas only at the age of twenty.

Afterward Papa wavered for a long time until he had his own children and his new ways were set in stone. Then he finally gave up being nomadic once and for all.

As for myself, I knew almost nothing of that bygone world; only through the old folks' stories could I conjure it up in my imagination. But what I'd heard was enough for me to decide that Grandma was right, and I practically held it as a grudge against Papa for having given up his free life for the wretched servitude of life in a hut. As if I'd been cheated and robbed, I grieved over my lot. Yes, this was my future, and I couldn't do a thing about it.

I felt the effects each and every morning, too, when Mama roused me from sleep saying I had to go to school. Sometimes things worked themselves out, though, in a way—Papa was locked up in jail for a bit in lieu of the fine that would otherwise have been imposed on us for me going neither to school nor to Levente Youth[10] meetings.

But Papa wasn't annoyed about that. No, all in all, he was happier to undertake a bit of jail time than I was to undertake studying. Mama was the real challenge; she knew how to use a whip. Sometimes she'd shout at me, "Son, you're Papa's kind, a kind without a country or a home! No wonder you were born on the road!"

Mama never let me forget that fact, as if it, too, had been my fault. A kid spends nine months taking shape inside his mom, and then doesn't wait until she gets home from the village next door. So I was born; Mama took me home in her skirt.

That's how Papa was born, too, Grandma told me. She had given birth sixteen times and didn't need a midwife once. On one occasion Grandma consoled me though. "If those people, the Zhidos, come, son, we'll head off with them on the road and leave this misery behind."

---

[10] Levente Associations were paramilitary youth organizations in Hungary during the interwar period and World War II. From 1939 on, the time period in which this novel is set, all males aged 12–21 were required to take part.

She dreamt of little else but sitting one more time on a horse-drawn cart.

"Grandma, why do people get their tongues cut out?" I asked in an attempt to take advantage of our intimate conversation.

"They won't cut yours out, son," she said, stroking my hair. "They'll love you, they will, on account of you knowing how to read and write. When you grow up, everyone will listen to you. Our kind like smart people."

"Grandma, what is a phiripe?

"Why, that's a dulmuta's territory, where the dulmuta filches gold, horses, and clothing."

"Do your people have a territory like that?"

"We do, but we don't go that way anymore."

"Why don't we go there to live?"

"Those whose territory it is never live there."

"And if others take it over?" I asked.

"Why would they do that? We never went on others' territories, either. Just let them try; they'd go before a *kris* and soon find out what Gypsy law is really about."

She tried reassuring me. I knew the Gypsies' respect for the law all too well for her words to be convincing.

"Why did your people steal other people's horses and gold when it wasn't yours? Weren't you afraid of the gendarmes coming after you?"

"We did our best not to meet up with gendarmes. If there were only a few of them, they kept their distance; if more, they took everything we had, set our carts alight, and sent us scattering every which way. Then we had no choice but to get new stuff to replace what we'd lost."

"I don't like horses," I admitted.

"Now where does that leave you?" she said, giving me a bemused stare. "You want to get around on foot? That's what beggars do. You've got to love a horse more than a wife, I tell you, because a wife can fool you and cheat on you, but a good horse will never leave you in the lurch.

"Take your father: If he didn't have horses, he might as well go to work making adobe bricks. Our kind feels good only with reins in their hands. And look at you, not even capable of taking the horses to pasture! Remember what old Fardi once said? If he and his clan come this way, he'll teach you to cast doorbells. Not a bad trade. You can travel the world, and wherever you go, you'll have a certificate in hand showing your occupation. Otherwise you'll be hounded at every step you take. It's not like it used to be. There was a time when we wouldn't meet up with gendarmes for years, and now you see them everywhere you turn."

"Grandma, did your dad know how to make doorbells, too?"

"They cast church bells, son, and got a certificate from the priests to show for it. Even the commissar bowed before them over that. And they never got into trouble, either; theirs was known as a quiet, peaceful dulmuta. Tsino Petro knew how to do things right, he did. Not like that character Ball, who had no respect for anyone. Your father left us precisely because he didn't get on with him. Ball was always getting folks into trouble, and he wasn't scared of anyone or anything. In the middle of the day he robbed the horses right off gentlemen's carriages, since they alone went about with real horses. We were always on the run. He'd pull a knife on anyone who said a word to him.

"He was a strong one, but he wasn't one for justice. He hated his younger brother, your father, because your father wasn't scared of him. Lots of times they got into fights, but your father, he beat Ball to the ground like a rotten little dog. Lots of times he showed him mercy, because Ball begged like a coward for his life even though he, if he could have done it, would have killed your father. Well, your father then got hitched and stayed right there while we moved on. We never did stop crying over your father, and when Ball was finally shot to death, we went back to get him. You weren't born yet, just your older brother and sister, but your father wasn't about to leave his kids behind."

"Grandma, is it true you have kids all over the place?"

For a while she just kept nodding, then she said with a sigh: "That, I do—in Serbia and Romania, too. And I'll never, ever see them again. And who knows when Fardi will show up around here with news about my children. We were scattered all over the world when Tsino Petro's eyes closed that one last time."

"You know, I'll be fifteen in four years. I'll tell Papa to give me the little foals. By then they too will grow up, and I'll take you to Serbia. I want to meet our kin there, too."

When I let Papa in on my plan, he just smiled.

"Okay," he said, "but then *you'll* have to look after the foals from now on."

Papa gave me one to tend to.

For the first time in my life I groomed a horse. True, I did so reluctantly at first, but once that foal licked my face so gently with its tender little muzzle, we began to hit it off splendidly. By the evening he was following me about like a dog. We shared my bean soup, but he wasn't interested in meat. I wondered what would make him grow quickly.

That night I waited for everyone to go to sleep. Grandma always perched sitting down like an owl; you never knew whether she was asleep or awake, but I wasn't scared of her, no; she always wanted the same thing I did.

"Are you asleep?" I quietly slid to her side.

"No. What's wrong? Are you sick?"

"No, I'm not. Do you have any cord?" She had no idea what was going on, but wordlessly dredged up some hemp cord from behind her head.

"I'm going to get some alfalfa for my foal."

Without waiting for an answer, I snuck out of the hut. During the day I had cased some green alfalfa in the fields, figuring it would make excellent fodder. It was a couple of hours past midnight; it was a moonlit summer evening, the soil of the cart track was still lukewarm, yet my half-clad body was covered with goosebumps. I must have been scared.

I fastened the cord, and began to divide the now wilted, dewy alfalfa into portions. It didn't rustle, its leaves didn't crumple; I picked the rows as if they belonged to us. I no longer thought about being scared, but nor had I considered whether I was physically strong enough for this endeavor.

I couldn't even lift the first portion. That is the curse of the thief's profession: you can't take as much as you would like, even if there is plenty. The second time around I couldn't manage to take out any of it. I crept under the bundle and, with the blood vessels in my neck all but ready to burst, I stumbled along under its weight. Halfway back the cord broke. By then it was all I could do to trudge along, but I got it home. Grandma was sitting in front of the hut, silently threatening me with her clenched fist.

"Your father will kill you if he finds out."

"*If* he finds out," I said, panting triumphantly. "My foals will get rid of it all by morning."

However, it seemed the foals were not used to being fed so early. They nibbled at the alfalfa half-heartedly; perhaps I myself could have eaten more of it had I not fallen asleep. I don't know how I ended up in Grandma's lair, but the sun was already shining brightly, when I was woken by the flies and Papa's thunderous cursing.

"Where have you been during the night, boy?" He chewed me out then and there, though he rarely did so. "Do you realize the warden was here? He followed a trail of alfalfa all the way here and then alerted the gendarmes."

At first, I just blinked blankly, but then I vanished from home without even washing myself.

I spent all morning bathing in the river. However, by afternoon I could no longer resist my curiosity or the rumblings of my stomach. I was bored with climbing trees; the musty old mulberries gave me awful bellyaches; the twigs tore at my skin; the berry juice had made me as sticky as flypaper. It would be good to know if Mama was at home or whether she had left before the warden arrived. She was not one to spare the rod. After a handful of green plums even that didn't worry me.

Carefully I slunk home, sat down under the window, and listened. Papa was in the hut, crooning to my baby sister, trying to get her to sleep. A couple of steps, and next I was on the porch, searching for some food. I tried to avoid making any noise that would wake the baby from her half-sleep, but when I finally found my little dish in the heap of unwashed ones, all the other dishes fell onto the porch floor as I pulled mine out. Papa didn't say a word but kept on crooning. After gulping down the last of my potato soup, I called out, "Got any tobacco?" I followed this with a belch while kicking aside the dirty dishes scattered over the floor.

"Don't shout," he said in a hushed tone.

"Give me some tobacco," I whispered.

He tossed over the pig-bladder tobacco pouch. I then tore a bit of paper off the salt packet, rolled a cigarette and, lying down on Grandma's stuff, began blowing smoke rings into the air contentedly.

I almost fell asleep to the sound of Papa's lullaby, but my baby sister preceded me. Papa came outside.

"Listen, you," he said, nudging me with his foot. "You've got to go to the gendarmerie—someone was here with a summons."

I got in such a fright that I couldn't even take the burning cigarette out of my mouth. I looked around, terrified, and felt like throwing up the soup.

"You'd better be going, son, or else it will get worse." He saw what was going on inside me.

Rarely did I give in to persuasion, but this time I couldn't resist his concern. Anxiously, I resigned myself to fate.

"Take off those grubby pants and put on the new ones." He brought out a pair of new trousers and a smart-looking brown vest. Mama had meant for me to wear this outfit in school. Cold shivers ran down me as I splashed my face and the rest of my body with water. Papa rarely bothered about us bathing, but now he stood there ready to dry me off, using my grubby old pants as a towel. He even tended to my hair, patting it down and parting it like Gypsy musicians do.

"Go ahead and tell them you took the alfalfa for the youngest foal," said Papa. Without so much as looking back, I just gave my new trousers a pat and headed off. The other Gypsies were looking at me as I walked on, head raised, watching my every step so as not to stir up any dust.

On entering the village hall I felt my heart leap into my mouth. The thought of escaping kept crossing my mind. I stopped for a moment by the door of the local gendarmerie office, but didn't have the guts to turn back.

I knocked. Staff sergeant Bacsa was pacing back and forth across the cold room with thundering steps.

"Good morning, sir," I said timidly.

Swords, keys, and truncheons hung on the walls. Goosebumps came over me.

"Good morning, sir," I repeated even more softly. Bacsa turned around.

"Hello, son, who are you looking for?" he asked with a paternal smile. I pulled my neck between my shoulders; I didn't really know who I was looking for.

"Well, then, tell me who you are."

I murmured my name, which didn't seem to mean anything to him. He only smiled at me even more encouragingly.

"Don't be silly. Tell me who sent you." He smoothed my unruly locks of hair.

"I'm here on account of . . . the alfalfa," I mumbled through my tears.

The smile disappeared from his face as he straightened up like a ramrod.

"Oh, you're Boncza's son!"

I nodded. No matter whose son I was now, I couldn't avoid what was coming. He chose the very truncheon I thought he would—the one with the spiked end.

"Hold out your hand!"

The first blow hurt a whole lot; after the second and third I no longer felt a thing, though he was pounding away at my bones. The blood flowing between my fingers splattered onto the floor in drips and drops. After each blow, I withdrew my hand with a groan, but stretched it back again.

"Hold out the other one!" he yelled.

I wasn't counting the blows, and it seemed he wasn't either. I sweated in my effort to hold back the potato soup I had guzzled down.

"Let's not meet again!" Out of breath, he motioned toward the door, but not before he gave me another blow through my new vest, whose shredded pieces had to be cleaned out of my flesh with a vinegar-soaked cloth. I then trudged on home like a sleepwalker, my outstretched hands dripping blood. I no longer recall my thoughts, only that I gave up the idea of raising that foal.

Luckily Grandma fainted when she saw my fingers all cut and bruised, or else she would have surely insisted on smearing them with cobwebs or warm horseshit, as she did with all wounds to stop the bleeding.

Mama sure had a fit. Her yelling was enough to draw every last Gypsy who lived in our settlement over to our hut. She called Papa all kinds of names except his own, and slapped my little sister for upsetting the pot in which she was mixing water and vinegar. As for Grandma, on coming to she took to blowing my fingertips and kissing them, as if that would ease the pain. I couldn't sleep a wink all night. I soaked both hands in the pots next to me, but all the while devils kept dancing before my eyes. By morning my wounds were worse. I had to see the doctor.

The doctor began by searching my clothes and hair for lice. Only then did he ask what was the matter. I had to sing Gypsy melodies as he daubed my fingertips with some sort of yellow, stinging ointment.

I wasn't allowed to go out for a few days, so my friends came by to visit. But Grandma shooed them away with a stick.

"Get away from here! Leave the poor sick child alone. I don't want you to get him into trouble again!" As if they were responsible. Well, someone always has to be punished for a wrong even if he isn't guilty. It is to Grandma's credit that she also included herself; she was tormented by remorse for having given me the cord I'd used to tie the bundles of alfalfa.

All this did not bode well for that trip to Serbia I'd imagined taking with Grandma. Still, even though Papa sold the foals after a few weeks, I never did give up the idea of getting Grandma together with her long lost son.

As for my new trousers, I was like someone whose appetite comes with eating. Wherever I now went, I dressed my best, and somehow or other my prestige had grown in the family. Mama and I changed places at the table; I now sat on the chair next to Papa. Until then, whenever we went somewhere I had almost invariably cowered in the middle of our horse-drawn cart to hide my tattered trousers that were worn away practically down to their seams, their more prominent rips stitched together by wire or string. No longer. Indeed, now I could walk briskly along, only one line of stitches visible on my vest, where the billy club had torn it.

Each market day our horse-drawn cart stood in the nook next to the market, opposite the post office.

"I'm going to the post office," I told Papa one such day.

"What for?"

"I want to find out how to send a letter to Serbia." He grumbled, but I didn't let that stop me from going in.

A thin, fiftyish woman sat behind the closed window at the counter. She stared at me but said nothing. I waited patiently. There was no line; I was on my own. Ten minutes passed before she finally slid open the window.

"What are you waiting for?" Judging by her unfriendly tone, my waiting had made her more nervous than me.

"I'd like to send a letter to Serbia."

"Where's the letter?" Her voice sounded like a gendarme's.

"It hasn't been written yet."

"Then have it written and bring along a pengő.[11]" She slammed the window shut.

---

[11] The pengő (*ő* as the *ea* in "learn") was Hungary's main unit of currency from 1927 to 1946. It was subdivided into 100 fillérs.

"Jesus Christ, a pengő?" I said aloud. My despair didn't bother the woman, who kept working. I went outside, back to our cart.

Papa noticed that something was worrying me. "What's the matter?"

"I need a pengő."

"One whole pengő?" I knew I couldn't count on him, that I might as well walk to Serbia; to him, money was a rare commodity.

I set out to the market, hoping I might find a pengő. It wasn't impossible: I'd once found some small change by egg sellers' stalls. Why not a whole pengő?

I looked so hard that my eyes almost popped out, but no luck.

The other Gypsy kids were hanging around a pile of melons. They waved me over to join them, but I didn't give a damn. I had other things on my mind.

A Gypsy man selling whetstones to sharpen knives and other tools was loudly praising his wares through crooked lips. There were no takers, but a bored, nosy throng—mostly non-Gypsy Hungarian peasants—was gathering around his stall all the same.

"A gift at fifty fillérs! Anyone using these here whetstones will live ten years longer! Here's your chance, Hungarian peasants!" Practically foaming at the mouth as he hollered away, he kept twanging at the blade of a rusty old scythe.

"Just watch this, *khandine*[12] commoners, you've never seen anything like it!"

Bober, one of my friends, was standing beside him. He watched open-mouthed as the man now proceeded to shave his hairy hand with the scythe.

Surely Papa would want one of those whetstones, but how could I get my hands on one? If I called out to Bober, the man would understand that I wanted him to steal it.

"Watch me, you khandel commoners!"

---

[12] stinking

I couldn't bear to watch as he slid that rusty scythe across his hand. I waved to Bober for quite a while until he spotted me in the crowd. He grinned, showing that once again he was standing closer to the show than me. I was worried the guy would notice me waving. Bober just kept shrugging his shoulders. He didn't understand what I wanted.

"*Char o bar!*",[13] I called out to him in Romani, figuring the vendor wouldn't understand what I really meant by "lick." Bober picked up a stone and examined it from all sides until the man gave him a shove, for Bober was obscuring his stunt. Bober pushed his way back, timidly licked the stone, and then put it back.

"Don't handle the merchandise, kid, or I'll cut your nose off." He pushed Bober away again.

I was so angry I thought I'd be sick. So much for the fifty fillérs I practically felt in my pocket. I left.

A few steps away, vendors were offering clay birds with colored feathers, paper horns, and all sorts of other gaudy toys.

"Ladies, girls, kids, come and buy!" sang one man in a hoarse voice.

I pressed through the crowd right up to the stall and stopped next to a short, pudgy lady who was dragging a pale little girl by the hand so she could choose a toy for herself. The sight of the yellow change purse peeking out of the lady's apron pocket made me feel hot and cold by turns. I no longer saw anything around me, only that purse. I waited a moment longer as the crowd pressed me even closer to the stall, and all at once the purse was in my vest. A lanky peasant lad and a loudly laughing girl with long braids pushed themselves between us.

Grabbing the collar of that peasant lad, the pudgy lady screamed for help.

"They stole my money, help! Gendarmerie, help! This kid was next to me—this is the thief!"

---

[13] Lick the stone.

The young man tried to free himself, but couldn't escape her grip. I was still standing in the crowd, which had closed in around the screaming woman and the vendor.

"Beat the thief!" came the calls from the crowd, but only from a distance, since no one dared approach him.

"Let go, my good woman," said Mister Tony, stepping up beside her. "This lad just happened to be next to you a moment before you took hold of him. Before that a young woman with a brown shawl was standing there."

Well, so much for an eyewitness. Too bad he didn't point at any particular woman: the pudgy lady would have clawed her eyes out. The pale girl was trembling beside her mother, her matted blond hair wet with tears. Her mother cried, so she too cried.

"Oh my God, I wanted to take my daughter to the doctor, I've already used up all I had. What am I to do? It was my last eight pengős; they've killed my baby!"

The little girl looked around in despair, She had no idea what was going on.

With my two thumbs I pulled at the elastic waistband of my pants, the big yellow change purse ran down my thighs like a rat, falling soundlessly on my foot. I waited for a few moments before ducking under the legs of an old man.

"There's the purse! There's the purse!" I shrieked.

The staring crowd parted in surprise as I ran with mock delight toward the woman.

"Lady, is that your purse?"

The woman didn't run; she flew toward me.

"It is, God bless you!" She smiled and cried, and could hardly count the money through her tears.

She hugged me and kissed my cheek.

The young man she had been holding by the neck shrugged indignantly. "Next time you'd better watch what you're doing!" he said.

The woman ignored him and only spoke to me.

"Aren't you clever! God bless you, my child!"

She took out a pengő. "This is for you."

I looked at the shiny coin in the woman's hand; her wailing still rang in my ears.

"Come on, take it!" she offered again.

"I don't want it," I said firmly.

The skinny little girl edged closer to me, joy bringing a bit of color to her face. She took my hand, her eyes glistening. I turned and left. *This won't work,* I thought.

It was a good market day. Mama had bought no less than thirty pounds of feathers and Papa carried two huge melons in his arms.

"Come, young man, give me a hand!" he shouted.

Any other day I would have turned cartwheels for joy, but now I barely shuffled along. I had already sensed that morning that it wouldn't be a good day for me. I'd awoken from a dream in which I'd seen a stark naked girl—Iza Verge was her name—and she'd already had her way with all the older Gypsy boys. Every morning I told Grandma my dreams, but this time I kept it from her.

Papa found my listlessness suspicious, but couldn't get the reason out of me.

"Listen woman, let's give the kid a pengő! He badly needs it!"

"Sure, when money grow on trees."

Money from Mama! It would have been easier to convince her to pull out a healthy tooth.

"Here's twenty fillérs," she said, handing the coin—one-fifth of a pengő—to Papa. "Go have yourself a shot."

Papa put the money in his pocket.

"We'll stop by the tavern."

He handed me the drive bar. The two young bay horses galloped head down. Papa just smiled at me.

"These horses are running well, aren't they?" he said. I nodded. "We won't sell them until late fall, son. For now, though, we'll get the old mare looking like her old self this afternoon and we'll fit up the two broken—winded horses at dawn—the ones that are heaving all the time—and then we'll get rid of all three tomorrow in Ladány. They have good markets there. You'll do the selling; folks will think you're a peasant boy. If we strike a good bargain, a pair of good leather boots will be your fee in the fall."

Yes, I thought, *if it were up to you. But the captain is sitting here in the middle of the cart.* The old man must have guessed my thoughts, or maybe I'd been thinking out loud, because he now looked back at Mama.

"Just go ahead and try it," she said to Papa, "and I'll cut your head open with the whip handle. When you get your inheritance from your own father, *then* you can order me around."

Papa's father had nine children-three sons and six daughters-and sixty-two grandchildren. Twelve of those kids and grandkids lived off him. His oldest son had been in prison for six years already; the other one was a soldier. Hardly any inheritance could have been expected, anyway.

But the point is, what Papa said about selling those horses wouldn't come to a thing; in the end it was Mama who made the decisions.

"Stop here!" said Papa. "Pull off the road. We're going in to Mr. Ginsler to get you a pair of pants."

Papa jumped off the cart. I didn't budge. Was it worth getting off? If Mama said there was no money for pants, this would only end up causing an argument.

"Well, come on! What are you brooding over?"

I wanted to hang up the reins, but Mama reached out for them.

"I'll take those, and you'd better choose a good pair, not too small."

Her consent surprised me.

"Good afternoon, Mr. Boncza," the old Jew greeted Papa. "What can I do for you?" he asked politely.

"Give the boy a good pair of pants, Mr. Ginsler."

Mr. Ginsler placed a dozen cotton pants in front of us, and then some made from a better fabric.

"Try these on!"

Papa picked a gray pair. I never had felt good in pants. These looked good, but I always preferred running around naked. He chose a gray one.

"Keep them on."

He paid for them and we drove to the bar.

"Aren't you coming in, woman?"

"No, and you'd better not stay too long. The kids at home are hungry!"

The bar was full of scrounging Gypsies. They greeted Papa deferentially, hoping to sponge a drink from him. He returned their greeting and went straight to the john, but only as a ploy. He returned within minutes and slipped the twenty-fillér coin Mama had given him earlier into my pocket.

"It's too hot for cheap booze. Let's go."

I was more pleased with the money than the pants. If we were to strike a good bargain in Ladány tomorrow, I thought, I might be able to wheedle another fifty from Papa and then I wouldn't need much more. My sisters were green with envy about my pants. They only got melons.

All afternoon the money burned my pocket. I was tempted to play heads or tails with the other kids, but I was afraid of losing. I'd already thought about how to make a coin that would never lose. It wouldn't be hard; all I had to do was file down two coins to half their thickness and glue them together so both sides had heads.

But I didn't have a coin like that, not yet. Maybe if I were to play, I'd win anyway. It was all a matter of luck. I knew all the ins and outs of the game, but the others also knew a trick or two. It was hard to be more clever than them.

I fingered the money in my pocket. Luckily they didn't know how much I had in there, for they would have pestered me like crazy. Szabó, a kid who was constantly teasing me, now went at it about my pants.

"*Oooh* . . . Looks like *you* . . . *who?* . . . *Yoo-hoo* . . . *gotchyerself* . . . *new* . . . *oooh* . . . *paaants* . . . *my* . . . *frrriend!*"

"Yep, *new . . . oooh . . . paaants,*" I mimicked him. "It's because I don't piss in my pants; I go outside even at night, not like you."

"Good for you, but I got money, hehehe . . ." He showed me a handful of small coins.

He did that out of pure anger.

I too was angry at myself for being unable to risk losing a couple of coins. I could have won all his money with one toss. I just wished that pissy Szabó didn't show off. Any money he got his hands on, he sure as hell wouldn't have given to his mother, though she could have used it. Ever since his father became deaf they hardly ever saw the color of money. The old man had been a good violinist. Now they made their living from picking forest grass to make whitewash brushes that could be sold at market, and from teaching violin to a few Gypsy kids.

Papa told me time and again that if I didn't like horses, I should at least learn to play music. I had no intention of doing so, figuring I knew as much as I needed to. Instead I'd learn to cast bells as soon as Mr. Fardi visited. With that, at least I'd be able to go anywhere in the world. When I grew up, I'd open a bell factory. The Fardis could sell all they wanted, because only Gypsies could make really good sounding bells. Grandma said someone wagered with old Fardi about whether he could forge metal spurs onto an ornamental egg for Easter, and damn if he didn't do it. Nobody could match him, and the count gave him a foal for it.

It would be nice if Papa too could do anything like that, but all he's good with is horses. But there's not a single cataract he can't slice right off the surface of a horse's eyes, and if a horse's artery needs cutting into, he's the one they turn to, because the vet sure won't do it. At the moment he was busy doing something just like it.

The old mare was already lying in the yard with its legs tied, Papa stretching its mouth open with a flattened O-shaped iron, which he called a mouth-stretcher.

He worked like a dentist.

"Where have you been loafing about?" he asked me. "Why aren't you here when I need you?"

He was dripping with sweat.

The poor horse was moaning. Mama kept a pot with holes punched into it above the horse's mouth, spraying thin jets of water onto its teeth, which Papa was cutting down to the size of a six-year-old's.

With all the sawing, the air was thick with the odor of burnt horn. The chilled water didn't help; it just kept warming up. After the sawing, Papa etched small grooves into the teeth and filled them with potassium permanganate crystals. The dentistry took quite a long time before all the teeth were properly filed to the same size. He obviously wasn't doing it for the first time. When they untied the old mare, the poor thing tried to eat, but being used to its long teeth, the fodder kept falling out of its mouth.

"Come on," he said to me, opening his wallet, "tell me which one of these cards in here is used to verify that a horse is a mare."

"This one," I said.

"Read out when it was born."

"One thousand nine hundred twenty-one.

"Which of the last two digits can be altered so it doesn't show?"

I thought for a while, shrugged my shoulders. Papa had never gone to school, yet he knew which numbers could be tampered with.

"Look at the number one! If you're clever, you can make a nine out of it that looks just like the other nine. Then she was born in one thousand nine hundred and twenty-nine, eight years later. Right?" Reproachfully he added, "A boy who's been to school should have realized that right away. Go on, now, make a nine out of the one. But make sure it's exactly like the other one. Be careful not to touch the pen to the paper where there is writing, because it shows. Just make a head for the nine." All I really had to do was to add a semicircle to the one. It turned out well, and I was proud.

"That's it, boy," he said. "At dawn we'll fit up the two broken-winded horses."

I knew what "fit up" meant; I had already paced broken-winded horses more than once. We'd make them swallow some henbane seeds, and then we'd have them walk until they were sweating. No one could tell for eighteen to twenty hours that there was anything wrong. There was no puffing, no coughing. Henbane is good not only to stop broken-winded horses from heaving so much, but also, if its smoke is inhaled or a tincture rubbed into the gums, to make a toothache go away. But you have to be careful not to let them swallow any, or else they go mad for a good two days. The plant can be unbearably smelly, almost stomach-turning, while it is green, but once it dries, it doesn't smell at all. Young horses do get better after eating it; you just need patience. It often takes a month before they are completely well. With some horses, though, you can only stop the symptoms for an hour or two. In such cases it's best to palm them off to someone fast, because even a little exertion can make them suffocate.

Sometimes we had horses whose marks didn't match the information in their registration booklets. The marks had to be removed. On one occasion it took us a week to figure out that the white "stockings" on a horse we'd bought had in fact been dyed into its hair. On went that horse, from one buyer to another. Indeed, we ourselves bought it more than once. Papa, pretending he didn't know the horse, would buy it at a bargain price. He then casually pissed on the horse's leg, and if it hadn't been smeared with anything other than hair dye, the color would run off. He would promptly demand a refund amounting to half the price. Its owner didn't dare to protest for fear of being taken to court. I couldn't keep track of everyone who had the pleasure of owning the old mare-turned-filly, but their enjoyment certainly wouldn't last long.

It was around dusk when Miss Hermina drank the lye. She was in love with a fellow named Koka. Her husband was in jail and her kids, eight of them, were with my grandfather; she'd been hanging out with Koka and having a good time. But for weeks already, Koka was no longer sleeping with her but with another woman, Terus, whom everyone called Blind Terus. Not that it could be said that Miss Hermina had a poor figure—her breasts and bottom were still firm despite having had all those kids.

But every single Gypsy around her knew that Koka had left big—nosed Hermina high and dry. He hadn't been in love with her in the first place; no, all he'd wanted was her money and the food she used to bring from the village. Anyway, that night lots of folks, including Miss Hermina and Koka and Blind Terus were sitting around our settlement, and everyone figured Miss Hermina was drunk. At one point she stood up. The others, feeling sorry for her because they knew she was suffering from unrequited love, gathered around her, singing and playing the fiddle and other instruments. She may have been crying, but she did join in the singing, as if enjoying herself.

"Come on, Koka, drink up!" she called, taunting her unfaithful lover.

She kept swirling something about in a glazed jug. Folks figured it was wine.

Koka was drooling after the wine, but Blind Terus, whose eyesight was incidentally quite okay, grimaced in a way that left no doubt that she would go after Miss Hermina given the chance. Koka had to put his foot down to keep the two women from having a go at each other. Otherwise he might have accepted the wine.

One of the musicians was playing *We Shall Part From One Another Quietly, As Is Fitting*, which was the tune all lovesick people sang at the time.

Miss Hermina waved the musicians to silence.

She raised the glazed jug and called out, "God bless you all!"

"You too," said the others reproachfully on account of the fact that she alone was emptying a jug they too would gladly have helped empty.

She could no longer thank them for their good wishes, though: she staggered backward as if really drunk, blood pouring from her nose and mouth. Everyone crowded around her.

"It's lye she drank!" someone shouted, and in an instant everyone else repeated it, along with this: "Milk, milk!"

The whole place was in turmoil. Everyone was screaming, but most of all the little ones, because all at once the vines by which they'd been clinging to their mothers were rudely ripped out of their mouths. That is to say, anyone who could get near Miss Hermina was milking her breasts into her mouth. Papa rode off to get the doctor.

Miss Hermina motioned to Koka, wanting to say something to him, but no sound came out of her mouth. The lye had mangled her esophagus; the bleeding seemed to have stopped, but she was no doubt still bleeding inside.

The doctor, when he arrived, looked at the residue in the jug. "It's lye all right. I can't do a thing. I'll give her a shot, and you'd better do what you can to get her to a hospital."

My aunt, know-it-all that she was, tried to reason with him. "*Well,* doctor?"

"What do you mean by 'well'? There's no other choice. You've got to get her into a vehicle." Everyone looked at Papa.

"Well," repeated the doctor. "There they might be able to help her. You do have good horses and a cart."

"And if she dies on the way?"

He shrugged his shoulders: "It's no good my trying to call for an ambulance. I already tried once in the afternoon and was told it was out of order."

There was nothing to be done. They put her quilt and pillow on the cart. My aunt sat next to her, I sat next to Papa, and off we went.

A long, wooded road led from our village, Okány, in southeastern Hungary, on south through the neighboring village of Doboz to the city of Gyula. The moonlight broke through the leafy archway formed by the tree branches stretching over the road, which twisted and turned like a giant, multicolored snake. The steady rumble of the cart wheels startled it from its slithering silence. Here and there a pheasant stirred up, wailing loudly as if being chased.

I was holding on to Papa, shivering with fear.

Miss Hermina had fallen asleep from the injection the doctor had given her. I didn't dare turn to look at her. In my mind's eye I could still see her writhing, blood oozing out of her mouth, painting her vest red.

"She is making rattling noises. Shouldn't we turn back?" my aunt asked. Papa cracked the whip.

"The doctor said they might still be able to help her in the hospital."

Not another word was uttered during the drive. We were all consumed in thought; only the patient kept making noise, rattling ever more loudly. If she were to die, I thought, I would never again sit on this cart. Fear overwhelmed me even more. I knew Papa had a gun, but this awareness brought no solace now: what use is a gun against a dead person?

Papa was sweating in his effort to keep the horses calm; they were puffing and snorting like mad. It was about ten-thirty by the time we arrived at the hospital. The doctors only shook their heads. And so we left Miss Hermina there for what now seemed a certain death.

On our return trip, Papa drove the cart right into the Körös River to wash the blood off it.

"We won't get home until dawn, anyway," he said. "Besides, it won't hurt the horses either. At least they'll be refreshed."

There, beside the road, we heaped a bunch of fragrant clover on the back of the cart, and I then burrowed into it like a pig. But still I couldn't fall asleep. Papa sighed, and spoke:

"God strikes everyone where there is a whore; she poisons even the air around herself. Our kind knew what to do about them; they used to burn the badness out of the whore's bottom with a hot iron. But this woman with the ram's nose could do anything with your brother, like some sort of wizard. And she wound up leaving behind eight orphans."

My aunt now spoke, indignantly: "What do you mean by saying she left them orphaned? Why, she hadn't much bothered about them so far, either. No, she shat them out and then my dad, he took care of them, he did. They didn't hanker after their mother for a minute, but their old man, what will he say when he finds out? He would have gone through fire and water if this woman ordered him to do so. What is he locked up for this time, anyway? He got three years in the workhouse for stealing a measly amount of iron, and he's been there now for six years.

Oh, they'll never let him out; whenever he says a word, he gets another year, and he is not the sort of man to keep his mouth shut. All his life he was always put away for zilch. For stealing fruit, chickens, wood. He will surely rot away in prison."

Day was breaking by the time we got home. "It's curtains for the market," Papa said. "They too are tired." He caressed the sweaty horses.

"Go to sleep, son. There will be other markets."

Some of the Gypsies woke up at the rumble of the cart wheels. They wanted to know what was up with the woman.

"There was hardly any life left in her by the time we got her in. The doctors just shook their heads. No, it wasn't worth going there. But we always think there are still miracles, don't we?"

Neither Papa nor the others could come to terms with the thought of Miss Hermina's impending death. They tried to talk about other things, but in the end they kept returning to the subject of the dying woman.

I was upset that we had missed the market day. I climbed into Grandma's warm den, but she too had been up all night, worrying about us. And she too was berating "whores who can't control their blood."

"Don't be so hard on her, Grandma," I said, "You were young once, too."

"I sure was, but I never did anything like that."

"I see," I said, half asleep, "you only married a Hungarian."

"I didn't want to marry him; he took me by force."

"Tell me all about it when I wake up."

I don't remember her reply. Her crooning reached me from somewhere far away, like a childhood memory, softly; I felt it rather than heard it. No one sleeps more deeply than me. Indeed, I could have slept until all hours if our little Gypsy Paris, which is how I thought of our settlement on the plains of southern Hungary, hadn't been stirred up by the news that a telegram arrived.

Miss Hermina had died by morning.

Even the oldest people couldn't recall a Gypsy woman having done anything like this. Yes, even though Death was a frequent visitor among us—taking the tiny, green, swollen-bellied children and the very old, for whom no one grieved—this particular passing counted as a great event. It stirred everyone's soul. Folks no longer called Miss Hermina a "whore"; instead they wept.

Koka set out in a clean white shirt to collect money for the funeral. He was shattered by what had happened and didn't want to mingle with people, but it was only fitting for him to do the best he could for Miss Hermina; after all, it was him she'd been closest to. Not that either the men *or* the women here in the settlement looked askance at him for the whole affair. No, they too understood that he couldn't tie himself down with someone he didn't like. And what of the fact that he'd taken her money, that he'd slept with her? Well, folks used to say, "Where there is no slut, there is no swindler." Sure, they felt sorry for the departed, but that was all they could do. In any case, she too should have known that love doesn't last forever if you've got eight kids, and there are not enough begging baskets in the world to make up for it.

Not that she had a problem tending to her kids, actually, seeing as how my grandfather had taken on that task by taking them away from under her like piglets.

Folks did, in the end, scrape together a few copper coins from their penury to give a more humane funeral to the dead woman. I too gave a little coin. In the end, the money Koka managed to collect was not enough to bring her body home, but then again, the earth is blessed everywhere. Here, too, only a hole in the ground and some ornamental crêpe paper could have covered her love. The further away memories are, the sooner they pass away.

There was no grieving in the settlement. The late summer evenings washed away everything. We spent half the nights singing outdoors, and then we teamed up with our groups of friends and walked over to the nearby vineyard. We knew it well; we knew what the grapes in the various parcels tasted like. Especially when they became ripe.

We were a mixed band, boys and girls together. Iza Verge served our group exceptionally well. She could sweep the vineyard guards right off their feet. She was very fond of boys, and the evenings that she did not go down to the clay pit with one of them were few and far between. She was blessed with an amazingly good nature; she wasn't choosy and could be endlessly patient even with the youngest kids. She was extremely experienced for her age and could liberate the boys in a masterly manner. Who knows how long this would have continued, had Ginar not trimmed her wings one afternoon.

Iza was lying in the yard, on her back, head tucked under a "broom bush," whose branches were used to make brooms. The sun shone brightly. The bushes had grown lately, completely obscuring her upper body; only her thick, bare thighs were showing, shining like freshly debarked fence post branches. She loved daydreaming, and on such occasions she broke into song with her magnificent voice, like her father's—even the dogs went mad on hearing it. Usually she began softly, choosing one song after another until one of them caught her fancy and then her voice resounded throughout the entire neighborhood.

Ginar followed the sound right through the broom bushes, whose wide-spreading branches stroked his chocolate skin.

Iza kept opening her naked thighs at regular intervals, as her song and her self-dictated rhythm required it. She saw Ginar stop in front of her, and now her voice rang out good and proper. The beats no longer concerned her. She spread her thighs apart as far as her joints would allow, pausing longer, and then, like a dog catching a piece of tossed meat closing its jaw with a sharp snap, she clanged her knees together.

Ginar watched this performance, munching on a head of garlic. An indelible "what-the-hell" consumptive smile was etched around his parched lips and made it impossible to tell whether he was in a good or bad mood. He could ease his asthma only with garlic, and on top of that he exuded the odor of sausage.

"Listen here," he said to Iza, "the deep-throated beast is showing."

"He who sees it should chew it, his mouth will get sweeter," Iza chanted to the tune she'd just been singing.

The bitter smile vanished from Ginar's blotchy face. Feeling like a lad again, he spat that garlic head into his palm—it resembled a clump of chewing tobacco—and pressed it deep between Iza's legs. Perhaps there is nothing more accurate than a chance hit; as the girl jumped up in fright, the garlic got completely stuck. Ginar disappeared into the bushes, trying to get as far away as possible from the hollering girl, who by now was jumping up and down and wailing in pain.

The settlement woke from its sleepy idleness, but despite their best intentions, the Gypsies gathered round her couldn't do a thing; for she was clutching herself in a spot that was not exactly fit to be put on public display.

"Oh my God! It stings!"

They stood around her helplessly.

"A wasp or a snake," guessed the wiser ones. "She has to be taken to the doctor at once. This is no laughing matter; there are all sorts of worms among these tall weeds. It might even cost her her life."

Margaret Verge pushed her sister breathlessly in a muddy wheelbarrow to the doctor. They were out of luck. Dr. Bocz gave both girls a good slap.

"If she didn't stuff so many sausages into it," he said, "it wouldn't sting."

They practically wiped the stairs with their behinds as the doctor kicked them out.

Folks wouldn't let Iza forget the incident for a long time, everyone calling her "Garlic Ass." Gone were the lovely nights she'd spent with one guy or another.

Ginar, on the other hand, gained in prestige. Everyone approved of what he'd done—at least he'd lowered Iza's libido. He'd been popular to begin with. Despite being puny and consumptive, he was full of life. He was the best dancer of them all. He adored the fiddle, and folks often had tears in their eyes when he sang. They couldn't help envying his slightly hoarse voice. As for the non-Gypsies who lived nearby, gentlemen spent whole nights reveling in the musical entertainment he provided, and so he was always being invited to festive gatherings.

At the time, there were two hunting groups in the area, one led by the Honorable Mr. Komlódy, the other by the school principal, Mr. Rácz. Ginar could be found daily at Mr. Rácz's place as his all-around gopher—master of the hunt, butler, shopper, and court jester. His right-hand man, in short. In return Mr. Rácz sometimes gave Ginar second-hand clothes, and gave him lunch every day; and, on hunting days, he gave Ginar just as much pay as anyone else employed to drive game. Festive nights depended on the luck of the hunt, and Ginar profited, too. The hunting party was comprised of gentlemen who knew how to do everything in style.

The school year had started long ago, and I could bear its constraints no more easily than could Grandma tolerate the captivity of our hut here in the settlement.

But I had no choice—a will much stronger than mine forced me to go. In any event, as a result it was only in the evenings that I could meet up with the other boys. Little went on at school that I could talk about with them, and they weren't interested. Sure, sometimes they would ask what I'd eaten at school. That was the only thing worth mentioning, for the school slaughtered a pig each week to feed us. When I talked about those food- and lard-filled days, their eyes lit up with yearning. They had never experienced the like of it.

They, on the other hand, went hunting three times a week. They talked half the night about the outskirts of the village as if it were a well-stocked pantry, where you could fill your belly freely with all sorts of fare. Compared to all that, my petty little school stories counted for nothing. I was constantly being ridiculed; even the grown-ups didn't understand what Mama was aiming at with all this school business, when the other kids could earn as much as one hundred fifty fillérs a week during autumn hunts. This got me all upset, too. Mama didn't want me to miss even a single day of classes.

In the evenings I did my own thing; no one told me what to do, that is. I didn't have to study, nor did anyone test me at home or, most days, in school. It seemed natural that I never wrote anything down; there was nothing to write it on, anyway. I never set my eyes on books or textbooks or notebooks. But when the school inspector stopped by our classroom—it was his job to make sure our teacher was in fact doing his job—I was the one the teacher called on to prove that we knew a thing or two.

"Let's see if our black little prince here can tell us . . ." he would begin.

And I did tell them.

"The buttons on pants are made of iron and copper, as is the coin the honorable inspector is holding in his hand," I said, "because Hungary is a rich country that has everything."

He gave me the coin.

School regulations didn't apply to me as much as to other kids, and I partly had Papa to thank for that. Exactly when I started to smoke, I don't recall, but I know I tried it in school my first year there: during a break one day I picked up a smoldering butt the teacher had tossed on the floor, and took some puffs.

My classmates were so incensed that they didn't even wait for the end of the break before telling on me. To their amazement, my potential demise didn't come to pass. Indeed, no sooner had the bell rung and we sat back down in class than the teacher coolly sat right on top of my desk, gesturing for me to get up and walk to the wood stove on the other side of the room. I did so. He opened the door of the stove and reached inside with a Hunnia—a notoriously strong, stinking brand of cigarette with which not only rats but also polecats could be exterminated. I couldn't refuse the now-lit cigarette, although I knew its toxic effects. I'd smoked Hunnias before when I had nothing better to do. For the fun of it I blew the smoke alternately from my mouth and nose. The sight of the contours of my irregular smoke rings made even my enemies overcome their prejudice, and they demanded a repeat performance.

After I finished, the teacher handed me another one. I tried letting him know in the most humble of terms that on account of my stomach and my head I could undertake the task only during the next break. It didn't work. He forced it on me with the burnt end of his reed cane.

I went through with it. In my own circle of friends, back in the settlement, I didn't count as a beginner, and yet I now felt the floor swaying under me.

"This is a warning," the teacher said. "If you ever smoke again, I'll make you smoke ten of these." I took him seriously, and for many years I smoked only at home or on the street.

It so happened that we got a new teacher in third grade, and not just any old one. When she became aware of my unhealthy lifestyle, she gave me several whacks on the head.

Papa didn't quite agree with this method. Indeed, he protested vehemently; if *he* didn't tell me not to smoke, sure as hell no one else had the right to do so. Maybe he didn't use exactly these words, but it worked. In the years to come, no one reproached me for my habits. It was just as natural as the fact that one of our teachers was always drunk.

I went to the movies every night, and when Mama didn't notice, by day I played hookey. She was the only one who didn't approve of my independent lifestyle, so I tried as best I could to keep my private affairs under wraps. It was in this frame of mind that, one day, I secretly vowed that I, too, would help them drive rabbits at the gentlemen's hunt the next morning.

My friends were just as aware of Mama's fiery temper as I was, because when she caught us together, she was just as hard on them as on me. So when I let them in on my plan to join them at the hunt, they would not have bet their boots that I would go through with it. True, I too considered and reconsidered the matter, but by then I was bound by my rash announcement. Indeed, I went home and told Mama that the next day my friends and I would be going on an "outing."

"Okay," she said, immediately giving me instructions: "Don't you dare climb any trees! Nor do I want to hear that you've wandered off somewhere or had a fight, otherwise you better not come home at all."

At the crack of dawn I left the warm family nest and, shivering, huddled in a ditch until my friends arrived.

"Hooray!" they shouted with admiration. My chest swelled with pride; even my shirt felt a bit tighter.

Fall was nearing its end, but the mornings were still glowing yellow in the sunlight, which, though it still provided warmth, no longer made us sweat. Here and there you could even find some frostbitten fruit, and if we could get at it, we didn't spare our pants from the thorns we had to wade through to get there.

We pressed forward through the brambles and wind-torn cornfields, driving the game with loud shouts. There were plenty of rabbits, far more than the hunters could shoot. For lunch, we took a rest in an abandoned farmyard.

The gentlemen started their meal, bragging to high heaven about how they couldn't get over their luck at hunting that day. Even those whose guns somehow always misfired got their share of praise. We waited patiently on the sidelines for the hunter and his dog to get their fill, counting on the leftovers. In fact, we didn't get sick from overeating, for we didn't get much. After lunch, everyone was in high spirits. Ginar diligently kept opening bottles, the gentlemen's insider that he was. The face of the school principal, Rácz, became more and more flushed from all the wine he downed; he kept laughing and drank like a thirsty horse.

"Come on, Gypsies," he called out to us. "Sing for Ginar, make him dance."

We didn't have to be told twice, hoping that we would get something. Unfortunately we didn't, but we still sang Ginar's favorite, lively tune.

"Come on, Ginar, get moving! Strike it, cut it! Hey, hey!" Taking big gulps from the bottle, they kept exclaiming, *"Hey, ho!"*

Ginar danced feverishly, tempestuously, slapping his palms to his legs to the soul-shaking rhythm of the song.

"Come on boys, let's go!" they called out to us, while they themselves kept stomping, beating their feet on the ground, dictating an ever faster pace until they kicked the rhythm right out from under our tongues.

Ginar, out of breath, was behind with the beats and his slaps no longer sounded the same. The song, having lost its leader, ended up like the howling of wolves. Ginar collapsed. No amount of encouragement helped; sprawling on the ground, under the masklike laughter his face contorted. When he tried to get up, his legs buckled, and he sank back to the ground. We kept on singing and, with Ginar no longer holding us back, resumed the beat until Bober whirled into the circle. He hopped and skipped with fresh energy, but lasted only half as long. He soon missed the beat, gyrated giddily for a while, and then sank to the floor, his facial muscles and eyes twitching frighteningly. The hunters burst out laughing at the sight of Bober's rigid form, foamy saliva bubbling from the corners of his mouth. The wine was boiling up in their brains as they forced whoever was closest to be the next victim.

"Hey, ho!"

The youngsters quickly realized that the gentlemen no longer needed dancing as an entertainment, for they had drunk far too much by then. What the gentlemen wanted was to watch them collapsing and writhing like shot game.

We somehow managed to pull Bober out of the circle. Principal Rácz gave a salute from his six-shooter Winchester in honor of each fallen dancer, followed by the hunters' roars.

I kept rubbing the area around Bober's heart until his stiffened limbs slackened.

"Water!" he said in a stupor.

"Water?" I asked in despair. "From where?" I could barely speak from all the saliva that had gathered in my mouth.

"Give me water, bro!" he implored, pressing my hand over his heart. I knew his illness; we had revived him more than once after running or while playing. Whenever tears came to his face, his convulsions ceased. This time the sight affected me differently than usual. The merrymaking was still going on, but only Bada, another Gypsy kid, was still dancing, comically, making the gentlemen laugh, while they were hollering, *"Hey, ho!"*

"Bring me water!" Bober begged me.

"Hold on to my neck," I said, wanting to lift his spirits lest he get sick again. "There's water in the canal. Everything will be alright." Holding him, I stood up with difficulty, at first crawling and then staggering along until I regained my balance, heading through the onetime farmyard toward the nearby canal. Midway there my legs began buckling, but I murmured to Bober reassuringly that we'd be there soon. Fiery circles were dancing in front of my eyes, and I felt a pressure as if my ears were rupturing.

The rhythmic shouts ceased, and Rácz's swearing stopped me in my tracks. I sensed it rather than heard it; perhaps it was my curiosity about the sudden, deafening silence that caused me to turn: Rácz aimed, rings of smoke appeared around the muzzle of his rifle, and I heard but a faint thud as Bober dropped off my neck. A searing heat suffused my body as I plunged into a dense fog accompanied by an unforgettably pleasant smell as every bit of my body now fell apart. All my fatigue was gone; invisibly I floated, like gray mist, and then everything died away together with me and only a slight, whistling noise remained like an inflated balloon being untied. I felt neither time nor pain; I only heard that whistle blowing, and after what seemed an eternity the sound metamorphosed into human whispers. As the voices grew stronger, so my body reformed: my flesh was burning in colorless flames and the pungent smell of vinegar hit my nose. I was lying practically naked on a sack, with the game warden, Peter Stefan, kneeling beside me. Using the tip of his huge knife, he was digging out the lead shots embedded in my body.

"Does it hurt?" he asked, pouring vinegar into each hole he'd mined a shot out of.

"It stings," I replied.

"This is how it's done; otherwise you could easily get lead poisoning. As soon as Ginar comes back from the village, we'll apply some antiseptic. Don't you worry, though. You're lucky! Had you been closer, it would have been worse."

Bober was crying next to me: he too had been hit by a few shots. The horses were still galloping as the cart arrived. Before they even stopped, Ginar jumped off with a bottle of iodine in his hand.

"You haven't told anyone?" Rácz asked. Ginar, pretending not to hear the question, gave the iodine to Mr. Stefan. They smeared the pigeon-egg-size bumps with iodine and got me dressed.

"Listen, you'll get a pengő each, and not a word to anyone. Understood?"

We didn't reply.

"Here's a *two*-pengő coin." For a while he locked eyes with us, then threw the coin on the ground as if expecting us to fight over it. We stood motionless.

"Ginar, tell them to pick it up!"

Ginar picked up the coin and threw it away with all the strength he could muster. Rácz, by now blue in the face, attacked Ginar, relentlessly slapping his face.

"You fucking Gypsy, I've had it with you!"

Ginar put on his weather-beaten, feathered hat and, pale as death, staggered over to one of the other gentleman, Géza Kish.

"Sir, have the driver take the children home!"

The hunt was now over, and Mr. Kish told the driver to make room for me on the game cart.

Back home, everyone already knew what had happened to me. Throngs of people were waiting at the edge of the settlement. Mama neither screamed nor moaned. She and the others just put me on our own cart and took me to the doctor. Dr. Kovács didn't even look at me.

"There's nothing wrong with him that two or three days of bed rest can't cure."

"Doctor, aren't you going to give the child some medicine?"

"There isn't any need for medicine. I told you there's nothing wrong with him."

"But his whole body is full of wounds and he has a fever."

"What is this?" he barked at Mama. "So you're a doctor, too? Now scram!"

I had to put my clothes back on in the corridor. We had not even gotten on the cart when a gentleman, László Moochi, walked up to us.

"Good evening," said Mr. Moochi, greeting Papa.

"Good evening, sir," Papa replied, tipping his hat.

"What happened to the boy?"

"He's been shot, sir."

"What did the doctor have to say?"

Here Mama took over. With her unfathomable unpredictability she could swing from silent calmness into total lunacy like a bolt from the blue. Mr. Moochi just listened to Mama's unbridled tirade, which certainly did not praise Dr. Kovács.

Obviously Principal Rácz had got there first.

"All right, ride on over to Dr. Bocz and we'll talk it over there," he reassured Mama.

We started out with little confidence, as the doctor was generally known to be crazy in the head. What we didn't know, however, was that he and Moochi belonged to a different hunting club, and the members of each of the two didn't get on particularly well in the gentlemen's salon.

The village had two doctors, both of them raving mad.

Throughout his entire working life, Dr. Imre Kovács, a member of Rácz's group, had been interested only in soccer. It had happened that a patient waiting to have a tooth extracted had to sit with his mouth open until the doctor returned from a soccer match. Then he wrote out a prescription for "two pairs of soccer shoes."

He was the director of the local sports club.

Dr. Elek Bocz was his direct opposite. He hated soccer but was passionate about hunting. As a member of the Honorable Mr. Komlódy's hunting club, he considered it his duty to deliberately annoy the other club. Now, through me, the perfect occasion arose, and not just any ordinary one.

We found this out only when, through Moochi's influence, we received a surprisingly good reception from the Dr. Bocz. He even reproached us flatteringly for not having looked him up first.

Mama told him that the only reason for this was that she had wanted to get me to whoever was nearest, since my injuries looked serious.

"Serious? Very serious indeed, and it will certainly cost Joe Rácz." Turning to Moochi, he added, "I think this was his last shot." First he jabbed two injections into me, after which he scraped out each wound with a gigantic needle, carefully placing every last bit of lead he got out of me into a vial. Not daring to shout, I just gripped the edge of the operating table. I nearly pissed my pants. He dug around in the wounds for at least an hour. He ascertained that I had seventy-three wounds in my left side—barely visible but half-inch deep holes where the shots had pierced my flesh—that required urgent medical intervention. My condition was life-threatening, and there was the risk of lead poisoning.

He himself pressed the official stamp on the findings.

"His weapon must be confiscated tonight!" Moochi suggested.

"It's only natural," concurred the doctor. "Guns must not remain in the hands of such people. Who would take responsibility for it?"

The doctor spread some white ointment on the wounds, and then sent me across to the gendarmerie. I almost got into trouble there, for the sergeant had not forgotten that I had once stolen some alfalfa. But when the Honorable Mr. Komlódy appeared, accompanied by Dr. Bocz, things took a different turn. All that had to be done was to sign the logbook. He firmly instructed Mama to negotiate only in his presence.

By the next day I ran a very high fever and the doctor gave me two more injections. Rácz's maid came to us every hour trying to see Papa, but he was out all morning. In the afternoon, on the doctor's prompting, he sent back a message that he was busy.

In the evening, Rácz came to us personally.

Papa seemed very calm, even though he had put a pistol in his pocket in the afternoon with the intent of shooting Rácz if I died.

They said that I was in a bad way. I knew nothing about it; I just felt I was dying of thirst.

I wouldn't let anyone near me except Grandma. She secretly moistened the corner of her kerchief with plum brandy to soften my lips, which were swollen and chapped from the fever. Then she wiped them not only on the outside, but on the inside as well.

She sat by my head with her hair loose, tirelessly murmuring a prayer in Romani, which had everything in it from repentance to vows. The curses she cast on our enemies were always followed by the first line of the Lord's Prayer: "*Amaro Del, kon san ando cheri*"—"Our Father, who art in heaven." The rest, she improvised. My head felt heavy; I couldn't keep my eyes open. I lay dazed for hours under the effect of the injection, but after a good sleep I felt better.

It must have been time to light the lanterns when Rácz, tired of exchanging messages, arrived. His face was entirely different than what we had known so far. It had not been an easy day for him.

His weapon had been confiscated by the gendarmerie, and my fate was not indifferent to him. He had summoned Ginar early in the morning, obviously to bring news of my condition. By evening, his nerves could no longer bear it.

He was probably still around the edge of the settlement when Mama began to sharpen her tongue.

"Just let him come here! I'll smash his head in with this pan!" She was just in the middle of doing the dishes.

"Come on, take the dishes out of here and stop yakking so much," Papa admonished her. "I don't want your voice to be heard inside."

Turning to me, he said, "And you'd better talk properly with the principal, who is, after all, an educated gentleman."

Rácz must have felt uncomfortable crossing the settlement; he had to swallow quite a few nasty jibes. They told him bluntly to his face: "You murderer, we'll kill you if the child dies!"

It was not surprising that he could hardly find our door handle. The news had spread across the village like wildfire that Rácz had shot dead a Gypsy child who was already in the morgue.

Papa offered him a seat, and then left the room. Grandma kept sitting by my head like an old owl, saying nothing, just stroking my hair.

Rácz must have felt the silence oppressive, for he lit one cigarette after another. He fidgeted for a long while until he asked, very timidly:

"How is the child?"

"Like this," said Grandma sadly.

Not that he gained much information from that, but at least it broke the silence. It had annoyed me, too, and I peeked out from under the blanket, licking my lips, which had grown to the size of sausages.

"What sort of medicine is he taking?"

"There it is," she said, pointing at the nook in the wall where it was kept. "Even its smell can make you sick."

Mama came in, put a wet cloth on my forehead, and walked out without a word.

I was wondering why Papa was not here. Half an hour passed before he entered.

"Well, that's how things are, sir. I guess you've had a good look at what you have done."

Rácz just nodded his head.

"I too have hunted for humans," said Papa, "but that was in the war."

"How can matters be rectified?" The principal's voice sounded awfully timid, his eyes still looking toward that nook in the wall.

"You'll be lucky if he gets well, sir. Two of my sons died, and there was no one to take revenge on. Maybe I could have, maybe not."

"You are right," said Rácz, pale as death.

"We are people who can put up with a lot of things, but there is such a thing as a last straw." Papa said these words as if he weren't speaking to Rácz at all.

"He'll be fine when the fever passes," said Rácz, comforting him. "You'll see."

"We are in God's hands."

"That's right," Rácz assented, "but I would like to help to get the child well. Then, after his condition changes for the better, I think we can agree on something."

Papa swallowed some rude word, and all he said was this:

"That is a matter for the courts, not me."

"Yes, yes . . . but if the court leaves the decision to the parties? Will you be willing to agree to a certain amount of compensation?"

Papa knew why Rácz had visited us, but he was still surprised by the offer.

"Look, sir," he said, turning pale, "life has taught me a lot, especially to be a good judge of character. I'd be very disappointed if I was wrong."

"What does this have to do with our case?"

"I'm sorry, sir, but you ought to know that it is not us you are up against."

"Then who?"

"Opponents more worthy of you. Do you really think we could have taken even the first step by ourselves? The matter would have stopped with Dr. Kovács. What does a filthy Gypsy kid matter, after all? He matters only to the extent that he allows you gentlemen to get your revenge on each other. I'm indebted to Dr. Bocz, no doubt about it, because he may have saved my son, but was that really so important to him? Or is he really out take the gun away from you?"

They each fell silent. A lot of things must have passed through Rácz's head, for his gaze was fixed far away.

"Do you think," he spoke after a long pause, "that they are behind it?"

"I'm sure of it. Otherwise, you know what he would have said? 'The child is sick because he and the others shit behind the outhouse.' That's what he tells all the Gypsies. Why would we have been an exception?"

"Did you ever go to school?"

"I did not, sir, but don't imagine that means I'm completely blind to things. Maybe, just maybe, we're human beings too."

"Don't get me wrong. I'm a teacher. I do not discriminate between man and man. Ginar can tell you."

Ginar stood next to the stove with downcast eyes.

"Ginar?" Papa looked at Ginar for a long time. "Yes, he can."

Whenever he was nervous, Ginar would get busy stuffing his pipe, and that is what he was doing now.

"You, sir, would not have shot your dog if it hadn't jumped at the first whistle, but you didn't hold a Gypsy who spoiled your frolicking in as high regard as you would have a dog. Do you know who my father is? The Honorable John Boncza. That's right. I'm a child of rape. Once, when we were in that area, all that my mother wanted was just to show me the man I was named after. But my honorable father beat us away with a whip and set the dogs on us. What could we do and who could we complain to?" Papa paused. "Our justice is like the beggar's cloak," he said with a sigh. "You can no longer see the cloth from all the dirt and patches."

"Look, my good man," replied Rácz. "I'll admit you're right. That is why I'd like to compensate you with something."

"What did you have in mind—money?"

"Yes. What else can I offer? You are poor people; you could surely do with some." After a pause he added, with a conciliatory smile, "And there shouldn't be any bad blood between us."

"We are poor people, that is true, but not so much that we would be willing to accept even a penny's worth at the cost of our child's blood. And what does it mean to you whether we are angry at each other or not? You straighten things out between yourselves. If two people of your kind have a quarrel, it is always a third one who has to pay the price. Don't expect us to be the ones. If Dr. Bocz finds out that we have been negotiating with you, he won't ever let us into his clinic again."

I could hardly understand anything of this. I didn't like their quiet conversation. Why didn't Papa hit Joseph Rácz? I couldn't make sense of it. At other times, he would slap Mama on the face for the smallest thing, and here he was talking nicely with this man who had almost shot me dead.

Their conversation gradually veered away from the original topic, as if they had lost their way.

Papa talked, Rácz occasionally asked a question.

We didn't even realize that the hut was filling up. Mama had come in, too, but did not get involved in the discussion. No, she just kept poking a piece of bread in my mouth.

My youngest sister was desperately trying to stick a toe in my ear, as if just that particular toe would not fit onto the bed.

In the weak light of the kerosene lamp the faces of the other Gypsies seemed even darker, their color like that of earth. The glistening of their black eyes cut through the smoke-filled air.

That many people usually congregate only for a vigil. They talked in whispers, as if not wanting to disturb the dead person's peace of mind.

Papa occasionally cast a glance about him, expecting a nod or word of approval, and then went on almost inexhaustibly.

They respected my old man. He never uttered needless words, and no one doubted what he did say.

Such meetings are rare for Gypsies. The topics that were discussed here went far beyond the limits of simple family problems. Papa avoided laying on the blame, but nor did he demean himself; the principal blushed often from the bitter truths he voiced. He had no choice but to nod even to those words that pertained to him directly.

"I came to make a compromise," Rácz said, as if he had just awakened, "but I see that all of you are right. It wouldn't be worthwhile for us to go to an attorney, or else you too would become victims of the revenge. We shall wait until the young man gets better."

Sometimes Papa called me a "young man," too, but that was different. I didn't like the principal's cajoling words at all.

"The boy is in sixth grade now, isn't he?" Rácz asked, glancing at me.

"Yes," said Papa.

"Each year, we send a couple of poor kids to high school at the expense of the state from among those who are good students or seem talented at something. If you want, I'll put the boy's name down for further education."

That's all I needed, I thought. I could hardly wait to rid myself of school.

Papa looked at Mama, whose eyes began to shine, ignoring whether I wanted it or not, adjusting her kerchief in embarrassment.

"We too have been thinking about it, sir," he said in awe. "Certainly if we could, we'd send him to high school. Even if we ourselves would be in rags, at least he'd get an education. But I really don't think they'd admit a Gypsy kid."

Papa was evidently sad at having said these words.

"You leave that to me," Rácz assured him, "as long as he wants to study."

No problem, I thought, because I didn't like to study.

"I'll take care of that," Mama looked at me menacingly, as if she'd read my mind.

All these words made me as sad as could be. Wasn't it enough that the gentleman had almost shot me dead? Now he wanted me to suffer even more, with another school? No doubt he was out to destroy me.

It took me a long time to fall asleep. Perhaps I didn't have to take Rácz's promise as having yet sealed my fate, but he'd put ideas into Mama's head, and now she wouldn't rest until she had her way.

How often she'd threatened to send me as an apprentice to a blacksmith or carpenter! And now she'd be devastated if I didn't go on studying. I was still hoping that all of this was almost a year away. It might take a month before I could go back to school, and what could they do if I failed? With that in the back of my mind, I eventually managed to fall asleep.

II

THE LATE AUTUMN NIGHTS, ENGULFED IN MUD, WERE SILENT. Ever since Miss Hermina had returned, the nighttime frolicking had come to an end. Everyone huddled in their huts, and the Gypsies didn't even dare to go outside after sunset to do their business.

Old Eva, who lived next door, saw Miss Hermina's ghost arriving every night—always dressed in pure white, a white crepe paper shroud hanging from her neck down to her belly, the toenails on her long white feet rattling like someone sprinkling gravel.

Each and every night Miss Hermina kept searching among her dishes, probably looking for the glazed jug from which she had drunk the lye.

She was looking for it in vain; the gendarmes had taken it with them at the time.

The Gypsies tried giving her the same sort of jug, though they only tossed it into her yard, which had no gate out front; not even in broad daylight did they dare enter her hut, which was by the pasture at the edge of the settlement.

It seems she didn't want it.

It isn't easy to mislead the dead; they know even your secret thoughts.

At night the musicians steered clear of the pasture to avoid getting close to her hut.

Hardly any Gypsies could claim to have never been haunted by her. Nearly everyone had seen her. Not for love or money would anyone risk entering her house after sundown.

Nor would anyone dare to venture outside on his or her own after midnight. Miss Hermina's ghost knocked on windows, tried to pry open barricaded or bolted doors, and leapt effortlessly from one rooftop to another.

Even mentioning her name in broad daylight gave people the creeps. She kept everyone in a state of panic. We all waited eagerly for nine weeks to pass, because until that happened the dead always come back to say farewell, even to their lost strands of hair.

After Principal Rácz had left, my parents talked to one another for a long time, discussing the matter. In the end they even felt sorry for him.

The lamp was on at our place every night from evening until morning, but only halfway, so the light wouldn't disturb us. There were little kids at home who could wake up any time and need some light, and besides, matches didn't come free.

Before going to bed, Papa always hung his pocket watch on a nail. It must have been a pretty old watch, since it had to be reset again and again to the whistle of the passing train. He also got out his pistol from under the couch and put it under his pillow. He didn't have a license for it, but he couldn't do without it.

"I'm a rambling man, a flea market man," he'd say. "I travel a lot at night, and you never know when you might cross paths with someone with malicious intentions. It's good to have something on hand to make you brave."

The gendarmes had already ransacked our hut several times looking for the handgun but had never found it, yet all they would have had to do was to turn over the sofa; the gun always hung on a nail just inside the back of its wooden frame.

Everyone was already asleep when someone knocked on the door—a low, muffled sound. I was just about to ask who it was, but then I remembered Miss Hermina and decided to keep my mouth shut.

A few minutes later the knocking grew louder, as if someone was hitting the door with a hard object. In my fear I grabbed onto Grandma's skirt; she was sleeping right up next to me, her feet by my head. I immediately broke out in a sweat on hearing that the door, made of weak boards, was creaking loudly.

"Papa!" I screamed, pulling the blanket over myself.

My old man sat up, thinking at first that he had dreamed my scream, but when he heard my sobs he came over to me.

"Are you feeling sick again?"

"No," I said through chattering teeth. "Miss Hermina wants to come in."

Hardly had I muttered these words when she began pounding the roof with huge bangs. Frozen with fear, we looked in the direction of the sound and imagined her stepping back and forth along the ridge of the roof in a galloping sort of way.

Papa grabbed the gun from under his head and hunched down next to me.

"At first she was trying to pry open the kitchen door," I whispered. By now the whole hut was shaking, and we were expecting the roof to collapse. I kept pulling at Grandma's skirt. What was the use of a gun against someone already dead? But I was certain that Grandma could send her away. After all, we'd never done Miss Hermina any wrong.

If only I could have pulled Grandma's leg closer, I would have bitten it, for it seemed she would otherwise never wake up. The ghost must have cast a spell on her, a sleeping spell.

Everyone else was snoring, but Papa and I kept listening to Miss Hermina with bated breath, expecting her to burst in any moment. Papa held the gun at the ready, but he sure didn't seem like the image of bravery.

At last Grandma woke up when I nearly swallowed her big toe.

"What's up?" Belying her ninety years, she sat up briskly and started caressing my face, but I sensed that she was still half asleep. I whispered to her in vain: she took no notice of me, muttering something about wet rags and plum brandy.

Our window was a single, round piece of glass. When the rumbling ceased, Papa fueled up the lamp to look outside. Sure enough, there, illuminated by the light, was a hazy lurking figure, a white face covered by thick hair. All at once Papa aimed his gun, but before he could shoot, Miss Hermina disappeared. I could hear her running into the squelching mud outside.

The sudden brightness banished the sleep from Grandma's eyes. Startled, she asked what had happened.

"The big-nosed woman was trying to visit us."

Papa's voice was shaking.

"What time is it?" asked Grandma.

"Half past midnight."

"Give it a rest, son; you can't do anything with the bad ones, anyway. Let there be nightfall where there's dawn. Go ahead, lie back down, don't you worry. I'll curse her away from here so she won't ever come back."

Grandma took off her upper skirt and vest, at the same time uttering her magic words of exorcism: "Why are you standing there, what are you waiting for, why are you haunting us? All good souls praise the Lord, so why don't you praise Him, too?"

She then pulled her clothes on, but inside-out. Hardly had she finished this strange ritual when the tiny knocks could be heard again.

"Here she is," I said, my heart in my mouth from sheer terror.

Papa froze at the edge of the couch as the knocking went on.

"Wake up, damn you!" Mama was snoring with her mouth wide upon. He poked her in the ribs.

"What is it, what is it?" she asked, waking with a start.

The explanation Papa gave her is unfit for print.

"Get up, bring the lamp!" With that, Papa set out for the door, gun at the ready.

Mama followed him, lamp in her hand, like a sleepwalker. She was no more beautiful a sight than Miss Hermina with her white crepe-paper shroud.

With my last bit of strength I hung on to Grandma, who was uttering curses and prayers relentlessly, interspersed with sighs.

At night, we always secured the main door with a sliding wooden lock. In humid weather it swelled so much that it was hard to pull it open.

Papa swore left and right as he tore it off its hinges.

The kitchen door was easier to open, but not a soul was out there.

Mama followed him without hesitation and shone the light into the stable, which adjoined the kitchen. She emerged in a nasty mood, as if someone had knocked the sleep from her eyes.

"Why are you so scared?" she asked Papa, who'd stopped in front of the oven.

Mama didn't know a thing; she just began sweating as the kitchen door burst open with an ear-splitting noise.

"What is it?"

"Hermina," Papa said impassively, giving up the ghost hunt.

"Hermina?" Only now did she realized what was going on around her. She looked at me as I clung, shivering, to Grandma, who kept casting the sign of the cross at me in her weird outfit, her hair disheveled.

Papa just stood there, arms at his side, looking helpless and even despondent. Mama grabbed the gun from his hand, and by the time we came to our senses, she was outside. We heard a shot, and then an awful bleating almost like a child crying.

"Damn you and your owner!"

The settlement's other Gypsies emerged all at once from their huts.

"Who was that?" they shouted almost in unison. "Boncza?"

Papa stood silently, overwhelmed by the supernatural powers, not paying attention to them, just staring witlessly at the corpse of a white goat.

The Gypsies approached timidly, complaining from afar that all night it had been trotting around on the roofs of their huts.

"It almost gored me, too," said Mama, "though I chased it away from the house on a couple of nights with a whip."

The goat lay in the yard until morning. We all waited for its owner to come forward, but no one came.

Papa wanted to announce the news, but no one would believe that the goat was not in fact an evil spirit.

It had obviously been this shrouded figure that Miss Eva had seen in Miss Hermina's empty hut as it had sought some scraps among the jumble of pots.

Afterward, I still dreamt of Miss Hermina a few more times, but no longer was I quite as scared as on that night.

After three weeks, I was completely well again and jumped into bed only when the doctor came. He treated me conscientiously, diligently recording how many times he came to us. Not disinterestedly—Rácz later told us that he had to pay a steep medical bill.

December 6th came—St. Nicholas Day—and St. Nick brought me a new pair of boots. It was no small pleasure, let alone for Papa, for until then I used to wear his boots in the evening on the ice, and he had to have new horseshoes nailed on them every week. Not to mention how many times I got his boots soaked. Ice could not always bear my weight, but who could see it at night?

My seemingly indestructible new boots had to be repaired after only a week; the soles had soaked off. Later on, Papa himself fixed them in a makeshift manner. By the time it became really cold, I had managed to wear them out.

Ever since I'd been promised admission to high school, my good life was over; I had to study. Mama implemented a strict routine. The school had leased me a book, and she took it out of the cupboard regularly. It no longer mattered that it had cost a hefty sum. Incidentally, I only saw it when she or Papa let me; after reading from it for a bit, I always had to hand it back to them. Indeed, such schoolbooks migrated annually from one student to another; it seemed to me that no one really dared to turn their pages too much, because if anything happened to them, the school ruthlessly collected the full price.

The first few days I spent in the company of that book, it still held my interest. I looked through the whole thing and discovered lots of new things about the curriculum. But within a few weeks I already knew what was on which page.

Mama sometimes quizzed me about what I'd read, and those days did at least break the everyday routine. She would have been a strict teacher. She picked up the book and expected me to repeat things word for word as they appeared on a given page. There were two possible outcomes: I either knew every word and got five cigarettes, or else I didn't, and got none. I tried to avoid that unpleasantness, because Mama added stuff I missed one day to the next lesson.

My freedom of movement was hindered by the fact that I could only grab a pair of better boots at night, when I wouldn't be noticed. The settlement's ditches lured me mightily, as they were fabulous ice rinks at this time of year. I couldn't resist my yearnings and ended up tying a pair of wooden skates onto my bare feet, speeding around as long as I could. In all its wisdom, Nature knew I had no shoes. It didn't abuse its advantage over me: never did I catch a cold or even have a cough. If the ice tore at my feet as I slid barefoot over it or if the big boots I sometimes wore rubbed them bloody, they soon healed by themselves.

The moonlit silvery nights compensated me for everything.

Once I glided over the glossy surface of the ice, slicing regular figure eights with a pair of makeshift skates forged from horseshoes. Tiny clouds of frozen dust swirled around me as I mimicked the galloping of a runaway colt, and even though protruding bits of ice sometimes knocked me down and made me slide on my backside, I kept trying ten times over until I managed to do it the way I wanted.

Failures could not break me. These words echoed in my mind: "to want" or "not to want." And, if I wanted, I knew no bounds, no obstacles; I was fixed only on my goal.

I often experienced the downside. Even if I'd reached my goal, I sometimes wondered if it might have been more in my interest to have given up, or else . . . ?

Unfortunately, these ideas usually occurred to me too late. If I went out in the evening, dawn drove me home, and I kept wandering around the settlement's shanties without eating anything.

People usually cooked in the evenings, but few evenings found me at home at dinnertime. Many times I stood with a growling stomach before old Khandi's door, the savory smell of boiled meat seeping from within through the gaping cracks.

I was always prepared to be set upon by Papa or Mama if they caught me there. But it would have been a pity to miss out on all the excitement that went on behind that door just for a meal at home.

Old Khandi was my great uncle on Papa's side. From fall to spring, he plucked chicken feathers. His hut was the only one in the settlement where everyone could go and not regret a sleepless night. Songs, dances, games, and stories alternated as if at a perpetual party. Sometimes there wasn't a bit of room, though his wasn't among the smaller huts. With a small frame, gray hair, and beard, Khandi held much prestige. Perhaps he wasn't respected simply for his age, though, but also for his boundless imagination. Every night he poured different stories into us. His tales, rich in adventure, bravery, and love, lasted all night.

We listened to him in awe; not for a moment did anyone doubt the veracity of his stories. We believed them, because life had only given us barely enough space to live next to one another; we had to escape into another world, where giants lived, enchanting old women rode on brooms, and benign or evil spirits decided our fate.

We imagined, we believed, that such a world existed: our shaman horses galloped about in the Realm of the Orange Sun, where we confronted even dragons with living swords that we pulled out from under our skin. We could barely wait for evening, so as to immerse ourselves into the mysterious world of tales, within which we ceased to exist as our yearnings effortlessly followed their wondrous landscapes.

We feared and, at the same time, loved this world; we summoned spirits to bring news from there, because in our narrow little world there was no news. On such evenings Khandi's rickety old table danced around half the night as we deciphered its scary tapping by which our dead friends and brothers communicated with us—telling us not only about their fate on the other side but also about ours over here.

Not that we wanted to see the future—no, it's said that it is not good to do—but all the same one evening we asked Mister Gene to voice these imploring words: "Come, spirit, come! The sooner the better! When you get here, tap once."

Seven pair of hands nervously pressed against the table's rough plank board. Hearts pounding, we watched to see when the table leg would rise.

We shook with excitement as our breaths grew quick. Our eyes stung red from sweat, yet we looked unblinkingly, our gaze almost scratching the table leg until it rose.

"When you get here, tap once!" And sure enough it tapped out every word. Sometimes well, other times not. There were also evil spirits. At times spirits came in pairs—a good one and an evil one. When that happened, we couldn't expect very precise answers.

True, we weren't too fussy. We didn't see how many of them there were, but Mister Gene did. Or, rather, he knew the most about it.

We marveled as a spirit tapped out how old each one of us was. Although it got it wrong in some cases, there was no time to argue. Besides, who was to say who knew better, the spirit or the person himself?

Indeed, many of those around the table learned this way how old they were, more or less. Before that, they had never given the matter a thought. The only problem with summoning spirits was that it was only until midnight that you could carry on a normal conversation with them. After midnight, they came in droves, even if they weren't summoned. Mister Gene spoke with them as with old friends. If the tapping of one of them wasn't to his liking, he sent the spirit away and summoned another. It happened that a spirit didn't want to obey. Well, then it had something coming!

"Harder! Turn the table on them!" he said if there was a compliant spirit among them. The table obeyed and reared up like a colt. The participants howled with laughter. Many of us, me included, were scared, but we kept on with it. This was a different sort of fear; we still felt safe. The worst thing that could happen was that the table would tip over. And, of course, if we wanted the spirit to go away, we could take our hands off the table.

I became preoccupied with the question of why the power worked only if we had our hands on the table. But my experiments were unsuccessful: even when I took my hands off, the table danced just the same. Nothing changed.

I was burning with curiosity, and I resolved to get to the bottom of things. The only upshot was that Mister Gene no longer allowed me to the table.

"If someone doesn't believe in what he is doing," he said, "he shouldn't do it. The good spirits stay away from nonbelievers. Don't spoil it for the others!" Reluctantly I kept a low profile because if I talked back, he'd send me home.

Old Khandi tried to let me in on the secret, but his explanation made me no wiser.

"Everyone's nerves get into the table, which is why it dances. Don't you believe Gene, he's nothing to do with spirits—he talks to the dead only to frighten those whose hands are on table. Yes, it's our nerves that do it."

"But you should know better," old Khandi chided me. "After all, you go to school."

This upset me. Whenever I'd ask something, I was told: "You should know better—after all, you go to school." As if they taught us *everything* there, from forgery to summoning spirits. Some folks lived to the age of ninety, even a hundred, and still couldn't read a single letter, while I was expected to know even what went on in the table leg while it was dancing. Why didn't Mister Gene tell me? Was he afraid that someone would take his power away, or didn't he himself know what he was doing?

He was just as big a liar as his grandfather, Wrinkled Rick, who too had caught a fish so big that twelve bulls couldn't pull it out. But he and his grandson managed it. That's what he built his house from; its bones were as thick as rafters, its scales the size of tiles. If he cracked his bullwhip, even the outlaws hiding in the Bakony Hills across the country could hear it. "That was Wrinkled Rick!" said the outlaws and took to flight. Yes, he stood up to a whole gang of outlaws by himself, bullwhip in one hand, knife in the other, lance in the third, something else in the fourth, and who knows what in the fifth, and he didn't stop until he counted thirty-two hands.

So they called him "Thirty-Two Hands Wrinkled Rick."

Mister Gene took very much after his grandfather.

"Don't get angry," Khandi said, trying to appease me. "I'll bring you some books from the village, and you can find out everything from them.

I protested: "I don't even like the books I have."

"These are different. But I'll only bring them if you'll sit next to me and read them out loud so I can hear everything too."

I always sat beside him on the bed in any case, massaging his legs. He walked a lot during the day, selling drills in the village. In the evening, exhausted, he perched on the bed in his long, baggy underpants, while I went about squeezing his outstretched legs. He hissed in pain, but bore it. He said it was good for him.

For weeks no one bothered to sweep up after plucking chickens. Feathers covered the floor of the hut like thick bedding, providing guests with comfortable seating, or indeed a bed for anyone who didn't feel like going home for the night.

Inside, the cob oven burned day and night. Every day Khandi brought home a dry acacia log that, when split, yielded a brisk, long-lasting fire. Nobody went to the timber depot to buy firewood. The forest was almost half a day's hike, and a bundle of wood would last but a couple of days.

If we were in a tight spot, especially when the weather turned wicked, even the grape vines out in the yard made for serviceable fuel.

Our huts had to be heated constantly, for the wind cut right through their thin walls; if the fire went out for an hour, the water would freeze in the kettle. The winters were very long, posing many challenges for us. Living honestly was not really an option. No, cold and hunger made the Gypsies do all sorts of things.

To stay warm and to eat! This, then, was our day-to-day concern. Each day brought its own hopelessness and growling bellies; the settlement's many hungry little mouths had to be satiated with food, and the cold and the lack of clothes on so many backs meant that getting our hands on fuel was ever on our minds. But what could we do during blizzards? Why, even dogs couldn't be sent out into the biting winds that would sometimes last for days. No, here, life was fit not even for a dog; it didn't give a damn what was acceptable, what was proper, and what wasn't. Life demanded its due, but from where? No one talked about that, and there were no options to choose from. To live—that was the only commandment, and there was no appeal. Anyone could starve or freeze to death, if they wanted, but to do so they had to bear the hunger or the cold.

Even in the bleakest reality, though, there is always a saving grace; if nothing else, the certainty of hopelessness itself. Here, too, such was the case. Our Gypsy settlement lay at the edge of a village that was surrounded by vast, aristocratic estates of sprawling farms, some of which raised livestock, especially pigs, which were fattened all winter long.

One winter it so happened that swine flu struck, and those pigs dropped like ripe fruit. Every day their carcasses were carried away by the cartload. It wasn't easy to get near them. By day it was completely impossible; any Gypsy spotted on an estate was shot at. At night, an armed guard would watch over the hog pit at each farm, lest someone carry a carcass away. But, if it was freezing, even the guard got cold, withdrawing to his hut to sleep the sleep of the just.

The worst weather favored the Gypsies, and there was no shortage of it, not that winter. Through waist-high drifts they moved toward the pit in wolflike packs, making it easier to scrape out the frozen soil where those dead but life-giving beasts lay.

Most every Gypsy hauled an entire pig around his neck, and there was no chance to rest. Once you picked one up, you couldn't put it down until you got home up to five miles away, or else it would stay right there on the road. Getting home as soon as possible was the key. Each man chose a pig whose size suited his strength, assuming there were enough pigs. If not, they cut a carcass in two, but in general there were several to choose from.

A feast was held that very night.

It was custom to give a loin or two as tasters to friends and relatives and to those who'd been unable to take part that night in acquiring the booty.

The aroma of roast and boiled meat permeated the settlement. Lard now glistening on their lips, folks laughed heartily and even joined in on the task of stuffing sausages. Not that much of a ceremony was made of it; a good sharp hatchet was used to chop up the meat instead of a grinder, and the meat was then stuffed through makeshift cones of paper, along with a good bit of garlic and salt, into the hastily cleaned guts we used as casings.

At times like those, our little settlement became a veritable fairy-tale land.

One afternoon, old Khandi received me with three huge books.

"Well then, my friend," he said fondly, "have a look at these. The Hungarians say they are very good."

I looked in horror at the tattered three-volume set: *The Black Horseman,* by László Jarosinszky. Each volume was as thick as the Old Testament and had a black cover.

Folks filtered into Khandi's hut, and I began to read aloud.

From then on, the spirit rapping ceased. Mister Gene's time in the spotlight was over, and I was glad, for he'd been all too full of himself, sending even grown-ups out of the room if they laughed at or expressed any doubt about his séances.

From the very first night, my readings were to everyone's liking.

The hut was packed every evening; coins were collected to buy kerosene, because the oil didn't burn brightly enough in the lamp to read by for long.

The story fascinated everyone, and I could pause only for a cigarette break or when everyone went outside together to take a piss. My reading out loud got better and better, and I quickly realized that emphasizing certain punctuation marks enhanced the excitement.

I got heaps of praise.

"He reads like flowing water," said some.

Here it was the reader, not the writer, who reaped the laurels.

Respect for books grew, as did the frequency of comments like, "How good it is to be able to read!"

Khandi put a separate little bookshelf on the wall, and I alone could lay my hands on what was there.

"Leave it alone," he'd tell the others. "The child gets angry if you bend the pages."

Those three books were the first I ever had. I became fond of reading, and the other Gypsies were sad when the story ended.

Longingly I would stare at the cheap, gorily titled thrillers displayed in the windows of the tobacconists' stalls in villages and towns.

My nighttime skating escapades gradually decreased.

Also, for the first time in my life, instead of making the rounds of the village on Christmas Eve singing carols, I stayed at home and read, even though the good fresh aroma of the kalach, or sweet bread, that was handed out to the carolers wafted right into our place, too.

The singing of "God's Holy Angel" came from every direction.

The carolers were coming home with full baskets and knapsacks.

Our little Gypsy settlement was filled with the succulent smell of stuffed cabbage.

Christmas was indeed celebrated, too.

Those who could not cook up a little feast for themselves at such a time were seen as poor even among the Gypsies. Many folks even sold their last blanket so they could honor the holiday properly. They welcomed anyone and everyone according to their means.

Around midnight, Grandma looked at me and let out a big sigh.

"What's the matter?" Mama asked.

"If my feet didn't hurt so much, I'd go out there to get some sweet bread for this boy of ours."

We all knew full well that it wasn't me who was hungry for kalach, but her. By then she was already sick. She hurt all over but didn't complain.

"Give me your pillow case, Grandma."

"What do you want it for?"

My parents too looked at me in surprise.

"I'm going out to carol. I need a bag to put things in."

"Now? It's almost midnight."

"That's exactly right. Everyone's getting ready for mass, so maybe they'll be a bit more generous."

Thinking it would be best not to go alone, I went over to Zolti's place; he'd already returned with a basketful of sweet bread, but he joined me all the same.

Just to be on the safe side, we began with nice big houses. We tried telling from a distance where the lights were still on, but no sooner did we start to carol than the lights turned off.

"Let us have something, master," we called out the usual way. "There's just two of us."

"Then scat in two directions," yelled the master of the house from behind the dark windows. Cursing, we walked on. We'd been wandering around for nearly an hour without any luck when a plump young farmer stepped out of a house, breadbasket in hand.

"Do you like dried sour cherries?" he asked.

"Sure we do," we said gratefully. A group of other young fellows were snickering away about something on the glassed-enclosed veranda.

"Well, then hold out your basket." He poured the fruit into Zolti's basket.

“Thank you,” we said. ”May God reward you.”

The moment we left Zolti put a handful in his mouth and spat it out at once.

“Maybe they’ve gone bad. We’ll have a look under some light.”

When we came to a street lamp, Zolti spat out his second handful, too.

“I knew this wasn’t real,” he said, pouring the sheep shit out of his basket. “I’m going home,” he huffed.

“Go ahead,” I said. “I’ll just go on over to the other side of the tracks—no one goes there, anyway. Since we haven’t gotten anything here, at least the poor folks will get a bit of singing, too.”

Zolti kept hitting his basket against the sidewalk, and then he followed me all the same.

The lights were on everywhere. It was quiet, dogs all tied up, as if those who lived there were expecting guests.

We began to sing that old Hungarian favorite, “Angel from Heaven,” right below the window of an old cottage with a reed-thatched roof. We did so in rounds—not like those who sing for sweet bread, but like those who sing because it’s Christmas.

Their light didn’t turn off, and a window was opened instead, revealing a young woman with a smiling little girl in her arms who waved to us with tiny hands.

“Come on in,” came a man’s voice as the door opened. A mustached elderly gentleman showed us in.

It was nice and warm and utterly silent inside. There were four of them: an elderly couple, the young woman, and the little girl.

“Sing here,” said the old man, pointing to the Christmas tree.

Both of us sang, quietly, so as not to wake the neighbors.

“Thank you, children.”

He handed us two glasses filled to the brim with an inky black wine.

“Drink up!” he said, pouring a second glass, and then a third—until the wine jug emptied out.

The old lady brought out a platter of sweet bread and doled it out fairly between us. The smiling little girl handed us four coins.

Turning to the little girl, the old lady said, "Let's say farewell to the baby Jesuses, who are leaving now."

By dawn, I could hardly hold the corners of the pillowcase, it was so full of the sweet bread we got while making the rounds of this neighborhood.

Among Gypsies, it is custom that on Christmas morning only men or boys can first enter a stranger's home. In the settlement, we did our utmost to honor the holiday in this way.

Wine was poured, followed by long, flattering toasts full of good wishes. If someone then offered something, you had to accept it graciously because it was done with good will. Being unable to feed a guest during the Christmas holidays was contemptible. Not so the rest of the year though, since poverty was nothing to be ashamed about.

Everyone endeavored to do their best. People had been preparing for Christmas for months.

To secure some cabbage, rancid bones, and other scraps of food the well-off no longer had need of, Gypsy women patched up the walls of chicken coops with mud, swept the attics, stoked the wood-fired ovens, and undertook other such jobs—anything to ready these ingredients for the holiday.

Traditional Gypsy custom forbade certain foods—such as cereal grains, beans, and peas, because they caused rashes—during the Christmas season. And Christmas for those Gypsies who followed the Romanian tradition lasted right up through the Twelfth Night to the Feast of the Epiphany. No matter how this custom got started, it's a really good one.

No one wants to break these rules. True, it's not hard to do so, anyway, since so much food had been saved up by Christmas that you could easily do without that which you aren't supposed to eat.

I've often thought how good it would be to have Christmas all year round. There would always be plenty to eat, and there would be peace.

But maybe if there was always enough to eat, there would always be peace even without Christmas.

The carefree days of Christmas quickly passed. We hardly noticed when the holiday was over. There was still some dry sweet bread left, true, but we sensed that lean days indeed would follow in short order after the New Year.

The first signs of those days soon appeared: one blizzard after another, the tiny huts verily groaning from the onslaught, some of them practically buried in snowdrifts. Moaning winds swept over the pasture, bringing with them every grain of snow, blocking our windows and doors. At night a wolf or two ventured out from among the now frozen reedy marsh, their plaintive howls swept along by the wind amid those prickly grains of snow. The temperatures inside our shanties dropped ever lower; in vain we kept stuffing wood into the insatiable bellies of our cob ovens. The layer of ice that grew thicker over the windows engulfed even the daylight into a mysterious twilight.

Families moved in together to protect themselves from the cold, bringing along their worries and their kids' intolerable behavior. And so they listened regularly to the growling bellies and the sizzle of steaming piss atop the rubbish heap swept behind the door, which gobbled up the hut's scant air supply.

Not all the shanties could withstand the weight of the snow. Their beams, no stronger than the latticework of grape arbors, were sometimes crushed by it.

The wind twisted fur coats of snow and ice around those who ventured into the outside world and hardened their raw pigskin sandals to stone.

That was the kind of weather in which the Zhidós arrived, frozen blue, practically fused together, all in a heap, wrapped in thick blankets. You couldn't tell which of them was male or female.

When old Fardi, his head all wrapped up, was helped off his cart, the scene reminded me of the earless dulmuta Grandma had once told us a story about.

They came in three godforsaken carts with horses so decrepit that even giving them away would have been a capital crime. So many folks poured out of those carts that they didn't all fit into our place. They put their luggage into the stable. Old Fardi was so cold that he lay right down on the oven. He trembled for hours.

Botosh beat all three nags to death; they would have been frozen by the morning, anyway.

"Eat up, Gypsies!"

They were thin, but there was still a little fat on their bones. The folks picked them apart, skin still on, as they couldn't be skinned in the cold. Within an hour, there were only three heaps of guts and three heads left to show that they had once been horses.

Neither old Fardi and his clan nor Papa had eaten any.

Papa didn't mind if we ate horse meat, but I don't remember him ever tasting any. He and some others believed that the horse isn't a pure-souled creature. Grandma was happy to see her daughter Zhidó and her siblings once again and to get news of her scattered children and grandchildren.

The Zhidós had set out for Hungary with spoils aplenty, but then they barely managed to get even themselves across the border. Hungarian Gypsies had given them those dreadful horses and carts.

Zhidó had brought me a smart-looking, side-stitched boot, but only one, as she had lost its pair. Her husband, Botosh, insisted that Papa give it to me.

Mister Fardi had strong, burly grandsons who got married that same night. The Gypsy women and girls of our settlement seized the opportunity, for they weren't bad looking guys. Within a week they all became widows, though, for their men left as suddenly as they had arrived.

Three days later, however, they came back once again from Romania, this time with handsome young horses—horses that could have made suitable in-training cavalry horses—to replace the ones they had killed. Then, once again they disappeared as if they had never arrived.

That's how it always happened: we never knew when they would appear and how long they would say. I don't think they knew it themselves.

By the time the gendarmes came looking for them a few weeks later, no one knew where they were, what names they were using, and what identifications they were carrying.

The joy of seeing them invigorated Grandma so much that it was she who was most upset that the Zhidós had lost the other half of my pair of boots.

"Buy some ink powder for it, son." With that, she handed me some of the coins her daughter had left her. "At least you'll have one decent boot on."

"What about my other foot?"

"I'll knit you a smart little sandal, and you can say your foot is sore."

Her eyes sparkled in the morning when I put on that one good boot, which fit like a glove.

"If you had its pair, you'd look like a little hussar."

Each night Grandma herself smeared my boot with the ink powder to make it shine, but her satisfaction didn't last long.

One morning we awoke to find that Grandma had died.

We hadn't even noticed it; she'd just fallen asleep forever.

I wasn't afraid of Grandma's body, and indeed I sat by her side until the funeral. I mourned for her for a long time hoping she would return or visit, but she was true to her word. She used to tell me:

"When I die, don't be afraid of me, I'll never haunt you."

Still, I hoped I would see her once more.

We'd been really good friends. She could read my mind better than anyone; if I wanted something, we both wanted it.

She'd spoken little Hungarian, and her convoluted words had brought smiles to everyone's lips; all the Gypsies had liked her.

For a long time the others didn't dare mention her name in my presence, because every time I heard it, my heart sank and I couldn't help but burst into tears.

Still, life didn't stop; it kept inflicting one trouble after another on us.

Six months' pregnant, Mama slipped on the icy road one day, and Papa had paid the price of a horse to the doctor by the time she was well again.

Of our four horses, only the two weakest ones remained by spring.

Even though he himself had meanwhile made peace with the rival Komlódys, Principal Rácz kept his word: he had me enrolled early on at the high school. He asked Papa to come in one day, and I too had to be there.

"Mr. Boncza," the principal said to Papa, "your dream can now come true. The school's Red Cross committee has recommended your boy for further studies. But although he will get free tuition, you must look after the boy's proper clothing, hygiene, and all extra expenses that might come up." Stroking my hair, Rácz added, "You can be proud of your son. He may have missed out on school for quite a while, but he excels even among the best of them. The main thing is that you, his parents, mustn't let him down. You're not as poor as the others in the settlement. Many Hungarian peasants who have nothing but a worn spade would be envious of your horses."

Papa only nodded; he was evidently both happy and not happy. He didn't say a thing, but it seemed as if I could hear his mental reply:

"Sir, you have no idea what you're talking about. You don't know that the difference between a peasant with only a worn spade and my horses is deceptive. Common folk can't sell their spades to buy food or shoes for their sons, because they wouldn't have a thing with which to earn money for the next day's bread. My horses, too, are just tools."

Indeed, for days there hadn't been any food at home. When Mama had gotten sick, there was no one to buy and sell for us; everything stopped, and we ate up every last bit of food we had. I myself did well, though, because I got a meal at school, and I took my knapsack with me so I could take the leftovers home for my younger siblings.

Papa didn't argue anymore with the principal, though. He only thanked him for the favor.

For my part, I wasn't exactly jumping for joy. Though I had an inner thirst for something, I just didn't know yet what that was. The prospect of high school really scared me, but what terrified me even more was the change of scene, of being among upper-class kids whose crowd included not a single friend of mine.

What is more, I would only be able to get home in the evening, as I'd have to take the train.

Every bone in my body protested. Papa was the only one who knew my true feelings. As much as I abhorred the idea, I would even have been willing to become a horse trader. But it didn't depend on the two of us alone. Papa tried to comfort me, but in secret his hopes, too, were shaped by self-interest.

"You should get a job issuing livestock licenses, son, once you finish your studies." Papa couldn't imagine a greater gentleman than the one he had dealings with at the village hall. Everything could be arranged with him as long as he got enough money.

Mama didn't mention anything about school, only that going was a must. In the opportunity she saw the family's future. Maybe she didn't aim for the stars, only to see me more educated and smarter than the others. I didn't want to upset her with my feelings, since she hadn't been well lately.

"We can't leave anything to you except our poverty and worries, but a smart man always lands on his feet. You won't be sorry," she consoled me.

The other Gypsies, too, had come round to the idea of schooling—for me, at least. Indeed, they wished various professions upon me according to their personal preferences. In their eyes, doctors and county clerks, for example, were all-powerful. No one thought about whether these wishes could be fulfilled in the case of a Gypsy. The mere possibility seemed to satisfy them, for there had never been anything of the sort in our world.

My anxiousness soon subsided, and after the high school entrance exam—which I passed with flying colors—I surrendered myself wholly to Mama's will.

Ever since the term "high school" had burst into my life, I'd been the object of ridicule at school. Everyone could have dirt behind their ears—everyone but for me, that is, because the whole class was laughing at me, including the teacher.

I often went home crying, telling Mama I'd rather become an outlaw than go back to school. But doing so was like talking to a brick wall. The upshot: she started scrubbing me down first thing in the morning so I'd look proper for my return. Bumming about with my chums, getting into fights? She made it clear that it had to stop.

My situation became somewhat easier when my teacher had a baby two months before the exam.

We got a lovely teacher in her place, Miss Panna. Though she too called me "My Little African King," she did so differently, in a kindly, pleasing way. She withdrew me from the school cafeteria, and from then on I had lunch at her place nearby every day. She gave me a pair of her own shoes, as she didn't let me go barefoot even in good weather. She lived alone, and in the afternoons, after I did a little gardening for her, she entertained me by reading to me from the *Eclipse of the Crescent Moon*—that classic historical adventure novel that swept me right back to the sixteenth century, to the Hungarians' heroic stand against the Turks laying siege to the Castle of Eger up north.

She virtually regarded me as her own son.

Although this did not exempt me from mockery, much of what *was* said was toned down through her influence, and she set me as an example to the children.

Now I really studied hard.

Then, like a malignant tumor, envy appeared.

The parents of the other children took to dropping by the school to lambaste the new teacher for "mollycoddling the Gypsy kid." But they couldn't accuse her of anything forbidden, like accepting eggs or fattened ducks in exchange, so she stroked my hair lovingly right in front of them. As she explained to me later, she did it to make them burst with envy.

All good and evil ended, though, with the final exam.

My freedom regained, within a week a laborer's work permit was in my pocket. This would allow me to do farm work over the summer at an estate well away from home, as Mama had arranged, except that my age qualified me only for children's wages. Thankfully, though, the months of education I'd received were now like water off a duck's back. I proved to be a good student of life: the same day I got the permit, I falsified my age on it.

Nor did I let my friends down; all of us had grown pretty tall and looked to be not a day younger than sixteen, so I performed the same service for them on their permits. Doing so would make a big difference, we knew, for we would receive women's pay.

Except that the foreman at the estate had his doubts. He'd never seen me; most Gypsies in the area had been there before, but not me, as I lived farther away. Standing beside me was Miss Mili, the lady Mama had told me to report to at the estate.

"Have you ever worked before?"

I was so startled that I could only tell the truth: "No."

"So there!" snapped the foreman.

"'So there!' What's that supposed to mean?" Miss Mili spoke up in my defense. "The kid is going to high school, so let him work if he wants to be with his friends. He can do so just as well as any skinny woman. I won't let him out of my sight; his mother asked me to take care of him."

"Where does he go to school, in a hovel?" the foreman asked sarcastically.

"Yes," a couple of the other women called out at once, whereupon Miss Mili added, "He has more brains than all the hired hands on this estate put together."

The foreman decided to quiz me: "Well, then, can you tell me what that ancient Greek guy had to say about water?"

I told him; I'd learned about Archimedes' principle in sixth grade.

"Okay then, here are two jugs," he said, giving in, "you'll be the women's water carrier."

Hundreds of local Gypsies were gathering on the estate. The non-Gypsy Hungarian peasants were busy harvesting, and day laborers were needed. At times like these, the estate people weren't choosy, but they were the ones who decided what constituted a day's pay.

The ox barn we slept in was huge, and it was full of Gypsies from far and wide. We made up spaces for ourselves from rancid straw—literally just spaces that seemed completely inadequate for sleeping or even resting. Falling asleep was not easy, anyway, on account of the flies. The singing and noise that could raise the dead, almost numbed me. I lay down on a warm haycock that stank of stinkbugs and slept there until morning all the same.

Miss Mili filled two foul-smelling jugs with water from the canal.

"Here's some water in case anyone gets thirsty."

I had a fine time: I slept when I wanted, and I innocently cavorted with the girls, who saw me as a little gentleman. I, however, thought of myself as an older, mature young man, as per the faked age in my work permit; and yet, I knew, something else was needed to *truly* become a young man.

I had to settle for the appearance of being one. That was better than nothing. In the eyes of the older folks I seemed like a serious, high-minded boy, one who took no notice of the loose Gypsy girls clamoring for my attention.

"My boy," Miss Mili boasted to the other ladies, "gives gals like that the cold shoulder even though they're practically all over him."

It's a good thing that one's thoughts can't be heard, otherwise their opinion of me would soon have changed.

After certain rainy nights, the fields were too drenched for us to work in them, and I had so little to do that I was bored. At such times Miss Mili invariably sought to distract me with something or other. On one occasion she found a couple of bird eggs and recently hatched skylark chicks. She began to dig a little nest of sorts in the soft, loamy soil to help them survive.

For a while this did hold my interest, but as Miss Mili sat across from me I couldn't help but notice something else vying for my attention, a brushlike lock of her hair. As she went about carving out that nest, a blade of grass got caught up in it, and it took great effort on my part not to reach over and take it out. If for no other reason, I resisted the temptation out of politeness. For better or worse, such was our world.

Public morality meant that folks around there, judging from their words, held sexuality in contempt. But sex was in fact the sole meaning of their lives. The young people, for example, were by no means forced by their financial circumstances to work on the estate. No, their lots didn't improve one bit as a result. But they had to satisfy their sexual desires, and here they had the opportunity to do so. That is why they migrated here in droves, just like certain types of fish that swim thousands of miles to fulfill their mating instincts.

I was really sorry that I couldn't pick such fruits. No, the thirteen years I had under my belt seemed insufficient for such salvation, and so I found myself only retreating from such stimuli, and my thoughts of doing otherwise were quashed.

My friends, however, who were just a few months or years older than me, threw themselves headlong into pleasure. Anyone who had the opportunity took advantage of it. Few indeed were not caught up in the general mood. Some guys were content to prepare for the real thing by pleasuring themselves behind a bush or at the foot of a haystack. Nor were the girls any different. We often sneaked a look at them as they did the same, and this meant something not only to us but, if they noticed us spying, also to them. And then there were the "petting nights" held without ceremony in the ox barns, evenings whose sole objective seemed that of determining who had a full growth of hair down there and who had not much, or none, at all.

The boys didn't leave it to chance: a glance at a girl by day sufficed to let her know to be on hand for a tryst by night. Sounds of protest sounded more like lustful growls meant to hasten time, for life was rushing on. The object was to drink up whatever could be had along with all the potential pitfalls—sexually transmitted diseases, TB, and the like.

The uninvited participants of such nights of debauchery were lice of all possible species and orders that had graduated from the academies of crossbreeding. Indeed, a fine collection of parasites could have been collected from among the chaff-trodden straw and the girls' disheveled curls. Some couples, marred by the itching and the festering rashes of scabies, could only gnash their teeth like souls condemned to eternal darkness in the nothingness of the universe.

Intimate conversations between guys and girls sometimes turned into vocal disputes when certain, shocking information was shared. There were no secrets here: eyes couldn't always see but ears sure as hell could hear. Girls who gossiped one night were sure of a visit from the guys the next night. After all, why else would they have talked but out of jealousy or to get themselves noticed? Not that it would have been easy *not* to notice them. As we saw it, many such gals deserved to be screwed in revenge. Which guy actually met with success was another matter, but the following night the girl was already quietly waiting for a repeat performance.

The first few days, the girls stayed together in small groups of families and friends. Under the same blanket they lay in communal brooding nests, lips painted pink or red using crepe paper they soaked in water.

Huddled together, the girls giggled as young men's lascivious gazes pulled their blanket off. In no time they made their own, individual nests, some so they'd be noticed, others so they wouldn't. After a while, the girls no longer even fit into the ox barn. Some in fact had to move outside—they did so resentfully, expecting to be pitied, as if they were orphans and outcasts. But most everyone had a good time. Before long, the nights quieted down and the petting nights ceased altogether, for every Jack had found his Jill.

At first, it had been a matter of blind choice, based on smell and touch alone—the important thing being that the gender was different.

Then, when the excitement began to fizzle, longer-term relationships took hold—whether for a whole night or even for two or three.

On Sundays it began all over again. New girls and guys arrived as some of those who'd already been there now stayed home or else had seen their desires satisfied, and relationships that hadn't been stable in the first place now came to an end. But those fervid feelings of love planted into each other's mouths still burned on their lips, filling the ox barn's air with heat, with she- and he-smells aplenty.

Never were such swarming and seething encounters brought about by mutual affinity, though, but rather by biological necessity. Ironically, every part of the participants' bodies seemed to protest. Still, they were unable to resist, like a tree whose branches have broken off under the weight of the previous year's fruit, yet which is blooming again, fertilized by outside forces, only to break down once more under the weight of the fruit nourished by its own sap.

I was exempt from all of this. Now, such feelings were alive within me, too, but the combination of my fear and Miss Mili, who guarded me like a lioness, ruled out any possibility of their being realized.

She complied with Mama's request to the letter. In the evening Miss Mili gave me just enough time until lights out before making me slip into the straw, from where I wasn't allowed to budge until the morning.

After a few weeks I tried to break through these barriers, though, for I had had quite enough of my friends' remarks about me always hiding behind Miss Mili's apron strings. Still, those remarks were not purely sarcastic but also mingled with some envy. Everyone saw me as a good boy—serious-minded and clever, prudent and far-sighted. This general admiration gained me prestige with the girls as well. They admitted me into their circles without reservation; they did not hide their secrets; in fact, they often asked me for advice. Gradually they forgot that I was a boy. It has to be said that I, too, often forgot. They made me the same type of large hat out of a kerchief as the one they wore, and they painted my lips.

Many a time I even found myself imitating their gait.

"That spotted kerchief really suits you," my male friends teased me. "Tonight we'll have a look at what's underneath."

I got used to such taunts and went on being friends with the girls, who were much more restrained than the boys. Not that their desire for male company had diminished one bit, but if they managed to corral a real man for themselves, they didn't exactly shout it from the rooftops.

It got to the point where I could have a sleepover with any one of the girls I hung out with; which is to say, they didn't have to worry about me getting hot and heavy on them. They saw me as their friend. Even Miss Mili wasn't worried about me being with them; for she had realized before even I did that I didn't exactly belong to either gender yet. What is more, she was delighted to see that I occupied a position worthy of my status.

Without intending to, I began to bring order to the chaos of the nights. I enjoyed the trust of both genders; they didn't hide their secrets from me, and I, like a central hub, sent everyone to where they were welcome.

By the time I realized my role as an intermediary, all of them had already long been expecting me to help their secret desires come true.

The sarcastic remarks fell by the wayside; even grown-up male lions now asked for my advice on how to approach dangerous-looking lionesses. It was the same with the women. They entrusted me with their secrets so I might create their coveted Garden of Eden.

I pursued my vocation selflessly, not even realizing its importance in resolving the nighttime worries of so many and in inspiring courage in the timid. And, like a good fairy, I guided aimlessly fluttering bees to flower gardens.

The rendezvous I arranged didn't pass without leaving marks. Within days, the signs of lifelong venereal diseases had appeared, and the afflicted had to spend their earnings, if any, from the labor they were taking on by day on potassium permanganate.

And yet every Saturday night, one mule-drawn cart after another bumped merrily along toward home. The few coins left in the occupants' pockets as a result of their labors made them forget all their troubles.

"One for the road!" they were soon calling out to the man busying himself behind the counter of a makeshift bar hastily set up for just such traveling laborers.

"Another and another for the road!" Long-necked bottles clanged against one another as they began singing a popular tune:

It's so lonely on my trail of tears.
Why oh why? It's not yet time to die.
My dreams have left me high and dry.

Indeed, tears came to their eyes as an untold number of drinks sloshed about inside of them. Then, not even reminiscent of their stalwart ancestors and relatives back home, they wallowed in their soul-shaking, mule-drawn carts like a slimy, choking, gagging mass of cells amid an inextricably putrid tangle of vomit, tears, and piss-soaked rags. The incomprehensible jumble of boozy singing and sobs mingled with the carts' ceaseless clattering.

All that was left of many a man by the next day was what the doctor could prescribe free of charge on being presented with a certificate of poverty: a syringe and a pack of potassium permanganate.

The mornings, noisy with arguments over card games, were painted bloody by the tongues of squabbling women. They kept piling up the past weeks' trash until the gendarmes came by kicking up a storm, for our rowdy Gypsy Paris had disrupted Sunday's pious silence, and at such times order had to be restored.

The day laborers' carts, widened to make room for additional passengers, arrived like guardian angels, allowing both the guilty and the innocent to escape. The long, unforgettable nights brought oblivion, erasing even our awareness of the fact that nothing had really changed; there had only been an intermission, a breathing spell.

There is no beginning, only continuation—the continuation of a big, never-ending night in which the past mingles with the future, where you never know what has passed, yesterday or tomorrow. Only one thing is certain: today. And whatever it brings, good or bad, it is always just about to pass, carrying us away lock, stock, and barrel. We live for its minutes, its moments, and if there is a promise of tomorrow, or rather, of a glimpse of tomorrow, all we can do is take that image with us today, an eternal today.

We arrived back on the estate Sunday evening. The sun was still hovering in the sky like a giant muffin, making our mouths water. Wouldn't it be nice to have a bite of it?

We dared only to touch the watermelon-size loaf of coarse bread nestling in our stinging nettle–fiber sack. Saturday was still far away!

That bread—which we couldn't put down even for a moment, lest the rats get at it—and two packs of cheap tobacco; those meant everything to us.

Farmhands in blindingly white, unironed shirts were promenading about the vicinity of the ox barn. They were itching to dance, and indeed the Gypsies were already strumming their violins to signal that the Sunday evening folk dance evening would soon begin. The farm girls, smelling of scented soap, arrived in groups, clutching white handkerchiefs, as well as the bread and smoked bacon that comprised the Gypsies' pay. It was always the girls who gave it to the musicians.

At the sight of those colt-hoof-size loaves of bread, the Gypsies began playing a bouncy tune. The farmhands whirled around with eardrum-splitting "whoops" until they and the girls were drenched with sweat.

We too danced—freeloaders, we were, trampling on one another's feet, but it was a good opportunity to get acquainted.

This marked the first time I'd taken part in this custom—stomping from one side to the other rather like a goose, sometimes to the beat, sometimes not. My hand slid its way right up to my partner's underarm; I was sweating and so was she. While turning, I felt her supple breasts on my wrists; she smiled, and I blushed like a saint who had found himself cursing.

The musicians were now playing something slower, a popular tune hardly a few years old. My partner snuggled closer to me, and I was no longer just holding her; I was embracing her. She leaned her smoke-scented head against my sweaty neck pretending to be asleep; she was heavy, but I carried her. Babi—that's what they called her—was not an ugly girl; she was a bit freckled, but it suited her. Rumor had it that she had already been married once, though she was not much older than me.

"I'll sleep with you tonight."

That was all I needed, I thought.

"You're too late," I said, trying to extricate myself from the situation.

"How about tomorrow?"

"Then, too, and always."

"Don't go telling me it's better with that old lady?"

I got hot under the collar and left her right there.

Seemingly unembarrassed, Babi soon found another boy, one older than me; perhaps he accepted her offer.

Still angry, I sat on top of a manure cart and looked down at the swirling mass of people. I was hurt that everybody was talking about Miss Mili and me, although there was nothing between us. She was almost as old as Mama.

I'd let all of you girls have it, I thought, *if I were just a year older, but as things stand you'd only laugh at me.*

Yes, Babi, too, had been chummy with me only for *that.* I had regarded her as the most decent of the girls. Now that her auntie wasn't there, she too had let passion get the best of her. It would have been good to be fifteen!

Babi left the boy and set off between the dancers, looking for someone. After turning her eyes this way and that, she finally headed my way.

"Are you mad at me?"

"Yes. So what?"

"They say you're well brought up."

"I don't give a shit what they say. They also say I'm sleeping with Miss Mili. And so," I looked at her inquisitively, "I'm a man or not?"

"No. You're still a kid."

"Me, a kid? You'd soon find out!"

I thought I'd boil over with rage. I wanted to jump up, but she pushed me back.

"I won't let you go until you tell me you're not mad at me."

"Then we'll sit here until morning. The Gypsies are already going to sleep."

"Let them go, we're gonna stay here, or I'll sleep with you."

"With me? You sure are a fool."

"I'd rather be a fool than catch something bad. I'm afraid I'd get it from one of them."

"No one's twisting your arm."

"You're wrong. I'm a woman, after all, and I wouldn't be able to resist among so many men. But if I sleep with you, nobody will accost me."

"Don't you go hiring me as your guard, okay?"

"No, not as a guard, but you can hold my boobs all night. You've done it before but pretended it was by mistake and I let you. I'll let you do so now, too. Let me sleep there, okay?"

I felt as if a trolley were moving under me; a feeling of dizziness came over me. In fact, I had touched her breasts quite often, but only while we were playing. They were small and hard, and I used to look under her blouse—and now she wanted me to repay her.

"It's not possible. Miss Mili is worried, too."

"But maybe I've already put my things next to yours. Miss Mili said she'd look after both of us. Don't be angry," she said, trying to placate me. "I'll also take care of you."

I didn't know just what Babi meant, but it hurt my pride terribly.

"I don't need any looking after; I'm not afraid that someone will knock me up."

Miss Mili was already looking for us; I couldn't even finish my tirade.

"Let's go to sleep, children!"

Babi grabbed my arm and pulled me into the stable.

People were still milling about and fixing their beds of straw, noisily teasing one another, giggling, screaming, and shouting, wrestling, and groping as they prepared for the night.

Some of them risked more obvious moves, but it was still too early.

Jokesters were looking for partners to make fun of, and the stable resounded of guffaws if a good quip found its mark.

No one was sleepy, and yet everyone wanted like hell for the lights to go out.

Miss Mili ran after us playfully, carrying a small rod. In fact, she wasn't old yet, surely not much more than thirty-six; she always looked relatively clean and neat. It was said she spent her younger years in a brothel.

Babi settled into the straw where I slept and covered it with a rosy bedspread.

"Mili," came a girl's voice, "your daughter got married, and I wanted to lie next to her."

"Come lie next to me," replied Miss Mili, "and you can paw my ass."

She could in fact be quite foul-mouthed. Anyone who messed with Miss Mili soon regretted it. She didn't mince words. She now stepped over and pulled up the skirt of the offending girl as well as her own.

"Have fun with this," she said, offering her own pubic hairs, which she'd pulled out. The girl quickly shut up, but one of her companions now spoke:

"We're moving in here tomorrow."

"Get the hell out of here," Miss Mili threatened them. "Or are you hankering for young sausage?"

Giggling, the girls scattered.

Embarrassed, I sat on the straw right where Babi had forced me to and looked pleadingly at Miss Mili, like girls who are scared of a wedding night's horrors.

"Go to sleep."

Babi took off her dress, draped it under our heads and, now dressed only in her long-sleeved shirt, arranged it maternally under me. I got under the cover with my pants still on.

The light was being clicked on and off to indicate that bedtime was near, and a few minutes later it went out.

I cowered next to the girl, holding my hands between my thighs, hardly daring to breathe.

Only the top of my head touched Babi. I used up practically all the air under that thick bedspread. The moment she fell asleep, I told myself, I'd go off to a haystack. I needed fresh air; my brain was pounding against my skull. I felt as if I was about to catch fire. If I straightened out, she'd pull me even closer. As it was, she was almost ripping off my head by pressing it tight against her bosom. I couldn't even try to resist, no, she'd wrestle me down—and who would believe that I wasn't the aggressor? And if they did believe it, I would be put to shame; I'd be called a coward. So I figured it was best if I kept quiet; she'd fall asleep eventually. But perhaps I'd suffocate by then. "Get out of here, if only for a minute," I pleaded with myself.

I'd suffocate under this damn coarse cloth. This bitch was trying to kill me! By now she had completely squashed my nose between her breasts, and I could breathe only through my mouth, and what did wind up in my nose reeked of body odor; which is to say, it seemed to have little to do with air.

I had to get out of there before it was too late! Straightening myself out, I turned onto my back and sucked air into my lungs. As if she'd been waiting for this move, Babi now snuggled closer to me, pressing me to herself with her arms and legs.

She wasn't a big girl, but was twice as strong as me. She played with me to her heart's content.

"Are you hot?" she asked, caressing me.

I just kept inhaling; I couldn't utter a sound or word of protest or otherwise. I let her caress me from my neck to my belly.

She pulled my shirt up to my chin and, after rubbing my perspiring belly all over as if just washing it, she dried it with the bottom of her shirt.

"Why don't you take off your pants, you'll die of heat." Babi got hold of my shoulder and turned me toward her.

I kept sighing heavily.

"You're not crying, are you?" She put my hand on one of her breasts. "There you go, hold it."

When I first touched it, a pleasant tingling sensation came over me. It felt good; I was happy. I'd previously sought every opportunity to touch her. Before I went to sleep I always thought how nice it would be if it wasn't Miss Mili's snoring I heard next to me, but Babi's breathing. And now she was here.

Why did I yearn for her? Maybe if I hadn't sighed?

But I had asked for it. It wasn't unpleasant, the feeling of my palm against her breast. Until then I'd felt it only through the rough cloth; now it was bare skin, and it was practically burning my hand.

Gone were the hard spasms that had earlier run through my fingers; she gently pressed her breast against my relaxed hand as it rested there, her little ball of flesh pulsating to the beat of her heart.

"Take off your pants, they're really scratchy."

She was bent on pressing her knee between my legs. *Great*, I thought, *at least you'll stop being so aggressive for a while.*

The nettlelike fabric of my sweat-soaked, thick winter pants stung my skin. I would have gladly taken them off, because I was also suffering from the fleas' insatiable feasting, defenseless as I was in my motionless position. I had to choose between holding Babi's breast and scratching myself. I already started to give in to her wishes when it flashed through my mind that the underpants I was wearing were not fit to be seen by others. They had no legs, no bottom, only seams.

Babi noticed that my hands had stopped as I was untying the cord.

"Are you bashful? I only want the best for you; the fleas are feeding on you."

I no longer had a will of my own. I was completely at her mercy as she pulled the pants off me. She threw the flea nest out from under the blanket.

"There we are."

Pulling even closer to me, Babi folded the fringy residues of my underpants right up to my belly.

My thoughts were utterly confused. How had my hand wound up on her breast? Was it Babi who put it there or was it me? All I knew was that I was holding it, this time more boldly than before. Squeezing and caressing it, I was looking for something—for that little protrusion at the end, which had often so embarrassed me.

"Hold on, I'll take my shirt off, then you'll be able to hold it better." I no longer remember how she took it off, but my search was fruitless.

"What are you looking for?"

Something irritated her, too. I was ashamed to put it into words, but she understood even so.

"Oh, what a child you are."

She tried to guide me, but I hardly felt a thing, Not that my fingers were insensitive, no. I could notice even the smallest fingernail scratch on a marked playing card.

I felt somehow cheated now; breasts always looked so pointy and tempting, and now it turned out that they didn't even have nipples.

"You're turning me on," she whispered in my ear, giggling as if tickled.

"With what? You don't even have nipples."

I noticed even in the dark that what I'd said was not to her liking.

"Why would I have real nipples? I haven't had a baby yet."

"You should have them all the same," I said.

"That just shows how many women you've had in your life. You don't even know how the girls' nipples grow."

Now it was me who was offended.

"So you think I hook up with all sorts of whores?" Sulky, I let go of her breast.

"What do you want with the nipple?"

"Nothing. It's just that they're so pointy the way they stick out when girls are dressed, I'd have thought they were real."

"Do you think I also use padding like the other girls to turn on the men?"

I didn't reply, but only kept my lips pressed tight as if offended.

"Do you want a nipple?"

I kept silent.

"Well, do you?"

She lifted her breast and brought it to my mouth.

"If you suck it, there will be a nipple on it."

She wrapped her arms around my neck, and offered me her breast as if to an infant.

No longer in control of myself, I was overcome by an aroma, like that of some long-coveted fruit-the forbidden fruit, it seemed as a blend of sweet and salty flavors now filled my mouth. Within seconds the taste pervaded our bodies at the speed of snake venom, and we were trembling in the fervor of our blood, kindled by our naked bellies pressing against one another. I felt as if I were emptying the cup of peace, of birth and death, from which eternity's inanimate material takes shape.

"Hey, we might get into trouble," she said, kissing my face. "It'll be yours again tomorrow night."

Her breast made a squelching sound as she pulled it out of my mouth.

My vanity didn't object to her mothering, and so I let her rock me in her arms like a baby. I cuddled up to her, smiling at the thoughts that ran through my mind. Childish thoughts, according to which time can neither be stretched out nor stopped. It was well past morning when Miss Mili woke up us.

"Get up, little bitches, how long were you aiming to sleep? Wasn't the night long enough?"

But she put the cover on us rather than pulling it off. Babi had probably been awake for some time, as she laughed when I cuddled up to her.

"It's raining," she whispered in my ear.

Papa picked me up in the afternoon.

"Let's go home, young man, school starts next week. We'll buy whatever you need; there's not much time left."

I didn't show it, but it was with a very heavy heart that I said goodbye to my acquaintances. Babi kissed me and accompanied me to the cart. I saw her waving to me for quite some time. I sat silently next to Papa, looking at the horses' legs as if counting their steps, but every now and again I forgot my own thoughts as well. Sometimes I looked back, watching to see if a familiar figure might appear for whom we should wait.

"Who was that girl who kissed you?"

"Babi."

I didn't know anything more about her, either.

"She didn't look bad."

The horses took big gulps from the sodden potholes. Puddles glistened everywhere as the sun emerged in the afternoon.

"There was a big storm last night; it made a mess of everything."

Yes, there had been a "big storm." Papa's words echoed inside me, stirring up a lot of feelings. Closing my eyes, I tried to recall every detail.

"Are you sleepy?" Papa asked me angrily. "Lie down on the hay."

I climbed onto the back of the cart without a word, but I couldn't recapture anything; it's one thing to imagine something and another to feel it. I was intrigued by my thoughts and feared admitting it even to myself that I loved everything that was happening around me, warts and all, together with the dark brutalities.

Every world forms its own people, and every person his own world. The two live within one another as best they can.

"Hey, wanna light up?" asked Papa, reaching back to offer me some tobacco. "You won't have much of a chance after this. They'll hardly allow you to smoke in school. They say eight years is a long time." After a pause, he added, as if answering his own question, "Well, that'll pass too."

It'll pass, I told myself. Centuries, too, have passed already.

"To be sure," sighed Papa.

He too was only thinking of himself—perhaps that he would be that much older.

"How old will you be by then?" he asked.

"Old."

"That's for sure. I already had a wife at that age."

I could also have one, I thought, even after only half the eight years are gone.

"You've still got time—you might even land yourself a real lady. That Gypsy girl wasn't bad, either. She would have been suitable for you, she seemed like good little gal, poor but good."

It was hard to figure out his thoughts; he promised ladies and sighed after poor girls.

Mama had saved every last pengő I'd earned on the estate.

"We're going to the market tomorrow," she said before I could even ask her why I had had to come home.

I should have known. Okány, the village we passed through going home, had been jam-packed with carts.

"This too could have been a week later, yes, you could at least have spent another week working on that estate."

This was the first thing she'd said in years that I agreed with.

"We ought to buy something for the little ones, too, but instead we'll spend all the money on you."

"You're the one who wanted me to go to school."

"Of course I want you to, else you'd become a tramp. You're just like your grandmother's kind, who only want to be on the road."

Mama didn't like her pronouncements to go unanswered. On such occasions she went on making her point with even more vigor.

"I know you don't feel like studying, but at least I won't have to worry that you'll end up in jail."

This was the climax. Apparently she hadn't had anyone to grumble at while I'd been off working.

"You'd better not fight with me," I said, unable to resist, "or else *you'll* be the one going to school."

"What?" said Mama, fixing her eyes on me before turning her head to the yard. "Come inside, you Gypsy," she called to Papa. "Your son doesn't want to go to school!"

This was the least of Papa's worries; it wasn't the first time he heard our bickering. He just smiled.

"He's become too big for his britches because you haven't managed to teach him not to."

"What am I supposed to be teaching him? It's your mouth that's always sounding off."

"So it's my mouth that's sounding off? Didn't you hear what your darling little son said?"

Papa was always pleased when I spoke the truth instead of him, even more so if I repeated it.

"All I said was don't shush me up," I said.

"What's become of this kid?" Mama, taken aback, asked Papa.

"He misses the woman."

"What woman?"

"It seems a Gypsy girl married your boy last night."

"Married him? No Gypsy girl would want this grubby kid." She looked me over. "Take off those clothes of yours this instant!"

Mama poured a pot of scalding water into the tub.

"Come on, why aren't you getting undressed?"

"Go outside," I said.

Mama wanted to speak, but the words got stuck in her throat; she could neither swallow them nor could she utter them. She became one big question mark; the world was spinning in her eyes until it fell out with a tear.

"You'd better wash that shaggy head of yours," she said softly, turning back from the door. "I'll comb your hair when you're done."

In the evening, Koka cut my hair by the lamp. Among the Gypsies he was the best at it. He gave me a hairdo like that of old Verge, with just a small mop of hair in the front, and even that, he trimmed like a foal's.

I never owned as many clothes in my life as what we bought at the market. Mama even picked a satchel made of good strong boot leather.

I was already counting the days; the time was getting very close.

"When do you have to leave, son?" the older Gypsies kept asking me with deep sympathy.

It was the sort of question one would ask a conscript with a call-up paper in his hand, suitcase at the ready.

The guys my age, though, avoided saying anything that could hurt my feelings; they simply sighed along with me. There was no more making plans, and then came a day when I couldn't even say "tomorrow," for that too had come.

I was tired by the time I started to get dressed; I hadn't slept all night. Mama hadn't slept, either, because hours ago she had started to clean my clothes again, although she had already done so until late the night before.

"Take care of your clothes," she said, giving them a pat. "The girls will like you better for it."

I could see myself only in her eyes and in her face, which was beaming with joy.

"Go on then, don't be late."

She didn't want to burst into tears in front of me, which was why she was hurrying me up.

I got to the train on time. There were still hours to go, but the ticket window was already open.

Parents stood in line to vouch for their kids as they got discounted tickets for the first time with student IDs; I had yet to be issued an ID. An adult accompanied almost every new student, and the kids were showing off by introducing their parents to other kids.

Silently I stood leaning against the railing. I wished Mama had come to see me off, for then I wouldn't have had to stand there all by myself. Why hadn't she come? Normally she wouldn't even let me go to the doctor on my own, no, she went with me everywhere. She sure had some strange whims; no one but Papa could have put up with her. She was like the weather—she had nearly burst into tears and yet she stayed home. In fact, it was quite early.

I didn't see a single familiar face among the group of students. It seemed no one from my old school had come.

The other kids were already talking about the curriculum; they must have known about it in advance. They were pretty cocky kids, though none of them were better dressed than me. Some wore boots that had been smeared only slightly with iron powder—rich boys, they were, who hadn't had to work for their boots.

Lo and behold, there among them was the fat-assed Molnár kid! Was he also coming to the new school? How would he fit into his seat? His father, who was standing there next to him, was the sort who would skin anyone alive if he could. It seemed he'd fattened up his boy to slaughter him.

Molnár's father glanced at my shoes. Folks could look at my shoes as much as they wanted, but they were new shoes, bought from a proper vendor! I only wished my suit was as comfortable, but Mama had ironed it so thoroughly that I could barely sit down. All night she kept pestering me not to get it crumpled up on the way to school! Did she imagine I'd keep standing on that train that would take me to school for years? True, supposedly the suit wouldn't wrinkle, anyway, because it was made of genuine wool. Wool, *shmool*, but if the necktie got undone there wasn't a waiting room window anywhere for me to stand in front of to retie it. Whom would I wake up every morning to tie it for me? If all the kids at school would be like the upper-class kids here at the station, why, Mama could talk her head off tomorrow in vain to get me to tie it on properly. *These proper clothes are for the dogs*, I thought, *and for music-making Gypsies. Yes*, I thought, *those who wanted to play gentlemen could feel free to do so.* I felt like taking off my necktie then and there.

"All aboard! The student car is at the rear."

"Hey, this is a car for students!" Molnár's father yelled at me—me, the Gypsy kid—just as I was about to board.

Luckily I had time to jump up into another car.

School promised to be very strict. A man in a black suit coat, standing next to the bell, warned us that we weren't allowed to run in the hallway.

Our teacher told us that we were to address him as "Teacher, Sir." We didn't learn a single thing all day; all that happened was that people introduced themselves to one another. In the evening I came home with a bagful of books.

All week I avoided the student car, but once I was issued my own ID, the conductor motioned me over. I still knew hardly a soul among the kids at my new school, and the two others in my class, Class 1C, who were from our village—the Molnár boy and Vayda Varjú—avoided me. Molnár and I couldn't stand each other; he constantly made fun of me. He, at least, had a friend in Vayda, who likewise received free tuition on account of being poor. They laughed their heads off together during breaks.

I was completely alone. Whenever they happened to get near me, they fled as if I were mangy.

Fat-assed Molnár walked through the student car stopping at each seat, whispering something, and then the remarks began:

"Which class are you in, Molnár?"

"1C."

"'C' stands for *Cigány*[14]," Molnár declared.

---

[14] Hungarian for "Gypsy," pronounced "tseegahñ"

Casting him a mean glare, I thought it best to move over to another car before losing my temper. Just as I was getting up, though, Molnár kicked his foot in front of mine, dirtying one of my shoes. I barely dared to walk in my new shoes as it was; indeed, Papa regularly carried me out of our Gypsy hut on his back to keep them from getting muddy. That being said, had I been in Molnár's place, I suppose I might not have acted any differently considering the look I'd given him.

Perhaps I even hissed something through my teeth, but I couldn't hear my own voice from Molnár's yelling. Standing there, I reached in my pocket for a handkerchief to clean my shoes with, and at that moment Molnár sprawled out on his back over the seat, flailing his hands and feet in the air.

"Please don't, please don't!" he howled like a banshee, and in no time his pants were soaked in piss. When he saw me swiping my shoe, he sat up laughing and wiped away his tears.

"What's happened to you?" the others asked, looking at the huge puddle of urine on the floor.

"I thought he wanted to kill me! My dad warned me not to make friends with a Gypsy, because they cut people's necks."

I don't remember what he did next. I looked at him, at that huge mass of fat, with pity. I sat back down in my seat.

Without a friend in class to this point, it was even worse after this episode. During breaks I strolled around alone in the hallway, and I didn't feel like going down to the yard, since kids from other classes also pointed at me. Not only did Molnár laugh at me but so too did the whole class and, indeed, the teachers, who never did manage to hide their smiles while passing me by.

THE WEEKS PASSED, BUT EVERYTHING AND EVERYONE remained alien to me. A dismal silence reigned in the hut, which used to resound with blaring conversation. The space was now like a crypt in which only gesturing shadow figures moved about; for I had to study. I got up early and went to bed late. I too became silent, as if in the grip of the atmosphere; I couldn't wait for Sundays to tear myself out of it. But that didn't work, either; gone were the stormy arguments, and those of my friends who dropped by kept quiet, too, as if bored by my company. They looked at me in surprise when I forgot about everything and wanted to be my old self. Still, they stuck with me.

If I went into a hut, those inside tried to hide their poverty from me as from a foreigner, tidying the bed or spreading a clean cloth on the table.

During the day, I was tormented by terrible headaches and was dizzy after classes. I always felt as if the teacher was talking directly to me, and I swallowed every last word of his.

When it came to oral quizzes—once a day, a student had to go to the front of the classroom to answer a question—the teacher ignored me, calling only on someone who had raised his hand. Soon there was no one left to call on, and I figured my turn would be next. Whenever the teacher opened the class record with our names in it, everyone looked at me, including him, and yet invariably he called on someone else. I would have liked to get over the ordeal—to hear myself answer, to assess the results of the agonizing nights and days, but I didn't have the courage to raise my hand. No, I was afraid of something, maybe myself. While others brought with them their inner courage, their homes, their milieus, I was a gutless alien. Each day I started out thinking, *Today! Or neither today nor tomorrow, and maybe never?* Such thoughts soon drove me crazy.

But once, almost involuntarily, in spite of my inner resistance, I raised my hand all the same.

"Well, well, so you know the answer, too?" the teacher asked as if I were a stranger from the street whom he now saw for the first time. Maybe it's just me who remembers hearing it that way, or maybe that was indeed how he said it. I tried to speak but, for the first time in my life, I stammered.

I felt as if I was playing a clown on an open-air stage.

"Sit down," said the teacher, waving his handkerchief, with which he'd been wiping his eyes.

I made up my mind that very hour. In my thoughts I was already at home among my friends, who received me like someone who had been to the end of the earth and whom they'd given up as lost.

This was not my world, I thought lucidly.

In the afternoon I gathered everything that could have left a mark of me; I didn't take leave, nor did the others try to detain me, although they knew I wouldn't return.

Molnár didn't dare travel in the same train car with me. The others were quiet; they knew that nothing really mattered now.

The first thing I did on getting home was to announce my intention to quit school. Mama didn't say a word; instead, she waited until everyone had fallen asleep.

As always, she had covered the filthy table with a clean tablecloth. Unlike so many times before, now she didn't shout at me but talked quietly instead.

"Alright, son, I understand you. I know it's not easy to be a Gypsy. So starting tomorrow you won't be one anymore."

"What?" I looked at her quizzically.

"You've been a Gypsy only in school, where you've been rejected and ridiculed. Back home you'll be different: a cowardly fool who is slow on the uptake even though his parents wanted him to have an education. A phony who swindled his siblings, his parents, and his people because he didn't want to be a Gypsy. If that was your only aim, you've achieved it. Do you really think you'll be respected around here as before? Don't you understand that everyone loves you and surrounds you with admiration, because they believed that you, who were the same as them, would remain for them and with them? A person shouldn't want to be someone other than who they are, because they can't; they should remain who they are. I thought you knew you were a Gypsy, and that that would have been enough for you as you go out into the world to prove what no one believes. Not even me, anymore."

"You think I haven't studied, that I haven't stayed up at nights? Look at these books! I can recite them all by heart."

She just shook her head.

"No," she added. "What I told you, I said not because I learned it somewhere; I said it because I know it. But whether you now go to bed or stay up is your choice."

I understood she wasn't really talking about bed or staying awake.

Without another word I got out my textbooks.

I may have read only a few pages, but her words echoed in my mind, and that was worth far more than the learning by rote I'd been doing up to now. At first I did so only out of a sense of duty, but later I came to realize that if I really did want to prove myself, I had to know twice as much as the others, and that meant staying up.

Back to school I went, and from then on, I raised my hand a lot. Nor did I just give an answer to the question posed to me by the teacher every time I did so; instead, I gave a veritable lecture.

The anticipatory smile froze on the teacher's lips when I proved in the simplest manner theses he had made complicated and difficult to understand. My rising voice silenced the muttering of the class—muttering that was to have been the harbinger of thunderous laughter. Their dilated pupils were pierced by amazement as I explained the logical connections of the course material.

"Excellent," said the teacher in spite of himself. He often approached me nervously as if I was hypnotizing him. Yet I was driven only by my desire for knowledge and to show that I, too, had been delivered by a mother and was a human child.

After a series of such episodes, I managed to overtake even the best of them. Mama burst into tears of joy when she saw my semester report card. However, she managed to overcome her touchy-feeliness.

"That's the way to go, son." Her words didn't surprise me, yet it seemed unusual that she now treated me like an adult who didn't have to be coerced, who not only knew what he had to do but also how to do it.

Her recognition of my innate sense of duty brought me far more joy than if she had pampered me for fulfilling her own aspirations.

"You can be proud of your son, Irene, he is the best in the class," Molnár's dad said to Mama as he brought us a huge container of pickled cabbage.

"If your son would help Imre with his studies, you wouldn't regret it."

"How?" Mama pretended she didn't know what this was all about.

"They could study together during school vacation. Miss Sophie cooks every day, and there would be a plate of food for him too. He is pretty skinny, anyway, and his fee would be forty pounds of flour."

I hated that Molnár kid, but twenty kilos of flour meant a month's worth of bread to us.

I never had a meal at their place because they had it at dinnertime and I didn't wait for it. In the morning, Imre gorged himself on garlic sausage and all he wanted to do was to go back to sleep. After a week, he was reeling from exhaustion. If we didn't manage next day's lesson, we exercised. We duck walked around the room, and then squatted on tiptoes for half an hour.

It was difficult for me too, but it was always him who begged to do it. A couple of times I also threatened to tear off his ear. At first he didn't take it seriously, but I quickly convinced him I wasn't joking. He couldn't wait for the school holidays to be over.

His brother, who last Christmas had paid us with sheep shit for carol singing, made me write his love letters for him. He'd been going to school, but had forgotten how to write.

For his part, Imre Molnár didn't become a good student, but at least his next report card was better.

"Not everyone has to know you tutored Imre," his old man pointed out while measuring the flour.

Lots of kids dropped out at the end of the first year. Only those non-Gypsy peasant boys whose parents were able to offer food for them to take from home stayed on. The class was less populated, but even so, there was barely enough room for Gypsies. The world I came from—what to my classmates was the dark, mysterious, strange-smelling world of the Gypsy settlement—still seemed to alarm them as much as before. But no longer did they mock me. And my hair-raising stunts in gym class, which conjured up the death-defying courage of the acrobats in traveling circuses, amazed even the teacher.

Indeed, my physical strength and audacity put an end to open ridicule; everyone thought twice before taunting me. When certain incidents did reach the last straw nonetheless, I didn't always act in a decorous manner against my impertinent peers. This temporarily enhanced my authority, but my circle of friends was even more limited to myself alone.

It was only in physics lab that anyone sat next to me at my bench, for there was no choice.

"The Gypsy has it good," they whispered, "because the teacher lets him sing solo."

Those little things with which I gained one or another teacher's favor, bred envy in the class.

The boys claimed I had it easiest. It was easy for me to study, because I had no other chores at home; it was easy to have a clean shirt every day, because Gypsies don't have to work for it. They beg and steal.

Whatever I did, everything seemed natural and they found a fitting explanation for it. If the janitor came in to report that someone had left a mess in the restroom, the eyes of the whole class were turned toward me. Even the culprit looked at me in shock, and if I couldn't prove my innocence at such times, I was not spared the teachers' remarks.

Not a single pencil could disappear in class without me being the first who had to turn out his pockets and empty his bags. Although there was never a precedent for it, I was automatically suspected.

Our lead teacher, Mr. Garabuczi—in charge of all the kids in my grade—was the only one who trusted me.

"You may find that sooner or later you'll fall victim to some student prank," he said good-naturedly.

I only found out later what he meant. On one occasion, I found a strange handkerchief in the pocket of my overcoat, with a coin knotted into its corner. At first I wanted to put it in another boy's coat, but then I felt it more prudent to give it to Mr. Garabuczi.

"Good," he smiled. "Don't say a thing."

Mr. Garabuczi stepped into the classroom during our Hungarian language and literature lesson. Holding up a drawing of an amphora that looked like an etching, he said, "It's fitting that he who made the best drawing get a reward. Let the artist stand up."

He didn't call me by name, but everyone was looking at me.

The drawing of that stone jar was indeed familiar. It had sparked a lot of controversy in previous weeks, not only in the classroom but also among the teachers. Opinions differed strongly, one group attributing it to my drawing skills, the other to pure chance. By now the controversy had started to calm down, but now that damn drawing had resurfaced. You could never tell here what was to your advantage and what wasn't, what could become really unpleasant. Such matters left me feeling quite insecure, even when it came to those whose goodwill toward me was absolute.

"Hey, don't you recognize your own drawing?" came the words of another student, loudmouth "Tihi" Garzo, whom most kids called by his nickname, Tihi. His words were, however, drowned out almost immediately by uproarious laughter.

I should have split Garzo's mouth from ear to ear long ago, and now he seemed even more deserving of such treatment. But the circumstances happened to be unsuitable.

At first, he cawed at me like some kind of crow only during breaks, but later he did it even during class. At the same time he would blow his top at anyone messing around in class. He also knew which of the teachers would tolerate his jokes. Tihi was unbelievably insolent with me, although he was one of the best students in the class.

"If you don't stop acting like a jerk, Tihi," I told him during a break, "I'll let you have it even if it means getting into trouble."

"How dare you call me Tihi? To you I should be 'young master'!"

Many times I felt like I'd had all I could take, but I always found the strength to swallow the humiliation.

Mr. Garabuczi's ever-present smile disappeared from his lips.

He looked intently at Garzo, whose ears were visibly burning from all the looks fixed at him.

"Garzo what is your father's occupation?"

The glib-tongued "young master" couldn't answer the form master's question. The boys were shocked; as far as everyone knew from Tihi's account, his dad was railroad stationmaster.

Garzo at first cast an expression suggesting an unwillingness to reply, but then he couldn't resist the form master's querying look.

"He's a railroad man."

"Am I to understand this the way the class whispers it? That he's a stationmaster?" Garzo's face turned even redder.

"Enough, everyone!" said Mr. Garabuczi, hushing the laughter. "Let us then clarify just what sort of 'stationmaster' Garzo's daddy really is—namely, because he is in fact only a switchman."

I, too, blushed at Garzo's disgrace at having it now revealed that he'd promoted his poor little switchman father to stationmaster.

"All quiet now, please." The form master's smile appeared on his lips again. "And now I shall reward the owner of the amphora with this."

He held up the coin for all to see.

Everyone recognized the money. The class hissed.

"There's a bit of ink stuck in the grooves," he said as he held it out to me. "Ágnes used the coin to draw bunny rabbits with."

He was always happy when he could mention his little girl, who, in his assessment, was extraordinarily talented at drawing.

Perhaps I was the only one who understood something of the whole affair, but not all of it. Our Hungarian language and literature teacher clearly didn't know what to make of the scene, and when the form master left the room without saying a word, he glanced at me before resuming his lecture.

During the break, Garzo stepped up to me in the hallway, looking mean. His genteel expression and presumptuous behavior were gone.

"Give me back my coin, you rotten Gypsy!"

I looked right back at him for a long time; I couldn't decide whether it was worth my while to resist and face the prospect of being booted out of school. The other kids crowded around us, pulling at Garzo's coat to indicate that they were on his side.

The bell had already rung to indicate the end of the break, when, all at once, the voice of our music teacher, Mr. Turóczi, screeched through the hallway.

"Everyone occupy their usual places!" The staircase where we sang our way through our music lesson was already free of kids milling about there during the break.

"The soprano, go to the bottom step. Hurry up, please!"

But the hive of students gathered round as Garzo and I locked eyes, all of us ignoring the bespectacled, insignificant teacher.

"What coin?" I asked just as brazenly as he would have.

"The one you stole. Give it back to me; I need it."

"Well now, the stationmaster's son needs a coin."

No one laughed at my words.

"One little coin," I repeated, louder.

"Give it back to him," the others hissed at me. "It belongs to him!"

"Isn't the weather nice?" I brushed off the front of my jacket nonchalantly.

I felt no anger, but if what I expected happened, I wanted to be in good form when venting all my bitterness.

"What's going on here?" asked Mr. Turóczi, shouldering his way through to us.

"The Gypsy stole a coin," the chorus resounded. Mr. Turóczi stared at me in astonishment from under his glasses.

"Please return the coin, and put an end to this unpleasant situation."

"Thief!" they cried.

"Quiet!" shouted Mr. Turóczi. "Please, give back the coin," he urged me, wanting to iron out the unpleasant situation without delay. His gaze jumped from me to the classroom doors that were opening one after the other, inquisitive teachers emerging and hastening toward us.

"Please do it—it will be better for you."

I just kept quiet, as if nothing was happening.

"What is this disturbance?" asked the principal, pushing everyone aside. "Who struck the first blow?"

"No one has hit anybody yet, sir," Mr. Turóczi smugly proclaimed, "I've been here."

"The Gypsy stole something!" roared the whole class in unison. The headmaster took no notice of me.

"What happened, Garzo?"

"He stole my coin!"

"How do you know that it was he who stole it?" Garzo just lowered his head.

"Who saw him steal the coin?" Everyone kept quiet.

"Please, go into your classroom. We don't want to disturb the others. We'll talk about this inside."

The teachers left us to ourselves for a few minutes before coming into the room. The class was silent.

"Come here, please," the headmaster called me. "You are accused of stealing a coin from Garzo. Are you prepared to admit it?"

I looked for help to Mr. Garabuczi, who just stood there, looking away from me.

I was by no means as confident as I'd been before.

"Are you prepared to admit it? Otherwise we'll have to search you!" the headmaster insisted.

I didn't have much to say, and there was nothing to admit, but the coin was on me. And who would be believed? Me? My mind raced; calculations ran through my head leading to various possible outcomes, but looming over each calculation was the one and only world to which I belonged. All other possible worlds were false.

"Get his bag!" the headmaster commanded.

Half the class jumped up to get it.

"And you," the headmaster spoke again, now pointing to one of the students, "bring in his overcoat!"

The merriment of old returned; everyone laughed and rubbed their hands.

"Here you are, sir, this is the overcoat."

"How did you know it was his?"

The startled boy's only response was to shrug his shoulders; he would have liked to escape from the uncomfortable question.

"You stay right here and check the suspect's pockets."

"Empty them!" he said to me. I took out the coin and put it on the table.

The headmaster was not all surprised at the sight of the coin.

"Is that the one?" he asked Garzo.

Garzo nodded, and the others responded loudly: "Yes."

"Strange! An hour ago nobody knew the occupation of Garzo's father, yet now everybody knows that this is Garzo's coin."

Things were fluctuating just as in a card game, where luck moves from one to the other. Now it was me who had the good hand.

"Let us put an end to this game!" The headmaster's voice became stern. "I need an honest volunteer, one who doesn't want to lose his credibility while part of our school."

All the boys were looking down at their desks, holding their hands in their laps. The headmaster glanced around the room.

"Please stand up!' He pointed at a small, long-haired blond boy in the front bench. "You do understand what I said, don't you?"

"Yes," replied the kid sheepishly as he bowed, stood at attention, and parted his lips to speak, as he knew he must. "Garzo said we should be ashamed for being in the same class as a Gypsy. Everyone calls us the 'Gypsy class,' so Garzo said we've got to make sure the Gypsy gets kicked out of school. Anyone who doesn't join in is a traitor and should be ashamed of himself for not defending the class's honor. It was his idea to put that coin with the ink marks into the handkerchief and then put it into the Gypsy's coat pocket. He said he didn't want a Gypsy getting better grades than him, that he too could get all A's if he wanted, but that he didn't want his name to be even mentioned in the same breath as that of a Gypsy because his father is a stationmaster."

"Alright," said the headmaster. "We've already clarified that his father is only a switchman. Is there anyone who did not share Garzo's views?"

Everyone scrambled to raise his hand.

"I mean, did any of you tell Garzo this is unacceptable? That no honest student—no one who proudly wears the emblem of culture and knowledge on his school cap—can join in on such a venture? No, none of you did. Garzo will be severely punished, but I want to remind all of you here in class that the honor of our school demands that we raise people, not animals."

The music teacher just smiled at me. "Let's go on," he called out, "the singing lesson is almost over, so let's sing now with the freedom of real relief."

He jumped around like a goldfinch and seemed much happier than I was.

Spring arrived. Back in the settlement, melting snow and spring rains conspired with decades of trod-upon clay that yielded massive puddles as far as the furthest hut. The more it thawed and rained, the more the fragile dams dividing the puddles collapsed until, finally, they merged into a semicircular little sea that wound its way around our Gypsy Paris.

It wasn't an unpleasant sight. The sea's blooming tiny islands were dotted with tall yellow sweet clover, and between the pointed leaves of the reeds, cattails swung their brown heads.

Other than for for drinking water, the "great pit"—for that was what we called it—satisfied all our water needs. It served as a marvelous place for the smaller children who were not yet allowed to swim in the Körös River, as its water was too deep. Even so, once in awhile a child drowned in the great pit, and then the adults forbade them to go near it for weeks—but who could go on resisting the yearnings of so many kids?

The bathing season was already underway by late April, and until the great pit dried out or froze over, come fall and winter, it was constantly in use as a place to splash about.

In the evening, when all was quiet, it became the realm of the frogs. We kids loved listening to their calls, wondering what they were talking about. A series of delicate "ribbits" were regularly answered by a deep, throaty one, just as when a group of our folks are chattering away about this or that and, all at once, one of the older men gives an approving nod and says, "That's right."

Forgetting all their concerns, the frogs regularly broke into a chorus of croaking until, finally, one of the oldest ones seemed to declare,

"Tomorrow is another day." The younger ones then either stopped or else went on making a racket, just like we were apt to do.

Our summers, too, were cheerful and virtually carefree. In the sweltering heat of the mornings we blinked as sleepily at the foot of our huts as the frogs from under their leafy umbrellas, except that we didn't stick our tongues out waiting for flies to settle on them. But we too panted through the mornings in that morass, drowsily, quietly, waiting for the old frogs to touch our tongues with food. Then we'd splash merrily about, now and then peeking out from under the thick weeds, keeping our eyes open for mosquitoes, until some jokester would invariably come along and throw a clod of earth at our heads.

Here, desires didn't take wing—no, they sank like millstones thrown into the water, under bellies and under skirts.

In the summer, folks from the settlement roamed about far and wide during the week, but weekends brought everyone back.

Fair-skied Sundays were preceded by nights overheated with little gasps, both dreams and the ticking of time disrupted by the sweltering embraces of lovers' trysts.

Women still lounging next to their husbands after sunrise were called lazy sloths. The rapturous moments of the night showed in the dark circles under their eyes, but at daybreak in the yard they were already smoothing down the wrinkles of their skirts.

Why the women had to get up early, I do not know. As for the men, only the inexorable siege of flies chased them out of their lairs. The kids disappeared from homes as they awoke; most were self-sufficient. Day had barely broken when some of them were already touring Gypsy Paris with cigarette ends wrapped in newspaper. They were looking for a light.

Mama was among the early risers. By sunrise she'd done some wash, and after that always found other work around the hut. One after another women from elsewhere in the settlement lined up in our yard, surrounding the fire—scraps of dung aflame, surrounded by blackened clay—and passed around a cigarette butt (chewing tobacco wrapped in a thick wad of newspaper) to reinvigorate their lungs.

"Is your boy still asleep, woman?" Nootsu, an old man, shouted from a distance at the top of his lungs.

"*Still?*" Mama was surprised. "The sun is hardly up; why shouldn't he be?"

"Why?" groaned the old man, dragging himself closer to the fire as if half paralyzed.

"What's wrong with this hairy-soled Gypsy?" asked folks among the curious crowd that had in no time gathered around him.

"I haven't slept all week. I almost scratched up the ground with my fingernails last night, my tooth aches so much."

It was hard to recognize his voice, that's how badly it was shaking.

"Your tooth?" they asked in amazement.

"My tooth," he kept moaning, while squatting with his feet tucked under him.

"It's a bad sickness, it is," lamented the others, as if talking not about a toothache but cholera.

"It's enough to drive a man crazy. I wouldn't even wish it on my enemies."

More and more folks emerged to offer their condolences.

I'd been awake for some time; I was used to getting up early. But I had no idea what that old man wanted from me. A shiver went up and down my spine whenever he shouted away like that. Some of the women were wringing their hands and crying along with him.

"Why don't you wake up your son, Gypsy woman?" they snapped at Mama. "He should do something for him—this old Gypsy is going crazy."

"What could he do for him?" Mama asked defiantly, but her voice was trembling.

Falling to the ground and turning on his side, Nootsu held his face in his hands and brayed like a donkey. By then a whole crowd had formed around him.

Nervousness and curiosity overcame their sleepiness. Some folks had no idea what was wrong with the old man, but they felt sorry for him all the same.

"You can't just stand there and do nothing," one of the men grumbled as those around him nodded. "Why don't you wake up your son?" he called out to Papa, who was busy tending to his horses.

Papa came into the hut, complaining.

"Get up, boy! Nootsu's howling is driving everyone crazy."

"And what am I supposed to do for him when I get up?" I asked. "Give him some chewing tobacco? Maybe that's all he needs."

Papa left, but came back within minutes.

"Come on, for Christ's sake—all the Gypsies are swarming around right here."

I didn't have a problem getting up, but I didn't have the faintest idea what to do with the old man; I myself had never had a toothache in my life.

"Take him to the doctor?" I asked, trying once more to pass the buck to Papa.

"On a Sunday?" Papa retorted. "What an idea!"

"Have you ever had a toothache?" I asked.

"Me?" he looked askance. I could see he was thinking. "I seem to remember I did, while I was in the army.

"What did you do with it?"

"Nothing."

"Well, does it still hurt?"

"Of course not," he said, adding, after a pause, "I think . . . ." Looking for the tooth with his tongue, he added, "they pulled it out."

"Sure," I said, "that's how they do it in the army. But what can *I* do? I have no idea what a toothache even feels like."

"What the hell *would* you do? Tell the old fellow to go to the pub."

"*I'm* supposed to tell him?"

By now Papa was also nervous, because the old man was braying more and more wildly. I could barely put my pants on.

Nootsu lay next to the fire, curled up, saliva dripping from his mouth. He looked the picture of misery. I stood next to him and didn't know how to console him.

"Help me, my child, bless your soul, I'm dying!"

Had Papa not pushed his way beside me, I would have burst out crying.

"Why don't you get some plum brandy for it? All you do is holler like a madman, you think that'll help?"

"I've put everything on it already," he moaned with a pained expression. "I've even tied garlic on my arm."

A massive blister hung on his arm, caused by the garlic.

"It'll have to be pulled out," said the old man, still moaning.

"I'll harness up, just stop yelling. I'll take you to the doctor; he might pull it out." You could tell that Papa, too, felt sorry for him.

Nootsu's face became even more distorted, this time with anger.

"You want to take me to the doctor, Boncza? Do you want to have me killed? I'll set your house on fire if your son doesn't pull it out!"

Now I understood why he came to us, but before I thought about running away, he caught my foot.

"Pull it out, my dear child!"

"Is it loose?" I asked in fright.

"*Aaah!*" He opened his mouth wide as if he wanted to swallow me.

I looked at the bystanders in desperation.

"Why aren't you helping him?" they asked reprovingly.

"But how can I help him?"

"With this!" Mama tossed over that little bag that held the dental tools Papa used on horses.

I felt dizzy. I peeked to see how I could sneak away. I expected Papa to intervene. But without further ado, he emptied the bag and picked up a pair of huge, curved pliers.

"Let me see which of your teeth is aching."

Bristling, old Nootsu raised his hand at him.

"Get away from here, Boncza! I swear on my child's life that I'll hit you, even if you kill me afterward, but don't take me for a horse!"

Frightened, I tried to find a smaller pair of pliers among the tools, but Papa had the only one, the one he used to pull horses' teeth. He was still clutching the large, jaw-locking pliers in his hand; he was pale with anger but didn't say anything. Instead he just handed the pliers to me.

The pliers, which evidently hadn't been used in years, would barely open.

"They need to be lubricated," an onlooker proposed.

I kept looking at the pliers' wide grooves, which were calibrated for horses' teeth. If I reached into the old man's mouth with them, they'd pull out at least three teeth in one go. Pale, Nootsu was kneeling before me with his mouth wide open. His full set of teeth, blackened by chewing tobacco, were lined up like sawed-off pillars.

"Which one is aching?"

"*Aaah!*" he called out with a shrug. He himself didn't know which one it was.

"It's sure to be that big thick one," said Mister Gene, bending closer. "The one in the middle."

Maybe it would have been easiest to pull it out with its two neighbors, because the pliers couldn't have reached just the one. By now Nootsu was only panting, not moaning.

"It can't be removed with this," I said, still trying to get out of it.

Mister Gene came up with a new piece of advice: "You don't need pliers for this, no, just take this puncher, and all you have to do is to fit it to the tooth and hit its end with a hammer."

"What if his jawbone gets broken?"

"It certainly won't," he insisted. "I've seen plenty of these at the fairs."

"Well then, here it is, do it."

He was about to begin when the others shouted for him to stop.

"You stick your nose into everything," said one man. "You think you're a doctor. Why, if you break his jawbone, he'll never be able to eat again. Let the kid think it over; he knows what has to be done."

"These pliers are too thick," I said, showing Papa. "They need to be filed down to size."

"You want to ruin my pliers?"

Still, after thinking it over, Papa consented. Khandi just nodded and went to pick up the file. The entire settlement was standing around us by now.

While they were filing off the pliers, I tried to find the sore tooth.

"Tell me when . . ."

I started to tap on them one after the other. Nootsu screamed at each tap. I could barely push aside his thickened tongue, which kept clinging to his teeth. Perplexed, I threw away the puncher.

"How should I know which one hurts when you always yell?"

His only response was a shrug of the shoulders and a big *Aaah!*

The others gasped. "Nootsu doesn't even know which of his teeth is sore!" came a voice. Slowly the others began to feel sorry for me.

I was nervous and drenched in perspiration but no matter what, one of them had to be pulled out. After a few minutes I started again, this time probing with a reed splinter, looking for cavities. I was prying out the petrified remains of tobacco from between the worn molars, but all of his teeth appeared to be healthy.

Then I saw a tiny bright object shining at the bottom of one of his molars. Sweat pouring off him, Nootsu hissed at each touch, but when I got to the shiny object, he bit the reed in half. Throwing himself to the ground, he scratched the soil in agony.

Relieved, I dried myself off.

By now the Gypsies had run out of consoling words, and were looking in turn at me and the old man as if he were giving up the ghost.

They let Khandi through without a word when he returned with the filed down pliers.

"Is that how you meant it?"

I didn't know myself, but it looked right. Only Papa shook his head reluctantly, sorry about his tool.

"Bring a cup of water!" I said to Mama, who was already tired of the whole thing and made absolutely no secret of wishing Nootsu to hell.

"You ought to hold his head," I said to Mister Gene, who was intent on giving a hand.

He grabbed Nootsu's hair on both sides, together with his ears; the old Gypsy stood it.

"I'll hold it, don't worry, just pull it; it'll be worse if you're scared."

But Mister Gene's mouth also dropped open when he saw that I was plunging the pliers into the smoldering dung fire. They gasped quietly.

"His hands need to be held down, too!" called out Mister Gene.

Two helpers volunteered for each hand and they stretched out Nootsu like a flayed skin.

The pliers hissed loudly when I plunged them into the water.

Dear God, I prayed silently, *please don't let his tooth shatter to bits.*

I waved the pliers in the air a couple of times to cool them down.

"Don't be frightened, my boy, just go ahead," the old man encouraged me, his face contorted with pain. He opened his mouth wide.

I used both my hands to fit the long-handled pliers around his tooth; I could almost hear the creaking sound. I twisted it from both sides, then, carefully moving it, eased it out from among its neighbors.

"This was the culprit," I said, showing everyone the tooth and its root, dripping of pus. A broken bit of a sewing needle was visible standing out of a small hole in the tooth. The old man wanted to nod his head, but to his surprise Mister Gene was still holding it and only let go when I told him to. The others, too, looked at the tooth in amazement.

Amid a lot of spluttering, Nootsu told us that it had broken off a week ago, and that ever since then he hadn't been able to eat or sleep.

"Rinse it with a decoction of privet leaves and bark," said Papa in a friendlier tone than earlier.

This whole affair turned out to be a disadvantage for me personally. From then on everybody came to me with their aches and pains. On some Sundays I had to cut open as many as two wounds caused by the men's bare soles having been chafed by clods. I either cleaned out the pus or let them suffer.

I had to prevent many a self-inflicted infection caused by superstitious practices; for they were apt to put warm horseshit, dusty cobwebs, and whitewash scraped off walls on open wounds.

It wasn't easy to apply vinegar or salt to effectively complement or counteract the more traditional therapies, but no other disinfectants were available. One possibility was to absorb the vinegar with some bread, sponge the wound, and finish the process with some sort of incantation.

It was likewise hard to clean the head of a child with impetigo, which, the people of the settlement believed, was not to be touched by water. A doctor's advice, if it ever came to that, was simply laughed off. Washing a child's head with soap and water virtually amounted to sacrilege. There was one remedy, like using the hair of a dog to treat a dog bite. So too it was believed that ringworms occurred on a newborn's head only if a woman in "that time of the month" chanced to look upon the infant. Over the years, the wound on such a child's head grew as large as a cap, but hastening recovery was forbidden. Instead, the child's head was occasionally wiped with a menstruating woman's rags, shirts, or skirts.

Almost all the settlement's inhabitants suffered from skin diseases, such as scabies and ringworm; many children's faces and upper bodies in particular were marred by palm-sized blotches of fungus. They treated both with urine, tobacco residue from pipes, and window sweat. Although the oily-pasty, nicotine-rich filth scraped out of pipes seemed pretty effective, where could you find that many pipes? Anyway, such diseases spread terribly fast due to so many people inhabiting closed spaces. I wasn't exempt from scabies either. Tiny pimples formed between my fingers, then spread over my whole body and later turned into huge, itchy wounds.

The ineffective or slow-acting medicines prescribed by the doctors did not eliminate the possibilities of infection at all. Those who tried the doctor became objects of ridicule in the settlement, because the brown, foul-smelling ointment betrayed the presence of scabies from afar. In this case one did not only expose oneself to mockery, but also to an unpleasant handicap, because the villagers wouldn't let such people into their houses. Thus the hideous festering sores caused by constant scratching became more and more infected under filthy clothes. I couldn't use the medication prescribed by the doctor, because I couldn't go to school smudged with black stuff and smelling from the unbearable stink emitted by the ointment.

To battle my own case of scabies, I had to endure the torture that came from a treatment we knew about using two powdered fungicides—copper sulfate, or bluestone, as well as sulfur. Whether used as an ointment or added to a bath, the pain was excruciating but worth it, because a single application was enough for complete recovery. Indeed, word spread quickly, and after a few days everyone in the settlement wanted to give it a try. Not only the children screamed in pain, but the adults too. They reproached me and threatened to beat me to death if anything bad happened to their kids or themselves.

Many decided to try it, as if after long persuasion they were finally willing to commit suicide, and they knew full well they might as well yell their lungs out; for that is surely what they'd do when treated with the stuff.

A few weeks later, though, only traces of the white scabies and of the black ringworm wounds remained. The treatment was cruel, but the infection could be fought off only if everyone applied it.

The village's grape farmers could not imagine why all the Gypsies were begging them for the bluestone and sulfur powder, which smelled of rotten eggs. Dr. Bocz just laughed when he heard how the Gypsies treated themselves, but when the symptoms eventually reappeared on someone, he too recommended it.

For their part, the settlement's Gypsies were all in fear of Dr. Bocz. One fine day it was rumored that a local doctor had died of bites from lice he'd contracted from Gypsies. We were sorry on learning that it wasn't Dr. Bocz, who barely ever bothered to pay house calls on any of us. Not one of the Gypsies wanted his help; they would rather have suffered or died.

"Is he alive?" he would almost always ask when one of us got sick. "Why didn't he come to the clinic? Call me when he's dead."

Dr. Bocz chased lice like a man obsessed; the only treatment he knew was the use of scissors. And he certainly used them whenever he could.

"Where is the body?" His howling could be heard before he even appeared. "Or have you eaten it? I'll burn down this breeding ground of bacteria!"

The Gypsies just hid among the bushes growing in the ditches. The doctor's fury always left a trail of destruction. Anyone who came within his reach had a cross cut in his hair. But then not even that meant a thing, really, for folks could cover up their scalps with a kerchief. Nor did they get too upset about Dr. Bocz kicking over cooking stoves and flinging pots full of just-cooked food to the floor. No, the people of the settlement tolerated all this without a peep, although there were plenty of big-mouthed, feisty women among us. Instead they judged it wiser to remain silent and keep their crowns; if, that is, there were still any unshorn ones.

Margaret Verge, who lived with her daughter Emma, was generally known as a sad, quiet woman. The older men looked in awe at her marriageable daughter though; their taste in women hadn't changed. The young ones, however, were not impressed by Emma because her ass had grown too much and they regarded her thick, crooked legs to be ungainly, whether shaven or not. She walked like someone constantly worried about stepping on thistles. Only the smell of good Hungarian tobacco lured the boys in.

Despite the fact that everyone regarded Margaret as a hushed, hangdog woman, she always landed on her feet. She asked for nothing from anyone, but neither was she generous. Her hand trembled when giving away a pinch of tobacco, even while offering something to a visitor. It therefore gave the Gypsies a double satisfaction when, one day, she had a fight with Dr. Bocz.

Margaret was in the middle of gutting a chicken, and had barely enough time to jump into her low-eaved kitchen. Bocz just happened to stop his motorcycle in her yard.

"What's this?!" he yelled, pointing to the chicken guts in front of the kitchen door, which evidently disgusted him.

"Come out, you damn bitch!"

They argued for quite awhile, him from the outside, her from the inside, hurling expletives at one aother. Margaret was lavish with her repartee: she not only told him where to lick her, but also showed him where by clapping her ass with her palm while the doctor pulled her out of the hut by her hair.

It wasn't such a shocking sight, really; this was not the first time Dr. Bocz had pulled a woman by her hair like a child pulling a sled. However, when Margaret had had her fill of it, she picked up a plank and beat the doctor within an inch of his life. He had to be transported home in the village's horse-drawn carriage.

At last Dr. Bocz had gotten some of what had been coming to him. Folks in the settlement hadn't really taken much advantage of the doctor's help so far, but after this incident they did so even less.

The children could cope without him. Those who were fit for living stayed alive, others were buried.

If they suffered colic caused by unchewed meat or other food, they were given a dose of bird shit or onion juice.

Mama, too, tried to collect bags full of this medication for us kids when necessary. If that didn't help, she would smoke the ailing child's shirt at night or, putting it on the threshold, beat it with an axe and then throw it over the roof. She did that until the child hushed up. Not a single night could pass without her putting the broom by the door. Perhaps it was due to this diligently pursued superstition of hers that the midwife didn't "switch" any of us. Sometimes the midwife charged so much that it took years to extricate ourselves from debt, but one child after another came all the same.

Still, if I sneaked outside at night and inadvertently kicked aside that broom, it never occurred to me to put it back in place.

"Will you never understand?" Mama would admonish me the next morning. "Look, the midwife switched one woman's child a year ago to a veritable monster. The three-year-old was skin and bone—full of hair but underdeveloped, unable to walk or speak and constantly crying; they couldn't feed it often enough. They shaved it weekly, and still it looked like a furry monkey. Nothing they tried helped, until they took it to the medicine woman."

"What did they do with it?" I asked. "They put its food into a mug and put a soup ladle in its hand. '*Small mug, large ladle, I would eat, if I was able*,' the switched child said all at once. The medicine woman had indeed predicted that it would talk. But that night the midwife switched the child right back. That's why I put the broom in front of the door every night."

Although Mama spoke sheepishly about such things, her faith couldn't be shaken.

Outwardly I despised these superstitious beliefs, but inside I couldn't rid myself of them. I spent hours lying motionless during many a night. In the flickering candlelight I watched the threatening shadows as they sluggishly or greedily bit into the faces of my young siblings. They then snuck back powerless, humiliated, repeating their unsuccessful attacks again and again, perhaps waiting for someone to upset the broom for a moment so they could, amid soundless joy, abscond with their tiny prey.

Was I the one everyone believed me to be? The one who didn't use his little finger to draw nine circles around their navels to drive off nausea, but instead forced salty vinegar into them to make them throw up the uncooked or spoiled food?

Who was I, then?

On the night of Good Friday even I was given to washing myself, and then, exactly at midnight, combing my hair under the willows so it would grow to my waist. I, the same person who didn't let people twirl cats' tails in their babies' mouths to cure thrush. I, who protested against superstition like someone protesting his own being. No, I didn't believe in it, and yet I feared it. Superstition entwined everything with thousands of threads; nothing could take its place. If a single thread were to snap, all that would remain would be shadows and a black void, an existence without faith or trust.

It was in *nothingness* that we believed, because for centuries its roots had become ossified; it destroyed, killed, and infected, and it demanded belief and fear. It devoured everything, obliterating and re-creating our existence, torturing us with fear until we became brave enough to endure the captivity of our manacles.

Where is this world's clear blue sky, under which long-haired black fairies unshackle the ties with which the *zhuklano manush*[15] has hogtied them in their sleep?

Many a time my friend Zolti and I sat silently next to one another, watching the Gypsy men as they fanned their horses. Dressed in trousers, they looked like half-human, half-animal monsters. So too the men caressed their horses and stole fragrant feed for them. Meanwhile their own kids clung all day like caterpillars from the branches of the settlement's mulberry trees. They didn't even get off, no, they just shat all over the branches, because their mothers got home late in the afternoon from the village and nobody else paid any attention.

Some kids eventually had no strength left even to pick mulberries—the diarrhea had turned into dysentery and had wasted them away to skin and bone—and, before long, they were stuffed with resin powder. More often than not, a crepe-paper shroud and a free coffin was their end.

In the evenings, our Gypsy Paris resounded with noise. Almost invariably some old woman could be heard above it all, cursing to high heaven at both earth and sky.

"Why don't you jabber away at home?" Papa or someone else would shout at her. "May disease gnaw your guts out! You're keeping the horse awake."

The horse meant everything to those Gypsy menfolk; it was their only desire. Honor, humanity, and, often even family and wife, were dwarfed by its worship. It demanded that neither friend nor brother

---

[15] dogman

should matter, for only then could a life of cheating, stealing, lying, and fighting reign uncontested.

We were already well into summer. I soon forgot the way of life circumscribed by school rules. Within a few weeks I'd gobbled up everything around me for which I'd hungered for so long and, having done so, I soon felt I was drowning in the boredom of inaction and idleness.

Try as we might to circulate through the village one Sunday when the hiring went on, we didn't manage to get work binding sheafs of freshly cut wheat.

"We'll be needed next week," the Gypsy guy called Bada consoled me. "When they are pressed for time, even Gypsies will be good enough for them."

In a way I was sorry, and yet I wasn't, not really. I kept looking pensively at my shapeless shoes that no longer even resembled their original state; I'd completely worn them down. I'd been counting on earning twenty pengős from work during the harvest; that's what sheaf-binders were paid. But it was strenuous labor: the days merge with the nights, the sun beats down mercilessly, and you bathe in your own sweat for up to five weeks straight. I wasn't quite comforted by these thoughts, and yet I was reassured that autumn would surely bring something new.

Bada started to talk about women; he too was delighted by his early puberty. He wasn't picky, which is to say that he picked up one older woman after another. They were promiscuous, the whole lot of them; their being so much older made them all the more so. I don't know how the one called Rahi condescended to sleep with Bada, who was seen by folks as a simpleton, but then again, her husband, Guchess, could just as well have been her grandfather. What could he offer a woman so much younger than him? And, even though Bada was considered stupid, he was young.

Figuring out what goes on in a woman's head is tough. Rahi had been afraid of frogs since she was a little girl, yet as a teenager she spent lots of time sitting out in front of her hut in the midst of them. For his part, old Guchess, ran about all day, because anybody who wants a young woman has to show his mettle. He saw her there. Earlier, when he'd lived with a woman named Leenka, he'd been well off. No longer. How long, after all, does a Gypsy fortune last? Until the sky clouds over.

Rahi was about fifteen when she eloped with the old Gypsy.

Somehow he managed to produce three children with her, and by that summer when Bada hooked up with Rahi, the old man supported his little clan by fishing all day. Why, they ate fish all the time, just like herons. He'd barely swallowed the last bite, and already he was asleep. So Bada could go there whenever he felt like it.

The next day Rahi would put her arms around Guchess, too, her skirt pulled up over her ass, for as they said, the world is so small that what happens is a secret only until it happens. Guchess just smiled, not even imagining that someone else was performing his marital duties instead of him. If he ever did find out though, death would have been the end result. He was among those Gypsies who used razors not just for shaving.

Only now did I understand what Mama meant when Rahi came by our place one morning for a light.

"Guchess will cut your throat if he finds out," she said to Rahi.

"I'll take care of him!" Rahi said in her short-tempered way. That same day they brought the old Gypsy home in a cart, because his woman had sent him high up into a tree to catch some crow fledglings for supper.

He fell and broke his spine.

On our way home we saw a large group of village folks, not Gypsies, standing at the edge of the main road. Curious, we pushed our way to the center of a crowd standing around a collapsed horse evidently in the throes of lockjaw.

"Nothing more can be done for this animal. We have to report it so the flayer can come take it away and at least put its skin to good use," said the vet who'd been called to the scene. "It would be a pity to just bury him."

The horse's owner, a peasant farmer named John Kish, just stood there, looking at his horse with deep emotion.

"There's nothing I can do," the vet reiterated. "It has to be removed from the road."

Bada winked at me, and approached the distressed man.

"Give it to me, sir, I'll buy it."

"What are you going to do with it?" asked Kish.

"We'll eat it. There are lots of us. I'll pay for the price of the skin; at least you won't have to bother about paying for the flayer to take it away. You wouldn't even get anything for the skin. But I'll give you ten pengős."

"It's not for sale."

"Why don't you give it to them, Mr. Kish?" asked the vet. "If they stab it now, they can safely eat it. It doesn't cause you any inconvenience and saves you some trouble."

"Doctor, I delivered this horse and I intend to bury it."

"Too bad," replied the vet as he shook the man's hand and left.

"I'll give you twenty pengős," Bada resumed the negotiation. "We could even do it all in writing, and if it dies it's my problem. We'll eat it—it won't go to waste."

"Go away," said the peasant irritably. "I told you, it's not for sale."

Everyone was on our side; some of peasants even told the man to his face that he was a fool. Still, he took out a long knife from his haversack, sharpened it thoughtfully on the hoop-iron, and slowly started to approach the horse.

"Wait, Mr. Kish!" Bada stepped in front of him in desperation. "We'll cure your horse."

"*You?*" The peasant gave us a smile, thinking that we wanted to console him. Anyone who knew anything about horses could see that it wasn't suffering from any dangerous disease, at least nothing so bad that it couldn't be helped. I'd been amazed that the vet hadn't seen that. Lots of times what looks like lockjaw is in fact a circulatory disorder, and at such times folks who aren't experts can be easily tricked; which is to say, if someone asks for their sick horse—thinking it's a lost cause, anyway—they'll give it away.

But, no, we hadn't pulled the wool over the eyes of John Kish. So far I hadn't said a word. Bada's cunning held the promise of making us some money, but luck had not been on our side. Just to be sure that we were now on the right track in offering to cure the beast, I checked the horse's eyelids. We had to act urgently.

"If you leave it to us, you'll be able to use your horse within half an hour. Or if you don't want it, you can really bury it."

Kish began to think it over.

"For twenty pengős," Bada interjected.

We didn't even notice that two other Gypsies, Zoga and his younger brother, were now on the scene.

"What do you want to do?" Zoga asked us in Romani. "If you dare to cure it, we'll knock your teeth out!"

Turning to Kish, he said, "Don't believe these kids, they just want to cheat you out of twenty pengős. They wouldn't be able to heal it; it's half-dead already. But I'll give you fifty pengős for it."

"Fifty pengős?" Kish looked at Zoga for a moment, and reached for his whip. "Don't you think that's a bit low?"

Zoga's eyes lit up.

"Well, what the hell, I'll give you sixty for it, and if it dies, it's my problem."

"So it's sixty, then."

Zoga wanted to mutter something else, but when Kish started to hit him with his whip, he only grunted while forcing his way out of the crowd.

"Go fuck yourself!" shouted John Kish. "You say it can't be cured, yet you'd give sixty pengős for it?"

Zoga was making his escape, his brother having already hightailed it out of there. It seemed for a second that we too would get it, but Kish calmed down and put the whip back in its place.

"Here are twenty pengős, and you'll get another twenty if the horse stands up."

We didn't even need a bloodletting gadget. Within minutes Bada punctured the horse's jugular, which he had previously fastened with the whipcord as a tourniquet. The blood flowed in a thin, even stream.

I watched the horse's upturned eyelids until the swollen capillaries became paler.

"How much blood should we let?" I asked Bada.

"Until the bucket is full," he whispered to me. "Don't worry, the twenty is already in our pocket. I don't give a damn if we don't get another twenty. It would have been nice if he had given us the horse," he lamented, "It's worth at least two hundred. He is a rascal, that *gadjo*.[16] He'd rather have killed it, even though it's part of his life." Bada stroked the horse's neck for a while, then whispered again: "His horse is alright now, to hell with him."

Bada undid the whipcord and deftly tied off the cut skin. Leaning on the cart, John Kish had been watching us, and came closer only when the horse began to pull its stiffened legs under itself.

"Give us a cigarette, Mr. Kish," said Bada, proudly wiping his bloody hands on the horse's mane.

Quite a lot of people were helping, but they could barely keep the horse down. Bada was watering all four of its legs, and spilled the remaining water in its face.

"It's alright now. Talk to the horse, Mr. Kish!"

The horse shook the water off itself noisily; it was still trembling a little, but its eyes and the way it held its head were perfect signs of life.

Kish handed over the twenty without us having to ask for it.

"Don't give him anything to eat today," said Bada. We gave the smiling farmer some more advice and headed home.

Bada almost hugged the breath out of me. I too was happy, thinking about how we'd each spend the twenty. Had we become sheaf binders, we wouldn't have earned any more.

[16] non-Romani man

Even before they reached home, Zoga and his brother got boozed up; they couldn't assuage their anger on account of us having intruded on their luck. We barely got home when we already heard the shouts.

"You either pay us thirty pengős or I'll cut you to pieces!" Francis Zoga's younger brother, yelled at us.

Everyone flocked to an adjacent yard, the Billats.'

"Why should we give you thirty pengős?" Bada retorted. "You weren't even there."

"I wasn't there, you snotty brat?" Francis tore his shirt off in anger and ran toward Bada with an open knife.

The Billats cooked all summer on an open fire, and next to the oven was the wreckage of a hollow barrel.

Bada grabbed a stave and, just as Francis lunged at him, knife in hand, Bada struck the back of his neck with the piece of wood. Blood poured out of Francis's mouth and he fell, his face hitting the hard ground.

The women lay down on top of Francis, because Bada's relatives came with pitchforks and scythes to kill him. It took hours for the murderous emotions to subside.

Francis quickly sobered up. The elder Zoga came to us in tears to beg forgiveness; it had all been due to drunkenness. By evening there was no longer any trace of trouble. Everyone sat around the fire as if nothing had happened; only Francis held a wet cloth to his black-and-blue, swollen face.

The others were heartily laughing at an old man, Palalo, who was squatting by the fire shivering, even in summer.

"Got that?" asked Palalo insistently. No one understood his rambling stories.

"Um . . . You got it . . . about how when they tied me to the buffalos that little girl saved me?"

"Who was that little girl, Palalo?" asked Hamster.

"Um. . . . Well, only you know that, you've got to know, Hamster, you bum. Do you got that?" Palalo looked for his stick to hit Hamster with. Kálmán Hamster was the only Gypsy whose presence he couldn't stand.

Palalo was a thin, towering man, more than six-and-a-half feet tall. Summer or winter he wore only underwear; the only time his skin saw water was when the rain caught him outdoors. Not that he ever entered anyone's yard without invitation, but he was in the habit of calling out over fences: "Outhouse needs cleaning?" People invited him in even if he wasn't needed and found some dirty job for him. He didn't accept handouts.

"One outhouse, ten fillérs, got it?" It wouldn't have done any good to offer him more, he wouldn't have accepted it.

Palalo had lived alone all his life. No one could claim to have ever entered his hut—no one except for a little girl called Munura, that is. Munura panted and squealed all the time. She gave out strange, sharp, annoying noises from between her huge teeth. People nicknamed her Mouse, because she was always gnawing whatever she could lay her hands on.

She couldn't walk, only crawl; no clothes could cover her bloated belly. She was in the habit of crawling out of her own family's hut, even at night, on her way to Palalo's place—the only place she felt comfortable.

"Well, sit yourself down." Palalo would tell the little girl, placing chunks of dry bread all around her. Munura sank her teeth into them one by one.

"You sure do have good teeth."

The crippled girl let out big squeals as she picked up handfuls of bread. Palalo just hummed.

"You understand what you are saying." He didn't let the girl leave until she had eaten up all the bread.

He had a fire going indoors even in summer. All you could find in his hut was firewood and a handful of straw.

On his way home from his dirty work, Palalo would regularly stop in front of the bar.

"Palalo is here, dear sir," he'd shout to the barman. He didn't enter; he knew that a certain odor accompanied his trade.

Two quarters of plum brandy were enough to make him chat with himself half the night.

"Got it, Palalo? . . . Um . . . Got it, you soot-faced Palalo? Why of course I got it, goddamnit!"

Sometimes he yelled so loud as we eavesdropped on him that he gave us a real fright.

"Got it? . . . Um . . . Got it, Palalo? . . . Um . . . Why . . . Hey, hey . . . Hey, Palalo . . . Um, he's not just anybody."

Palalo always lay on his back on the floor of his hut with only some hay sprinkled there for bedding, his head against the wall. He must have had an inexhaustible stock of topics. We never did manage to find out what he was talking about, though.

"Um . . . It'll work out somehow . . . Don't you agree, Palalo? Yep, Palalo, things always work out in the end."

He spoke this way even when he fell off a merry-go-round one day.

"Let me go," he said, when asked to produce money for a ticket. "It'll work out somehow."

After just two turns on it, Palalo was lying on the ground.

"Um . . . I said it would work out somehow. Well, it did."

These were his last rational words. That night he perished in his burning hut.

It was noticed only at dawn, when his hut caved in. They pulled him out from among the red-hot glowing logs with a pitchfork. His charred remains were still sizzling, his hands and feet standing on end, his fingers burning with blue flames like candles. He looked like a little roasted pig.

We wholeheartedly lamented his passing like that of an endearing clown.

After that, he was seen for a long time where his hut had stood, looking for something at night between the cold cinders and ashes, until it all became overgrown by grass.

He took everything with him, leaving behind nothing and no one. For us, his memory conjured up mirth more than moroseness.

Seeing Bada made everyone think of Palalo. With his dark, desiccated body, like a piece of cured meat on giant feet, Palalo was his perfect lookalike, although there was no family connection. But it was said that, when pregnant with him, Bada's mother had come to adore Palalo.

It was the custom among us that we got one or more lifelong nicknames as kids on account of whom we resembled or our faults and foibles. We used our real names only for official purposes. Most of the time if someone was looked for by his real name even we didn't know who it was. Few children got as many nicknames as Bada—one of which, not surprisingly, was Crazy Palalo—but the one he liked best was Dotty.

Why, Bada even had a document to prove he was an "idiot." He kept showing it like a birth certificate. His parents had been forced to have him declared insane, because they had had more than enough of having to pay the penalties for their son's behavior.

Incidentally, though, Bada had many attributes that proved his resourcefulness and gumption. These good qualities of his manifested themselves already in his early years. He cheated, lied, and filched whatever he could lay his hands on—even from his own mother—and he had the potential of a sly, wily savvy, cunning child, whose main interest in life was playing cards.

As he grew, this predilection became even more finely honed. As Bada entered manhood, the opportunities for him to pursue his passion expanded. He remarried weekly, or if it worked out, daily. The nuptials always depended on how much money the newlywed bride owned. Age was of no concern, only how much she had for Bada to spend on a card game. The women didn't complain if the game didn't turn out to be a lucky one, for he was by nature good at redeeming debts. In fact, losing always provided another opportunity.

I liked hanging out with Bada, though Mama was dead set against it, worried he had a bad influence on me.

Bada always raged with the desire for revenge; he wanted to win the very life of whoever had made a clean sweep of him that day. Usually the rematch didn't work out for him, but did that dampen his spirits? No. As a last resort he would gamble with his own clothes, and if luck was against him, well, the other kids accompanied poor naked Bada with great fanfare until he managed to slip home between the settlement's huts.

"Open up!" he'd shout, banging on the door. His mother had locked it on purpose.

"Get away from here, you soot-faced Palalo! Don't you dare come in here where the children are. Go around naked if you've gambled away your clothes."

"Give me something to wear!" he shouted.

His mother eventually threw out a shirt.

Here you could do anything—steal, cheat, be a card shark. The point was, if you hit the jackpot, share a bit of it. No one asked to whom it belonged, where it came from.

Bada wandered around practically naked all day until the winners had laughed enough. Then they gave him back his rags. Apart from him, no one took those card games too seriously. There was hardly any money around, anyway; for the most part only old, useless stuff changed hands. But cards were, at least, an ideal antidote to idleness.

Cards satisfied every need. They provided entertainment, thrills, a reason for a fight—and sometimes someone who hadn't set eyes on food all day could eat his fill because some players were apt to game away their food right off the fire. Bada was entertained by the game only while he played it. Sometimes he was bored by the foolishness of it all, but he couldn't free himself from the bondage of his passion.

"I'll buy a horse," he once said with serious intent. "I'll show those Gypsies that while I'll be drinking wine, they won't even get water."

He kept his word and brought a horse that even the Gypsies didn't dare to approach. He killed it after a few days because he couldn't keep it without a registration. He sold the meat on credit, and could only make some money on the skin. The first thing he did with that was to buy some new cards.

Everything went on as before.

Barely a week went by, and he brought home another horse. He had done some work to earn it. The poor old skinny nag was almost blown away by the wind. The whole of Gypsy Paris surrounded it, reeling with laughter.

"Get away!" folks shouted at the curious kids. "It might kick one of you to death."

Bada smiled; he knew they were making fun of him. He tied his horse to a boxthorn bush.

"Come here!"

He drew me aside from the others and, as if it were a big secret, pulled a box of Herzegovina cigarettes from under his shirt.

"Light up and put the rest away! And read this!" With that, he opened the horse's registration booklet. Have a look what sort of a stamp it has!"

"Nothing, only 'bay.'"

"Does it have my name on it?"

"It's written on the back."

Bada smiled when I read out his name. He looked around again, saw that we were being watched, and drew me even further away.

"How old is it?"

"Eleven."

"Eleven?" he repeated, grinning. I guessed his thoughts.

"So that's why you bought me Herzegovina cigarettes? Here you are." I held out the box to him.

"Oh, don't be silly, I myself don't know what I want."

"Yes, you do. You want to rejuvenate this old goat."

"This one here?" He looked at the horse. "My axe will rejuvenate it. Are you coming to the movies?"

Bada had hardly ever been to the movies. His generosity was suspicious.

"I'll tell you something on the way there. I swear you won't be sorry. We'll have so much money that we won't want to change money even with a Gypsy. This old nag will bring us luck. Trust me, I know where the money is."

Usually I'd take anything Bada said with a grain of salt. But it struck me that, though the others had invited him to do so, lately he hadn't wanted to play cards.

"Come on, Dotty, let's play!" the others had called out, coaxing him. They too figured he'd acquired money somewhere.

"I'm not playing. I made a vow to the Virgin Mary that I will never play cards again."

Bada lied left, right, and center. He often swore on his mother's and siblings' lives that he wouldn't play, but the next moment he forgot about it. His word was worth as much as a plugged nickel.

He was mulling something over.

I could hardly wait for evening, but Bada was even more impatient.

"Hey," he called into our yard from a distance. "Let's go!" Bada didn't dare to come over directly, for he was afraid of Mama.

"It's a good movie; we won't get any tickets."

On the way we stopped at several places for a smoke. We weren't in a hurry. Bada spat between the eyes of the snarling dogs just inside the fences.

"Good afternoon, sir!" he shouted into each and every yard as if he were Palalo.

Bada was pretty tall, too. Granted, he didn't ask, "outhouse needs cleaning?" For all my efforts to call him to catch up, he lagged behind me at every step.

"Okay, okay, I'm coming."

He caught up with me for awhile, but then stopped again-this time right in front of the bailiff, Mr. Kurucho, who happened to be standing there. I got sick and tired of having to yell at him.

"Listen, if you won't walk properly, I'm going back. What the hell are you gaping at other people's open windows for?"

"Well, then, let's get a move on; I won't stare anymore."

Bada strode on with big steps, even overtaking me. We had almost reached the main road and, due to the clatter of the homeward-plodding carts, I took notice of Mr. Kurucho's heavy footsteps only when he grabbed me by the shirt collar. Bada tried to bolt, but it was too late; Mr. Kurucho—a big, thickset peasant—caught him as well. I almost choked the way he pulled my linen shirt over my neck. He shoved us ahead, pressing us together.

"I'll give you something to remember, you little Gypsy bastards!"

We had to proceed at a good pace whether we wanted to or not, for those large boots of his were kicking our behinds. No sooner did I manage to get some air and yelled than Mr. Kurucho held me even tighter. By the time we got to the village hall, I was virtually choking. My feet barely touched the stairs; only the table stopped me when he flung me into the office.

"I've caught the stork thieves."

Two coatless gendarmes were smoking in the room.

"So you're the ones who stole that stork? . . . Why, you sons of bitches. . . ."

They set upon us, hitting us left and right. Within seconds I was hurting like hell; from table to oven we flew as chairs fell over one after another together with us.

I have never heard a howl like the one Bada let out. The gendarmes quickly closed the window. He just kept on howling even louder, and it started to pierce even my brain. The siege stopped for a bit. At first the gendarmes threatened him, but then they told him almost pleadingly that if he didn't stop, he would really get it.

"Where's the stork?" All three of them set upon me. I couldn't get a word in edgewise; I sprawled after each blow.

"So you stole a stork? Here's a stork for you!" I fell. They stood me back up. Bada struck up with renewed vigor, perhaps even louder. I couldn't tell the difference; my sense of hearing had become rather dulled.

"Get out!"

They tried to get rid of us. I don't remember whether we left the door to the room in its place or whether we took it with us to the streets. We sprinted down the road, dust rising behind us. In vain had Bada's legs grown so long, he could hardly follow me.

"Don't run," he panted. "Stop already!"

"Come on!" I hardly dared to look back.

"No . . . I can't run . . . I haven't eaten a thing today."

I had to stop so Bada could catch up.

"Well," he said, completely out of breath. "It wasn't worth it."

"It was you who were so keen on the movies. I don't know why you talked me into going, but they sure left us looking pretty. I needed the movies like a hole in the head."

I fingered my cracked lips.

"It wasn't the movies; it was that rotten stork."

"Damn that crazy Kurucho, what sort of stork was he demanding from us?"

"This one."

He took a painted plaster stork, the size of a chicken egg, from his shirt.

"I stole it for you," he said, handing it to me.

"For me . . .?" I said, flying into a rage as I took that plaster stork. "May maggots eat out your crazy heart!"

Had he not bent down, I would have hit him in the eye with it. As it was, the stork broke into tiny pieces as I jumped on him like a dog, ripping and biting him wherever I could reach him. Bada ran away.

"Stop, you idiot, you son of a bitch! You had me butchered by the gendarmes! You murderer! You stole the stork, you dickhead! May your bones rot in a dungeon! Catch him, people, he's a murderer!"

I made so much noise that people streamed out into the street. They laughed when they saw me hitting the back of the tall Gypsy with fist-sized lumps of earth as he ran away. Unable to run anymore, I sat down; I blubbered with fury. Bada also stopped.

"Don't cry, dear brother. I didn't do it out of malice." He came a few steps closer to me.

"I shouldn't cry? Go rip out your mother's guts!"

I broke into a run again, ready to fling more lumps of earth his way, but I no longer got near him.

I gave up the chase. I was still fuming for a while, but as I regained my breath, my anger dissipated.

Bada was silently waiting for me between two yards. He joined me without saying a word. He only cast me a sidelong glance. My face was smudged with blood, tears, and dust, and I was still choking back tears. I regarded the beating by the gendarmes as undeserved.

"Give me a cigarette," said Bada. I tossed him the pack, as if wanting to get rid of all his memories. "You're not smoking?" he asked.

Silently I reached for one; I already regretted having thrown the pack back to him.

"Matches?" He was inadvertently crumbling the cigarette while twirling it between his fingers, not daring to look at me.

"You have them."

"You're right," he said, reaching into his shirt pocket.

I would have liked to go for him, but I was afraid he could easily thrash me then and there. Bada insisted on giving me a light first.

"You're right to be mad at me, I'm to blame. But look!" He pulled out a bunch of horse IDs from under his shirt.

"If you want them, they'll all be worth a hundred."

"Where did you buy them?" All of a sudden I forgot the stork affair. How many are there?"

"Fourteen. I worked for two days at the flayer in Okány until I was able to filch them. It was him who gave me the bad horse in place of wages."

"Who do you want to sell the IDs to?"

"No one," he said, staring me in the eyes. "You think I'm crazy? We too can use them. If you're smart, we'll be loaded in two weeks. Did you see the horse I killed?"

"I did."

"Where do you think I bought it?"

"Nowhere. You stole it." I flew into a rage again.

"True. But where did I steal it from?"

"The Hungarians."

"No way. From the Romanians. It took me a day and a night; it flew like a magic steed."

"Oh my God, you want to go into horse rustling?"

"Yes. No one is going to look for them over here, on our side of the border. And if they have IDs, no one's going to bother us."

"Why us? Do you think I'll go with you, you yellow-belly? Do you think you can trap me again like you did with the stork? You screamed like a madman, and meanwhile they were just about killing me."

"Don't go thinking it was the beating I was scared of! I was worried that if they searched me they would find the IDs. Besides, why should I let those farmhands beat me up?"

"Even if you yell your head off, I'm not taking another step with you."

"You don't have to come with me; you're an idiot candyass."

"Maybe I am. I don't take part in such things."

"Will you listen to me?"

"Keep talking, but I'm not going. I'll alter your old nag's ID, but that's all. I'm scared."

I was so nervous that I even lit the cigarette at the wrong end.

"I've told you already that you don't have to come along."

"So what do I do, then?"

"Nothing. You just have to take a look to see which registration best matches the horse I'll bring, and if need be, just make a few changes to it."

"Don't you try and fool me. Do you think I don't know that if you get caught, you'd put me straight next to you in jail? Perhaps they wouldn't even put you away; you have a paper to prove you're are an idiot."

"Have no fear, they won't catch me. I'll cross the border in the middle of nowhere. I know about this stud that's outdoors all summer long with no one guarding it. The pasture is surrounded by water, so I wouldn't even leave behind any tracks."

"And what will they say at home if you turn up with a good horse? Will they believe you found it?"

"It's none of their business. What would they have said if we could have bought the one we bled? They would have said fortune favors fools. Tomorrow I'll have the nag's registration transferred to my name, and at least then they'll know at the village hall that I own a horse. Besides, it's not as if they'll bother to look at what it's like."

I always knew there was more cunning in him than in all the Gypsies put together, but I hadn't known him that well.

"Haven't you thought that one of the other Gypsies might rat on you?"

"They didn't do it with the other one, either, though they knew I stole it."

"Why would they have betrayed you when you gave them the meat? You brought it for them. But what if you don't kill your new horse?"

"Don't you worry! They'd testify for me and tell them where I bought it. They'd all say: I too knew about that horse, but the Hungarian wouldn't sell it to me at the time. Fortune always favors the fool. You think I don't know the Gypsies? They'd say anything for five or six pengős, like Francis. Everyone would swear that I bought the horse right under their noses."

Bada stopped talking, and we went on silently for a while. He must have been musing over something intriguing; his white teeth flashed and his limbs hung loose as he walked. Then he looked at me, wagged his head, and smiled. He seemed in a good mood. Money had completely gone to his head, I thought, and the wretch now had no idea what to do.

"Know why I'm laughing?" He shook me by a shoulder. "The way they grab at the meat, when I let them have it on credit. . . . Five horses wouldn't have been enough."

"They're hungry."

"They're hungry. . . . If someone else sold it, most of them wouldn't have bought half as much. They knew a fool could be fooled."

"Why did you ask for money? Everyone knew you stole it."

"But they didn't think I might have paid for it with my life."

"They didn't ask you to do it."

"A marvelous lot. First they pull a fast one on somebody and then they laugh at him."

"Why, what should one do with somebody like that?"

"Nothing," Bada said more seriously. "They howl like dogs for me for just one pengő."

"Tell me, are you angry with them?"

"Me? Why would I be angry?" He pretended to be surprised at my words, but it seemed like he wanted to say yes.

"Listen . . . does it hurt if someone is seen as an idiot?"

Evidently taken aback, he paused to look me over, and then waggled further.

"Do you also take me for one?"

"Don't ask right now-answer! Does it hurt if someone is seen as an idiot?"

"Yes."

"And do you think that if you lose your clothes playing cards and then beg your mother for a skirt, and if you squeeze toothless Zsuzsa or hairy Irma night after night for thirty fillérs, they'll think you're clever?"

"You don't know why I do it."

"Sure I know, I know you very well. It's not passion for the game that drives, you—it's vengeance. To make the others lose their shirts, to tear them up, to burn them, and let them also walk around naked. You believe that if there will be more idiots, you'll be able to blend in with them."

"What good would it do me? They'd still say I was mad. Don't go thinking I want to swindle everyone. I never once wanted to trick you."

"Oh yeah? Look at me. My head looks like a bruised pear. Do you see this?" I pointed to my mouth. "It's still bleeding. If you didn't manage so far, you've sure made up for it."

"Not at all. I could have done it lots of times. Even when we bled that horse, I didn't have the heart to. I did everything. I could have fobbed you off with five pengős. But I like you because you don't laugh at me, but scold me when I do something stupid."

It was hard to believe Bada, but I felt sorry for him. Everyone knew he wasn't really crazy, but what was there to do? He made himself look ridiculous, after all.

We plodded along in silence for a while, and then all of a sudden he stepped into an apple orchard.

"There's the warden!" I shouted after him.

Bada didn't even listen; he just bit into the apple he'd picked. The old man gave him a wide berth and stepped over to me.

"Tell that idiot to get out of the garden, someone might see him."

Bada stepped closer to the old man, his cap heaped with apples.

"Hey, how you doing, buddy?"

"Get going, get going," grumbled the warden. "To hell with you."

We sat down a little further away.

"Come on, eat up," said Bada, offering me an apple from his cap. "See, sometimes it's good to be mad—you can get away with more than if you're clever. You understand?"

We went home late, when everyone was asleep. There would be hell to pay when Mama saw me, I knew.

Lucky for me, she left early the next morning; I pulled the covers over my head so she wouldn't see me when she returned. When I emerged from my lair, as usual around noon, I could see Papa chatting with someone at the other end of the settlement; the hut was cool, for Mama had put green acacia foliage over the window. A mid-morning stillness had descended over Gypsy Paris.

The early risers hadn't come home yet, and the late risers were contemplating whether it was worth getting up yet. Always depending on the position of the sun, the people gathered in the coolness of one of the huts. Bada sat patiently under the box-thorn bush opposite our place. He was peering at me, dozing off every so often. His "big plan" didn't leave him in peace.

"If I'd only bring two horses across the border, that too would mean a fortune," he told me the night just before we parted. "It's hay harvesting time, after all—those horses will sell like good wine."

The same thought occupied my mind during the night, but when I looked in the mirror in the morning I was no longer in the mood for anything. I only ventured to poke my head out of the kitchen because of the black and blue marks under my eyes.

The settlement remained silent, as if everybody had moved out. A group stood around talking quietly, only one voice audible in the crowd, that of a fellow called Taltosh; he boasted about something. The slab of smoked bacon he was waving about sufficed to keep everyone's attention riveted on him. He'd been showing it off all over Gypsy Paris, while his wife kept shouting at him.

"Get you home now! Bacon bring, I want cook for the kids."

Her Hungarian was pretty poor, but she was as good as any village woman. She was the kind of fine-looking young lass whose butt the peasants liked to fondle, in return for which they gladly give her a basket of potatoes. Begging can't feed five children when one hasn't earned even ten fillérs in a month. But then, whose wife had not been "fondled"? No, not one of the settlement's army of multicolored children had been delivered by the stork.

Everyone knew it about their neighbor's wife, but no one believed it about his own. Anyway, the men had no topics of conversation during the day other than women and horses. They regarded both as livestock; a woman, though, was more profitable, easier to obtain, and free to maintain. What's more, she could maintain and support her husband, meaning what work she did could get them by. That is why each man tried to get himself a *harniko*[17] woman. But there weren't many of those around. The shiftless gals weren't worth a red cent, or only until their money lasted, after which they were left high and dry.

If a beggar or itinerant tinker turned up from somewhere, the settlement's women fought over him like cats and dogs.

Many Gypsies were drafted, and the women and girls consequently suffered from a lack of men. A gal didn't mind if she found a one-handed or one-legged companion as long as he lay down beside her. The gals would dance all evening, swaying their hips to lure in the boys before getting mounted. First, though, they would spread cucumber peels all over their faces to get rid of their wrinkles.

Bada noticed me.

"What's up," he said, sneaking into our kitchen, "has anyone seen you yet?"

"Not yet, and I don't want them to see me." I moved back in, because Bald Rosie was after me, always lurking around the house.

"What does she want?"

"Her pants are on fire."

"Lure her in, bless your soul, and I'll look after her needs so well she'll end up in the hospital."

"To hell with her, Bada, she's full of disease. Go tell my father that we're taking the horses out to pasture."

Bada took advantage of the opportunity, and by the time he returned, he had his nag with him.

We managed to get out of the settlement without meeting a soul. Long, silky grass covered the space between the ditches. Bada, grinning, threw himself down on it; he was in a good mood.

"Hey, you know who I slept with last night?" he asked, trying to cheer me up too. "Margaret Verge's daughter. Man, that woman isn't too bad at all. There's plenty to look at, yep, she's all fat. Your groin won't

---

[17] capable, industrious

get sore. You'd better get yourself a woman, too—why are you so afraid of them? Or do you want to stay a virgin? At your age I was already screwing Hairy Irma."

"That's why you can't get rid of her."

"So what? Why should I get rid of her? She saves everything for me that she brings back from the village. Would it be better if I starved?"

"I hope you thank her very much for the food she gets with her ass. The old Hungarians screw her good, and then she brings you the greasy pan. 'Here, Dotty dear, eat!'"

"I couldn't care less what they do with her! None of them have left it in her yet. Don't worry, once I have money, I won't even speak to them. I'll get myself a good *mashari*[18] woman—at least they don't sell their asses."

"Yes, but they're picky about who they marry."

"Picky? When I have a cart and a horse, I'll be able to get a whole stringer full of them fish. You think I don't have a way with women? I could have gotten some before, but they knew I was broke. Now I shit on it all; I don't give a damn. I've got my fortune in my hands, and I'll deal with it wisely. You'll see."

"I won't see anything. I'm not interested in your fortune. Count me out."

"Well, then you're a fool."

"Doesn't matter, but I don't want to go to jail. Come on, let's go for a swim instead."

"Okay," he sighed, "but you'll be sorry."

Folks from the settlement were shouting excitedly at Bada when he got undressed. He just showed them his ass.

"Look at this! You can pick up the picture tomorrow."

He plunged into the pit and only emerged at the other end. He stepped ashore and did another pose.

"Hey! Have you ever seen a Gypsy priest?"

---

[18] Rom who live by fishing

He was hopping around like a billy goat, slapping his naked ass so hard that it made a clapping sound. You couldn't tell whether he did it in anger or high spirits. He played around until the kids started throwing things at him. He jumped back in the water, his head and feet submerged; only a bit of his bottom was visible, as if the water were carrying some unknown object.

Bada was always counted as the best swimmer, and could do two or three laps without stopping, though it took fifty steps to walk along the pit from one end to the other.

"Come on, I'll race you!"

"Let's bet." I jumped at the chance. Bada seemed tired to me.

"Whichever of us gets back sooner wins five cigarettes."

"Okay."

At first it looked as if he was really tired, but halfway he began to gather speed. He was only making a last effort, I thought. I too picked up my pace, and we turned at the same time. I was certain he was falling behind.

"Whoa, we're not gonna play that game, buddy."

By the time I got out of the water, Bada had already been standing on shore for a while. During the big race I hadn't heard Papa shouting.

"Come home, stork man!" he waved to me.

"Stork man?" I asked Bada as if I'd misheard Papa. "How on earth does he know?"

"Come on," Papa called again. "They're looking for you!"

"Well, Dotty, here they are again."

"Well, let them be. Don't tell me you'll just sit back and let them bash us, will you?"

"What do you mean by 'let them'? Don't you understand that I'm being called?"

Papa kept standing on the opposite shore until I got dressed.

"Ignore it. Let's go somewhere. They'll soon get tired of waiting and leave."

"Oh sure, so at worst they'll take it out on my old man instead. . . . Don't you think?"

"I swear on my mother's life you're crazy. Why would they do that? It wasn't him who stole the stork."

"No indeed," I said. "May the rot eat that skinny flesh off you, it was you. You're like that scrawny old nag of yours."

Bada didn't say a thing as he quietly put his clothes under his arm. From under his matted hair he was staring into the wild blue yonder, where in addition to scorching sunlight only the night can be found.

After kicking at the soft molehills between patches of grass, he took his crumpled clothes from his armpit and flung them in a rage at the ground, kicking them in every direction.

"What's it you want?" I asked.

"I'm going with you."

"Go back to the horses," I told Bada, "because I'll tell them that it was you who stole the stork."

"I'll tell them myself," he said while smearing himself with handfuls of mud. "At least they'll let you go, and they won't beat me because I'd muddy them up."

"Great, then they'll beat me twice as hard again."

"Then tell them I did it—let them come and get me."

I was glad to be rid of Bada. Papa, who had meanwhile gone off, soon reappeared at the edge of the settlement. But I didn't see any gendarmes among the crowd of Gypsies that surrounded Kurucho.

"What sort of stork did you steal?" Papa asked.

"That fellow knows," I said, pointing at the bailiff. "Look how they beat me up yesterday. He claimed I stole a stork." There was an outcry from the people standing all around us when they saw the marks on me. Kurucho thought it best to keep his sword at the ready.

"Let's be off to the gendarmerie!" he said, again grabbing me by the neck. But Papa too got hold of me, releasing me from his grip.

"You're not going anywhere," Papa said to me. "Go take the horses out to graze." Turning to Kurucho, he said, "As for you, if my boy has caused any damage, I'll pay for it. Here you are." In Papa's upturned palm were two pengős. Taking no notice, Kurucho only followed me. I began to hurry.

"Don't you dare run away; I'll catch up with you! Get going to the gendarmerie!"

No way, I thought. Let me just get out of the settlement, and he'll give up on the idea of talking to me. As I now prepared to run, the sword blade hit me once. If I hadn't then bolted, the second blow would also have reached me; I only heard its swish. Kurucho tore after me.

"Don't you dare hit the child!" Papa shouted, running after us with a pitchfork. The other Gypsies followed. Bada was running toward us barefoot, looking like a clay devil, flourishing some sort of a stick.

"I'll hit you, you son of a bitch!" Bada shouted at Kurucho.

The swishing of the sword sounded closer and closer; Kurucho was stumbling, but kept up the pace. He was yelling, which is why he didn't hear the shouts of my people-otherwise he might have realized that a lot was at stake. Bada came closest to us, but he was still too far away to deter Kurucho, who by now was furiously trying to hack away at me with his sword. He was practically groaning from the effort to get just a bit closer.

The bastard will kill me if he reaches me, I thought, *or he'll cut me to bits and I'll never be an able-bodied man.*

I was still managing to keep up the pace, but fear was taking its toll on my legs.

If only I can get to the water, I thought, *I'll drown him.* Bada was getting closer, which encouraged me. Perhaps it was thanks to that that I managed to jump out of the way of a fatal blow. Its momentum made the bailiff stumble, but he regained his balance.

Having gained a few steps' advantage, I ran toward the water across a field of scattered garbage whose bone fragments and other sharp objects pierced at my bare feet. But, unable to take notice of the pain, I continued on my numb soles as well as I could.

I had to weigh the distance between Bada and Kurucho; my own strength was waning. The years I had spent in school had softened me, undermining my resilience. The Gypsies running after us began to lag behind, then stopped and only shook their weapons and hollered at the top of their voices as Kurucho kept chasing me. He made up for lost ground and pushed forward, his sword ready for a blow. I didn't have enough courage to stop suddenly or throw myself in front of him. Despair and momentum carried me forward in the hope that Bada would intervene before I'd be cut into half.

Maybe it was the Devil who threw before me that old horseshoe with its rusty nails staring into the sky like a centipede lying on its back. I didn't think at all of picking it up, and I wasn't at all glad when I noticed it. Nor did I have time to think of it as a means of escape. It was my instinct at work; I only sensed the heavy piece of iron in my hand and, not even hoping for luck, I flung the horseshoe blindly behind me with the last of my strength. I threw away all my willpower; the earth turned with me and, bereft of purpose and hope, I looked back without thought or resolve.

Kurucho flung the sword away and, staggering, pressed both his palms to his face. He then slid first on one knee and then the other before landing head-first in a heap of mucky chicken feathers. Bada stopped next to me looking in turn at me and the bloody, feathered face of the writhing bailiff who, struggling unconsciously, had managed to roll over onto his back. Papa was leaning on the handle of the pitchfork, panting.

"Jeez. . . . Goddamnit," he drawled, "you sure have bungled up this time." Crying fits clutched at my throat; I couldn't even reply to Papa's desperate questions. The others also arrived on the scene in small groups, wordlessly watching Kurucho as the air that exhaled from his nose and mouth turned into clotted bubbles of blood on his face.

"Let's get him out of here," Papa pleaded still in a desperate voice. "We can't leave him here on a garbage dump!"

Someone brought a linen sheet that had been washed to tatters, and they tried to stanch the bleeding. The skin dangling from his forehead covered his eyes, a shapeless hole without incisors gaped where his mouth had been, and all that remained of his angrily curling mustache were two tufts sticking out on both sides. He didn't resemble the old bailiff at all.

"Well, you sure did take care of him," an onlooker remarked.

I crouched at the foot of the same box-thorn where Bada had been waiting for me hours ago. People cussed at the bailiff even while trying to resuscitate him. They gathered every bit of white cloth they could while Khandi and his wife, bloody up to their elbows, were stemming the bleeding. They couldn't bind up his mouth, though; he would have choked had they done that. At other times everyone would have wished Kurucho to the Devil; now they were praying for his life.

Their anxiety was soon dispelled, as he came to and, half dazed, shouted for a doctor. Then he kicked old Khandi in the stomach and, had he had his sword handy, would probably have wounded the people around him. They scattered like little chicks as he ran staggering first after one and then the other. Kurucho waded into the crowd of staring kids, but before he could kick one of them to death, two robust Gypsies grabbed hold of him and took him home. It was my turn now, though I didn't need any nursing; my snot and saliva had mingled with my tears. In my despair I was unable to do a thing.

"Get a move on!" cried someone. "Run away from here, or else your skin won't be fit to use even as a sieve!"

"Where should he run off to?" Papa asked as if he wanted to dissuade me. "He's not the one to blame."

"You sure are making light of things, Boncza," another onlooker shouted. "Will you be able to defend the kid if the gendarmes come for him?"

He started to say something, but his clenched teeth made his voice raspy.

"Don't sit there looking so helpless!" Bada urged me on. "Let's go before it's too late!" Papa no longer held me back, but gave me the two pengős he'd offered Kurucho only a little while ago.

"Look after the child like the apple of your eye, Dotty!"

I heard Papa's voice from among the strident crowd as we left the settlement as fast as our feet would take us. My shirt became sodden as we crossed the arid pasture to avoid the main road, going over a hedge and a ditch in the direction of a distant tower. Bada was leading the old nag by the halter, encouraging it, while I kept running after them.

The cluttered thoughts in my head stopped me from feeling fatigued; I kept looking back as though ants were crawling on my back. I dreaded the gendarmes. By the time Bada quieted the nag down, we had already passed the next village. His hair hung in muddy tufts over his neck, which was washed white by sweat, and his white teeth flashed within his grimy face as he looked at me with a grin.

"Don't you be scared anymore."

He too was panting, but he seemed happy. His eyes had become much larger. The joy of satisfaction was blazing in them, as if to say:

"You've come with me, after all."

IV

WE PLODDED ALONG THE DUSTY ROAD. Bada talked about something, while I tried to make sense of the events of the last few hours in my mind. The misgivings that had surged through my whole being at the sight of Kurucho's bloodied face had somehow disappeared during our long run.

He was a big *khanchesko.*[19] I no longer regretted one bit that I'd gashed the bailiff's face. Papa had promised him two pengős, yet still he preferred to fight.

Well, I had done the right thing. In my anger I gave the nag a slash with a stick, and the three of us went trotting along.

We jogged past a seemingly endless yoke of oxen; the farmhands, dozing on top of the carts creaking from the weight of the shocks of wheat on top, let out big whoops at us. Then we ran again into the silence, only the rhythmic chug of our feet accompanied us as the soft, fine, gray dust splashed under our soles. The countryside floated in a golden juice; sun and sweat blinded us, and the withered leaves of the solitary parched acacias hung limply like vegetables in an overcooked broth.

"I wonder where this road leads?"

"Does it matter?"

"No. Certainly not, because this road," I tried to look for an appropriate notion to give myself a satisfactory answer, "is the way of escape."

---

[19] good-for-nothing, rascal

I smiled at the untrue, meaningless thought. The way of escape? This? I shook my head, lamenting my own fallibility. To escape from this world? Where to?

In the distance, below the curve of the sky, was a narrow black stripe, out of reach of the human eye. Between my brows and under my dust- and sweat-matted eyelashes, I sensed that I knew that island; the deceptive lawn surrounded by century-old trees, where the difference between man and beast disappears in the dark quagmire of ox stalls, and stench and grubs are inextricably mixed together. Everything there merges timelessly. The alternation of day and night is only that of light and shadow; cold or warm complement each other, and eternity is without minutes and hours.

I have been to that island. Its memory is revisiting me now as a series of images, and they are the color of smoke, as if I were looking at them from a distance of not three, but thirty or a hundred years.

Numbed by the haphazardly heaped figures flickering in my mind and amid the boiling heat of flavors, colors, and smells flowing around me, I do not have the strength to bond with these memories, because I equally love, hate, and fear them. Familiar shapes appear in the flashing pictures. I'd swear I have never seen them; they move closer or farther away, react to invented names, yet I cannot place them. I've gotten on a road where each moment has significance, because time is made up of these; it passes and rushes along, and does not take anything or anybody with it. Whoever doesn't keep up is mercilessly left behind.

Having sighted the Tisza family estate, we were no longer in a hurry. The old nag was slowly ambling along, touching the soil with its nose, sniffing each clump of earth like someone who is already enjoying the scent with which it will unite forever.

Somewhere the irregular sound of a cowbell sought to rouse the farmhands from their midday rest. But only silence awakened to devour the sound and to continue digesting it in its slow, scraping furnace.

Who was to say how long we'd been running? We might as well stop or lie down in the shade of some tree and sleep until hunger forces us to run again. Because we are always running for one reason or another. Ultimately it didn't make any difference; we were approaching the same objective either way. Perhaps there weren't any objectives at all, and we were just running and then stopping somewhere in the belief that we reached a haven, and then set out with renewed zest, perhaps to where we started from.

The nag stopped in its tracks; Bada crouched in front of him like a gun dog, then, bent in two for fear of being noticed, he dashed to the pea field. Two bloodied birds, bustards, disregarding the lurking danger, were clinging to one another and beating each other with their wings.

In their fight to the death they did not realize that Bada was about to attack them. It all happened very fast. The huge birds, blinded by fury, delivered themselves to their own downfall. Bada kicked himself off the ground, made a small arc in the air; you could hear the crunching sound as the bones of one of the bustards collapsed. The bird's outspread wings caused the earth to rumble, and while it instinctively tried to escape it held the other's swollen, bluish-red dewlap firmly in its beak.

It never occurred to me to help Bada; I was completely fascinated by the sight. Another fight began. Dust and brown down swirled in the air, while Bada rolled about on the ground, clinging to the bird that had dragged itself out of its opponent's beak. The bustard with the broken bones managed to pull itself along three or four paces by its wings, lifted its swaying body off the ground and fell back feebly. The other one still fought, trying to escape; it struggled and thrashed about with its wings, but couldn't rise due to its weight.

By now Bada was completely exhausted, stumbling about while clinging to the bustard, torn feathers swirling around them. The battered big bird dragged its attacker with incredible force, kicking his eyes and mouth full of dust. Clusters of its strong tail-feathers remained in Bada's hand, but—half-plucked—it managed to escape and took off with sluggish wing-beats. Bada looked after it sadly, and then turned to me with a reproachful shake of his head.

I nodded approvingly; a little help would have come in handy. He tried to fix his disheveled appearance by hawking loudly, then stopped beside the dying bustard, got hold of it at his neck with both hands and raised it in the air. His flashing white teeth showed that he had already forgotten his earlier setback.

"Hahaha! We'll eat you soon!"

You couldn't tell whether Bada said it in kindness or malice. It no longer made any difference to the bird. With one last twitch it gave up its soul with all its might. Its gray nails got caught in Bada's shirt collar as a soft crack sounded, and the shirt together with its collar got scrunched into the waistband of his pants.

"Wow. . . . Damnit!"

In his sudden fury Bada spun the bird around until its head was ripped off. Blood flowed down his chest in regular streaks; at first he tried to wipe it off with the plucked head of the bustard and then plastered it with blood-soaked mud that was still on his body since morning. By the time he stepped back my way he seemed to have forgotten everything and just laughed.

"Look at that!"

Bada's heart was evidently swelling with pride as he lifted the headless bustard into the air.

"It weighs at least fifteen kilos."

I too lifted it approvingly; it did have plenty of meat on it.

"We'll take care of it in the woods," he muttered as he hung the bird on the horse's back with strips of his ripped shirt.

After we took to the road again, I couldn't think about anything but my stomach. The forest appeared only after we slid through a line of trees that looked rather like a hedgerow.

Tiny farms huddled along the lanes. At one time the adobe hut dwellings had been built with purpose, but the descendants of the orchard keepers who'd presumably first lived there and who'd been paid in kind, had wrecked the place. The huts were half-swallowed by the earth, and only the smoking chimneys could be seen among the thicket of shrubs.

"How are we going to eat it?" I asked.

Bada, not even jolted out of his thoughts, replied: "Roasted."

Idiot, I thought, *I know that.*

"And bread?" I pestered him.

"Are you hungry?" Bada asked, his voice becoming softer.

I spat a big one, indicating that my mouth was watering. Rising on tiptoes, Bada gazed across the surroundings until his eyes caught a seemingly inhabited farm.

"Alright, you'll be eating soon."

He said it as if he were searching for some invisible knapsack among the alley's dense vegetation. He let out huge groans as he hacked off a thick acacia bough with his pocketknife, cleaned it carefully, and cut its two top branches to fit his armpit between them. He rolled the peeled, white stick into the dust to make it seem old and dirty.

"I'll be back, wait here!"

Bada started off like a born cripple leaning on his newly made crutch. Where he thought that he couldn't be seen along the way, he carried the crutch on his shoulder. For a while my eyes followed him. Then I led the nag to the ditch, where the grass was fresher and thicker. The beast gobbled it up as fast as he could. "A horse that eats fast is built to last," so the saying went. The nag's molars made a strong sound.

I wondered what the beast was called. I'd taken to calling it "the nag." But every horse had a *real* name, too. Indeed. I had one, Bada had one, and everyone I knew had one, yet nobody used them. For people, real names were good only so they could be called up into the army. Horses were called up too. Only the good ones, though. The same went for humans. Oh dear. Being chosen to be a gendarme, a soldier, or an army horse means you're good, for you know how to give a good kick.

"That's right, isn't it, Handsome?" The horse pulled back his ears and looked at me; he stopped chomping the green grass, and his eyes were blinking. Could it be that he was really called Handsome? Of course it could—he was. I'd opened his registration booklet only yesterday, if it really had been his. I myself had two birth certificates; Mr. Fardi's grandchildren were using them so they wouldn't be drafted.

I stroked the horse along his bony spine, and he leaned toward me as if enjoying it.

"You're exhausted, aren't you?" I said, patting his neck. The reply came as a sluggish rumbling of the belly. I just didn't know whose belly it was that I'd heard. Hunger was clawing at mine with sharp fingernails; it was around this time yesterday, before we set out to the movies, that I'd last eaten. A large swarm of flies was feasting on the neck of the bustard tied to Handsome's back. Here and there you could see heaps of yellowish white eggs; the flies were piling on their future generations as well.

"Jesus Christ," I exclaimed, "what a lot of meat!" I squeezed the bustard's huge thighs with pleasure. The forest seemed quite close; its huge expanse filled the horizon. A string of slow-moving ox-carts shrunk into broken lines at its feet. The din of a hovering flock of crows swallowed up the whooping of a farmhand's singing.

I counted more than fifty of those carts, each carrying stokes of wheat. An occasional guttural sound from one of the carts cut deeply into the crows' revelry, but I couldn't determine the melody the farmhand sang, because every time he started up again, he always did so on a different note.

Handsome tore at the grass vigorously, the leaves fluttering as a stray breeze tried to hide between them. I was deeply absorbed in my thoughts; they slowly reached up to my eyes. Handsome's monotonous grinding was still beating inside me for a while, and then that too flew away.

Soon, the dogs of a Gypsy settlement surrounded me, whining away; their feet were so small that they couldn't walk from their bellies, and they practically slid along the ground.

Sweet little pup, I thought, *how did this piece of metal get into your back?* With blood-soaked hands I stroked what was in fact a piece of sodden loam, and as I touched another dog, all of them turned into pieces of loam. The Gypsies were watching from a distance, shaking their heads. My entire body was sticky with mud; I tried to unclench my fingers, but the mud wouldn't let me; I felt tiny pins and needles in my arms, and I wanted to say that this is not me.

"*Na vorbi!*"[20] shouted Bada to me.

"You see, sir," he called out to a peasant farmer standing nearby, "the poor devil isn't deaf, only dumb."

I was sitting at the edge of the ditch, dazed from the dream, but still I realized that it was all about me.

"*Kode phendom, sar tu muto san.*"[21]

What was my fool of a friend up to this time? Why did he want to make this other miserable fool believe I couldn't talk? Bada sat on the rickety cart, grinning like a Cheshire cat, impishly pointing with his crutch at the old peasant, who was pulling the cart, straining between its two handles.

"Whoa!" The man stopped and helped Bada off the cart.

"Well, this is it. It's really gentle. God himself meant it for you. It doesn't kick, it doesn't bite, and you can stroke it even with your nails. Lead it up from the ditch, you dumb-dumb! You can tow away even the church with it. Undo the dead turkey off its back; his shape can't be seen properly on account of it."

Handsome was being unruly.

"Its teeth are like rice. He's a bit broken-winded, but that won't stop him from living until Judgment Day."

The man must have been past middle age. Under his red stubble the wrinkles formed into irregular rectangles; they grew deeper or shallower in turn as he examined the horse.

"He's skinny."

---

[20] Don't talk!

[21] I told him you were mute.

"True," said Bada, "he's not overweight, but if he finds a good owner, he'll show his gratitude for the feed he gets."

"He's weak."

"You call this weak, sir?" Bada pulled the horse's tail with both hands. "Why, he could pull that hill away." Feigning offense, Bada angrily rubbed the horse's protruding ribs. "It's not compulsory to buy it if you don't want to. Come on, kid, we've still got a long way to go."

Bada swung the crutch above his head and was about to throw it away when he remembered that he was supposed to be lame. "Is Geszt that way?" he asked, referring to a village by the woods, as if he had swung the crutch only to pinpoint a direction.

"Well, how much do you want for it, chum?"

"You know, boss," Bada said, as if about to give in, "I'm really reluctant to part with it, he's grown dear to us, like a child. We've gone through many a good and not so good time together, because beggars like us always have their troubles. I'm only putting it up for sale now so I can take some medicine to the wife. Believe me, boss, I wouldn't give it away to anyone else, but I know it'll be in good hands with you. By God, next time I come this way again, you sure won't have to drive me off your farm because I've cheated you."

He shook the man's hand firmly.

"It's yours for ten pengős."

"Too much," the man said curtly.

"Well, what's it worth to you?"

The farmer walked around the nag once more, felt his legs, and then went back to Bada. For a time he seemed to be calculating something, never taking his eyes off the horse, and then struck Bada's outstretched palm.

"Five pengős."

"What? Five pengős? May my wife rather die where she is, but I'm not parting with my horse. Hear that, Handsome? Five pengős? I'd get more for your skin if I flayed it."

"No one can find fault with this here horse," said Bada, poking its side with his crutch. "See, he's gentle as a lamb."

Handsome slept through the entire bargaining.

"Its last price is eight pengős," offered Bada, hobbling back to the peasant. "May my wife drop dead this instant if I knock off another fillér. Just harness the horse to the cart, and you'll see how well it starts off. You'll remember me as long as you live, for you've never had a horse like this since you've grown out of your diapers. May it drop dead right here if you can't get two tens for it at the markets."

He held out his hand again.

"Well, what's it worth to you?" Bada looked at the old peasant expectantly.

"Six." The peasant shook Bada's hand as if to say goodbye.

"Wait, let's not rush things. You're a poor man and I'm a poor man, so let's compromise and cut the difference in half. You can't say now that I didn't give in."

"I've got no more money."

"It's okay, boss, we can agree in another way, too. I saw your missus baking some lovely wheat bread. Let's make it six pengős and a big lovely loaf of Hungarian bread."

"Well, that's it then." The man shook hands with Bada. "You'll get a nice slab of smoked bacon to go with it."

We hadn't gotten much use out of Handsome, anyway; it just meant there were three of us. All the same, I'd somehow grown fond of him the past few hours, as if he'd been a serious old guy who didn't talk, but just went about his business or was lost in his own thoughts in his free time, chewing over his chores and then doing everything just as it should be done.

"Well, mate," said the peasant, "if the horse works out well, I'll stand you a drink next time around." He resumed after a pause. "By the way, don't call me 'boss'—the Jew is the boss around here. He owns the land. The neighborhood Gypsies all know me—John Székely, Bad John Székely, is everyone's mate. Call me Mister John."

Oh dear, I thought. *Bada, you've just sold coals to Newcastle.*

He winked at me from the rickety cart where Mister John had sat him, and introduced himself and me too.

May that sooty Palalo flesh of yours rot away! I thought, angry with myself for being pulled along by that miserable fool Bada. He could tell that I wished him to hell, and laughingly pointed to his feigned lame leg.

"May you become a cripple!" I hissed at him and threw the dead bustard at him.

"Let's go, Mister John, the dumb-dumb is hungry!"

I would have liked to give Bada a good hammering with his crutch, but then it occurred to me that, when it came down to it, he'd been driven by the pleasure of making a good bargain; besides, Mister John was already jogging alongside the cart. I was, after all, pleased that Handsome had found a new owner. Who was to say what sort of ideas would spring up in Bada's head, though? He could have easily decided to kill off Mister John.

A portly housewife in filthy clothes received us. She sat under the eaves, legs spread wide, while three children—foster kids, from the look of their clothing—peered at us with frightened glances. Around them flies were buzzing over fresh child shit that had been trampled into the ground.

Handsome, head held high, neighed at the incredible shambles of the farmyard. He was guffawing until the woman, arranging her dress over her ass with swift movements, stepped toward us.

"You didn't by chance fall for some swindle pulled by these black-souled folks?"

"We're not like that, lady," Bada moaned as Mister John lifted him off the cart.

"Nah, your kind can't really be trusted."

Bada, his head awry, limped around the woman while Mister John clarified our identity.

"Don't tell me you know them!" The woman said incredulously. "Well then, tell me, how much was it?"

"Six."

The farmer tried to satisfy the woman's curiosity briefly, whose questioning gaze shook his faith in the good bargain.

"Well, John Székely . . ." She probably wanted to say, *These kids are crazy*, but instead she thought about it for a while, gathered her silk crepe dress, sticky from grease and filth, and rubbed her ass with slow, steady strokes until she found the right answer.

"You can't buy properly if I'm not there."

Bad John Székely smiled modestly. He realized from the woman's voice that she was pleased, but that's how it is in the horse-trading world: folks always put down what they are buying and praise what they are selling. The two of them knew each other well; the wrinkles lurking under their noses couldn't hide their pleasure.

"You have a good piece of a healthy woman here, old mate," said Bada with a nod. "I bet you've got plenty to do with her."

"As if he could," said the woman with a laugh, "when he works himself to death all day."

"Don't tell me that, lady," Bada said flatteringly, "I see that he's managed to give you three children."

"Yeah, from the orphanage."

Despite the fact that the children were wearing orphanage garb, Bada pretended not to believe it.

"This little one in the shitty shirt does look like his papa."

John Székely beckoned to the three silently staring children.

There was a large wound on the cropped head of the blond child. The peasant patted their backs with a sort of love due to children in general. He looked at the wound, scraped some grease off the cart's shaft with his fingertip, spread it on the whining child's head, wiped the rest on his pants, and waved the children back inside.

"The wife will look after the payment," said Mister John. "She's the one who takes care of these little brats, so she's got the money."

"Indeed, John Székely," she said, "you wouldn't be anywhere if it wasn't for me. Fifteen pengős a month is all we get. What hired man's wife would put up with that? You, John Székely, also took your rifle each dawn, and you, Juli Gargya, can go mad with your foundlings. Then there's the baking, three loaves a week as big as the wheels of a cart."

"Okay, okay," John Székely said soothingly. "That's just why you need the horse; your legs aren't as strong anymore."

Paying him no attention, Miss Juli just kept rebuking her husband. Her father was head of the farm back when Count Tisza owned it, she explained, and now she had to bother with other people's brats.

"I wish I'd never met you, John Székely! There was no other girl like me at the farm; when I started to sing, even the bailiff's assistants went crazy."

"*But zhanel, xoxavel,*"[22] I murmured.

"What's the dumb-dumb mumbling?" asked Mister John.

"He says it's going to rain."

"What the hell! He can sense that?"

"He sure can. He came out of his mother with teeth in his mouth. Miss Juli, you'd better bring the money; I wouldn't like for us to be caught in a storm."

True to his promise, Mister John gave us that slab of roast bacon, too. Miss Juli clearly begrudged our taking the sack it was in with the bread, though it was old and worn. But she then insisted that I carry it, because she felt sorry for poor Bada being so young and a cripple.

"You can't get anywhere with this one, ma'am. Once he bristles up, no one can talk him into anything. And don't worry about the sack, when I come here next, I'll return it."

We went on in silence for a long time. Bada had thrown his crutch away awhile back, but I continued to play dumb just out of spite. I had decided not to eat Miss Juli's bread-her hands were so filthy-but by the time we got near the forest, I'd changed my mind. I kept getting a whiff

[22] She's a good liar.

of the fresh bread, after all; my mouth watered, and only my stubbornness kept me from taking it away from Bada.

We set up camp next to a stack of cordwood overgrown with morning glories. While Bada was busy making the fire, I was already elbow deep into the soft bread.

"Don't you get sick, now!"

Bada curled up next to me, his eyes full of tears—whether because of the smoke or the sight of my hunger-tormented face, I couldn't tell.

"There's food now, cheer up."

He tipped out the contents of the bag. Miss Juli had also packed us salt, pepper, and red onions.

"This will sure make a real gentleman's feast," said Bada, patting the dead bustard. "Cut me a piece of bread, too."

"What beautiful legs!"

He kept patting that bird, as if a beautiful girl were lying between his legs, and took large bites of the fresh bread with its crunchy crust.

"You've got plenty of time to leave; we could finish off even three such bustards before day laborers get back from work."

At first I thought he was talking to the bustard, but when I grasped what he meant, the food stuck in my throat.

"How about you?"

"Me?" Bada looked at me in surprise.

I tried to force the last bite down my throat, but I couldn't; it turned out of my mouth with a long thread of saliva. I have never felt the weight of loneliness as I did at that moment. I had already become more or less reconciled to the thought of flight and roaming; it would perhaps be easier to bear it in the company of another, but I felt unable to take a step forward by myself. Tears ran thick and fast down my nose, and I was ashamed at being so childishly emotional.

I wanted to voice my thoughts—thoughts that had been on my mind ever since we'd left home. But all I did was hiccup, sob, and tear at the grass around me, although I'd already decided to turn around and follow our route back. What could they do to me, after all? Beat me to death or lock me up? Even that would be better than living in perpetual fear among strangers. With bated breath I somehow managed to cry away my tears.

"I'm going home."

Bada was hurriedly tearing out the bustard's feathers. He kept touching his nose, as if bothered by moths, sweeping off the bustard and his pants with the palm of his hand and hissing and groaning by the time he found his own voice.

"When you've had your fill," he said, "cut off a couple of two-forked sticks, like the one for the crutch."

Save me, Lord, from fools, I thought. *Bada has completely freaked out. He doesn't even care if I race against wind; all he cares about is to have two crutches*. All at once I sprang up in anger and said, "Carry off this whole damn forest as a crutch! I'm no longer playing this game with you."

I made a rush for the stubbly field we'd crossed.

"Hey, where are you going, you idiot? The forest is this way!"

I just kept running without looking back.

"Can't you hear me?" his voice resounded. "If I catch you, I'll give you a flogging!"

Just you dare to come, I thought, *and I'll give you such a flogging that they'll cart you away in two bags.*

I did indeed want him to come after me; at least I could then alleviate my bitterness by taking revenge. I could hear the stubble crackling behind me; Bada wasn't running, just striding along.

Slowing my pace, I rummaged through my pockets for some hard object, and for a moment I was glad, but then I shamefacedly pulled out the money for the horse, tightly wrapped into a piece of rag. Bada was already walking beside me. He couldn't speak; he was just sobbing.

"What are you crying for now?" I asked, choking down my tears. "Don't worry; I don't need your money. Take it!"

He declined the money with a wave of the hand. I couldn't keep on holding it out to him; I too was overcome by emotion, and it took quite awhile until we finally got over our weeping bouts. Soon we didn't even know what we were crying about. We tried to take comfort in little mutual reproaches uttered in quavering voices, until I realized that Bada was right.

My sixteen years had proved insufficient for me to recognize those ruses with which he had prepared his plan. My supposed muteness and his lameness were a mystery to me, but what I had least understood was why Bada had bartered away Handsome, when he had received it in lieu of fifteen pengős from the flayer.

"I can't take you with me," he said sadly, when we went back to the fire. "I'm crossing into Romania tonight; the border is only a stone's throw away. Don't think that because I'm crazy I'm looking for trouble. We can't afford to risk anything. The reason I'm not going along with you to the estate is because we could meet hundreds of folks we know, folks who'd betray their father or mother at a gendarme's angry glance. If we've managed so far to get away looking like two miserable beggars, we'd better not spoil it now."

Meanwhile he'd gutted the bustard and made me cut narrow strips of bacon from the slab, strips he then stuffed into the slices he'd carved into the bird meat.

"There you go."

Bada kept stroking the meat with growing good spirits. He wanted to say something, but then he started out for the woods, returning with two crutch-like sticks and a sharpened skewer, which pulled lengthwise through the bird's body.

"You'll have to rotate that," Bada told me as he fitted it between the forked sticks, "and I'll be trickling lard onto it."

Roasting the meat as if it were a veritable hunter's feast made us forget everything, and we didn't even notice that the sun had hidden itself on the other side of the forest. I couldn't take my eyes off the crispy bird as it shone with the fat from the lard, giving off a heavenly aroma.

"Tell me when it's done!"

"If you like, it can be done right now," said Bada, waking with a start from his thoughts. "Meat tastes best if it's half-roasted, half-boiled."

I stopped rotating the spit while Bada carved off one of the legs and put it on the grass to cool.

"Carve off the other one, too!"

I gave the spit another turn. Bada looked at me, and for the first time in my life I met with a look on a person's face that radiated a kind of intelligence similar to that of those domestic animals that follow or guess a person's thoughts from a single gesture.

Bada plunged his pocketknife deep into the sizzling meat, the splattering fat raising tiny bubbles on his hand. Some sort of light flashed in his narrowed eyes; you couldn't tell whether it was in anger or sorrow. He placed the second bird leg on the grass beside the first.

"Okay like this?"

I didn't say a thing. These moments did not allow for much talk. At other times we would perhaps have asked each other what the other was thinking, or else we'd dispel the silence with coherent or even incoherent words aimed really at driving away our own bad thoughts. Instead we surrendered ourselves to the enjoyment of eating; chattering, boasting, swallowing our bitter worries with tasty morsels, forgetting everything that minutes ago had etched itself into our thoughts. Only one sensation remained: amid the endless hammering of our sharp teeth, we had to belch, because the bag is full, so to speak, and what would happen to the leftovers? We couldn't keep them for tomorrow.

Who was to say what tomorrow would bring?

The legs were cooling, and we watched them as if they were two glasses filled to the brim that must be emptied. That's how it's done whenever a farewell is at hand-gorging yourself with food or drink so you don't feel the moment of parting.

This is what hurts the most. These are the moments that have to be numbed so that the operation shouldn't be painful when fate with its merciless knife slashes our souls. After that, the lame can get used to their crutches.

Bada and I were indeed saying goodbye to each other. We couldn't clink our glasses, there was no heartfelt *t'aves baxtalo.*[23] We silently chewed the legs to the bone as if we could crush every trouble, every danger with our teeth so that nothing could hinder the other's way and that his return be safe before the last morsel might turn bitter in our mouths.

Bada left first, waving back from the forest's undergrowth before the vastness swallowed him.

It was evening by the time I arrived at the estate. The flickering electric light gave only an inkling of where the lines of the small-windowed barns were, but I could already feel the pulsation as hundreds of cattle breathed in and out through their dilated nostrils.

I drank my fill from the ever-flowing artesian well and splashed my face with the tepid, plain water until I felt like washing. The soles of my feet were swollen after the long trek, and the puddles of dung water surrounding the well stung my already cracked toes, causing a painful itch. One of the farmhands was again singing the strange tune from close by, as if he wanted to annoy only me.

Sulkily I sat on one of the posts, my legs hanging into the water up to my knees. The farmhand's good mood knocked those earlier thoughts out of my head. I might have been thinking of the weeks that I had spent here years ago; perhaps of that night when Babi's childish mothering led me to a river swelling with unknown feelings, a river whose waves of blood are enough to flood even the highest brain. I had not managed to fall into that river ever since, almost voluntarily avoiding those shores.

Bouts of laughter came from the stables. The people inside were telling stories or had found some fool to entertain them.

I listened for a long time to work out which stable the sound was coming from, and then my thoughts veered in another direction, chasing

---

[23] good luck

the other, now to the past and now toward the bleak future. I liked the silence, the solitude, and I followed the rolling spool, unraveling the entangled strands, which ended somewhere beyond our world.

I held onto those thoughts for hours, it seemed. Events woven by me came to life like some dazzling reality, and in the featherlike atmosphere of their music I felt that years had swept past me. That I had stepped back into time as a tough, resolute man, who wanted to reduce everything around him to cinders in order to create a new world over the smoldering ruins, until another childish thought urged me in the opposite direction.

Who was to say how many men Babi had embraced in her motherly way, and how many of them hadn't stopped what they began. I now thought about her a great deal and tried to visualize her, but all I saw was a mother similar to a sow surrounded by tiny squealing little brats.

That is the fate of them all—why would Babi be an exception? Men fleece them because they love hundreds of them. If one happens to get a decent husband, she despises him and calls him a simpleton, a fool. The real ones are the ones with a hard fist.

By now I was soaking my feet in a nearby trough. All at once a knotted *kamzhi*[24] cut into my naked back, making me spring right out of there: at its other end was a cursing farmhand.

"Damn you! You expect the oxen to drink from that after you?"

In my sudden rage I swung half a brick into the air; all I would have had to do was to let go of it. I don't believe that one can think in such a split second, yet my nails dug deeply into the wet brick as I held it above my head as if I wanted to rip it down from there. I flung it angrily to the ground when the man disappeared into the dark. I had recognized his voice as that of the singer who had come close to sharing the fate of Kurucho. Although the sting of the kamzhi was still sore, it was better this way.

I couldn't dispel the thought that what we do does not depend on our own resolve, but that some omnipotent power in whose hands we are only tools forces us to act. Now, too, if it had wanted it to be so, the

[24] rope-woven bullwhip

man would lie bloodied next to the well, and I would be on the run again. Sometimes that thought comforted me; sometimes it made me want to revolt. For once I trusted fate that someday it would deliver him into my hands, and then I'd be able to get even with him. I hissed as the bag I was holding touched my cracked skin, but I no longer cared. I walked toward the barn from where louder and louder laughter could be heard.

The night watchman, leaning on his cane, peered out from behind the manure trolley that stood in the wide-open doorway. I greeted him, but he didn't respond; he was preoccupied with the spectacle. With great difficulty I squeezed my body and my bag through the narrow gap between the trolley, which was laden with a soggy heap of cow dung, and the edge of the door.

As I now stepped inside I whispered another hushed "good evening" to no one in particular, but no answer came, even though people were standing three-deep along the two rows that marked the manure trolley rails. Only the area where the narrow track crossed the center of the barn seemed empty.

I saw nothing that might have accounted for the outbursts of laughter and the mutters of tense expectation I could hear. Perhaps the sudden light confused me, but not so much that I couldn't see across the barn. Only a single man approached, kicking a bundle of rags in front of him.

I didn't find this sufficiently interesting to laugh at, and the blow from the kamzhi still smarted. Listlessly waiting for the main attraction, I realized now that the approaching man, who brandished a thick length of rope in his hand, was none other than Bluelip. His face shone black even in the dim light; he had been given this nickname because of his thick, blackberry-hued lips that seemed to be ever whistling, although his otherwise wide mouth just barely covered his protruding gums.

He had lost his nasal septum as a toddler, and the space below his bulging eyes, which were constantly bloodshot, was adorned by a flattened sphere, with two holes at the top. I was always surprised that the rain didn't fall into those holes. Anyway, Sophie Bodnár had earlier brought him to these parts from, well, from somewhere. Nobody had ever asked Bluelip where he came from or just who he was; he'd been honored with his own special name and he lived among us like any other. He would live here as long as Sophie didn't get bored of him, that is, because if one thing was dead certain, it was that he would not settle here permanently. No man had yet been born with whom Sophie Bodnár chose to live for a whole year.

The bundle of rags kept springing into the air with Bluelip's every kick.

What kind of a game had this homely Gypsy devised?

As I got closer, that bundle of rags turned into a crouching female figure, two bricks hanging from her hair down over her breasts. Groaning, she was duck-walking along between the rails at a faster and faster pace, as dictated by the kicks being leveled against her back. Bluelip was grinning as the crowd burst out in raucous laughter: he was kicking and beating the woman to make sure she'd keep crawling or hopping along. Each time she set out again, silence fell as everyone anxiously eyed the distance between her and the hoe handle laid across the rails.

"Shit," a Gypsy next to me muttered through a bitter smile, "she sure can take it well. This is the seventh pass. She'll croak before she finishes."

You couldn't make much out of the woman's bloody swollen face. I pushed through the throng in front of me to get closer to the turnaround indicated by the hoe handle. The view didn't intrigue me particularly; I felt the blood rushing to my head, like earlier, when the farmhand had whipped me across the back. No one seemed to notice that there was an unknown newcomer among them, as everyone was trying to get further ahead; some pushed me aside while others clutched my shoulders, peering over my head.

Ignoring derisive comments and curses, I flung my bag into the nearby manger to free both my hands and began to press my way forward through the crowd.

Everyone took me for a girl rather than a boy. My hair had grown pretty long and my thin mustache had nothing much to do with facial hair; it only became visible when I blackened it with a burnt match or pencil, as I'd done that very morning, except that there was no sign of that by now. It had come off when Bada and I had our swimming competition.

I didn't see much while pushing forward, and could only deduce what was happening from the bursts of laughter or the sudden silences. A number of people tried to make it clear to me—some playfully, some with barely concealed anger—that it was bad manners to stand in front of others or to push them aside. But everyone was doing it. Anyway, I had come late, so why shouldn't I find out what was happening?

You couldn't argue with anyone, so I didn't give a damn about the scornful glances. I even cast a mean stare right back to someone behind me and, before the recipient could do anything about it, I slipped under the arm of whoever was in front of me as I pressed on ahead. A number of people indeed no longer watched the woman, but growled at me or inadvertently elbowed the one nearest.

With a kick, Bluelip knocked the woman over and, with arms akimbo, looked around.

"Is there anyone here by any chance who doesn't like this? Let him come forward! As long as I'm sleeping with her, I can do to her as I please. And if it hurts someone's feelings, let him sleep with her."

Everyone grunted approvingly; everyone but me, that is. I pushed ahead until I got to the front. Bluelip looked around again, blinking, still looking for the culprit.

The woman tried to rise, though very timidly; the ground was crimson from her blood. The bricks tied on both sides to her long, black hair were full of tiny blood clots as she lifted her head from the stone floor, her face contorted in pain. Suddenly I sensed the barn begin to sway around me. I could never come to terms with human blood. Whenever I was near it, its smell immediately assailed my nostrils, yielding queasiness at first, and then a retching nausea.

I was already sorry that I had pushed to the front, but I couldn't take my eyes off the battered woman, who tried to raise her arm imploringly. I saw a flicker of light in her eyes, reminiscent not only of a plea but also of hope.

The heavy bricks pulled her back onto the ground and, hands outstretched, she began to slide on her belly toward me.

"Save me, brother," she wailed, "save me from this Gypsy, Bluelip, so his bones get swept right out of the hospital. You see what he's done? He's murdered me! He's made a fool of me in front of the whole world! May the Lord never give him strength and health, and may He take away his good fortune when he least expects it."

Only snatches of her further curses reached my consciousness. Bluelip's startled eyes flashed as the hoe handle sliced through the air with a buzz and broke in two above his eyebrow. He made a dash for the post and a tremulous, female sound came out of his throat. He wanted to hold on to something or someone, but his squirting blood frightened away the bystanders; he staggered and sprawled across the tracks. For a while I looked at the pieces of the broken hoe handle; tough acacia wood, I thought.

Once again the almighty power! The surprise caused by the sudden unexpected change was still tangible. Everyone stared at Bluelip with his bloodied face as if no one could fathom what had happened. I didn't understand it, either. I looked. My fingertips were blue as I was gripping the remaining piece of the broken handle in my hand; I felt uncontrollable tremors inside me, like a cat watching its tortured victim, ready to pounce again at its smallest move.

Instead of the queasy, retching nausea that almost burst out of me a few moments ago, a sweetish sap swam in my mouth, and I had to spit. The short Gypsy with the bitter smile standing next to me caressed my cracked back; I felt no pain, just a warm hand that thawed me from my petrified state.

"You are a true man! And you," he said, turning to the others "are pieces of shit. You were laughing when he tried to kill someone else's child. Even if he sleeps with her a hundred times, a man should remain a man! Let him tie her to his belt if he is jealous and not make a mockery of her in front of all the world!"

He uttered the last words very forcefully, in a manner implying that those words were his final words on the matter. His voice hadn't quite settled down when, turning to me, he asked:

"Who are you, son?"

"It's the kid, don't you know him?" someone shouted to him reproachfully to give something back for the former reproof. He looked me over skeptically; I was at least a head taller than he. He shrugged his shoulders, indicating that I didn't belong among his memories. While the women, scolding the men, freed Sophie Bodnár from her load of bricks, the little old man walked up to Bluelip and poked him with his naked toes.

"Get up, mate, kiss Mara's ass!"

There was not one among the many Gypsies who would have felt the least pity for him, although he had heartily entertained them just a little while ago. He was wiping his cut forehead in a daze with a vacant look on his face. Perhaps I was the only one feeling sorry for him.

"May your blood ebb away!" Sophie jumped at him, scratching and slapping him until the others pulled her off.

"Listen to me, Gypsies!" She knelt down and raised her hands, sticky with Bluelip's blood. "May the Good Lord never give me luck and happiness, may I have to crawl on my knees to beg for every piece of bread, let him take from me whom I love most, may the earth become fetid wherever I go, if I ever in my life again let Bluelip put his pants next to me. *Bahter!*"[25]

"You see, brother," muttered Bluelip, looking at me, "doesn't she deserve to be killed?"

I didn't respond; I just tore off part of my shirt and threw it in front of him. A shaggy-haired girl picked it up and wrapped it around his cracked forehead.

---

[25] Amen

"May your stinking flesh rot from your bones!" she said. "The woman doesn't want you and you're still terrorizing her. I wouldn't want you, either, even if your dick were made of pure gold."

"So now it's me who is the bad one in everyone's eyes?" Bluelip tore off his shirt in anger.

"Didn't you see that she cheated on me with everyone right under my eyes? There's no man on earth who can satisfy her, she's got a white liver, I swear!"

The little man with the bitter smile didn't leave my side, but began to quiet the bursts of laughter. I was struck by the way they listened to him. I found out later that his five stalwart sons and two sons-in-law ensured his authority. Besides, judging by his white hair, he was capable of playing the part of a magistrate or some sort of an enforcer.

"Now listen to me," he said, tapping Bluelip's shoulder with his long-stemmed pipe, "you don't tame a woman with a white liver by beating her; what she needs is a real man next to her ass."

"Your son couldn't tame her, either," Bluelip interrupted the old man angrily. "Though he slept with her, too."

"You're saying I slept with your wife, you son of a bitch?! Just you wait! I'll put your guts in your hands in a minute!"

A boy, who emerged from behind the post, waited with his hands dug in his pockets for the other to repeat his assertion. All eyes were fixed on them, and knife-edge silence competed with the anticipation of raucous laughter. Bluelip trembled, his eyes flashing from side to side, and he pulled his thick, blackberry-hued lips tight over his gums, lest some ill-advised word slip out of them again.

"Keep quiet!" said the old man, pointing his pipe in a commanding gesture toward his son. "He didn't say you slept with her, did he?"

The boy blinked in embarrassment when he noticed that his young wife was coming toward him.

"So what if he did sleep with her?" she said, holding down her husband's twitching hand. "It was to his liking and to Sophie's. At least she got a taste of what a real man is like. Be a man to her, and then she won't cheat on you. We're not angry at each other, Sophie, isn't that so? And if somebody doesn't like it, he can kiss our asses." After a pause she turned to her husband and added, "Come on, my pet, let's go to bed," pulling him away affectionately.

When they got to the edge of the crowd, she called back jeeringly:

"Where there is plenty, there is enough to spare!"

It was no longer only the beating that hurt Bluelip, but also the lack of sympathy. The fast-moving events had made a mockery of his every word. Uncontrollable laughter was the reaction as he struggled to try and prove the rightness of his actions. People responded with cruel irony to his list of names, with Sophie taking the lead. The woman came out on top in their battle of words. Perhaps I was the only one there who believed Bluelip.

I had known Sophie since my early childhood and knew that there were at least as many men in her life as months.

It is easy to bleed to death in a knife fight, in which the victor invariably is praised even though it is not always strength that prevails. Still, there is always the possibility for the loser—if he survives—that his fickle luck might return some day. But for a crazy, humiliated womanizer like Bluelip there is nothing left but to creep under a barn manger and avoid the company of men—if, that is, he doesn't want to become the butt of jokes for the rest of his life—or else hang himself.

No one worried about him anymore. Most folks had dispersed, looking for their places on the thick straw litters next to the edge of the barn. I found many old acquaintances among them, who welcomed me with warm, manly handshakes.

"How you've grown, kid!"

I felt as if not even a minute had passed since when I was among them—the same old rags, shaggy heads, and unshaven faces. Only the women looked more worn out, their clothes exuding the scent of fermented milk, their faces showing the ravages of time and the entrenched traits of old breeding sows. They say there is no permanence, that everything changes and evolves perpetually. But does that apply to our world too?

I hadn't seen these people in years. If it is true that there is constant or changing motion here too, then—after the passing of some time—one should be able to determine the distance traveled, unless this motion occurred in one spot or, say, on a circular path. Since learning a thing or two about physics, I'd become interested in our world's speed of movement. No matter how tempting the idea of "petrified immobility" might seem, I don't believe in it. It may be that this sort of motion is like that of a rotating disk, which, despite its speed, gives the illusion of immobility. But then, what becomes of the projectile force created by that speed?

"Do you feel any force that wants to coerce you out of this world?" What would that shaggy-haired girl have answered, were I to have asked her that? She'd probably ask: "Where to?" And she'd be right. Where to? I settled my gaze on her as she just stood there looking down at her dirty feet, hiding her blushing face from me. She was younger than me, and already choosing her man.

She wouldn't have wanted Bluelip, either, even if his dick had been of pure gold. Nervously she poked at the straw with her toes, looking in turn at me and the men around me. We smiled, embarrassed; she smiled back at me, then shouted at me angrily, "Come on, kid, Grandpa is calling you!" She ran away like the wind. I stared blankly at the others.

"Go on," said one of them, encouraging me. "Their place is around the middle of the barn, there you'll find the little old man."

I wasn't tempted by the hospitality, no, I would have preferred to sprawl down on the straw, but they were so tightly squeezed together that it seemed almost hopeless. Waving to friends, I went to look for this Grandpa. As I walked through the empty center of the barn, looking at the folks milling about to the sides I now noticed lots more acquaintances.

As I nodded their way, they smiled, some of them shouting after me:

"How are you? . . . You've grown a lot!"

"Well, yes," I replied modestly.

In fact, I felt a little inner pride that I hadn't noticed until then. As I looked out at those older than me and saw the top of their heads,

I had to acknowledge their astonishment. I had suddenly, without any transition, crossed the threshold of my age. They no longer saw me as a smart, serious-minded child, but a man capable of independent action.

All at once a girl I knew sprang up from the now seated crowd while hastily throwing on her blouse. Running over to me, she fell upon my neck and kissed me on the mouth. It was the first time that had happened to me. I expected the usual spiel, but instead she hugged me for a long time; I expected her to burst out crying. Swallowing her tears, she held her airy blouse tight against her flat breasts.

"Babi died last summer." I couldn't even give voice to my surprise at the news, as she continued: "She wanted to get rid of the baby inside her, and things went wrong."

Had I been a little more prepared for the news of Babi's death, it might have touched me more deeply, but this simple communication only informed me about something that I couldn't grasp as yet. Perhaps because I had imagined Babi's fate so differently I just couldn't or didn't want to believe it.

"Do you now have another wife?"

Her question stunned me even more than the recent news. Only at that moment did I become aware of the full reality of something that was natural to her. Here, the years didn't count.

"She talked about you all summer; the poor thing hoped you would take her back."

I was no longer surprised. Her words had to be understood as referring to those husbands whose wedding intentions comprised no more than a couple of nights. It didn't count as a despicable attribute at all. It was at least as natural as the fact that if two individuals of different sexes sleep together for one night, they are referred to as a married couple. Hence I had already been married. Had I objected, I would only have demeaned myself.

"You haven't changed," I said, touching her arm.

"Ah!" she said, pulling aside her clenched mouth and signaling with her eye toward a young, grinning Gypsy boy sitting on the straw.

I didn't dare say goodbye to her with a look that promised anything, so we just shook hands warmly.

Increasingly I became convinced that for years I had been suffering from "childhood disease." Indeed, it now began to irk me how brazenly that disheveled girl had hurled, "Come on, kid!" at me.

Who cares about her grandpa? I was already wondering whether it was worth my while to give her another chance to insult me. That's how these young gals try to show off.

These thoughts faded away in no time. It seemed almost impossible to stick to any topic, even for half a minute, with so many strange new sights all around me, and with my being in the spotlight of so many different glances. Never had this world looked so colorful to me. I had lived in it, I had grown up with the colors; the monotony of its forms were ingrained in me. Only a few clans constituted the narrow circle in which I had run here. The constant intermixing washed away all differences. Why, some dogs even looked like their masters.

Grandpa waved impatiently. Stripped to his long underpants, he sat on multicolored rags spread out over the straw. At the edge of the lair an old woman, whose several layers of gaudy skirts made her look stout, was ladling out freshly cooked grits. She used a makeshift wooden spoon to beat back the attacks of her squealing grandchildren, who were dissatisfied with the unequally measured portions.

"Scat!" She put the sooty pot in front of her husband and spoke indignantly, in broken Hungarian: "Even the county welfare office wouldn't be able to cope with you. It's been barely an hour since I dished out a potful of food to you all." The children stared sulkily at the steaming hot grits in their laps until their appetites overcame their hopes of getting more.

I greeted the old man with all kinds of lengthy, fulsome good wishes.

"*Nayis,*"[26] he said curtly, and only let go of my hand after I sat down next to him.

---

[26] thank you

The adult family members settled down around the pot. It would have been impolite to refuse the spoonful offered to me, even though Grandpa's wife had first wiped it with the hem of her skirt. I kept licking and blowing on the grits, which I didn't like at all. My stomach was still bloated from the bustard; I craved only water.

"Where is Vorzha?" Grandpa asked a man with the drooping mustache who sat next to me, eating away.

"*Shun,*[27] how should I know?"

"The beggar who is timid is left with an empty bag." Grandpa was still munching the grit under his mustache. The children crouched next to us, ready to pounce. I turned my head but didn't see the shaggy-haired girl.

Sitting next to the man with the droopy mustache, a woman gave me an occasional look; her eyes spoke more than her mouth. There was something in her glance that reminded me of the girl. She nudged her husband with her knee and pointed toward me.

"Eat, brother, don't be shy, there's plenty here." For a while scraping noises could still be heard from the pot; they talked, wiped their mustaches, and burped. Then, all at once, the clatter of spoons fell silent. Grandpa had barely swallowed his last bite when he began looking for his pipe.

"Mára, take this pot away!" Instead of Miss Mára, a surprisingly clean young girl in a pink dress reached for it.

"Where have you been?" shouted the wife of the man with the droopy mustache. "Don't tell me you're too shy to eat? At other times you'd swallow the whole world. See, boy, if you weren't here, she would own the barn."

Their eyes locked for a while; it seemed that the pot was ready to fly out of the girl's hand and land on the woman's head, but instead she threw it in a huff in front of the children. I recognized her from her movements. She had smoothed down her hair and plaited it into two

---

[27] listen

braids with red ribbons; it was still a little wet. Her face was flushed, and the unconcealed anger drew dark circles around her eyes. Miss Mára brushed the ashes off a *pogacha,*[28] and handed it to the girl, who furiously snapped it in two on her knee and put it where the pot had been.

"Don't you want to eat?" the woman teased her again.

"Listen, talk to your wife, because I swear I'll do something to her!" The fellow with the droopy mustache just smiled and shrugged.

"Now, if you were a clever girl, you'd offer the boy meat, not just plain *bokoli*."[29]

She didn't reply, but leaned up against the post and stubbornly pursed her lips. Her face seemed somewhat longer to me than that of the usual average cat-headed gypsy girls. Below her sharply squared brow was a softly arched, narrow nose with nervously flaring nostrils. She was drawing circles with her toes on the brick floor, eyeing her heartily laughing mother with withering glances.

"Eat up, boy," said the woman, offering me half the pogacha. "This here girl kneaded it."

"Aye, bless her soul," said the father as he munched away. "If only it had salt!"

"Where from, if there wasn't any more? We needed some for the grits too," said Miss Mára, sticking up for the girl.

I watched the girl's face; at the sound of the word "salt" she smiled shyly. Other girls her age would have run away, but her stubbornness tied her to the post. *You're still a child*, I thought. *If you knew that this was the way they wanted to bring you down to earth from pretending to be older, your nostrils wouldn't be flaring, and you wouldn't scuff your toenails drawing invisible figures. There is no appeal against time; it makes no difference whether it waits or stops, you can't overtake it.*

---

[28] A savory, round puff pastry common in Hungary and the Balkans (Hungarian spelling: *pogácsa*), where it is made with varied seasonings and toppings such as dill and cheese. Traditionally baked in the ashes of a fire or fireplace, it is sometimes translated as "scone," but scones are leavened and generally sweet.

[29] Romani for pogacha

Her smile couldn't escape her clenched lips; it was silently writhing in the corner of her mouth under the grip of an adult reduced to a child. The conspicuous signs revealed by her tight-fitting pink bodice justified her awareness of being a "big girl." Maybe that's what the mother wanted to conceal. She still held the pogacha in her hand.

"Come on, taste it!" said the mother, holding one out. "Don't snub our daughter."

"He'd be mad to," interrupted the old man. "Only once Vorzha has tried it. Who knows what she's put into it instead of salt?"

Grandpa said it so seriously that she didn't even try to hesitate. Laughter broke out as Vorzha spat out the first mouthful in disgust.

"This is full of salt, Grandpa!" she said to her grandfather, whimpering. "I swear on your life and Papa's that it was your wife who told me to put in all we had."

"May your crazy Grandma's head rot right off! Don't you ever listen to her again. Old age has already robbed her of her mind."

"You're wrong, old man," Droopy Mustache's wife interjected. "If her grandma told her to jump in the well, I bet Vorzha wouldn't do it. She shouldn't keep her head only in the clouds but also on how much salt a pogacha should have in it."

"You just keep your mouth shut," said Droopy Mustache, putting his wife in her place. "Even the dog's gotten sick from stuff you've baked."

"Yeah, but I could cook meat so well that you licked your chops afterward."

"Yeah, when I brought some home. But it's not as if you've ever gone out of your way to bring home enough for a potful."

"I would've had to be a fool! If someone wants a woman, he should stand up for her."

"Then don't be surprised at your daughter. It's your teaching. Let her think about the clouds; it's high time. At her age you were already nursing Vorzha."

"Nursing . . . ?" she asked uncertainly. When the others nodded, she preened herself with forced laughter.

"Whether I was nursing or not, I was a woman."

"That's true," her husband retorted, "because you eloped with me when you were thirteen."

"She's so full of herself," said the woman, lashing out at her daughter, "because her papa always takes her side. May the rot eat his scooped-out flesh!"

Vorzha leaped behind Grandpa.

"May it rot the flesh off tinkers," she shouted back, referring to the itinerant menders that represented the young woman's ancestry. "Grandpa, tinkers are all mad, aren't they?"

Grandpa's face beamed with joy. He was pleased that his granddaughter set his kind before that of her mother.

"You're also laughing," the young woman turned mockingly toward her husband, "but it was fun making seven kids with the tinker's daughter, huh?"

"It was," said Droopy Mustache. Flashing his white teeth, he embraced his woman and gave her a conciliatory pat on the back.

"And what kind are you, son?"

I thought Grandpa would ask me, which is why he didn't reply to the girl. His sons were still laughing, and Vorzha was hugging her grandfather's neck. I could see her eyes clearly now; they were large and black.

"*Petroeshtyo, muro nano,*" I said, telling him I was of Tsino Petro's stock.

The boys fell silent. Droopy Mustache grabbed my shoulder and turned me in his direction.

"Did you say *Petroeshtyo*?"

"I did," I answered calmly.

"Well, a man coming from afar can say whatever he wants."

"You think I'm lying?"

"Not really, but you know . . ."

"*Azhuker.*[30] You've made a big claim." Grandpa looked at me and tilted his head. He hummed for a long time, puffing his pipe, and then shrugged his shoulders.

"Well, now, God knows."

Droopy Mustache wanted to say something, but Grandpa's raised pipe silenced him.

"Which side?"

"My father's."

"Who was your grandfather?"

"I didn't know him."

"You must have heard from your father."

"He didn't know him, either."

Tiny wrinkles appeared around the old man's parched lips; it seemed as if he wanted to bite his pipe stem in half. He scooped out a hole at the edge of the straw lair and spat into it. Seeing the family's wry smiles, he too broke into a grin.

"It's no good, I'm too old."

He pulled his neck apologetically into his shoulders. Vorzha got up from behind him and sadly went back to the post and began again to draw invisible figures with her toes. Uncomfortable minutes of silence followed. I would have gladly walked away. The boys looked pityingly at their father, whose great wisdom had failed him now in his old age. He had shared his meal with a man who was lying without reason. Yet in this world it is permitted to cheat, steal, and lie, and in most cases they praise you for it and regard you as smart. Well, then why not now?

I looked at Vorzha, seeking in her the shaggy-haired girl. I wanted to make it up to her for those unpleasant minutes, because the others saw me as a good-for-nothing boastful liar. She noticed me, looked around, and smiled at me bashfully. Her face mirrored so much beauty that I suddenly forgot my thoughts. Her mother looked in gloating

[30] wait

laughter at her husband, who only saw the girl's blushing face. Crunching his drooping mustache between his teeth, he looked at Grandpa, who, God knows why, was staring blankly ahead.

The coarse hairs crackled between his clenched teeth as he hissed right into my eyes:

"Hey, you, then you come from the dogs."

This counted as such an insult that it would have entitled me to cut his throat.

"That's right."

I jumped up angrily. I grabbed my bag by its neck. If he said anything offensive again, I resolved, I'd hit the back of his head with the remainder of the bustard so hard that he'd swallow his tongue. For a time, we looked at each other. I thought, *If you're so interested, you can find out for yourselves whether I'm telling the truth. I don't care what you take me for, kin or foe.* I repeated, "That's right, our people were also known as zhuklano manush.[31]

Grandpa looked at me as if he'd woken from a dream, and gestured toward his son with the pipe.

"*De Zhelko so phendom tuke?*"[32]

Droopy mustached Zhelko shrugged his shoulder.

"Alright, then, I'm sorry!"

The wrinkles became tighter around the old man's eyes; he looked at his son until Zhelko could no longer meet his gaze.

"You're saying sorry? You apologized to me, too, when you mixed up our blood." Pointing to his other sons, he said, "Look at them, boy! They too call themselves Petroeshtyos when they're together. But every last one is a coward on his own; all they know is how to *engedelmo mangel!*"[33]

With downcast eyes the boys endured their father's scolding.

---

[31] dogmen

[32] Well, Zhelko, what did I tell you?

[33] beg forgiveness

All around us in the barn the hullabaloo was still in full swing. People sang and cavorted, and girls' flirtatious giggles were followed by male guffaws. The night's strange stupor floated in the air, giving the impression of uninhibited merriment.

And yet the moonlight of eternal spring evenings stumbled on the mirror of their blood: hiding behind their own shadows, they were already paying duty on creation's forbidden honey.

"You can't stand a stranger if he's not to your liking, but you don't despise the skirt no matter *whose* daughter it covers," Grandpa scolded his sons. "Not a single one of you felt ashamed when you embraced that *Romungritsa!*"[34]

They didn't speak, but waited patiently until Grandpa relented and let them sit next to him.

I myself didn't have to do any explaining, for Grandpa had disentangled the threads. His words comprised the unwritten and yet unforgiving laws of a world born outside the universe, where the guilty judges his own sins to spend his self-imposed captivity in freedom.

He fumbled in his white stubble, moaning and rocking his upper body, as if seduced by visions in the intoxicating creaking of slowly moving carts. I accompanied him in his thoughts.

Along the roads of the endless plains that lead from the sky, I greeted with silent compassion my acquaintances, who in Grandpa's youth wielded their bludgeons with fearless courage. Life was still blazing inside them; time did not shackle their derring-do, but I stole their fates from Grandma's memories. I knew the mysteries of their ways, their grandchildren's names, and even the mounds that covered them in their youth or old age.

"But where are these now?" he asked. "Some of them were racing with the wind; others were devoured by their children. This will be my fate, too."

---

[34] Hungarian Romani woman

Yawning, he stuffed his pipe, mixing a dried green grass with the thick-cut tobacco. *Lindralo drab,*[35] I thought. I smelled it and felt slightly queasy; I feared, and at the same time hoped, that the old man would light up again. That is how they are able to dream back their youths.

"I raised eight kids," said Grandpa, "and all of them still call themselves Petroeshtyo. But they say so only until . . ."—he looked askance at his sons—"until they catch sight of a skirt! My poor father, God rest his soul, used to say that a man in whose own blood that of a hundred other men is flowing doesn't belong anywhere. The plains are too empty for him, the forests too dense. May this be the last pipe I smoke if I'm not telling the truth."

Pointing at the young Gypsy men burrowed into the straw, Grandpa observed, "You won't find a single wise man among them. No, they're just looking for holes to crawl in, like rats. They eat if they have food, and keep their mouths shut if there is none. That Romungritsa on account of whom you hit that Gypsy over the head was right. Why should she live out her life in a bread hut?"

"She's a bad-blooded woman, Grandpa."

"Bad-blooded? Which of them isn't if she has a bad man? Only that one does it openly and the other, in secret. Besides, it's said you can always exchange a good one for a bad one."

"It's a different world now, Grandpa, than in your youth."

"It's not the tent that's new, son, only the stakes. That doesn't stop the wind blowing in. In my time, every bush still gave us shelter, but in this different world we soon won't have enough room to lay our heads down."

He blew large wisps of smoke from his ancient meerschaum pipe. The smell of the lindralo drab made me feel like I was being gently rocked and slowed down the images in my mind, as if each of them were a separate world enclosed in its own frame that I could choose from. It is a strange grass that turns even the wildest horse into a meek animal.

---

[35] sleep medicine

Grandpa's sons stared blankly ahead; the old man's words made it easier to build up the multicolored misty world of their imagination. They conjured up the tiniest details of their childhood; only their bodies moved forward in time, their souls remained in the past.

They went to sleep in a torpor. Vorzha was still standing next to the post, having listened persistently to our conversation.

"Have you got a place yet?" Grandpa asked.

"He has," Zhelko's wife answered for me. "We won't trust him to you. You'd talk all night if you had him there to listen."

She tore a multicolored skirt in half: "There you go, girl, spread it under him!"

I could view the sleeping people from the top of the tightly packed straw lair of the manger. The scene was like that of a children's playground in which badly dressed rag dolls are lying in disarray. The fresh smell of dawn snuck in through the broken windows of the barn, mixing the pungent odor of manure with the sweaty-steamy air. The skirt spread under my head awakened manly thoughts in me, and I watched the usually dreary and monotonous images with interest.

Vorzha lay in front of the manger. The brown-skinned breasts peeking out of her ribbon-strapped shirt banished every normal thought from my mind. I sensed that she wasn't asleep, either. She took deep breaths amid the tangled mass of children, and in the ensuing persistent silence embraced the little ones. A bald toddler, scratching himself, slipped out from among the others to go piss all over the post, then stood around for a while sniffling until Vorzha pulled him back by his shirt.

On the other side, Muto's asthmatic lungs whistled away while his snub-nosed wife, mouth agape, grunted to the mournful music. Her dress had ridden up to her armpits, uncovering her corpulence, and patches of various shapes bloomed on her faded thick panties, covering Muto's hand as it rested motionless somewhere on the woman's pubic mound.

Now and then the chugging of the old gas pump that drove the aggregator machine missed a beat, and when that happened the naked thighs appeared elongated, the pubic hairs blurred into black smudges, the breathing became harder, and they pulled the blanket off one another with long, drawn out groans.

Here and there the swamp-odored gas of half-baked rye bread escaped from someone's behind with a bang, causing the others to shift around and curse. The world around me was full of naked asses and uninterrupted scratching. The rustle of woolly hairs mingled with the brisk galloping of rats across the barn, searching for food. If a louder cry interrupted the monotonous music of a dream, the cloud of flies that had settled on the crossbeams went at one another with angry buzzing.

I envied these people. Topsy-turvy they swarmed in undifferentiated sameness; it was impossible to tell which was male, which female.

Vorzha's scent spilled over the edge of the manger; I was burning in the heat of my own blood. I cursed the light and whoever had built the manger so high. If it were only half a span lower, my hand could have reached her naked shoulders. My thoughts pushed the sap throbbing in my body into my arteries, forcing my senses to revolt; and, despite my crunching ribs and the scarred, stinging wooden edge of the manger, I managed to hang on until my fingertips touched her hair.

"You're not asleep?" she whispered, looking up at me, her eyes bulging from feigned sleep. All that remained of my bravery was a "No" that rang of tonsillitis. Scared, I threw my numb arm to my side, turned on my back on the tantalizing gaudy skirt, and looked at the planked, densely cobwebbed ceiling. Perhaps the only desire remaining in me was that that ceiling should fall on me together with the sky. I heard the straw rustling under her. Everything became timelessly blurred; I could have sensed the approach of her hot body only later or that very instant. She leaned over the edge of the manger, her black hair covering my face small, and in my dark oblivion fiery circles began to cling to one another.

"I'm coming to you," she whispered.

"Come," was my brief declaration of love. The restrained fire flared up in me, and I lifted her next to me, my fingers searching under her skirt.

We stuck together with bated breath; her teeth, together with my coarse linen shirt, dug deeply into my flesh. Passionate thoughts that had been stirring for hours now fused us together, and we trembled all over like frogs hit in the midriff, until we torpidly regained consciousness in the sweat-soaked vapor of our bodies.

There were intervals of silence: I lifted her bosoms out of the ribbon-strapped shirt, and her tiny waves became faster with a delicate vibration, as I touched them with my soft mustache. We did not have the strength to protest; our will was expropriated by our senses. The insatiable thirst caused by the layer of salt around the thickened bumps of our chapped lips led us to repeated acts until we chased the night away.

The day threatened us with pale purple colors from the barn's iron-framed windows, as if it too was annoyed by the rapid dawn. The flickering lights became dim and, mixed with the morning light, painted Vorzha's face a gray, earthy color, drawing deep shadows around her eyes to break the dignity of those moments with disrespectful, drowsy blinks.

We'd both fit into the manger only by my lying partially on Vorzha's belly. Dawn arrived soon indeed. I could barely keep a big enough gap between my eyelashes to take in the early risers' surprised looks. They looked at us as if we were ghosts that, in the delight of earthly happiness, failed to hear the first crowing of the rooster. Here, nothing was regarded as sinful, but it was the night's demand that the dawn should not wallow in its secrets. Vorzha ought to have gone back to the children before we became the living advertisement of our rapturous moments. But did we have the resolve? *May the dogs take that part of me,* I thought, struggling with my desires, *that wants to keep holding her tight.*

Now and then I dozed off for a minute, but each time I had the eerie feeling that Zhelko's gaze was fixed upon me.

What would Zhelko have said if he caught sight of us pressed to each other in the narrow manger? He certainly wouldn't have felt sorry for us. It was futile to think about; my day was ruined in any case. I knew I might as well face up to him and say, "Get up Zhelko; I've married your daughter! Come on, let's have a drink!"

Unwittingly I thought of the money. It had become tightly wedged between us. The packet of coins, wrapped into a ball, could have elicited a new sensation from the girl; she kept fidgeting until it reached her softer parts, and she then pressed herself with full dedication into the base of my thigh.

The big moments, promising virtually eternal happiness, blunted me to such an extent that I only just started to take notice of everything. I didn't want to think about anything as long as the silence of the barn was not disturbed. Although from the first moment, anxiety had already been squirming in my subconscious, like a thief, I told myself: whatever will be, will be. But as the astonished gazes increased, so did the fear burgeon inside me.

Zhelko would kill me when he awoke. On the other side, Muto nearly choked on his makeshift cigarette, yet he wouldn't take his eyes off us. He looked blankly, coughed, cleared his throat, and motioned to indicate that Droopy Mustache would cut my throat. *May your stinking flesh rot from your bones*, I thought, though he had done it out of concern. Still, I showed him Vorzha's butt.

I gently pried off my fourteen-year-old wife's embrace; the radiance of full satisfaction shone from her angular, smooth forehead. In spite of all the danger, I was happy that it wasn't some old bitch that had violated my virginity. So far I had resisted every temptation humanely; could it be that I had just stood this great glory on its head?

Oh, was there anyone in this wide world who could tell me what was down and what was up? I was surprised by my own sigh. I pulled the twisted multicolored skirt from under Vorzha's head and covered her bare shoulders. *Get some rest*, I thought, *and get a feel for whom you've taken as your husband. They haven't rung the wake-up bell yet.*

For a long time I stroked the creases imprinted on the front of my pants; I tried to do honor to my father-in-law by looking presentable. I was both happy and annoyed that he wasn't awake yet, although most people were already on their feet. It would be best to get this over with as soon as possible. All my confidence was in the eight pengős tied into Bada's piece of shirt.

V

G*et up, Zhelko, I've married your daughter! Come on, let's have a drink!* I whispered to myself. I had to repeat it a few times before I found just the right haughty, imperious, gendarme-like tone—a tone I didn't want to forget.

If a man is jolted from sleep, it always has its effect. After a pint of plum brandy I'd have the advantage.

I had a great surprise when I didn't find Zhelko next to his wife. My mother-in-law, lying there in the fetal position, seemed to be smelling her own belly, her head barely visible under the dirty canvas.

As for Grandpa, I wasn't surprised to see him out cold as well: the night before he'd blown the smoke of the lindralo drab into our heads, and he himself had surely inhaled enough of that green grass that he would hardly sleep off its tranquilizing effect until midday. The poor little old man. He was indeed so hushed, so still that it seemed that someone had cast a spell on him.

Persons so bewitched just sleep and sleep, dreaming whatever they desire; some live to a hundred, until they're so shriveled with age that they fit into a jug. While it was evident that Grandpa hadn't always been as wizened a figure, I didn't believe the stories about his strength and courage that he'd told us the night before. Strong, courageous people are, after all, impervious to spells.

But where the heck was Zhelko? Hadn't he noticed that I was sleeping his daughter?

Old Mára, just like poor Grandma used to, was crouching with several layers of garish, rosy skirts pulled over her head in the inimitable way of old Gypsy women.

"*Lashi detehara!*"[36] she greeted me in a low voice and motioned me to come closer, pulling a white bottle of medicine out of the straw.

"Drink up! It's real plum brandy." She smiled while offering it to me, sloshing the bottle. Her teeth, as if they had grown out overnight, were flashing with brilliant white uniformity behind her lips, wrinkled like a prune.

"They'll be back soon."

The women were stretched out without their men under filthy, mottled coverlets, some of them with their fist-sized or school-age successors dangling from their breasts.

"They stay up all night playing cards with the deputy bailiffs. Drink!"

She didn't have to force me; I took another big swig from the bottle and hurried back to Vorzha, who looked at my bulging cheeks with sleepy, blinking eyes. I leaned toward her and she folded her arms around my neck; our lips stuck together, I formed a channel with the tip of my tongue, and she drew the spirit into her mouth with slow gulps. As the drink started to run out, so her embrace became tighter; she could hardly get enough of it, although my mouth is pretty big. It was the early morning wake-up bell that finally separated us. Vorzha pulled my head back for a few smooches and, like a really self-confident young woman, sprang out of the manger.

The Gypsies' astonishment was soon over, and they accepted us as man and wife. Vorzha pulled on her pink blouse, brushed as much straw out of her hair with her fingertips as she could, and then we huddled down next to the kids, looking at each other lazily.

The metaphorical music of our youth drowned out the noise of the comings and goings around us, and we wandered in silent bliss over

[36] good morning

the free open plains of our thoughts, where nothing curbed our passions.

I tucked my feet under her skirt; flies were stinging furiously. Rain was in the air. It seemed the weather was arranging everything. The towering clouds animated the people, most of whom were crawling back into their warm nests, praising the Lord's generosity with a heartfelt "Thank God" invocation. Cracks of thunder shook the barn, lightning flashed, and in no time rain came down in buckets. Scared, I pulled my feet out from between Vorzha's thighs. Not that any human could have seen the impropriety occurring underneath her skirt, but the heavens could.

At times like these our people like to be quiet and, with a calm, pure spirit, to not think about a thing. The Creator knows everyone's sins, and it would be futile to harp on them by begging. He smites the sinners and lets the others live.

It is also an unforgivable sin if a woman is bareheaded when there is lightning. I've never understood why. The omniscient Creator knows who is a virgin and who isn't whether or not she covers her head. Vorzha didn't understand that, either.

Muto's wife now shouted from the other side of the barn, "Cover your head, little woman! Can't you hear the thunder and lightning?"

All around us, the great saints—who had done the same as we had last night—spoke up one after the other. But they too covered their heads.

Vorzha had to tear a big enough piece off the skirt that had served as a sheet during the night to use as a headscarf, because slowly the men, too, began to get grumpy.

We didn't notice when the Zhelkos arrived. True, we weren't particularly worried about what was happening around us, but were nestled together in the manger, dozing off and keeping each other warm.

My mother-in-law's screeching shook us awake. Zhelko, ignoring the woman's cursing, stared into space like a penitent saint. In some cases these silences don't last forever. Unless everything isn't already too late.

If you don't tie a knot on a woman's tongue from the start, it'll eventually grow far too long. Then there's really only one option left: for the man to keep quiet. If he can. I don't know how long the one-sided debate had been going on; what is certain is that it had begun with less noisy questioning.

From the time that we became aware of my mother-in-law's well-chosen curses, it didn't take long for Zhelko to lose his patience. He hit his wife on the back with the sooty pot the children had kicked aside last night.

"Well done," whispered Vorzha. "God bless him for it. Had my father won a lot of money playing cards last night, she wouldn't be sounding off like this."

My mother-in-law looked at things quite differently.

"So you've hit me, Zhelko?! May a beehive move into your ugly rotten guts, you mustache bug! You won't ever eat my cooking again. If you took the last penny out of my children's mouths, then go to the one who's won it."

"I'm telling you, you Gypsy woman, stop it, or else you'll see your own blood!"

"You want me to stop? Well, did the deputy bailiff and those other gentlemen you played cards with need the money more than your hungry kids do? May hunger and lice eat your neck up all your life."

Apparently my father-in-law had found it difficult only to get started; he now began to hit her until she slipped from his grip.

"Just you wait, Zhelko, just you wait!" she yelled back from behind the third post, stroking her ruffled hair. "You'll regret this a hundred times over. Can you see, people, what this beggar is doing to me?! He wouldn't have anything if I didn't cheat and steal for him."

Zhelko lay back in his lair and covered his head with his jacket, ignoring the woman's shouting. He was mistaken, though, in believing that she would sooner or later get sick and tired and stop. Far from it. She crept closer and closer to him, shouting her head off. She stopped to take a breath only when she noticed a tuft of his mustache peeping out from the jacket. As soon as he covered himself again, she continued her tirade.

"You think I won't go right away to the deputy bailiff? I want my money back or I'll have you all arrested. It was my money you stole, damn you!"

The sooty pot clattered along the length of the barn's paved floor as Zhelko flung it toward the woman—without scoring a hit. After that, things quietened down. My mother-in-law decamped, and Vorzha slipped out of our mutually warmed lair. I stayed on, since I didn't judge the circumstances at all auspicious for confessing our decision to the enraged father. Evening would be soon enough. And what if he heard it from someone else? That would favor our nuptials even less.

My worries returned when I realized that matters weren't as simple as I'd hoped. My mother-in-law had spoiled everything. A good half an hour had elapsed by the time Vorzha returned.

"Would you light a fire?" she asked with a young bride's smile. "Grandma gave me some flour for pogachas. The children are starving, and so are you. Grandpa knows we're living together."

"He knows?"

"Well, of course. Grandma told him."

"What did he say?"

"He couldn't care less. He said I did the right thing."

"Do you think Zhelko will say the same?"

"Papa," she pulled her neck between her shoulders sheepishly, "will beat the shit out me when he wakes up."

Um, I thought, *some consolation.*

"Wouldn't it be better if we ran off while Papa is asleep?" she asked with an anxious look.

"Run off? Should I abduct you now, when we are already living together? You think I won't dare tell your father?"

I wanted to leave. Anyway, I had already decided to get it over and done with as soon as possible.

"No, don't go just yet; wait until he wakes up. You see, my mother has spoiled everything, and I would only make things worse. If he hadn't lost the money, everything would have been alright. Now he'd say we've brought *prekaza*[37] on him. Come on, light a fire, the children are crying."

As soon as he saw me emerge from the manger, Grandpa came quietly over to us.

"You two didn't do it the way it should be done," he chided us. Looking at me, he added, "You have a tongue; no one would have bitten your head off if you'd told them your intention." I nodded contritely. "The Devil is inside this Gypsy now; you can't confront him."

I shrugged my shoulders. I'd never been in such a tight spot. More and more I regretted everything, and if Bada had suddenly shown up, I sure would have hightailed it out of there.

"But if you love each other," continued Grandpa, "then everything will be fine."

Vorzha was not taken with Grandpa's consoling words.

"You know what he's like about money," she told him. "He'd kill even you for it."

"Money, money. He'll get it if any is to be. Don't you worry about it, just cook something for the kids."

"There is food here, Grandpa," I interrupted. "Yesterday we only pulled the legs and wings off the bustard." I emptied the bag onto the straw.

"Oh my God, what is this?" Vorzha watched in amazement.

"What else, silly? Roast turkey. At least that's what it was yesterday." Now it was a pretty disgusting sight. It was thickly coated with the Gargya brood's decade-old flour and bran residues. The carefully kneaded Hungarian white bread had collapsed when Vorzha and I had settled on top of it. My mother-in-law had put it under the straw when preparing my bed the night before.

---

[37] misfortune, bad luck

The bustard didn't look too tempting, but the bread threw all the children of the family into a frenzy. We had made friends with the little bald kid already, and now, at the sight of the bread, he almost ripped my pants off to get at it.

"*Bokhalo som!*"[38] He tugged at me and at Vorzha. He didn't understand a single word of Hungarian yet. The other kids were fighting over an onion that had rolled away. Vorzha straightened them out with a few well-aimed whacks.

"Anyone who's hungry should sit in a line on the edge of the manger," I commanded. "But I don't want to hear a peep out of you!" I didn't have to repeat my order. They sat down without a word, and only their sniffles and the rustle of the encrusted sleeves of their coats or shirts were audible as they drew them along under their noses.

"That's it, kids," I said, "just keep sitting quietly. Anyone who moves from his place might as well go away, because he won't get a thing."

You could see from their faces how they struggled to stay put at the sight of the bread being sliced. They had to use all their willpower, clinging to one another by their rags, lest one of them throw himself recklessly at the pile of sliced bread and the chunks of smoked bacon.

The little bald one was already munching away, while some of the others kept swallowing or salivating. One of them started sliding off the manger's wooden edge, desperately clinging to his neighbors' clothes until they managed to haul him back up amid whispered rebukes. I cut pretty thick slices; each portion was close to a pound. I started with the smaller ones.

"There you go!" I served the kids one at a time. "Enjoy!" Saying that was perhaps superfluous: the bacon was gone in no time, as they barely even chewed it before swallowing. Grandpa kept looking in turn at me and the children, nodding his head.

"Their father should see them now!" he remarked. "If it weren't for the old woman they'd all starve to death. His wife is all talk and no

---

[38] I'm hungry

action; her mouth would get all moldy from her humaneness. All she's good at is lying next to her man until noon. If ever she flavors her children's mouths with a slice of bread, she thinks she owns the whole world. She's eaten Zhelko's head. Still, God punishes in his own way. He could have had as many *harniko*[39] women from his own kind as he wanted. Instead of which he tied his life to this *prekaza*. He came off badly. And they are the ones who are paying for it"—Grandpa pointed to the children—"because she shits them out one after the other."

Grandpa was clearly not delighted by his daughter-in-law. Perhaps because she wasn't their kind? Mind you, after what she'd done to her husband, she didn't win my approval, either. I didn't want to inquire more from Grandpa; I had already learned a fair bit. Anyway, I'd certainly become involved with an unusual family.

"She couldn't cook a decent meal in all her life, yet she wouldn't put her foot on the ground if she could avoid it, because she is so *phukyardi* [40]."

In fact, it seemed Vorzha might well have inherited quite a few traits from her mother. The pocketknife sat in her hand like a feather duster in a dog's mouth. She scraped off the dirt from one part of the bustard and promptly smeared it into another. Grandpa noticed it too.

"Take it outside, dear; the warm water of the well will clean it off."

Vorzha looked at us bewildered; washing meat here was not customary, because supposedly it lost a lot of its flavor that way. It was up to me whether I'd eat it clean and tasteless or dirty and unappetizing. Vorzha's acquiescent shrug indicated only that she wanted to please me when she wrapped it into the same piece of cloth she had worn on her head; she probably wouldn't have performed this sacrilege solely for Grandpa.

The smallest kids were still nibbling the bread, each keeping it pressed under a rag lest another snatch it away. They held their ground; the sour smell of the remaining bread tickled their noses, and while we

[39] capable, industrious

[40] arrogant, haughty

talked, the onions, too, disappeared one after another. I kept looking at what was left of the bread, but it was impossible to distribute it among all the kids. There were three times as many by then; all the children from the barn were crowding around us, as were some of the adults, expressing their astonishment at the beautiful white bread.

"Get away from here!" Grandpa chewed them out. "Even the county welfare office wouldn't be able to feed you all!"

Some of the kids understood him, some didn't, but even those who spoke Hungarian were scandalized by this little old man threatening them with his pipe. Then, as if he didn't exist, their eyes again fixated on the bread.

In their minds, perhaps they were already tearing it into crumbs, and only me, whom they didn't know well enough to test, restrained them from falling into temptation.

Grandpa angrily threw the bread into the bag.

"As long as they can see it," he said, "you can talk to them all you want, but it will be like talking to dogs." I counted. Twenty snotty kids in rags were standing in front of me.

A little while ago they had still longed for life that was hardly an arm's length away from them. Everything had now broken inside them in one fell swoop, and their entire beings had become characterized by sheer disappointment and reproach. I wondered whether this silent contempt—which could just as well be called hatred—was directed at me or the pipe-wielding old man. It was also possible that they didn't even hear the old man's voice, but instinctively tore at the hateful bag that hid the world from them.

Twenty pounds of bread costs two pengős and twenty fillérs. So I'd have to borrow no more than twenty fillérs of Bada's money.

"Kids," I called out, "which of you is the cleverest?"

"Me!" they shouted in unison. They couldn't yet guess what this was all about, but within seconds they became cheerful and boisterous. Their instincts, like lightning, let them know that there was something in the offing and that it couldn't be anything but bread. Especially since

I'd asked them about their skill. They all felt clever, while the poor things were on the verge of dying of starvation. They quieted down at my signal.

"I need only one clever kid."

"Me! Me!" each of them cried, jostling one another again.

"Enough! Choose one yourselves, or you can all go together to see how much bread there is in the store."

"A lot," said one of them with a sad expression. The others, too, now lost their enthusiasm; everything turned topsy-turvy inside them.

"You sure?" I asked the glum-faced child.

"I went to get some *duhano*[41] for my mom, I saw the bread there, too." He wiped his nose across the back of his hand.

"Follow me!" I said. "Come on, Grandpa, you too!"

I met up with Vorzha at the barn door; the washed bustard's fatty-watery fluid was trickling down her skirt as she held it together over her groin. She'd covered her head again as befits a young wife, and—with such a Gypsy woman's usual smile promising eternal happiness—asked me:

"Where are you going?"

"I'll be back soon."

"Don't be long!" Had I said that I was running away, she might have replied the same way. I left with the children without a rejoinder. Vorzha's voice resounded in me for quite awhile. It sounded familiar, but definitely not like her. Where had I heard that unpleasant voice before?

We met my mother-in-law in front of the estate's small grocery stand; she didn't even notice me amid the buzzing group of children. She grinned at Grandpa all the more sarcastically, proudly holding a pair of tattered high boots and a bundle tied up in her kerchief.

Grandpa looked at my mother-in-law with raised eyebrows as if to ask what was going on.

[41] tobacco

"I've been to the deputy bailiff—or should I have left the money with him? I sure didn't. I took this suit from him." She exuded pride as if she had performed, God knows what, a huge miracle.

"And now I'm waiting for someone to come along to *drabarav*[42] so they give me a pint I can use to wash away my anger with that Gypsy."

Grandapa just looked at me as if to say, "See, this is your mother-in-law."

"Come on," I said to her, "I'll pay for it; you don't have to read anyone's palms."

"Look at that!" she exclaimed. "I didn't even recognize you among all the kids." Having said the word "pint," she tried to clarify matters. She already had quite a few under her belt; the children cast astonished stares at the screeching woman.

"What do you want? There are clothes in it!" She swore at them as they were fiddling with the bundle she held on her arm. "All you'd do is eat all day, but your father has gambled away the money; may the iron eat away his neck!"

I tried to satisfy the children's hunger as soon as possible, and as they received their portions of a pound of bread, they disappeared one by one.

The grocer seemed delighted to get rid of the days' old dry bread, which was the color of coffee. True, he said he wanted the money in advance rather than putting it on a tab to be paid up another time. But he'd already noticed my handful of silver coins as I ordered drinks from him, so he no longer had any doubts in making this request.

Muddled, inarticulate sentences oozed out of my mother-in-law's liquor-smelling mouth. Each time I ordered more plum brandy, she would show me the worn, white linen suit that she had wheedled out of the deputy bailiff.

"It is meant for a slim man just like you. If Zhelko would be a different kind of man, even his foot cloth could be made of silk, but the cards are eating up his life. God always smites good women with such

[42] tell a fortune for

bums. I'd show a real man what a harniko woman is like!" She capped off her words with an angry swig from the bottle. The strong liquor took her breath away, and she could only point at my feet with her finger until she finally managed to groan hoarsely, "Try on these boots! Even if they did fit Zhelko, I wouldn't give them to him. And I wouldn't barter them away for just anything," she continued in a whining voice, "and anyway, who here could afford them?"

"You're right," Grandpa agreed with her, while looking at me with a mischievous wink. He had noticed that my mother-in-law was determined to woo me. "Try them on, son; they look like your size."

Grandpa's assertion encouraged the woman, who embraced me and forced me to sit on a wooden crate. I couldn't protest; I had to put on the boots. I had barely slipped one foot in, and my mother-in-law was already gushing with delight. When I pulled on the other one, she seized me by my neck and kept kissing me on my mouth until I gasped.

"Oh, you look good enough to eat! Those boots look so good on your feet." Turning to Grandpa with a reproachful glance, she added, "This man is not your son."

"Be done with giving him those boots already. He is your son-in-law, after all."

My mother-in-law froze for a moment, and I could almost see the liquor fumes oozing out of her head. The blush of a woman lusting for a young man faded away; two pairs of eyes stared at each other, the one with hatred, the other wallowing in *schadenfreude*.

"Don't you know your own son-in-law, Balush?" asked the old shopkeeper, bleating like a sheep. That was the first time I'd heard my mother-in-law's name.

"How come he's my son-in-law, huh?" She looked at the grocer with narrowed eyes, who averted her questioning glance with a shrug as if to say, "I'm washing my hands of this."

Humming and hawing, Grandpa stuffed his pipe as Balush's questioning gaze turned toward him.

He lit a sizzling, poisonous red match and moved it closer to my mother-in-law's face to get a better look at her eyes. "Because your daughter married him last night."

"Vorzha?"

"Who else?"

The flame of the match, like the candles on so many black nights in our huts, glimmered with a quivering light in my mother-in-law's eyes until its tiny flame glowed into a fireball.

"Then you're my son-in-law?" she stated with crazed laughter. "Why then, procreate, like Jerusalem artichokes!" That was how she gave me her maternal blessings, with some noisy backslaps thrown in for good measure.

I sat, rigid as a statue, on the coffinlike wooden crate, and—like the eternal reproach—I kept asking myself: "Lord, is this why you shed your blood?"

She slapped a pengő on the counter with a big bang.

"Give us a drink, mister!" Hands on hips, she began bouncing about.

"Now that I have such a gallant son-in-law, I'm not just anybody."

Grandpa winked at me.

"Did the deputy bailiff return the money?" he asked.

"You're not kidding he did. Twice as much!"

"Ahem. . . ." The old man nodded.

By now the grocer no longer served us shots, but put the bottle in front of us. I didn't drink. What my mother-in-law chugged down was enough to make a man drunk. So far she'd only sought the opportunity, but now she felt that she had good reason to be all over me. I had the feeling that the fiery bottle was slithering from my ear to my mouth, dilating my swollen lips, sometimes pressing itself angrily between my teeth and sometimes slightly sucking them in.

"I'll make a man out of you—just take my advice!" She gave me another kiss.

Just you wait, I thought, *you won't get me sick with drink.*

"Give me a cigar, mister!" I called out.

"Give my son-in-law one on my account," she said, "one of those really good ones!"

I could hardly wait to get my cigar between my teeth. *Come closer,* I thought. Finally it was wedged in my mouth like a fire-tipped stake; it stung, and I felt like spitting, but I didn't mind; I preferred to swallow my own tobacco than that plum brandy of hers. I looked at my mother-in-law proudly, like a horseman at a pedestrian. She pummeled my back and chest whenever she wanted to draw my attention to something more emphatically.

I didn't care, and just kept the end of my cigar glowing. Each time she tried to come closer, I directed it right at her nose. I really enjoyed the gnashing of her teeth, until she realized what was going on.

"Give it to me, sweetheart. Let me smoke it, too; it smells so good."

"Mister, give one to my mother-in-law. I'll pay for one of those really good ones." So I bid the grocer with one eye closed, clenching the cigar between my teeth, as if I were God-knows-who.

"Who the hell wants that?!" With that, she threw the bundle at me. "Put on this suit!"

For a moment I was surprised by this about-face, and—half-amused, half-feigning indignation—I gestured to her: *Here?*

"Yes, here! You don't mind, mister?" The grocer was glad if someone brought money to his shop; it didn't even enter his mind to protest.

"Put it on!" he said. "May the good Lord strike me dead if you don't put it on!"

Not even the cigar was of any help now. I tried to keep my cool at all costs so as to behave within the boundaries befitting a newlywed husband on his impromptu wedding ceremony. God was my witness; this wasn't up to me.

No, my so-called wedding present elicited no embarrassment or humiliation in me; after all, it was in a far better condition than what I was wearing. Frankly, I quite liked it. But the way my mother-in-law wanted to put it on me! That was indeed too much. I shook her off and left her in Grandpa's company.

My nerves were ruffled by the time I got back to the barn. This was only increased by Vorzha's withering glances, not to mention that her reproof really got on my nerves.

"Where have you been?" she drawled. "Papa has been up for a while."

"So what? Do I have to marry him and Grandpa and the whole family too?"

"You don't have to marry my father," she sputtered in a shrill voice like her mother's, "but it's customary to make an agreement with him." I didn't answer, but motioned to her to follow me. We stopped at the end of the barn, where everyone relieved themselves. She had a smile on her face. I gave her two slaps on the face.

"So, what do I have to do with your father?" I demanded.

"I don't know, my pet," she said, snuggling up to me to avoid any more slaps, her arms around my neck. "You've got to know that; you're the man."

"Am I the one who has to know?" I said, feigning the uncomprehending simpleton. "A few seconds ago you knew perfectly well and asked me so nicely to make an agreement with your father."

"To hell with any agreement, my pet. He'll let you know if he has any problems. I'll never again tell you off; I love you!"

During the whole courtship, marriage, and family fracas, this was the first time the word "love" had been mentioned.

While I was away, Vorzha had carefully smoothed down her mop of hair; only a few unruly curls frizzled around her forehead. Sensing that my fury had faded, she nestled up to me. Surprise and love melted into a languid smile in her eyes. She couldn't get enough of kissing my palm, while red spots lit up her face.

"Your hands are as soft as if they were made of silk."

"If you watch your tongue you'll have a long life," I said, trying to comfort her, "but if you don't, I'll skin you alive."

"You can do with me what you want; you're my master."

"Me, me. I am your lord and master, who, if need be, can torment the straw you sleep in along with you into the morning, beat you to death, skin you alive. Just don't ask me for any bread, because I am not the master of even the smallest piece of bread."

"Listen, I don't even like bread. I don't care for it however hungry I am. I'll bake you some pogachas. And don't worry, I won't oversalt them this time."

"Oh, Lord," I prayed aloud, "hast thou truly created us, or have our seeds been strewn into your garden as a revenge to belittle your glory? Whoever took pleasure in this? And how long does the great trial last until you give your judgment? Or are we the verdict? And see what you have done? Is this how you punish the evildoers?"

"You pray so beautifully. I've already seen the little god; Papa keeps it in his wallet. I'll steal it from him; you need it more."

"Okay," I concurred, "maybe it will tell the truth."

"Do not sin, my pet! What I love about you is that you don't say so when you're mad; one of your eyes gets smaller, that's all, and you don't care if the other hits the sky. The kids told me you're rich, that you bought bread for them. You're sorry for them, aren't you? I'm sorry, too; my heart breaks when they cry from hunger."

"But your father still gambles the money away, and your mother spends it on drink."

"My mother?" She looked at me, surprised, and continued with a wry smile: "She sure does."

"I wonder how Grandpa has put up with her in the family."

"Papa is dying for her, even though she's gotten married a hundred times to others. He goes beating her, but it's all the same to her. She doesn't love him."

"Why does your father live with her, then?"

"There was a time when he chased her off and married another woman. He badmouthed her, had her beaten by the gendarmes within an inch of her life, and had her sent to jail. Men want her only while she sleeps with them; no one except Papa can put up with her temper. Though she claims that Papa has cut out her sex."

"He must have made a mistake when he did it." She looked at me uncomprehendingly, and I added: "He didn't cut it out well."

"That's possible. Would you do it, too, if you had such a wife?"

"What for? The bad remain bad even if you take their blood. Throw her out and let her have a swing at being on her own. She'll learn her lesson when she feels she doesn't belong to anyone."

"Hmm," she said with a smile. "Grandpa likes you because you belong to the kind who always knows what to do."

"I do. That's why our kind have only themselves to blame that soon there won't be anyone to tell the tale to. Among the many Gypsies they were the ones who always regarded themselves as the *chache Roma.*[43] That's what your Grandpa bemoans. He doesn't think about the fact that there is a limit even to the real man. If he oversteps that, you can't tell whether he is proud or a fool."

"Our children won't be such chache Roma, will they?"

I couldn't comfort her, but I didn't want to upset her. I shrugged my shoulders, as if to say: it's the secret of time. She felt happy anyway. She kept embracing and squeezing me until Zhelko's children surrounded us.

"Come on, Vorzha, cook for us!" they pleaded in unison.

"So what's my mother up to?"

"She's singing."

"Singing?" Vorzha asked mockingly. "Let her puke her lungs out on the road!"

"Go on," I urged her. Only the night before I had questioned Vorzha's behavior. No longer was I surprised at it. Enough had happened to convince me that it was just as natural as loving a good parent.

It was Balush's behavior that had stirred up yesterday's emotions as well. No matter how hard I tried to regard her as a completely strange woman whose only connection to me was that I had slept with

[43] true Roma

her daughter, I wasn't able to. Because of her brazen behavior and the shameless pawing by which she'd tried to undress me, I decided to refrain from calling her "mother" or "mother-in-law," however short or long my marriage would last. A woman who wouldn't hesitate to sleep with her son-in-law can only be called by her name, which was Balush.

Poor Grandpa was also embarrassed whenever Balush paid the grocer. She always seemed to forget in which skirt pocket she'd put the money. She lifted up all her pleats as far as her belly and then folded them back one by one. And it was downright shocking the way she blinked indifferently as Grandpa and I blushed to the roots of our hair.

Anyhow, I'm not surprised that Grandpa hated her. In a family with so many healthy young men plus a hot-blooded female, the usual family order is easily upset. *Zhelko,* I thought, *what good did it do you if you really cut out her sex?*

The morning rain had cooled the air. Grandpa was making a fire, the children were hauling wood, and Vorzha was kneeling next to a tablecloth kneading dough.

"Sit down!" the old man said, gesturing for me to do so. "You look sad."

I shook my head like someone unaware of it. In fact, the setting in which I'd wound up without any intentions good or bad did make me sad.

"You must be hungry, my pet," said Vorzha.

"No, not at all," I said to allay her concern. While I was searching at the back of the barn for an answer to the absurdities of my situation, I had forgotten about my needs.

"I can see it on your face," Vorzha whined. "You're as pale as death."

She acted as if many years of experience had convinced her that the change in my complexion could only be due to whether or not my stomach was full or empty. At the moment, though, her motherly care felt good. My totally strange environment was becoming oppressive.

Not only did Vorzha's parents make me nervous, but it seemed that wherever I looked, I saw a different image.

Then I realized that what seemed new to me were merely old images turned upside-down and inside-out. Willy-nilly I too was in the picture, in which voices turned into colors, colors into speech and sentences. The incoherent whisper of the bright, gaudy colors drowned out the pale gray, clearly comprehensible crying and wailing.

The fire burned and crackled as Grandpa, his long-stem pipe resting on his knees, fed it with dry twigs; while Vorzha, flushed, wrestled with the cart-wheel-size dough. As if small fires were burning in the children's smoke-stung eyes, the light refracted on their film of tears with a thousandfold radiance, behind which were the gray, smutty, ash-caked pogachas.

I was haunted by the merciless revenge of pretense. Had I already contemplated all that was ensnaring in this pretense and already tasted the root of the ripe fruit, I should not have been disgusted. Or I might have been content to leave everything as it was and let it proliferate in the manure. Others were doing so, too.

My own roots had grown from here, from this ever-cheerful world. I was well aware I'd always breathed its suffocating, mendacious air, but as I'd been born into it, I could imagine only that this was as it should be. My thoughts ran thus: *Why should we bemoan? Why would we expose our festering sores, our truncated brains to the world when, after all, every human being suffers from the same condition in some degree? Some deny it, others don't.*

What good would it do if I flaunted the unmendable rags of my bleak destiny before my own eyes? How much sweeter would life be today if I knew I'd die tomorrow? There would then be nothing enviable about my fate. Without that, there is no good. Liars are so often envied, at least those who seem happy-those who dress up their misery in gaudy colors so its hideous images should not frighten others.

What if we did lay it bare one day? Why, those garish skirts would shed blue-red leaves like trees in autumn; yellow roses the size of a child's heads would gobble one another up amid green flames; barefoot club feet with scabies-caused black scars would stomp the earth, and the rusty spoons—which have never touched food—would stop in the hands of the mustache bugs beating tam-tam gongs as they sit around the fire.

What colors would be needed to paint the gurgling made by Grandpa's cherry-wood pipe as the tobacco juice reaches his brain through its narrow channel; or the fear from which he flees into the world of dreams? What colors, to paint his disgust and revulsion with the world, not that he is aware of it, though he does sense that his life is narrowing and sees its morsels getting ever smaller? What colors, as he keeps quiet when screaming would be in order, and when he fears for his seed, which is already lost in any case?

What if we *would* take the glass out of Balush's hand, the glass she feared only before tasting it, until she realized that life is awfully short and that drinking all its dross and filth is pointless, anyway?

In a world of hypocrisy and gaudy colors that's all there is: you either drink, or you die of thirst before you've even lived—not giving a damn about salvation and eternal bliss no one has yet proved. But even if such fate is in the cards, what good is salvation if your soul has already been torn to shreds by misery? And what to give in return? Yourself? How many "yourselves" has life created? Or what has it added so you needn't give too much of yourself in exchange for the slightest bit of good? If life has been so stingy in doling out the good, why then it should be content with what's left.

I didn't want to admit that Balush was right, because there were other ways of dealing with it all, too, but somehow I now looked upon her actions differently. Who was to say who was right or even what was right? To be sure, I didn't get any more clever however hard I sought answers to my questions.

The disheveled Gypsy guys gathered around the fire were chuckling away merrily indeed, as if their lot was the finest in the world. Most hadn't taken their eyes off the baking pogachas. They must have been hungry, to be sure, but did that get in the way of their happiness? Not at all. Had there been a Gypsy woman beside them who didn't mind being pawed, they would have renounced even the heavenly vision of the food before their eyes.

Grandpa stoked the fire. We watched his movements as he doffed his hat and solemnly held it to his heart, while trying with his left hand to push his pipe away as far as he could.

"Dear God!" he exclaimed. For a long time he then kept muttering unintelligible words, before he spoke again.

"Look!" Startled, he stared into the setting sun.

The afternoon wind had scattered the clouds, and here and there small wisps floated in the sky; one of them had an ear, another a tail, but most had neither. We followed Grandpa's eyes. The vision froze us.

Sitting around the fire, we trembled together with the flames, and some folks fell to their knees and hiccupped until the old man began his incoherent Gypsy prayer. A dark blue cloud in the shape of a cross had settled on the sun's copper disc, framed around its thinner edges by a light purple glow. Then, almost unnoticeably, its uppermost vertical arms puffed outward, as if boiling, into the shape of an egg, while its two horizontal arms bent down-transforming the cross into a giant bird with outstretched wings that covered the sun. Then, like a continent painted on to a globe, it lost its shape.

"There will be war, you'll see . . . a very big war." Grandpa pensively stroked the ashes with his wooden poker. "The eagle that has covered the sun will consume human flesh. There will be so many dead that the living won't have enough time to bury them." He voiced his thoughts mainly to himself, and at the same time he tried clumsily to draw the shape of the bird with the outstretched wings into the flattened ashes. Lots of folks didn't know a thing about wars, but Grandpa's very words were enough to fill everyone with fear and dread.

If I hadn't seen with my own eyes all that had evoked these feelings, I might have doubted Grandpa's wise credibility. Not that there was any need for a sign from heaven to conclude that war was coming. The overwhelming majority of the men had been drafted; those remained at home, like Grandpa's sons, had chopped off their index fingers before conscription or burned their lacerated bunions with caustic soda.

"There are many sinners," Grandpa pronounced, looking at me sadly. I was convinced that he, like me, was thinking of Balush, whose shrill voice could be heard from the stables as she offered herself with filthy words to Zhelko, telling him where he could kiss her ass.

"So shouldn't there be a war?" I asked rhetorically with a nod.

We kept silent, watching the horizon and squirming with relief as the ominous red disc disappeared from our sight. It was hard for the earlier good mood to return, but we didn't have to wait for long. The people questioned Grandpa about the old war, and he smilingly showed his palm as his crippled finger fit into it.

"I would have been mad to go. You can't imagine how many men never came back. Back here we went hungry a lot, but it was still safer at home than where the shooting was going on. As for the hunger, well, darn it, when aren't Gypsies starving? Never does everyone get their fill. The clever ones will always land on their feet, anyway. As for the fools, let them perish; there are always plenty of them, after all."

Alright, I thought, *but if God inflicts wars as a plague, why then does He let people outwit Him? Or are only the fools guilty?* I was about to begin openly doubting the truth again, but then I didn't dare to. By now Grandpa too had turned his reminiscing to his youthful memories. His jovial tales made everyone forget the somber mood after the sign from heaven and, as usual, everyone found a way of entertaining themselves. As far as my mood was concerned, it was considerably dampened by the battle of words emanating from the stables, a battle in which Vorzha was also participating.

Balush had probably sobered up by now, but—holding on to her earlier rage—she was still calling the shots. From the wisps of conversation drifting toward me, I concluded that the two women were standing up for me. I wasn't certain, but I presumed that they were facing off against Zhelko.

Swaying her hips, Vorzha emerged from the stables looking angry and red-faced. In the heat of the argument she must have forgotten the implicit promise to feed me suggested by her earlier words, "You must be hungry, my pet." It seemed that she did remember it, though, before I would have starved to death.

Vorzha signaled something before squatting down next to me, but neither I nor the others took any notice; we only looked at the pogachas as she scraped the smoothed-out ash off them. Grandpa struggled to get on his knees again, and everyone cast a petrified stare at the charcoal outline of the celestial sign's clumsy spread-out wings on one particular pogacha, one that had turned out flatter and wider than the rest. In their eyes was the dumb expression of repentance, like so many brute beasts looking on as a shepherd skins other members of the flock.

I was unable to control my thoughts, and salvation interested me even less than the bird shape etched into that pogacha. I flew into a rage.

"Have you gone crazy, old man?" He must have had the same opinion of me, as he looked at me askance. "You were drawing in the ash before-didn't you notice that pogacha under it?"

"Oh, Devil take my foolish mind!" He picked up hot pogacha. "Go to hell!" He wiped it off with his hat and threw it back into the embers.

Vorzha, not knowing what this was all about, squinted with puzzlement at the petrified Gypsies, and when the atmosphere became more relaxed, she waved a hand toward the barn. The strident laughter with which the old man's terror was now being mocked annoyed rather than amused me. I was just about to leave the crowd when Zhelko appeared, confronting me in a fury.

"Hey there, you're rich and you've married my daughter."

"So what?" I asked provocatively, because nothing else came to mind.

Balush set upon her husband with a gaping mouth; traces of the afternoon's heated debate were visible on her disheveled hair. She was screaming bloody murder, and the only words that I could understand were these:

"And if he's married her, good for him! You and that filthy thing between your legs should be happy to have such a son-in-law."

Zhelko shut her up with his hand on her mouth, and shoved her behind him.

"It's custom," he continued with forced coolness, "that you pay. That's how it's done."

"How much?" I too found it hard to be calm, but I managed to get the words out.

"A hundred," he said insolently. The Gypsies around us gasped. The wooden poker with the burned tip was right next to my foot, and I wouldn't have minded using it, but Vorzha interrupted.

"Why should he pay you a hundred pengős if I wasn't even a virgin?"

"It's my due even then."

"He'd be mad to. So you can gamble it away? You want to eat your cake and have it too?"

"Why not?" said Zhelko, gritting his teeth and grabbing hold of Vorzha's hair. "If you don't pay," he looked at me with flashing eyes, "I'll cut off your wife's hair!"

"Two pengős," I said.

"Ten," he said, opening a huge pocketknife with his teeth.

"I won't give you a cent," I said, enraged, "but if you don't let go of her this instant, I swear on Grandpa's life I'll cut your throat with my razor."

I didn't have a razor, but if he'd cut Vorzha's hair I would have killed him if I'd lived that long.

"Will you pay or not?" He held the knife to Vorzha's hair. I didn't know what to answer, as all I had left were two pengős; I'd spent the rest. Vorzha didn't move, quietly enduring the sharp knife pressed to the roots of her hair.

Pure, sincere hatred poured from Balush's eyes toward her husband. I couldn't do anything but the same. If a satisfactory deal wasn't reached, old customs gave the deceived father the right to take revenge by disfigurement. It would be entirely up to him whether he cut off her nose or her hair. Nonrelatives could intervene only if they paid up.

I stood in the crossfire of the gazes and the knife. If I revealed that I had no money, he would hand me the shame of having been hoodwinked together with his daughter's hair. Everyone would agree with him, even Balush, whose eyes were fixed on him at the moment like daggers.

Zhelko needed money and was in no rush to finish the process; you can't play cards on credit, just as you can't to buy a wife. He rather snarled at me with his white teeth until Grandpa broke the wooden poker on his head.

"Goddamnit! Do you want to die for money? How often do you want to sell you daughter?" Zhelko clutched his head and released Vorzha.

"Hey, what can I play cards with tonight, then?"

Disgusted, I threw the twenty copper coins that made up the two pengős right before his feet. He threw himself on the money with both his hands.

"Let me wither away in the dungeons if that doesn't bring me luck," said Zhelko, and with that he scooped up the money together with the rubbish.

Here too the others knew the human forms of self-humiliating greed. But no matter how deeply they sank, they didn't lower themselves to dismiss their ancient instincts for small change. They watched in disgust as Zhelko scraped the coins together with his nails. Vorzha snuggled up to me, and Balush, gathering her disheveled hair, looked around the staring Gypsies.

"See, this is my husband, this grub."

"But I won't be a grub if I bring back a lot of money for you, will I?" Zhelko struggled to his feet and wiped off his dusty knees.

"You'll bring lots of money?" Balush spat in his direction.

"You bet I will," he said, jingling the money in his hands. He left us, laughing.

"God has taken away his sanity," said Grandpa, gazing after him.

Muto now joined the circle, slapping his palms together as if to deal cards, and then shook his head solemnly. Droopy Mustache was mad, he signaled.

"That he is," Balush answered impassively. "Marry me, Dopey; you're smarter."

At first Muto didn't understand, and looked at Balush with calf eyes until she repeated the signs.

"Nyim," he uttered incomprehensibly, shaking his head in protest. Flattening his nose with his fingertips, he looked around, and indicated the big-assed woman. "Nyim," he repeated, now flailing his arms. It wasn't a bad way to lighten the atmosphere. Muto was aware of this. He looked around, made a shy face, and then, grinning, embraced Balush.

Hearty laughter seemed to lighten the air around us, but Vorzha's remarks about her lost virginity echoed within me with a brassy chill.

"Don't be angry, my pet, none of it is true. I'll tell you all about it."

What can you say about nothing? I asked myself.

Balush watched Muto's game without a trace of sympathy. Not a single wrinkle marred her face-not after seven children, scores of men, and Zhelko. Zhelko, the desexer, the gambler! In her case there was no scraping off the paint to find the real person under the gaudy colors. This was the real thing.

The bystanders kept tugging at Muto amid loud, heartfelt laughter, but his good humor didn't abate even though they half stripped off his pants.

People were singing all around us as if nothing had happened. Grandpa wept with laughter; he liked the mute man's antics.

"*Sheebe, sheebe!*" he yelled, once again incomprehensibly, while leaping into the air, holding onto his pants with one hand and slapping his leg with the other. "Sheebe, sheebe!" He kept jumping about, his belly protruding, his two hands folded behind his neck as he pretended not to notice that his pants had slipped down to his ankles.

Vorzha looked on, too. The women laughed heartily with long, drawn-out whinnies. Miraculously, Balush didn't take part in the game. Turning her back on the whole thing, she stared straight ahead, her hands occupied with her hair, letting it down, and then putting it up in a bun; as if this wasn't the same Balush whose voice had made me nauseous just half an hour ago.

Muto pulled up his pants, strung them together on his waist with some wire, and asked her for a dance. She accepted without a word. The game ceased in one fell swoop, and the men took the women to dance with masculine bravado-a whirling, crackling dance. The sinuous flow of diverse colors combined into a whole, the colorless spots blending into it like a stretched, gaudy canvas whose bottomless depths absorbed everything.

I swirled inside their sooty cauldron in the stupor of the perspiration vapor oozing from under the women's loose breasts; the beats reverberated in the tunnel of the swirling ruffled skirts with a dull rumble, and the clapping of hands aroused our overheated blood to a frenzied pace, while our rags became drenched with sweat. The slippery embrace of smooth, naked arms encircled us as I flopped down, panting, dazed by fatigue, beside the flickering red flames.

Brooking no dissent and feigning anger at my shy wildness, Balush motheringly pulled off my shirt and waved it over the fire with expert movements.

"Do you want to catch a cold?" she asked.

I didn't respond, but instead kept wisely silent as a young, black-eyed gal now dried off my back with the hem of her skirt. The events of the afternoon had made me more cautious.

I shook the thoughts from my mind to let other thoughts replace them. I became more weary and hungry.

My heart sank when I saw Balush let go of my shirt; a black ball of smoke arose, and the shirt was instantly devoured by the fire. I was the only one who remained sitting amid the commotion, partly out of fright and partly because the black-eyed gal—taking advantage of the confusion—now clung tightly to my neck.

"Don't let it get to you," she whispered, "So she threw it in the fire. But she'll buy you another one."

Even though the girl's whisper didn't comfort me, at least it proved what I had seen. I was fuming, but I laughed along with the others.

"It fell out of my hands, bless your souls." Balush spread out her hands, asserting her innocence in front of everyone. "What'll happen now?"

"Nothing," I shrugged my shoulders disparagingly. "It wasn't much good anyway."

"Have you got another one?" asked Balush as if momentarily surprised.

"What for? Others go around half-naked here, too."

"You're right, bro," several of the men shouted almost in unison, "we *are* Gypsies." With that, they threw their tattered shirts into the fire. "Let the *zhuvya*[44] warm themselves." *Easy for those guys,* I thought, *they have jackets.*

Balush, seeing that I wasn't really comforted by their empathy, pulled me up by my arms.

"Come on, I'll give you a shirt like you've never worn before in your life." On our way to the barn, she pressed her face against my naked skin, trying again to persuade me of her innocence. Having had enough of her cunning, I stopped her in the doorway where the electric light shone on her face. She blushed at the sudden change in me, but looked into my eyes.

"Don't be a whore," I said, "if you have no brains." Something flashed in her eyes; she pinched my arm and ran away.

It isn't easy to hide our thoughts from ourselves, especially when they are coupled with a desire for revenge. All of Balush's movements recalled her daughter's, except that her limbs were fuller and rounder.

"Come on, eat," said Vorzha, coming up to me with a smile. She took my arm, which still showed Balush's pinch.

---

[44] fleas

"Are you hot?" She asked, caressing my chest.

"Yes."

"Are you still mad at me?" she asked with an inquiring squint. "I can't help it that my father would do anything for a game of cards. And what I said *wasn't* true; I just said it because I didn't want him to keep harassing you."

I could have argued with Vorzha about matters of marriage. The words that had been inadvertently voiced in the heat of the argument had let me deduce a lot of things. I wasn't in the mood for anything. This was the first time I'd come so face-to-face with my own mistaken convictions.

Everything and everyone around me forced me to believe that it was all good just the way it was, that I should just take from it whatever I liked. That I should see and hear not a thing, and I should hold my nose if something stank, for what was there was dependent on neither me nor anyone else.

Balush was already waiting for me with the shirt. The sight of the woman awoke a certain stubborn pride in me, but when I got there, I slipped on the deputy bailiff's shirt without a word. Its clean smell reminded me of another world, one to which I'd have to return sooner or later—who was to say at what price? I didn't long to go there, nor did I want to stay here.

Questions stirred within me, with answers nowhere to be had. Why, I'd had greater confidence in approaching the unknown while sitting on a bench in school, where I had to fight a life-and-death battle for space, than in confronting the known, here, amid unlimited possibilities. The very environment in which I knew I ought to loosen up was in fact suffocating.

"Come on, sit down!" Grandpa didn't like it if people looked down on him. "Why are you always so down in the dumps?"

"I'm usually like that, Grandpa."

"That's not good, son. Sorrow and anger are bad counselors. I know you're furious on account of Zhelko."

"Because of the cards," Balush coyly squeezed my back as if wanting to placate my anger against her husband.

"Yes, he did it because of the cards," said Grandpa, his voice raised to signal offense at a woman having interrupted him. Balush shrugged her shoulders; she understood.

"And because of all the old customs," he continued more calmly. "We still believe socks are full of gold, only that other people press theirs to their hearts. Well, those days are gone." He nodded to himself with a wise mien, and then broke into a wry smile. Perhaps Grandpa now understood his own delusions. He realized that he was a relic from the past; he was the yesterday, the tolerated enemy of today.

"Whatever there was has been lost with the past. Every era eats up its own customs, and whatever is left of them isn't worth a damn."

Vorzha was beaming as she presented her first dinner of our marriage. She offered the cleaned-off and unbroken pogacha to me, the male with the strongest hands. There were only the two of us, Grandpa and me; the others had gone off to play cards.

Some of the children were already hiding in the straw, while the others stood around quietly. The women formed a small circle around the sooty pot, and Grandpa found himself a place at the highest part of the straw lair so his short frame wouldn't impair his authority.

Vorzha had been right to give the bone-dry pogacha to me, not Grandpa; it took quite an effort to break it in half. I handed half to him and the other back to Vorzha, gesturing to her to hand it out to the children. There was no need to wake sleeping kids, though; in an instant they were standing in line without anyone telling them to.

The women looked approvingly at Vorzha on seeing the pot heaped with fried meat.

"This man brought a turkey," she waved at me, "but I had to fry it in some lard; I don't like it any other way." She pulled her face into a disparaging, feminine grimace. She surprised me. Yesterday's blushing little girl who didn't know how much salt to put in the pogacha had today become the perfect housewife. And not just any kind. I recalled

Grandpa's earlier words: is that really all that remained from yesterday? A smoky, faded image that bore no resemblance to today? Despite all my bitter feelings I had to don a smiling mask to accept the affable nods I was getting in acknowledgment of Vorzha's skill.

The day-old bustard—which had been cooked and fried over fire and smoke, and that we had involuntarily tenderized by our bodies half the night and that had now been fried in plenty of lard—had accumulated so many zesty flavors that I couldn't get enough of it.

The women's appetites were likewise voracious. Not that they ever seemed to be lacking at other times. No, I had noticed them wolfing down the grits the day before, but somehow the spectacle now caught my attention even more. They cut the pieces of meat with their nails into thin slivers and put them back in the pot. They did the same with two or three more pieces, and only after that did they gobble down whatever came to hand. I saw that all the women did the same, and I nearly followed their example. I thought it must have been some sort of custom to keep gluttony in check.

But if this was custom, why did neither Balush nor Vorzha do the same? I saw that nobody was watching me, so I pretended that I found all to be in order. I only kept watching to see what would happen to the pieces they had marked. They just pushed them aside as if they had been gnawed to the bone.

One by one they stopped eating, stretched themselves out with an evident sense of gratification and, having wiped their eyes and mouths, they now started to chat. Only Grandpa was still eating; the pogacha had not been baked with his frail teeth in mind. He tried to soften it by dipping it in the fat to keep up with the others, but even so he remained far behind them. Each time he dipped, he upset the meat that the women had so carefully put aside, and they put the pieces back on top of one another on the side of the pot.

At last I realized what this custom was all about! I broke off a mouthful of pogacha and, as if I was doing it out of boredom, I began to dip it in a leisurely way. The looks they cast at me and at one another were worth the trouble of repeatedly mixing up the pieces of meat. Again and again they rearranged them with amazing diligence, carefully separating their portions. I would have loved to see them make a mistake. I was sorry I wasn't successful, and would gladly have gobbled up everything—if for no other reason than to make sure there was nothing left with which the women could appease their husbands when the men returned from having lost their money instead of spending it on food.

Meanwhile the children live like chickens, getting something thrown to them once a day while the women squirrel away the choicest bits for the men. *Well, if this counts as custom*—I thought—*it won't last until tomorrow, because I'll feed the meat to the children today.*

As soon as Grandpa closed his pocketknife, I saw the women curving their claws like falcons. I preempted them by barely a second, but that was enough for me to stop their hands in midair.

Pretending I hadn't noticed a thing, I picked up the pot and took it to the patiently waiting children. Without being told, they lined up according to size. I threw the emptied, sooty pot back among the women. There was no need to hear what they thought; their eyes betrayed everything. I wasn't gloating, but I really enjoyed their poisonous glances that didn't even spare the children.

"This son-in-law of yours is as slippery as an eel!" barked the freckled Zholi at Balush. Grandpa winked at me, and Balush threw herself on the straw, choking with laughter. As for me, I acted as if I hadn't understood a thing. I looked innocently at the scarecrow of a woman who was slapping her mouth in anger as if trying to squeeze back the insults meant for me.

"You're laughing?" the woman snapped, throwing scornful glances at Vorzha.

"What should I do, cry?" Vorzha asked, blushing.

"Don't cry, girl!" said Balush, still gesturing toward her mouth. "But I won't know what to give that Gypsy; he'll give me hell when he comes home."

"You know what you'll give him?" Vorzha narrowed her eyes. "What you're sitting on. You don't have to press the straw all day, you could lift your *bul,*[45] and then your children could eat their fill."

"You've sure found your tongue since you got a man."

"That's right. Even if your husband won at cards, you didn't cook for your children; you preferred to have a sing-along. If my husband hadn't spent money on them, they would have starved."

"Oh no, they can look after themselves, they always find enough food for their needs."

"Of course, in old Mára's *trastya,*"[46] said one of the gals, blue-eyed Rilandri, all at once, siding with Vorzha. "If you have any money, you press it to your heart."

"Your husband plays cards, too, so why all the fuss?"

"He can play if he wants; he hasn't got any brats, yet he often feeds all of you."

"I'll see when you have kids how you'll manage to fatten them up."

"You sure will, sister." Rilandri laughed out loud. She couldn't have been more than a couple of years older than Vorzha. Her big blue eyes exuded a kind of candid warmth; she always seemed to be cheerful and was evidently saddened only by the others' idleness. She had a glib tongue and her voice carried, yet it was somehow more pleasant than those of the others, who wanted at all costs to wrest the truth for themselves.

"Easy for you all to talk," said Zholi before piping down. She saw that she remained by herself, with no one on her side.

Rilandri ignored Zholi's grumbling, and laughed at the other disheartened women, until they too got angry.

"Oh, *Devla,*[47]" Rilandri, exclaimed, "I'm so sorry for these poor women! What will they give those wretched Gypsies of theirs when they come home in the morning?"

---

[45] backside

[46] sack

[47] God

Zholi turned to me. "Listen, you little Gypsy man, you certainly did a good job. These"—she pointed at the women—"will all be so strung up by tomorrow that the men will be able to play them like a double base."

Zholi exploded with laughter, and bit her shawl to muffle it. Her hair fell onto her shoulders in long ringlets, radiating a black luster, and the laughter dug small dimples into her round face. At such times, beyond the black fence of her eyes, an unusually pure world opened up, where the grass, the earth, and the sun were blue and where the air became a dense light blue as in a bottomless crystal ball.

The shawl solution didn't work for long, for she threw herself next to Balush and both of them writhed with laughter. Vorzha ran away, and I stood next to them with tears in my eyes, chewing my hands to resist my own spasms of laughter.

The three women, holding back their anger, shot vindictive glances at Rilandri, whose gaiety they ascribed to her "immoral, mixed" blood. For that matter, women who constantly laughed and giggled were traditionally despised; for even a smile was considered as tempting the men, and if they found a way they used all kinds of slander to keep those women away from their own husbands. Rilandri wasn't interested in any of the husbands, and they respected her for that, but her eternal cheerfulness got on their nerves.

"See how she's mocking us?" said one of the women, "May her father string her up! Why are you laughing at us, you Jewish whore? Huh?" The woman blew her ugly nose into her skirt.

"*Youuu* . . ." yet another woman, Berbe, drawled at her in a deep guttural voice, "were made by a Jew . . . a *Jeeew!*" A thick thread of snot hung from Berbe's nose as she glanced up at a tall woman, Mulo, like a hatching chick searching for the sun.

"A Polish Jew," Mulo blurted out, encouraged by Berbe, exacting her revenge.

As if aspiring to something spectacular, Grandpa's sons had chosen their wives in a strange manner. The oldest and the youngest married real beauties; despite having given birth to seven children, Balush's beauty had not disappeared entirely. For the others, the only condition was that each have a hole between her legs.

Like any community, the Gypsies' is built on property. The difference is that, while in other communities we find thousands upon thousands of assets that count as public or private property, the Gypsies have just one asset, one piece of property: the woman. Among her people, she counts as private property. Only her treatment and utilization varies from one community of Gypsies to another.

I don't want to explain anything to myself, because the real world undermines all musings anyway, but I am unable to understand a woman who, at any moment, could refuse being forced into the role of a breeding animal, but doesn't. Why not? Maybe even the woman herself couldn't give an answer. But if she did answer, I maintain that she would protest against any other treatment. Who knows, she might even be right. I was no longer in as rosy a mood as before. I considered the sadness of these three women, whose faces didn't seem to reflect a fear of their husbands, but rather more generally, a mind-blowing mix of hate and pain.

I regretted what I'd done. I wanted to take revenge on their depraved husbands. It was the wives who ended up getting slaps. Those gathered here had really wanted only to find some joy in an appreciative smile or nod. Although their eyes were still flashing, they had calmed down by now and weren't even interested in the other two laughing at them; they gave them time to let off steam, if that was what made them happy.

The great jollity didn't last long. They saw that they could no longer force any reaction out of them, so they slowly gave up giggling but didn't lose their taste for teasing. The lovely-eyed Rilandri tried everything to provoke her sisters-in-law to renewed anger, but without success. Finally she realized I was the only available victim.

"Sit down, for heaven's sake, you're standing here like some bailiff in your lovely new shirt. It shows that you've got a good mother-in-law. Tomorrow she'll put some pants on you, too." She expected me to be embarrassed and, trying to help, took my hand and pulled me down next to her.

"Where are you from? We don't even know who and what you are; you just showed up and forced yourself among us." She kept silent for a while. Then she added, but now addressing Vorzha, turning her eyes to her, "My God, have you married a mute?" Rilandri then continued her questioning of me.

"Well, are you mute or proud?" I could tell from her eyes that a little annoyance had mingled with her playful teasing. "See," she turned to Balush, "that's how those cheap creatures get above themselves whose bodies have never been covered by a decent rag."

By now her mirth had faded completely; she even tried letting go of my hand, which she'd been holding, except that I maintained a tight grip. She looked into my eyes, apparently regretting the misfired joke, just as the three crouching woman did. She was able to control herself for now. But she hadn't given up her plan, and was just waiting for a favorable moment. She didn't make any secret of her feelings, indicating it by pulling faces and frowning at Balush, who was sitting behind me.

All at once I spoke.

"Why are you called *Ril*andri[48]?" Her eyes widened with astonishment. I didn't wait for her answer. "Is it because you fart so loudly?"

"Goddamn you," Rilandri said, furiously jerking her hand away "Did you hear, Balush, what that son-in-law of yours wants to know? If the old Gypsy wouldn't be here, I'd sure give him a piece of my . . ." Before she had a chance to finish, though, everybody burst out laughing; only Rilandri was glaring at me.

Maintaining my inquisitive expression, I awaited her answer to my question. Instead of replying, she wanted to jump up, but I pulled her back by her skirt.

"What do you want from me, Gypsy man? Balush, talk to your son-in-law! I swear I'll do something bad to him."

---

[48] In Romani, *ril* = fart

"Why would you, huh?" my mother-in-law asked, choking with laughter. "And tell me, what *would* you do to him?"

"May my dad drop dead if you're not all crazy!" Blushing, Rilandri lowered her eyes; she didn't dare to look up.

"Well," said Berbe with a shrug, "let me hear you laugh now! You're always wanting to pull one over on everybody, but now you've met your match."

"Go to hell, Turkey Nose!"

By the time Vorzha returned, the squabble was over. Rilandri said to Vorzha, "You sure got yourself a good man. Zholi was right when she said he's as slippery as an eel."

Music could be heard from the other end of the barn, and Grandpa left our group.

"Will you tell me now?" I asked Rilandri yet again, taunting her.

"What, Gypsy man?"

"Why you're called Rilandri."

"Who the hell knows?" She laughed. "They gave me the name when I was little. And why do you care?"

"Never mind."

"Well, Vorzha, you'd have done better to marry Muto, who only ever says: *sheebe, sheebe*." Keeping a straight face, she began to imitate Muto's voice, and then she continued to complain to Vorzha.

"You see, at first we thought you got yourself a nice, quiet Gypsy boy, and then it turns out he's full of devils." She turned to me. "Say," she asked seriously, "why were you so interested in my name?"

"I wasn't interested, silly—I was just curious whether you yourself knew."

Rilandri now looked at Balush. "Listen, Balush, do I look so crazy that he would have wondered that?"

"No, not at all. Too smart, in fact. That's why I warned you. A woman should not go asking a stranger who he is. He'll tell you, anyway, if it's safe. And if it isn't, you're just forcing him to lie. Ask the men how often they've asked. And as for whether a poor guy has a shirt or not, I say give him one if you've got one to give. You never know when you'll meet him again. Maybe he'll feed you, let you rest, and won't watch where you're going."

Rilandri's eyes opened wide. Behind the ever-jolly-looking fake cheer, there lay an endless barren desert where feelings had been unable to take root. She was driven by the mood of the moment as her whims dictated; she was accustomed to having the feelings come only to visit and then they always devoured everyone's leftovers.

There were only four of us remaining; the other three women had left us, giggling away and nodding their heads at me, as if I hadn't been the cause of it all. Rilandri now kept quiet, with downcast eyes, thoughtfully massaging her round arm with her fingertips. I wasn't in a talkative mood, either; the sounds of the fiddle coming from the other end of the barn were more tempting than was listening to the women.

Vorzha's unease began to abate, and she clung to me wearily, as if sleepy. But she too was interested in the riotous music. We waited for a favorable opportunity to leave our sad company. Balush surely noticed this, too, but she looked at me quizzically when we moved to leave.

"How much money did you give that Gypsy?" She meant Zhelko.

"Two pengős."

"Let him spew out his lungs to the dogs! He had the cheek to take everything you had."

"He might just win," said Rilandri, trying to comfort her.

"Not bloody likely. Here, girl," she said, and threw that morning's bounty to Vorzha. "Go outside, let your husband try these on! May God grant it that he should win; I'll scratch his eyes out if he doesn't split it with your husband."

Vorzha was thrilled by Balush's generosity. I let her drag me outside; I didn't want to put her off.

When we reached the stack of straw, I let Vorzha pull my pants and underpants off, just like Balush had wanted to that morning. The rustling of straw next to us didn't bother me, nor did the sounds of panting reach our ears. We locked ourselves into our own bliss, until the raging fire Vorzha's naked ass had stoked in me died down. After that, I began to dress up leisurely.

There was a bit of a problem with putting on the boots, but Vorzha solved it ingeniously. She tore off the hem of her long strappy shirt, and disgustedly ripped off the damp part together with the rough, hand-sewn stitching. She had a good laugh at my blundering, and helped me wind it around my feet so the boots fit better.

"You're clever," I said appreciatively, and embraced her to show that my words weren't empty. We went back to the barn in a good mood, if slightly paler—though only the initiated would have noticed.

"It took you quite a while to dress your husband!" said Balush with mischievous laughter. "There you go," she said, stroking the suit on me. "It fits you like a glove. Now you can tell him, Rilandri, that he looks like a bailiff."

"So he does." Rilandri agreed. "Like a real gentleman," she added with little enthusiasm.

Hearing Balush's admiration—which could have been either sincere or fake—the three other women also slunk back. They emerged from under their blankets, their undergarments barely covering their dangling breasts, over which they crossed their arms like caricatures of so many Virgin Marys. They too looked at me in awe, but in the meantime they also contrived to repay Rilandri.

"You see, young lady, that's why you shouldn't make fun of anyone; you never know who you're facing."

They had plainly forgotten that what I was wearing was thanks to Balush's encounter with the deputy bailiff. They were eyeing me like people do good horses. Vorzha, red-faced, kept shrugging her shoulders, as if ashamed to reveal how I came by my clothes.

"Alright," said one of the women to relieve the girl's embarrassment, "it makes no difference how you got them; the main thing is that you have them. You're not ugly, either." Amid the women's yacking, none of us noticed that the barn had become quiet.

"Can you write?" Rilandri asked me. Searching in her skirt pocket, she pulled out an ink pencil. The women, crouched around Balush, entered into a peaceful conversation. Vorzha was entitled now to take her place among them. Just as well, as they could provide her with a lot of helpful advice, especially how to always please a husband. These are all benevolent pieces of advice worth listening to, even though most of them are of the one-size-fits-all variety. Apart from love, keeping a husband demands a hard, self-sacrificing lifestyle, because husbands, no matter how depraved they may be, do wear the trousers. And even if they make a mess in them, they are still considered men, whereas if a woman's belly rumbles, folks say she's shit her pants. There is a kind of human Ten Commandments that hasn't been put into numerical order, yet every woman knows it better than the Lord's Prayer:

Don't be lazy, because your husband won't stand it for long.

Honor your husband, for he is your master.

Do not get into an argument with your master, and do not want to be right, because he is the man.

Do not be jealous.

One could endlessly list the prohibiting and commanding sentences that ensure men's advantages versus women's duties.

Rilandri stretched out her round arm toward me.

"Write *feri*[49] here," she said, pointing to a patch that she had licked clean and rubbed until it was quite red. "I'll have it etched with a needle in the morning."

"In Romani or Hungarian?"

[49] only, just (In Hungarian, *Feri* is short for the male name Ferenc, or Francis, hence the protagonist's confusion.)

"Romani." I didn't understand why she wanted to have a word branded on her hand that would never give an intelligible answer, but then there were so many things that I didn't understand that it didn't really matter. Instead I mustered all my drawing skills and started to write with nice, even letters.

"Stop moving your arm!" I rebuked her as she pulled back her hand with a soft cry before I could finish writing. Her voice was unusually sharp, and she had goosebumps on her arm. At first I looked at the tip of the pencil and then I searched her frightened face.

"*Le shingale,*"[50] she whispered. Two gendarmes were walking in the middle of the barn accompanied by Grandpa. They were summoning all the young Gypsy boys, and ordered them to stand in a row next to the trolley tracks.

"Pretend you're reading the boy's palm!" Grandpa called out in Romani.

We were numb with terror; *this was the end*, I thought. Rilandri's nails cut into my palm; her trembling fear rubbed off on me; I could almost hear my own heartbeat.

The gendarmes eyed Grandpa suspiciously. He was still looking at us and turned to them only with an apologetic smile, when he saw that Vorzha had nimbly picked up his jacket from the straw.

"I'm too old, honorable gentlemen," he said, pulling his neck between his shoulders as if feeling chilly. "At my age a man's blood is no longer hot." Without even glancing at Vorzha he took the jacket from her. The gendarmes continued to beckon the youngsters to them. I squatted ashen-faced before Rilandri, not hearing a word of what she was mumbling. My mind was racing. What luck that Vorzha had taken my pants off. Bada's horse registration booklets were inside them.

"Listen to me," I said to Rilandri, putting a halt to the confused words still coming out of her mouth. "If they take me away, go to the woods with Vorzha early in the morning. Take my bag with you; my

---

[50] the gendarmes

pants are in them. At the other end of the woods there's a stack of cordwood, and there you can find my brother. He is a tall, thin, black-skinned Gypsy; give him my things. If he isn't there tomorrow, go back the day after, and both times wait until noon."

I had hardly finished my sentence when the gendarmes came up to us.

"Good evening, sir!" said Grandpa, removing his hat with a flattering smile. "They're no good at reading palms. Go to my old wife, young sir, she knows how to tell your fortune! These here are only good for working and for lolling about."

I stood up, clicking my heels a little in a classy manner, and greeted the two gendarmes with a smiling nod. They feigned strict gazes that promptly softened somewhat, and they reluctantly raised their fingers to their hats. I couldn't tell what my expression was like, because I didn't see it, but the thought that I didn't have anything to lose reassured me. I took one step closer to them, with an ever so slight, elegant bow, so that the one with the silver star could reach my outstretched hand.

"Michael Rota," I said by way of introduction, clicking my heels. I don't know what made me think of that name. Yesterday, when we ran across Okány, I saw it on a grocer's sign. It had caught my attention because *rota* means wheel in Romani.

All I could make out of his mumbling was that he was a sergeant of the Royal Hungarian Gendarmerie. I acknowledged that with another nod, and then shook hands with the other man.

"So you are from Okány?" he asked with a grin. Now I really felt my face burning; if he knew his way around Okány, then I was really lost.

"Yes," I said, modestly reaching into the cigarette case he offered me, and clumsily rummaging for matches in my pocket, knowing full well that I didn't have any.

"I filled in for a few months at the gendarmerie outpost in Okány."

"Thank you," I said, clearing my throat. I held the cigarette between my finders as awkwardly as possible. The corporal smiled as he stomped out his still-burning matchstick. "Yes?" I said, trying to mask the blood rushing to my face by coughing.

"It was only a temporary stay, but I remember quite a few people. Including your dad, bless his heart. The shop is somewhere around the marketplace, isn't it? Although I thought he was much older."

"That's my uncle."

"Oh," I replied, "I get it now. I hardly remember the place—it was at least five years ago."

Changing the subject, he asked whether I'd already finished school.

"I wish I had." I assumed a glum expression. "I've got another pretty tough year to go. This is only a summer experience, and the pocket money comes in handy."

"That's natural," he said with a nod.

"Can I help you with anything?" I asked less loudly.

"Yes, I think you can." He reached for his briefcase. "We are searching for a vagrant Gypsy." He got out his booklet, and began to read from it. "There is a warrant out for him; actually it was originally for two of them, but it was the younger one who committed the crime of assault on an officer of the law. Sixteen to eighteen years old, hobo-looking, tall, round face . . ." After a pause, he rattled off this much more: "normal nose, teeth, mouth, and eyes."

"Oh!" exclaimed Rilandri with evident alarm, clapping her hands to her face. The two gendarmes looked at her almost at once. I just smiled, sadly. "You know, sir, that's my husband." Everyone thought Rilandri had lost her mind. Only the two gendarmes went closer to her.

"Your husband?" asked the sergeant.

"Yes, sir. I recognized him from what you've said. A tall, scrawny . . ."

"Scrawny? My ass!"

"Well, you know, sort of skinny and always looks like he's angry. There's a big scar on his side."

"Who the hell cares about his side? Where is he?"

"Search me. This morning when the warden wanted to rape me, he just ran off and never came back. He went off to another village, Geszt. I never ever want to see him again. Tell me, what sort of a man is he, who lets his wife be screwed in front of him?" The gendarmes couldn't stop themselves from smiling.

"Did the warden really rape you?"

"Yes, and good for him, sergeant, sir. God bless him for it. If a man runs away while his wife is being screwed before his very eyes, he doesn't deserve any better."

"That's right," the women around her buzzed, "such a man deserves it." The gendarmes looked quite embarrassed by what Rilandri had said. It was obvious that the sergeant would have liked to have a go at her had his uniform not held him back; his eyes were ready to tear her clothes off.

"*Devla, sar dikhel!*"[51] But Rilandri went on with her flirting. "Have a look, I'll show you how he left black and blue marks on my thighs."

She stepped between the two gendarmes, turned her back toward the others, and pulled one side of her skirt up as far as the top of her thigh. As her brown skin gleamed under the electric light, the two gendarmes touched her almost simultaneously. Nothing showed on her smooth, tight skin, but the red-faced gendarmes kept nodding as she turned her leg around and showed them the nonexistent marks with her fingertip. She even hissed as she touched them.

"Should I have let him hurt me even more?"

"You can report him for that," the sergeant advised her with a serious face.

"Come on, sergeant, sir, how can you say that? After all, I enjoyed it, too. I haven't got a husband now; he's gone to Geszt."

"How do you know he went to Geszt?"

"Because, when he saw that the warden started to grope me, he told me to go with him. But why should I have gone? If you're a man,

[51] God, how he is looking at me!

you should stand up for your woman. I'm not interested in his relatives in Geszt."

"What's his name?"

"The warden's?"

"Your husband's!" he yelled at her.

"Who the hell knows? I don't care." The sergeant shook his head and put his notebook away.

"Did you know him, sir?" he asked me.

"Yes, I remember him. The description corresponds exactly with that person, but I can't tell you his name because he hasn't received a number yet."

"Does everyone have a number?"

"Those who are here from the beginning of the week."

"Those too?" he pointed at the young men standing in the middle of the barn.

"Each and every one of them."

"It wouldn't hurt if we checked them out."

"The head bailiff has the keys to the office."

"Doesn't matter—just from memory."

"As you wish." In fact, everyone had a number, which they were given when they started work here; if someone didn't know it, he didn't get paid. I knew that from the time when I was here years ago. As I accompanied the gendarmes on their newest task of checking the men's numbers, the Gypsies looked at me in awe as we passed by them and greeted me respectfully as "sir."

My new clothes were paying off. If the gendarme pointed at a suspicious-looking fellow, he would tell me his name and number; I would nod, and we would move on. At the barn door the gendarmes again offered me a cigarette; I accompanied them all the way to their horses, which were being looked after by the night watchman next to the sprawling old oak trees.

The watchman greeted us, and then complained that the Gypsies always messed up the straw bedding during the night. I also found out from him that I was the on-duty intern.

"I envy you, young sir," said the sergeant by way of farewell. "You must have had a pleasurable summer holiday."

"I'm sorry it's over tomorrow, but school starts in two weeks."

"It would be a shame to miss out on that blue-eyed Gypsy woman—she's worth a night, believe me. I have quite some experience with women."

"Thank you so much, sir, for the cordial advice, I shall try to make use of it. I am pleased to have met you."

We shook hands, and they galloped away.

Uproarious laughter could be heard from the barn just like the same time last night, only now it seemed much more cheerful and sincere. I didn't know what to do with myself; I needed time to find my way on the intersecting roads of disaster and luck. I was now convinced more than ever that fate plans the turning points of our minutes according to its whims, whose secrets cannot be revealed by pondering them.

What an amazing game: when the rope around the hanged man's neck breaks, he thinks he's lucky. Balush must have enjoyed it when she dressed me in those clothes. Is that why she'd done so, or did she have other intentions? I could see Vorzha approaching with soft steps from the barn. As she reached the trees, her figure became blurred in the black shadow of the foliage.

I lay down at the foot of the old oak. I always enjoyed gazing at the sky when the time was ripe for shooting stars, because so many thoughts were born in my mind then that they could fill the empty moments of my tomorrows. Now I was the one who was empty, and the moments were filled with excitement. It was amazing to see how these folks around me could respond to a crisis. Any reasoning used to assess their situation would have just scrambled the clear mind. Instead, in seconds they acted with convincing passion.

I'd done the same. It wasn't only the gendarmes I'd deceived; I deceived myself, too. I felt human warmth in their farewell handshakes, and yet I was convinced that they were poisonous reptiles, that their touch caused suffering and pain. Their words embedded themselves into my thoughts; I really desired the beautiful Rilandri's thighs.

Vorzha's dark shape leapt across the beaten-down trolley tracks, disappeared with noiseless leaps behind the tree, peered around, and then, before I knew it, her figure, amorphous in the dark, was sitting next to me. I mellowed as she put her warm hand on my forehead. I was no longer interested in the shooting stars. I snuggled closer to her and dug my face deeply into her lap, my breath mingling with the lightly fermented smell of urine. Something ran through her, then me, and I reached under her skirt. Her smooth thighs relaxed, and she slowly leaned back, drawing me with her, while her nimble fingers freed the front of my tightening pants.

By the time the light of recognition squeezed through my befuddled brain, it was too late. Balush had achieved what she'd wanted. I found no reason to sigh; sooner or later everything comes to pass. Anyway, it had been on my mind all day, whether for revenge or simple curiosity. It seems that revenge is followed by revenge, and each time she found a way, she let me know that she couldn't be evaded, and that, when the occasion arose, she would show no mercy.

She was right in her own way. We had put a spike in her wheel. The night before she'd tried everything she could, and it was not her fault that circumstances had evolved quite differently; no one can be smart enough. It is to her credit, though, that once she got something in her head, nothing and nobody could sidetrack her. I neither wanted to ease my conscience nor did I see any sense in making a problem of it all. I let her play her role. It was dark enough for me to accept her deceptive game; by now it made no difference, anyway. Moaning, I picked myself up, patted her buttocks, and she chuckled softly, but remained silent. I tried to position myself so as to avoid any possibility of recognition, and after a few steps, Balush's figure appeared only as gray, shapeless blob.

"Go inside," I said. "I'll follow you. We didn't get much sleep last night; it's high time we make up for it tonight."

At first she just moved, waiting for me to finish, but then she got up and stumbled over to me. I realized that the ruse had failed.

"Do you take me for a fool, or are you crazy?" She stood before me. "Do you want me to believe that if a dog lies down next to you, you don't notice it? You knew from the first moment that it was me, and you still went on with it."

I'd counted on her brazenness, but I hadn't thought she was quite that depraved.

"So, why is this good for you?"

"Because you know and I do, too." I was convinced that Balush was mad. I shuddered, and before I knew what was happening, my fingers were around her smooth neck.

"You can strangle me," she said, "but even then I will die on account of Zhelko's revenge."

"Whoring has taken away your mind." I pushed her away from me.

"Whoring?" she asked. "You don't know this family. You won't talk like this when they'll mock you; you'll come to hate even their babies, like I have."

"You came to hate them? That's why you let them all make babies for you?"

"That's why," she retorted.

"Not bad—this sort of hatred can somehow be endured."

"You're making fun of me, but do you know what they did to me?"

"I know. They gave in to your badgering; only Grandpa resisted."

"The old *phumba*[52]?" she chuckled. "If only you knew how often he groped me. That's what he's been itching for, but he can go on itching! God, don't you give him peace until I sit on his mouth, at least he'll then get to see what he wants."

"Hasn't he seen it yet?" I asked mischievously. "You've shown it often enough to him this morning."

---

[52] pus (literally), here used in a pejorative sense of "slimeball," "slimy"

"He's seen it that way, but he hasn't tasted it yet like his sons have; no, he hasn't tasted that hacked up hole of mine, which they've spat on in front of the whole world."

"I get it now. So you thrust yourself into the bull herd from sheer hatred, and raped them one by one in revenge."

"Yes, one by one. I'll show Zhelko—may his bones be swept out of a jail—that they'll have to pay with their blood for what they've defiled."

"Come on, don't try to fool me. You wanted them and they wanted you; they all have ugly wives. As the little bulls grow, so you teach them the know-how of life. All in the name of your revenge on Zhelko."

"Yes. I've sworn that anyone who sets foot in this phumba of a family should have to flee from his own disgrace." She lifted her voice, indicating that she'd finished, and jumped up. Instinctively I grabbed onto her before she could get away.

"Wait, let's discuss this fleeing of theirs—don't hurry!" I forced Balush down to the ground by her hair. "Tell me, why should I have to flee from my own disgrace?"

"So there won't remain any seed for the phumba line."

"Then why do you shit out one kid after another?" I wound her hair tighter.

"They won't be proud of their heritage—they were born in infamy," she groaned, the roots of her hair creaking under my hands.

"In *your* infamy."

"In theirs."

"If you're lying, I'll pull out your hair by the roots."

"You're still too much of a child to force anything out of me if I don't want to tell it. There aren't as many hairs in your hand as beatings I've gotten." She pulled her head away as if to prove it.

I had to let go of her.

"I swear on my Vorzha's life that I'm telling the truth—she's still clear of any infamy. When I came into their family, my mother-in-law was in prison. She was telling drabarimos[53] all her life, and her kin was getting into one sort of trouble after another. Old Phumba was having a good time going after all the women. Except that I was saddled with all the children, because the old Gypsies were still living by their traditions. That was what ate away their minds and their luck. I was the young woman who, according to their customs, had to show how capable she was, because if she isn't resourceful, her husband is disgraced.

"They're right: let the woman be clever if she wants a man. I tied my Vorzha around my neck, and summer and winter I walked the village with next to nothing on, often barefoot. The only time I had something to cover my feet with was if someone gave me a rag or a worn-out shoe. The weather didn't make any difference; rain or shine, Balush had to go. Their two marriageable daughters were sitting at home, singing all day, and didn't lift a finger even to sweep the hut. They both needed men, but no one had come along to raise their skirts. You know what it's like where there are lots of children? I was knee-deep in trash. When I got home, Zhelko would punish me for their faults. He didn't want to hurt their feelings. Alright, then, to hell with it, I figured—I put up with it, though I was always full of children. Not once did I blame Zhelko for me having to look after all those kids. I loved them like my own children, and they loved me like their mother. My father-in-law wouldn't have given a red cent even if they'd all died of hunger. He used to say, *'Nai xurde love'*.[54]

"Often I went home half beaten to death by the gendarmes. What could I have gotten by honest means? I cheated and stole whenever and whatever I could. My father-in-law praised me for being clever. I was happy as a clam on account of that. He called me a true Gypsy woman, but one time when I passed by his cart while he was sitting in the driver's seat, he slashed me with his whip and called me a 'tinker whore.' In his eyes my honor was only as much as I took home in my *trastya*.[55]

---

[53] fortunes

[54] There's no money.

[55] sack

"When I joined the family, Khulo and Gosha still looked like children, and we often played with each other like kids. Zhelko wasn't an adult yet, either. No, he was just about like you, except that he'd been crazy all his life. All he knew was how to eat and how to make children. Three years, three children. One of them, I took home in my skirt frozen. May the poor little thing rest in peace. Three years later Khulo married Berbe; and Gosha, the hairy Mulo. Both of them looked like my grandmother. Okay, I was glad, they helped me out a little, after all, and I didn't have to do everything myself. Except that whatever food the old bitches brought home, they stashed away for their men, and neither my children nor the others got a bite to eat.

"In the end, Khulo built himself a little hole into the kitchen, and they moved there. From then on, he and Berbe lived well. Whenever Berbe went to the village, she would be back in no time carrying all sorts of things. Not only the men, but we too were furious. Begging didn't bring us much. I, with my big belly, managed somehow to plead for something, but hairy Mulo wasn't even allowed near the houses, no, she was constantly chased away. Lots of times she came home empty-handed. And when that happened, Gosha let her have it. Zhelko did the same to me. What they'd been happy to get before, they now made fun of, seeing as how it was nothing compared to Berbe's pickings. No wonder envy was killing me.

"Well, I thought, I'll nose around. She was never any good at fortune-telling, and now she's making fools of us. Who was crazy enough to believe that this *djunga*[56] Berbe could do a thing? But whether they believed it or not, the fact is that she brought back food by the bagful. Dry meat, sausages, bacon, money, whatever you can imagine; and meanwhile we were starving to death. Add to that that I was wading waist-deep in the snow expecting my child any minute. Well, early one morning, Gosha and Zhelko were arrested by the gendarmes for a burglary they had nothing to do with. The gendarmes tortured them for weeks until they found the real culprits. Gosha and Zhelko came home half beaten to death. You can imagine that after that, they were afraid to leave the hut.

---

[56] ugly female

"Two days after the baby was born, I got up. Everyone was so hungry that they were lying about by the salting tub; even Mulo was off her feet. I myself had been racking my brains since dawn that morning about what to do in this weather; I mean, it was so cold you could hear your own breathing. I was worried that this child would also freeze to death. Wherever I looked, all I saw were sick people. The older boys had sores on their feet from the cold; they were the ones who searched the woods for twigs, which they exchanged with the crippled shoemaker for potatoes.

"I wish I'd let them stew in their own juices.

Anyway, I spied out Berbe, saw which house she went into and stayed a good long time in, and saw her leave with a bundle she could hardly carry. She noticed me in the neighborhood, too, going from house to house, begging away with my two-day-old baby tied to my breast. But did she even say hi? Of course not. *Just you wait*—I thought—*I'll oust you from that goldmine of yours!* If misfortune throws itself at someone, you can't keep out of its way. That night I told Zhelko: 'Listen, you Gypsy, I figured out where Berbe hangs out.'

"Get going then," he said. "She shouldn't be eating that much while others are starving to death. Well, aren't you going?"

"I went. I figured out in advance what I was going to say. The child kept crying, it didn't stop all the way. Dear God, I couldn't say a word because of it.

"I went early; it was so cold that your spit froze instantly. I kept knocking, my hands and feet were numb from hanging around, but there wasn't anyone at home. Where to go now? I could see that someone was peeking out from behind the fence.

"'Hey, let me in,' *phendom.*[57] 'I've brought you a message.'"

"'What kind of message?' the fellow inside asked."

"'It's really important.'"

"*Just let me in*, I thought. As soon as he opened the gate, I was in."

---

[57] I said

"'What do you want?' I didn't take any notice, but headed straight to the kitchen. Oh my God, even my heart got lighter in the lovely warmth. The skirt almost broke on my belly; the baby's piss had turned into thick ice."

"The man leaned against the door and just looked. He was as ugly as sin. He had a face that would scare a dog out of a butcher shop. I didn't care, just as long as I could fix up my baby; it was getting blue from crying and from the cold.

"'Where's the lady? I want to talk to her.'

"'You got the wrong house.'

"'You live here, young man, or are you the owner?'

"'Yes.' *Well, Balush*—I thought to myself—*what now?*

"'Could you tell me when the lady is coming home?" He started to laugh.

"'Never. There's no woman here; I'm by myself.' That's when my jaw dropped. 'I told you,' he said, 'you got the wrong house.' He went on laughing.

"'I've come because the spirits have sent me. Sir, your luck has been tied into knots, and there's no one else in the whole wide world who can untie it. I couldn't settle down all night; Grandma Shaman made me follow her to all the crossroads and didn't leave me in peace until I promised to come and see you. Now, you can either let me untie your luck or lose the little that you still have. But, apart from this, she can do a lot more harm to you. Grandma Shaman is really sorry about your luck, which is hogtied and crying for you.' He couldn't take his eyes off the baby, as I was suckling it.

"'Bring me a fresh egg, sir, one that's just been laid.'"

"'Don't bother,' *phendyas,*[58] 'I know that trick.'"

"'Just bring me one, young man; you have to see for yourself how much misfortune and danger is awaiting you.'

"'I've told you, I know this trick.' *To hell with you,* I thought.

---

[58] he said

"'"Well, where do you know it from?'

"'"Liz showed me. She didn't come off badly, either.'

"'"Oh, Devla. Who is this Liz? Do you mean Berbe?'

"'"Yes.'

"'"She's no good at telling your fortune.'

"'"So when did *you* calve?' He sat on the stool in front of me. That's when I noticed he wasn't watching the child but my nipple. *Um,* I thought, *so that's how Berbe was telling* drabarimos. *Just you wait, you pock-marked* gadjo,[59] *I'll cut your mouth.*

"'"The little one is only three days old.'

"'"Three days?' His eyes glazed over.

"'"That's right.' Now he was really looking at the baby.

"'"Is there anything in it to suckle?'

"'"There is nothing in it, nothing."' There really wasn't. I pulled it out of the child's mouth. 'Come on, see for yourself!' I held it out to him, and he looked at me in amazement. 'You can touch it, just don't squeeze it.'

"His eyes were burning like a cat's. He reached into my vest and pulled out the other one too. He was fingering them, like doctors do. *To hell with you,* I thought, *you'll cum in a minute.* The child began to cry, and he let go of it. He brought a bottle of wine out from the larder.

"'"Drink,' *phendyas,* 'you can do with it.'

"I had a tumblerful. Oh, but it felt good. That's when I really thawed out.

"'"How old are you?'

"'"Eighteen.'

"'"You're more beautiful than Elizabeth.'

"'"If the baby would be older, I'd sleep with you, too.'

"'"When will it be alright?' he asked. What on earth was I supposed to tell him? If I gave an answer that seemed too far off I'd scare him away. 'When will it be six weeks?' I asked him.

---

[59] non-Romani man

"He started counting: 'Early April.'

"'It'll be alright by then.' *It will be springtime by then,* I thought—*as long as he helps us out in winter. . . .*

"'Don't you want to bathe the baby? In the meantime I'll find some clothes for you, else you'll freeze to death.'

"'That'll be good, God bless you for it. But I have to hurry; the children are dying of hunger at home. They'd need a little food, too.' What can I say, I was scared—who was to say what he had in mind?

"'There'll be some of that, too. Just go ahead and wash it, otherwise it'll get sick.' I knew why he said it; we were drowning the kitchen with the smell of urine.

"'The water is already warming for it at home.' What a joke. I'd washed it only once since it was born, and then from my mouth; there wasn't a fucking washbasin at home. The gadjo laughed; he could tell I was scared.

"He filled my glass.

"'Drink,' he said 'don't be scared; I am a human too, not an animal.'

"I drank because I was frightened. If I made him angry, we'd die of starvation—I didn't have it in me to go anywhere else that day. He brought two skirts from the room. I've never seen anything like them in my life.

"'Here's a little pillow also,' he said. 'Swaddle the child in it.' I couldn't believe my eyes. As soon as I put my poor little one into the warm water, it fell asleep. The gadjo knew more about swaddling than I did. I hadn't done it with any of my children. What on earth would I have used? Nothing, that's what. He loaded me up with food like a mule.

"'When are you coming again?'

"'When can I?' *phendyas.*

"'When you run out of things.'

"*Sun,* I thought, *then I could come back in the afternoon.* 'There are many of us, dear.'

"'Don't come tomorrow. I'm butchering a pig. But any time after that.'

"Who was in trouble now but Berbe? No longer did she carry home bagsful of food. Only sometimes did the gadjo let her in. She was beside herself, and Khulo kept at her constantly. I was glad that her good life was at an end. *Fuck you, Berbe,* I thought to myself, *now you'll find out what real poverty is.*

"Well, I sold the clothes I got from him and I sold the pillow—everything. How long did things last with us? Not long at all. I didn't dare go back; I was afraid. So I went begging again. Winter left us somehow and the hungry spring arrived instead. The countryside was becoming green again, and Zhelko kept pestering me with his sighs.

"If only I could put my hands on a *bogo,*[60] I figured, it could graze so well now. At the time, horses had been Zhelko's passion; now it's gambling. He knew about one that was cheap. He kept pestering me, but he was flat broke. So what could I do?

"I'd risk it once more, I thought, come what may. I went to the gadjo like someone terminally ill. It wasn't easy to pacify him; he didn't even want to let me in. I didn't take the baby with me; I said it was very sick, and if I couldn't pay the doctor, it would die.

"'I've been very sick,' I told him, 'although I've always wanted a man like you.' It took a while, but he became quite docile. He got excited again, and I let him paw me. After all, I figured it wouldn't get me pregnant.

"'I need ten pengős for the doctor, so I can get well as soon as possible.'

"'I'll give it to you,' he said.

"Who could have been happier than me? You've never seen as much meat and sausage as he packed on me. The old bitch Berbe guessed right that I was the one who'd muscled in on her territory, but she didn't dare say a word. When Zhelko bought that horse, Khulo was

---

[60] broken-down horse; a nag

green with envy. Christ has been in agony, but Berbe finished second. She kept going to the gadjo in vain; she couldn't even wheedle a couple of potatoes out of him. In the end, the beatings she got and her fury made her yell it out at me. *Bater!*[61]

"What more did these *chache Roma* need? We swore by heaven and earth, but they didn't believe us. My father-in-law never gave a flying shit about us.

"'You've brought shame on us,' he said. 'We will sit in judgment over you.'

"I'll never forget it to my dying day. They called together all the Gypsies at Easter. Those we'd saved from starvation passed sentence on us. Khulo cut Berbe's nose off. I was strung up by my feet and in front of all the Gypsies, Zhelko cut out my private part and threw it to the dogs. They spat at me before the whole wide world.

"That's why I hate them. That is the moment I swore that I would take vengeance on them using what they humiliated me with.

"Old Phumba often wanted to make peace with me. Sometimes he hated me; other times he too would have liked to violate Gypsy law for the disfigured hole even if it had cost him his head. But he was already doomed; all that lindralo drab had eaten away at his life. They all hanker after me, and I shit on their customs. I've humiliated them hundreds of times, and they've ripped one another up with razors, but they haven't dared say a thing to me."

I finally spoke. "How do you think all this will end?" I asked Balush. I really sympathized with her, and while she was telling me her story I felt a sort of regret. But still I couldn't forgive her.

"There won't be a thing. I'm not afraid of them, no, they're in my hands. Do you think Zhelko wouldn't like to snuff out my candle? I would have long been six feet under if he wasn't scared. But then his own brothers would cut him to shreds. Every single one of them has a kid with me-who'd look after them?"

The words stuck in my throat.

[61] So be it.

"I'm repaying them in kind. If they ate my bread, I can eat theirs."

"What will your daughter say when she finds out?"

"Vorzha? The same thing I said to her when she married a Gypsy to pay off one of her father's debts." She paused, and then continued, sighing. "Although she knew I was sleeping with him. . . . When they were little it was drummed into them to hate me for my whoring. They don't regard me as their mother—only what their Grandpa says counts."

"You don't love them, either." She didn't react.

I went on: "How long did Vorzha live with the Gypsy?"

"One night."

"Can you tell me that nothing happened between them?"

I couldn't see her face, but the laugh that accompanied her words was strangely forced.

"Do you think a dog lies down next to a piece of meat and doesn't bite into it?"

"That means you slept with the gadjo and deserved your punishment."

"Why did I deserve it?"

"Because you are a rotten stinking whore. If the punishment was severe then, you deserve it a hundred times more seriously today. It's a pity your maimed hole has become so dear to this phumba of a family; your blood has long been ripe for the dogs. I believe that all sinners get their punishment in due course."

She grabbed my leg when I wanted to leave.

"Don't tell Vorzha; I'd die of shame."

"If I knew that was true, I'd cry it from the rooftop, but your shame always ends up running down your legs."

"Wait, don't go yet!" Balush held onto my legs and started to search for my fly with an insane, suppressed laughter. She almost wrestled me to the ground before I could free one of my legs. I kicked, hard. I don't know where my foot struck her. But her groan came at practically the same moment as the thud of my boot. Whining painfully, she clung to me, wincing at every kick I then delivered—for I kept kicking—and then burst out into ever crazier laughter.

"Do you think you can get rid of me?" she laughed. "Whoever gets a taste of me can never forget it. You too are among the players now, and you'll fight with the others for the pot, but I won't show my hand until there are a hundred of you. I'd rather bear a child for each of you. In the meantime the dogs will gorge themselves on the blood you'll shed."

A cold shiver ran through me; it was the first time in my life I'd met a maniac! My God, I thought, I hadn't realized it until now. Balush's whole body was shaking, and I couldn't tell whether she was sobbing or laughing.

Her embrace slid down my leg, and she pressed her face to my boot. All I felt was her shoulders twitching; her voice sounded like the waning yowl of a dog until she fell silent with a last whine. She dug her head into the grass and loosened her grip, and when I pulled my leg out of her arms, she toppled over like an inert piece of stone. I stood there petrified, not knowing what to do.

"Are you sick?" I asked when I could no longer gather my thoughts.

"Why would I be sick?"

"You're right," I agreed. "Why would you be sick? I could be just as sick, except I can't diagnose it myself." I left her.

Inside, they had long forgotten that creatures like gendarmes existed. Why think about them, indeed? They'd come if they want to, and anyway, they are so unpredictable and grumpy, it's best not to think about them.

Vorzha rushed to meet me. We often do not notice our luck, although even a flickering light can make us happy. It can conceal the telltale signs on our faces that our conscience or some inner anxiety force on us.

"My mother?" she asked.

I was in no hurry to reply; I had to gain some time not to betray myself by my unease.

"Wasn't my mother with you?"

"Yes," I said, embarrassed. "I was with her." The ambiguity of my answer made me uneasy. Even though it was frank, I still feared that she would query my actions. She smiled like someone whose only joy is to know everything.

"I thought something was wrong," she said, clinging to me. "You don't know my mother yet."

"I know her. I am among those lucky people to whom she introduced herself." I couldn't keep secrets from Vorzha.

"Oh, that's nothing," she gestured disparagingly. "She's behaved pretty decently with you."

Never one to be overly curious, I have always given more credit to self-confessions, because there is more truth in them than whatever you can force out of others. I was now beset by such damn guilty feelings that they made me nauseous. Oh my God, what was that old slut making me do?! Pretending to be mad, she had outwitted everyone. I couldn't come to terms with my own thoughts. What was I to believe, her madness or her desire for revenge?

"Do you know that your mother is a rotten whore?" In my sudden fury I squeezed Vorzha's arm.

I hoped she would defend her mother's honor, if only by kicking up a feigned fuss. It would have been easier to reply to her lie with another lie. After all that happened, I no longer had the right to sleep with Vorzha, but if I left her without a word, I'd automatically make myself look suspicious. She shrugged her shoulders; she wasn't at all interested, and took it so much for granted that she didn't even bother to reply. I utterly lost my patience. If someone wants to provoke another, silence is just as annoying as talking back.

"Didn't you hear what I said? Your mother is a rotten whore!" I twisted Vorzha's arm.

"I heard it. And what do you consider yourself? Some sort of a saint?"

"No, I don't, but I'm disgusted by this whoring."

"Such a man shouldn't lie down next to a hole. You know, there's not a saint on earth who wouldn't fall for her. And a man doesn't have to be ashamed of anything."

"I didn't fall for her."

"Does it matter?" she asked quietly. "It's all the same to me whether she set you up or you fell for her. Balush's blood is hard to resist."

"How do you know that?"

"She says so. And also because she corrupts people. She's done it with my father, too. After so much disgrace, any other man would have buried her long ago, but as you see, she's still around. She's not afraid of anything or anyone. And you are gritting your teeth even though you're leaving tomorrow? Anyway, you're not at fault."

"How about you?" I asked.

"Me?" She looked at me. "I don't understand."

"Why did you sleep with your mother's man?"

"Ha!" cried Vorzha with a wry laugh. "You see, that's why they don't kill her. Mad people can say anything."

"Do you believe that what she says is true?"

"No. So far it hasn't been. And it hardly ever is true."

"Then why does she say it?"

"Because that's how her mind works."

"What she says about your siblings isn't true, either?" The blood rushed to her face, and she looked around.

"Did she tell you that, too?" Vorzha squeezed her eyes together and no longer looked as calm as before.

"Answer me! What is the truth?" She kept silent. Suddenly she jumped up, but Rilandri beat her to it and ran toward the door holding a blanket.

Vorzha pointed after her with a painful smile. Everyone around us fell silent. There was Balush, walking down the empty middle of the barn, her clothes crumpled under her arms, her naked body covered by disheveled hair that hung down to her buttocks.

"Can you see now what the truth is?" she sighed.

Rilandri wrapped the blanket around Balush while a group of women gathered around and slowly led her to the lair, as if she were a convalescing patient. Balush, in turn, asked the women how they were.

"I didn't like it in the hospital," she then mumbled out of the blue. "They treat people like dogs there. But thanks to my dear Lord, luckily the doctors managed to sew it back. I can tell you, though, that as long as I live, I'll never let Zhelko near me; I'd rather be the world's greatest whore."

"There won't be any more trouble now," said one of the women, seeking to comfort her. "Get some rest, Balush. It's happened to other women too, you know. Men are all like that."

They expressed the familiar words that they had repeated a hundred times, a thousand times, with as much regretful compassion as if the incident had happened only yesterday.

Vorzha sat wordlessly next to me rather than going to tend to her mother. She gazed before her; if I'd had the strength just then, I would have been able to read her mind. Rilandri sat next to us and broke our silence.

"That's what she does if something disturbs her. To hell with that rotten drink, she should never touch it."

"She'll sleep it off," Vorzha said without empathy. She stood up and left us.

"Will you take her with you?" Rilandri asked me, pointing at Vorzha.

"No."

"She's a good girl. She hasn't inherited her mother's blood. Don't you love her?"

I didn't want to lie; I kept quiet instead. That said, had I asked myself the same question that had just been posed to me, I wouldn't have been able to reply. Somehow there hadn't been enough time for such thoughts to ripen in me. I'm not well versed in such matters, but I don't think that desire is the same as love.

"Why are they after you?"

"Because."

She looked at her hand. The black writing was still intact on it. She smiled.

"I'll have it etched with a needle in the morning."

Rilandri looked at me for quite a while. Her face was smiling, but her eyes spoke of something else.

"Don't go home—go to my brothers and sisters. They'll welcome you, and no one will be looking for you there. How old is your brother?"

I shrugged off her question. Once again her inquisitive nature found me in a bad mood. This time not only wasn't she furious, she even seemed to enjoy it.

Vorzha returned, and Rilandri pretended to be in a hurry.

"I'll go with you tomorrow," she told me in a muffled voice.

"Why?"

"Because." She left us.

I realized now what made her so curious. She was interested in my brother. *Well, you'd be good for Bada,* I mused. I was somewhat cheered by the thought. Vorzha however, remained in a bad mood. It would have been good to comfort her with something, to tell her about the incident, exactly how it had happened; to whitewash my integrity, to blame Balush for everything; to explain how she'd taken advantage of the darkness, my inexperience, my fiery blood, even the hunted man's fretfulness for every free moment, his flight from fear and worry.

This epitome of leave-taking might have lasted for minutes or hours, since we could have held tight to memories of joy and everything else that fits into the hideous, disgusting gut of this black world. I wondered to what extent it would have comforted Vorzha if all the pain and loathing that she felt toward us was directed only toward her mother.

I struggled to think with hatred of Balush, whose confusion had ended with convulsive unconsciousness. She was sleeping now, her face deathly pale, her naked body clumsily covered by the clothes that had been thrown over her; her disheveled hair still gave the impression of a madwoman. Was I supposed to hate her? Why? What had she done to harm me? Grandpa slunk toward us, sat down on the edge of the manger, and kept quiet for a while.

"Vorzha, get the kids' beds ready for the night!" He waved a hand toward Balush. "That's what she's like. I noticed it on her already at the shop. That's what her mother used to do sometimes, may she rest in peace. She saw all sorts of weird things, and then she threw all her clothes off and ran around stark naked, wailing."

I'd heard about old Vorzha—Balush's mother, that is. That's what they said about her. Except that nobody knew why she did it. It was rumored that someone had put a curse on her.

"Grandpa, may all your children die if you don't answer me truthfully."

"Bater, son, go ahead."

"Do you believe that old Vorzha was cursed?"

"No," he said emphatically. "Her husband buried her alive because of her whoring; her children dug her out. That's when she went insane."

Both of us thought of Balush. He gave her a few furtive looks with his shadowed eyes while mumbling something from between his trembling lips. Then his glance turned to the multitude of children. Years seemed to flash before his watery eyes—irretrievable, incomparable years.

"You'd better go to bed too; it's late." Grandpa struggled to his feet, his body bent over.

Vorzha took a long time getting things set for the children; most of them had to be put under the covers fully dressed and half asleep.

The barn sunk into a single muffled snore; here and there lovers' arguments disturbed the quiet monotony, until they too became seamlessly drowned into sighs and moans.

The skinny little girl had moved to where the Mutos had been. She perched with her feet tucked under her the way crows do, digging into her hair with her fingers, and letting her flashing eyes dwell on us. She was only roused from her thoughts when Rilandri snapped at her:

"Why the hell aren't you asleep yet?"

"She needs a man," Vorzha remarked softly. "She was rutting after you all evening, as if her panties were on fire."

I knew she was right, yet I was still surprised how clued in she was about events. The grimaces with which she accompanied her remarks seemed affected. Rather than react, I just stared ahead rigidly.

"What are you thinking of?" Vorzha asked me in a changed voice.

"Nothing." I evaded her question indifferently. In fact, I was mulling over where she had picked up on all that information. She must have guessed what was going on in my head.

Vorzha looked at me up and down; interesting thoughts must have crossed her mind. Then she smiled and continued to arrange our bed of straw.

"You can get undressed," Vorzha muttered over the rustle of the straw. Maybe she didn't mean it sarcastically, yet I felt as if she had dug her nails into my heart.

My fingers clung desperately to the edge of the manger. *Please, not now,* I implored the invisible omnipotent being, *for once let me overcome my rage; I don't want any more trouble.* I tried with deep breaths to get rid of the cramps clogging my chest.

Vorzha bent toward me; her face turned ashen. Words are not always necessary to express feelings; our impulses settle candidly onto our faces when they flog our souls.

As I went about throwing off my clothes, which had been acquired by bull money, I chewed my lips until they were bleeding. So that was how life conducted its business. It bought and sold good luck, never asking what deal we wanted.

Regretting everything, I put on my rank-smelling trousers, draped Juli Gargya's tattered old sack over my shoulders as a makeshift shirt, and left Vorzha behind in the barn.

The night was still quiet, its stars blinking sleepily like so many distant lanterns whose countless multitudes gave the August sky a pale, utterly silent sheen. My stack of straw lay disheveled and bereft of human company beside me; at least I wasn't haunted in it by the desire to love. It rustled as I dug myself into its fieldbug-scented warmth, wishing I could submerge myself into darkest ignorance for a respite from my perpetually churning thoughts.

Before I drifted off to sleep, a thin hand crept under my neck, entwined my body with the flexibility of a snake and, shivering, held my head to her loudly hammering heart.

Let your blood kill you, I thought. "So that is why you stayed up all night: to wait for an opportunity! Vorzha was right when she said your panties were on fire." The strong odor of onions reeked from her smoke-smelling hair. She covered my naked body with her thin frame, as if her only purpose were to protect me from the cool dew. She didn't say a word yet, just held me tight, and the air from her thin body rushed into my ears as she burrowed under my straw blanket with the agility of a worm.

While she was fidgeting, I wondered whether I wanted this girl—or was it the devil who threw her at me? I kept quiet and waited patiently for matters to develop.

"Vorzha has already gone to bed," she whispered, as if to dispel my fear.

"Why aren't you asleep?"

"I can't sleep," she said, heaving a deep sigh.

"It's high time, though. And now that you're here, stop that squirming!"

"Are you leaving in the morning?" she asked.

"Yes."

"'I'm going with you. I'm as good as Vorzha, only she is fatter. I love you more. Do you think I couldn't have pretty dresses if I wanted to? She has them not because she's so clever, you know; her father bought them for her. I don't have anyone!" She commiserated with herself.

"You sure don't have a thing, not even any hair down there." She hissed as I pulled at her peach fuzz.

"It'll grow out. Last year I didn't even have that much. You know, Rilandri told me she was leaving with you, too; she hates this family."

"Why would she come along?"

"She'll marry your brother."

"First of all, I have no brother; second, keep quiet or I'll send you packing!"

"You'll be careful with me, won't you?"

"Why should I have to be careful with you?"

"Well, when you do it with me."

"Absolutely not. Get away from me!" I tried to pry her off, but she stuck to me like a leech.

"Don't send me away, please let me sleep with you!"

"Go away, I don't want to be badmouthed by the Gypsies."

"I won't tell anyone, I promise. Do it, please! I swear on my mother's life that afterward I'll leave you in peace and go back to the barn."

"You're going back anyway. I'm not interested in your pleading." She pretended to cry, but I felt that it was all just mischief. She couldn't squeeze a single tear out of her eyes and just sniffled.

"You'd better stop it!" I snapped.

"Then why did you get me all excited?"

"How on earth did I get you excited?" I wanted to stay serious at all costs, thinking it would be easier that way to scare her off. I didn't succeed. She was so ridiculously childish that not a single word of hers could be taken seriously.

"Is that why your tears are falling from down there?" I asked.

"Are you making fun of me?" she asked irritably. "Do you think that just because my pubic hair isn't an inch long, I'm still a child?" She angrily peeled her tight bodice off one shoulder. "Why, isn't this as good as Vorzha's?" She pushed her tiny breast under my nose. It had a bit of an unwashed smell, but also some sort of fragrance that made my mouth water even though I tried to resist.

"Take it in your mouth a little!" she started pleading again.

"What do you want from me, you little whore?" I couldn't continue; it was hard enough to take a breath.

"You'll be careful, won't you?"

Meanwhile the nest had completely engulfed us. She kept on pleading with me even after my willpower abandoned me and I'd fulfilled her desire.

"I love you more than Vorzha and will never leave you while I'm alive."

I thought to myself: *That's all I need, to be stuck with you for good.* But I said only: "How do you know that Vorzha doesn't love me anymore?"

"She said that she too wanted to go with you, but after what you did with Balush, she no longer wants to. I even told her that the old bitch sneaked up on you and that you kicked her for it good, and that even if someone killed her, she'd still remain a whore. Oh, Vorzha says she still loves you, but I don't believe it. She knows what her mother is like, so why does she have to make such a big to-do about it?"

"Where do you know all this from?" I asked.

But she fell silent, as if regretting that she had given so much away.

"Talk to me, or I'll break your bones!"

"Didn't Vorzha tell you?"

"What should she have told me? That you were tailing me?"

"Yes," she answered bluntly.

"When did you come there?"

"You were still talking to the gendarmes."

"Then it was *you* who told Vorzha?"

"Yes."

"Well, now I'll really take you with me; I'll bury you somewhere on the way."

"I told her it wasn't your fault, that you thought . . ."

"Shut your mouth, and get out of here!" I threw her out of my nest by her hair.

Yuck, what a swamp I'd gotten myself into. I ran away from my stack of straw as fast as possible. But then I had to go back, as I'd left my bag there. Finally, a bit more composed, I began to head toward the woods.

Dawn broke suddenly along the way. The farmhands on top of the steaming dung heap were scratching themselves with sleepy yawns. The estate started to bustle; googly-eyed servants and day laborers lined up in front of the steward's quarters. I didn't stand out from the others; some were even more tattered-looking than I. True, I was wearing hardly anything; the only thing that covered my body were my pants. At least the weather was still good.

Approaching the edge of the forest, I waded through a thick carpet of grass that the morning's large dewdrops had flattened down. By the time I rolled up my pants legs they were sopping wet; somehow I'd forgotten that there would be dew. Musingly I looked down at my feet; the moisture had soaked the filth out from its folds. Wouldn't it be nice to always have such clean feet?

So I'd seduced her! What a cunning little slut! How old could she have been? Thirteen? Fourteen?

Summer would soon be over, and the time of starvation would return. This world would shrink even more; there wouldn't be any place or opportunity for mating, for mere looks to awaken desire. If only there could be an eternal spring with neverending summers, then perhaps there would be more prospects for life and more room in our minds to fill up with other thoughts.

For a long time I wandered around the edge of the forest. I knew Bada couldn't have arrived yet, but was still disappointed. I didn't even dare to think what would happen to me if he got into trouble. The world might have been my oyster, but I couldn't help feeling sorry for myself; as I considered my appearance, all my hopes collapsed.

I had to resign myself to the fact that if Bada was lost, so was I. Ever since we'd separated, I'd given him hardly a thought, and then only when I was angry and wanted to escape from my surroundings. I'd left Vorzha without a goodbye. That is how it had to be. Nor had I said goodbye to my own mother when I came here, after all.

Our joy would be all the greater when we met, Bada and I. *If* we were to meet!

VI

NO ONE HAD BEEN NEAR THE CORDWOOD SINCE. The pile of ashes left over from our fire stood out between the two poles, and a creature of some sort had made a nest from the bustard feathers. I thought of Juli Gargya with heartfelt gratitude; were it not for her patched-up sack, which sufficed for a shirt, the mosquitoes would be feasting on me.

What about the money? I felt a twinge of conscience. I fidgeted for a long time on the bright side of things until I managed to digest my shame. I had bought a mare replete with foals, but the mother was more in heat than her filly. Now I had neither money nor principles left. How did Bada benefit? It was his money I'd wasted.

Two nights, three women. I was only sorry that I hadn't given that bald-assed girl a good and proper beating. She had the gall to lie down next to me. *Let me just get my hands on her once more,* I now thought to myself, *and I swear her skin won't even be fit for a sieve.* I don't know why, but I felt I had to blame someone—her or someone else, as long as I could forget about myself, who was just as much a part of it all as were they.

Only a few weeks earlier we'd played make-believe circus like carefree children. The whip, spun from rags, had urged my horses to a fierce canter. They were decorated with colored paper ribbons, stomping about in the invisible arena with heads held proudly aloft, and they provided their own music for their dances. Their tiny breasts took on the color of the moist crepe-paper bows, and I dried off their sweat-beaded bodies with the hem of their long shirts without my blood flaring up at the sight of their pubescent fuzz.

I'd still been a child. A child who'd cuddled the girls all in good fun and, if I did have any vague thoughts of something more when the warmth of their bodies came into contact with mine, well, those thoughts had not been coupled with courage.

Yes, I had imperceptibly crossed the threshold of adulthood without having felt even a spark of desire to do so. Something kindled the great fire in me and burned everything around me to dust. What caused me to be thrilled that dawn, when Vorzha offered herself? Did she perhaps do it for me? Now I know why we never talked about love. The sudden desire that captivated us was looking only for gratification.

Men are strange; they are happy if women are willing to sleep with them, and yet none give a thought to the fact that women do so not as a favor. They are often capable of self-denial in the spirit of love just to make the other one happy. Why?

There was no time left for a reply. The rustling of the forest forced itself behind my eyelashes, where my thoughts turned into tangled dreams. I do not remember them; I slept through the entire morning without waking.

It is said that if someone has more than his fill, he'll have bad dreams. So far I haven't had the opportunity to attest to this, but I can tell you though that the hungrily growling stomach is just as vindictive.

Thin threads of saliva hung from the corners of my mouth; an aroma of cooking meat was in the air. I felt like I was awake: I heard the cawing of the crows; the soft, dignified rustle of the trees; and all that I would have to do was to open my eyes and turn on my back for the dream's appetizing game to fade away. But it didn't. Happy female giggles suggested that something *was* really cooking nearby. No longer did I try to delude myself that it was all a dream. Suddenly such anxiety came over me that it would have shaken me out of even the deepest sleep.

Cautiously I circled the stack of cordwood. What I saw made me rejoice: in place of the pile of ash a fire was blazing, and there was Bada, lying down, leaning on one elbow like some sort of stud farmer after a hard day's work, his brown fingers playfully fiddling among the fluff of his thick, sheepskin coat. His unusually clean face bore a wide grin as he eyed Rilandri, who stared back blankly. His snow-white shirt, gleaming from under the fancy buttons of his waistcoat, lent his black face a certain glow; only his eyes suggested weariness as they kept drooping shut, and yet his porcelain-white teeth kept flashing.

Rilandri sat with her back to me, but judging by her movements, it seemed she hadn't come in vain. I could have imagined them as a married couple if I hadn't then met with Balush's lunatic eyes. At first she pretended not to notice me, carefully glancing at Bada and Rilandri, and then, circling the cordwood, she stationed herself behind me.

"Wait!" she whispered. "Your brother has come to take you home."

"Yes?" I asked, feigning surprise.

"Yes. Except that the gendarmes searched through the whole farm looking for you."

"Have you told my brother?"

"No. He would fall straight into the hands of the gendarmes right along with you."

"Rilandri?"

"She doesn't know."

"How did you know I was here?"

"Your little whore brought me here," she said with ringing irony. I didn't get angry at what she said, and just waited to see what she was driving at.

I was convinced that what Balush had said so far was a lie.

"Your brother is a handsome man," said Balush. "He says you brought the horse registrations and twenty pengős with you." I figured Bada had dished them up some story. Balush looked at me for a long while, a strange smile in her eyes. I wasn't sure whether it was suspicion or gloating that it mirrored.

"You are really something," Balush chuckled. "It seems you were born a man, but if you won't have the brains to go with it," she added in a more serious tone, "you'll wither away in jail." She leered at me in the same lecherous way as yesterday at the grocer. She pulled a handful of paper money from her *posoti*.[62]

"The money you gave Zhelko was lucky. Go on; return the money and the horse registrations to your brother!" With that, Balush handed me two ten-pengö bills. "If you don't want to fall into the hands of the gendarmes, then we can have a drink tomorrow morning in Nagyvárad." After a pause to let the thought of my crossing the Romanian border sink in, she added, magnanimously, "Here's another ten. Let your brother have a drink, too."

A pity that Rilandri is here, I thought, *I would let Bada have a go at you and then I'd string you naked to a tree and let the mosquitoes feast on you.*

"Don't hesitate. It's for your own good. But if you want to go, I won't hold you back. You'll see; you'll be the loser." I could feel the threat behind her words.

"Is Vorzha coming, too?" I asked.

"Vorzha is still young; she'll find herself as many men as she wants."

Apparently I'd miscalculated when I tried to appeal to Balush's feelings. She had already proved on several occasions that only one feeling dominated her, and that she was unwilling to share it with anyone. I stuffed the money into my pocket.

"Alright," I said. "When do we leave?" She looked at me, tears came to her eyes, and she awkwardly embraced me. She pressed herself to me in silence and fixed her eyes on mine, straining to stop her tears.

"You won't regret it," she whispered, overcome by emotion.

"How much money did Zhelko win?"

"Shh!" she silenced me, her index finger over her mouth. Then she looked around and crouched down on the bag.

"Come on, count it! He may be a stinking rotten mustache bug, but he was right; you gave him lucky money. He won everything from everybody. And I took every last bit of it out of his pocket. It's the first

---

[62] pocket

time in his life that he was lucky at cards, but he won't get anything out of it."

I felt the cordwood rustle. Balush, preoccupied with her revenge against Zhelko, was feverishly stroking the crumpled paper money.

"Count it!" She urged me. The very thought made me sweat, too, and it changed my thinking in no time. I'd decided not to argue with her; let her be happy, I would walk out on her at the first opportunity anyhow. As for the gendarme story, I didn't believe it; she had only made it up to intimidate me and, as it later turned out, it wasn't true.

The money, however, completely overwhelmed me, and I kept wondering what it would cost me to get hold of it. I didn't want it together with her, but I would be a fool not to seize the opportunity. Anyway, as far as that was concerned, I had a right to it. Balush had played foul from the very first; why should I be fair to her?

Had she offered that much money the night before and only then herself, I swear I would have accepted neither the money nor her. But she had deceived me, and now at least we could settle our mutual debts. The only gratitude I might owe her was for having freed me from further exile. If Kurucho saw this, he'd even let his head be chopped off. Fortunately, there was still time to arrange matters.

"How much?" she asked.

I was so overcome that I wasn't able to answer her immediately. I had to count again, because in my mind I had been counting the days.

"Two hundred and thirty pengős."

"Is that a lot of money?" she inquired.

"Well, it's a neat little sum." I feigned indifference.

"There's plenty of loose change, too," she said, shaking her posoti. "Will you have a look at it?"

"Yes." I said curtly. I really only looked at it as she handed it to me. I pocketed it without counting. We stared at each other for a long time without saying a word. I didn't want to hide my own intentions, and as for her, no matter how she tried to hide it, her face spoke of desperation. Out of sheer curiosity I would have been glad to know just what was going on inside her. Otherwise, I couldn't have cared less. As regarded the fate of the money, I had made up my mind irrevocably; at what price, that depended on her.

It wasn't difficult to fathom from Balush's astonished look that she had changed her mind about me. She didn't say so, though it seemed she no longer regarded me as an innocent child who could easily be duped by a bit of cunning, but instead as a bloody-handed rogue. I too had come to some conclusions. I knew that Balush was cunning, not overburdened with scruples, lied left and right, and that every bad trait vengeance can muster was present in her. I felt sincere gratitude for her when I experienced the opposite. I certainly didn't want to make matters worse, but I could easily imagine that she could force me to do so.

"Alright," she said. "It's yours, you deserve it." Her words sounded reassuring, but her unconditional agreement seemed too simple. Could it have been fear that forced her to relent?

"Did you tell the truth?" I asked, stepping closer to her. I pulled her horsetail-size hair out of her kerchief, and the blood in her thick jugular began to throb faster as I stroked her goose-bumped neck.

"I'll stay here until you've left," she said, her voice trembling, "but if you want to . . ." She shrugged. "You already wanted to do it last night."

"You wanted to flee with me? Where could I take you?"

"Even prison is better than rotting with these people. Or kill me!"

"I don't need your life, or you. I want the money."

The harshness of my voice surprised even me and made me swallow the rest of my words. Balush just stared ahead without surprise or sense until the light broke in her eyes. I watched her for a long time as her face turned paler by the second, waiting to see when she would begin her whining. My fingers trembled nervously on the corner of her shawl.

"It doesn't matter," she muttered to herself. "My dear God—let me kiss his holy precious red blood—will help me, and I'll get well again." In my surprise I got hold of her shoulder and drew her closer to me. The world became blurred in her eyes, she unbuttoned her blouse from top to bottom in slow motion, her head started lolling, her eyes closed, and I could no longer understand a single word of her moaning.

Startled, I stepped back and looked at her, perplexed. Her sluggish fingers were trying to undo her skirt, and I only just managed to catch her before she would have fallen face first into the sharp-ended twigs of the cordwood. By the time I lay her down, she was fast asleep. I felt my face blushing; I began to feel ashamed by her turn for the worse. Perhaps the poor wretch was in fact in a more desperate situation than me.

How many times could Balush have set out on her escape, over and over again, never realizing that it was not only the ship that was sinking, but the water as well. She thought that if she could only get out of here, she could get to shore. But then, who doesn't believe that? Rilandri was looking at opportunities in the distance, waiting for help from somewhere, while the black-eyed girl gave away her virginity impatiently; she wanted admission to a tomorrow, because here everything belonged to the past, even what had yet to be born.

Balush's face looked pale, and her deeply sunken eyes and loose jaw gave the impression of death. The past few minutes' crazy thoughts drifted through my mind. Dear God! I raised my hands to my face: was I the one who was insane? I couldn't remember. The locks of hair stuck to Balush's sweaty neck looked like black bruises inflicted by cruel hands. I felt nauseous.

"What have you done?" Bada asked in a hushed voice as he stepped out from behind the stack. He looked anxiously at me and then at the woman lying on the ground. I clung desperately to the protruding dry twigs; I felt like I was about to faint.

Bada must have seen the protest on my face; he asked no questions, but instead just motioned me to silence with his eyes and, ear pressed to Balush's chest, listened for a long time. Eventually he got up, evidently relieved.

"She's alive," he said firmly. "But if you ever have similar thoughts, forget about Gypsy women, and be sure there are no witnesses."

Bada couldn't have guessed my thoughts. The earlier panic still lingered in his smile, which he tried to hide as he chastely rearranged Balush's skirt that had ridden right up to her groin. Then he cast me a bemused expression. The woman's breast now undulated regularly and, as the minutes went by, her face eventually regained its brown tone.

"You sure took care of this one," he nodded curtly with more recognition than reproach. I noted with a smile that his brainpower would never rise higher than the ass of the woman lying here.

"For your information, she's my mother-in-law."

"So what?" he said with a wide-eyed stare.

"What do you mean? You can see she's sleeping!"

Frowning, he started to shake his head.

"I don't know if I'm the fool, or you. When I arrived, this woman sat next to you and said *you* were sleeping. The other gal welcomed me as if she'd known me for God knows how long. Maybe the next minute I'm going to wake up. It would be high time to find out what's real and what isn't."

"Did you manage to bring horses?"

"Well, if all this isn't a dream, then yes."

"I don't think we're both dreaming the same dream. But you've got to believe me that this outfit suits you very well. You stole that, too?"

"Not intentionally," he answered, fingering his vest. "I found it in the saddlebag, but didn't feel like taking it back."

"What are the horses like?"

"Let's just say they could be better," he said modestly, "if we didn't have to stick to the information in their registration booklets." Gesturing toward Balush, Bada whispered, "Is she sick?"

I replied in the affirmative.

"Too bad."

It seemed as if there was an apologetic look in his eyes. Perhaps in another's case it wouldn't have been worthy of attention, but this look appeared so unlike Bada that it piqued my curiosity. He bent down, gently wiped Balush's sweaty face, looked at her naked breasts for a long time, and then, blushing, buttoned up her blouse.

Bada didn't take his glace off the woman, even when he scrambled to his feet. He took a few steps back to take better stock of her, and then turned to me.

"She's a very beautiful woman," he sighed. "The other one's eyes are too large. It's not such a good thing if a woman knows she is beautiful. She devours a man with her eyes like bottomless pits, and then others, because she can devour hundreds at a time. Such a woman is always available."

"This one isn't any better than Rilandri."

"Is she called Rilandri?" he rolled his eyes. "Phew, what a smelly name!"

"You think this one doesn't sell herself? Maybe she no longer devours hundreds with her eyes, but she sure has devoured thousands with her ass."

"She would make a good wife now just because she has done her thing, like a hot-blooded horse, and now she needs a man who has the whip hand. Believe me, there's nothing more grateful than an old horse. This is the type of woman I always preferred. You couldn't pick a better one from a stud farm."

To hell with you and your old horse, I thought. *Who cares? But the money! If you so much as mention that you want to marry her, Balush won't play hard to get for long, and then she'll want the money back.*

The situation had changed from one minute to the next. I couldn't make up my mind. So far, I only had to steal from Balush, but if he teamed up with her, then it would be a matter of cheating both of them. Whichever way I looked at it, Bada had put a spoke in my wheel. I tried to get hold of myself; I couldn't be hasty: I had three hundred pengős in my pocket. I knew I was unlikely to be so lucky ever again in my life, nor have such a chance. Being all wound up wouldn't help me when I'd have to run. And if I didn't grab this opportunity, I would have to run until my feet wore out.

I watched Balush with disgust; there was only enough of a shadow next to the stack of cordwood to cover her face. She was still sleeping happily, moving her legs until her dress slid up again. Bada sat down on a hollow tree-stump, peering intently at the space between her legs.

It didn't surprise me. Her shapely thighs, which were almost as white as snow, gleamed seductively in the sunlight. I smiled. Many a time have I also played the role of the cat. What would I not have given, had the skirt slipped up another inch? Compared to their brown, tanned faces, their thighs, forever kept in the shade, always elicited some excitement.

Yesterday, even the old Gypsy's eyes flashed with the Devil's fire, though it certainly wasn't the first time he'd seen Balush's thighs. The whole family was crazy for her. *Damn her!* I thought. *Even when asleep she makes people lose control.* I felt a real urge to belt her with a twig. Now I understood why Bada wanted to give the other up. Less than an hour ago he'd looked into Rilandri's eyes as if into a mirror, but as soon as he saw this one, he wanted her instead.

My mind began to clear. What could he have seen before stepping over here? Nothing. I was sure that he hadn't *seen* a thing. Then again, the stack of cordwood had rustled twice. The first time Balush had been only whispering, the second time we were already counting the money on top of the bag. The rascal had been spying on us! Spying or listening. Yes, he heard something. He'd heard Balush. "You already wanted to do it last night," that's what she'd said. *Aha,* I thought, *so that's when you fell for the woman. If you didn't, I will. But just you wait!* He kept looking at her so intently that he hardly blinked, and only frowned when I knelt beside Balush and began to stroke her.

"What are you doing, man?" he asked hoarsely.

"She's hot. She is boiling in that skirt. How stupid of me not to have uncovered her sooner!" I started to wipe Balush's belly while baby-talking to her. "There, there, you'll cool off in no time."

"She's your mother-in-law!" Bada shouted jealously.

"So what?" I looked at him impassively. "God doesn't look under skirts. And if he does," I said, patting her thighs, "he sure can look at this one."

Bada was petrified; I thought he would fall off the stump. His lips moved for a long time before he managed to utter something intelligible.

"Did you rape her?"

"Me? On the contrary. She raped me, last night. But if you want her, I'll give her to you."

"To *meee?*" he asked. He jumped up suddenly, as if overcome by nausea, and ran away.

I used Balush's colorful shawl to improvise a little tent over her head. *Keep on sleeping, sooner or later the mosquitoes will wake you up.*

I went over to Bada, who was already smiling again. He poked at the fire, shaking his head; he couldn't get over things.

"It's a strange world. A man can't get up early enough without someone getting in first. Well, never mind! Come, let's eat."

He took the sooty pot and placed it between us on the sheepskin coat. As quickly as I had lost my appetite, it returned just as fast. I looked to see what was in the pot and chewed hard on whatever I came across unseen; and whatever my teeth couldn't cope with, I threw away.

"The big-eyed gal cooks well, doesn't she?"

"Where is she?" I could barely ask, my mouth was so full.

"She'll come back."

Unfortunately, she didn't come; *they* came. She brought along her skinny little sister, who didn't even say "boo," but went straight into a tirade.

"Look what your rotten old whore did to me! No one wants her anymore. The only time she gets someone is if she rapes him. Shame on the bitch! She stole the man from her own daughter. May her stinking flesh rot from her bones! Look what she did to me!" Her hair looked like a haystack. "She pulled me up and down by my hair because I live with you. All she wants is a young man. You've done it with her already, so what does she want? May you pull her insides out!"

Bada watched, wiping his eyes with his fists as if he didn't believe for a minute that he was awake. Rilandri whispered something to him, and they disappeared into the woods. The girl gestured wildly a good ten feet away from me, ranting incessantly. I tried hard to force a friendlier smile onto my face to lure her closer. All my efforts were in vain. Every time I beckoned, she just shook her head. No, not for all the world; she just kept on without letting up.

Yet somehow I felt as if she were coming closer and closer to me.

Come on, another two steps. . . . I tried to mesmerize her as much as my weakened willpower would let me. *If I can catch you, there won't be a single hair left on your head!*

What a little grub! She'd dared to follow me! "I live with you," she'd said! And not just any old way, but so loud that she woke up all the crows in the woods. How did she manage to outshout them? She hadn't taken a single breath since arriving. Meanwhile she kept alert like a farmyard fowl, strictly keeping her distance to avoid getting dangerously close to me. I was fuming, and perhaps only my youth saved me from having a stroke.

She stood there lopsided, one leg forward like a sprinter, her right hand leaning on her knee so she could hightail it at any moment.

I could no longer follow what she was saying. It didn't make any difference, anyway. Had I moved, she would have disappeared like the wind. I rather listened to the startled squawks of the kestrels circling above the top of the forest, until she forcefully admonished me:

"Do you understand!" she shouted. "If you don't do away with even those big tits of hers, I'll have you put in irons."

How the hell hadn't I noticed the sooty pot before? Why, it had been right in front of me the whole time. The odd thing was that she too discovered it at the same time. But I beat her to it by a second.

A loud thump, a brief moment of silence, and then a mighty holler fit to waken the dead.

The pot hit her exactly where I would have liked to kick her all this time. If I was ever ashamed of anything in my life, I outdid myself now.

There wasn't even as much hair on this girl as on a felt ball. The repulsive sight of her skinny legs kicking skyward appeased my accumulated desire for brawling.

Jeez, what the hell have I let myself in for! Balush told the truth even though she didn't believe it at the time, but now I'd proved it: *If a dog lies down next to me. . . . My God! What had she put into my mouth? There's not enough meat on it to satisfy an old crow.* Since I hadn't taken the trouble at dawn, I was now itching to have a look at it, if only to soothe my conscience. Unfortunately, this desire was not fulfilled. No sooner had I taken a step than she, that skinny girl, was already shouting anew from behind a bush.

"Just you wait! May they sweep your bones right out of prison! Zhelko and the others will smash your head to pieces! This way, Zhelko, here's that killer! He broke my bones. Murderer, murderer!"

Nothing is as nerve-racking as when we are completely powerless against something. There she was, taunting me from behind the bush, and I couldn't do anything about it. I couldn't shut my ears; I couldn't stare at the birds circling above the forest. The things she'd said about Balush, she now repeated with minor changes.

"Hahaha!" came her satanic laughter from the bush. "This time you won't get away; Balush is bringing the men. I don't care that you've put me to shame; at least I'll see how they'll bash out your brains."

I instinctively ran behind the stack of cordwood, but found only Balush's shawl there. The girl's shouting made me have serious misgivings; this crow wasn't cawing for no reason.

"You're scared now, aren't you?" she started again when she saw me.

"You were after your mother-in-law? Come on, Zhelko. They're coming. They'll drink your blood any minute now. That's what you deserve! You raped the poor Gypsy woman even though she is your mother-in-law; you've ruined her. I saw it with my own two eyes when you did it; she begged you in vain, and you had no pity for her."

This was a bit harder to swallow than what I was ready for. I flung the pot in the direction of the sound. It rattled a little while longer, the bush moved, then all was quiet, and all that could be heard was the crackling of the fallen dry twigs.

May the rot eat up that little slut. A minute ago she was still vilifying Balush, and now she wants to shove it all on me.

I didn't have much time left to wonder over the girl's duplicity. The remote sound of breaking twigs was coming closer and louder as if a whole herd of wild boar was clomping toward me. My heart was beating in my throat as I turned around. It was Rilandri coming out of the bushes.

"Come on!" she said, hurriedly picking up Bada's sheepskin coat. I followed her without a word. The approaching noise convinced me that the girl was not lying, and now it seemed that Rilandri had also known about it. That was probably what she was whispering about to Bada.

It seemed a long way; I ran after Rilandri, hiding between the bushes as I went. Whenever her brightly colored skirt got caught in them, I could see her brown thighs, but that was the last thing on my mind. I simply didn't have any thoughts at all. The fact that I was running away from something had not filtered through to my consciousness yet. No, I just followed the fluttering skirt that proceeded with firm resolve toward the interior of the forest until Bada stepped out from behind a tree with a freshly cut cudgel.

"What's up?" he inquired.

"They're there already," Rilandri panted.

"How many?"

"The whole lot of them." Bada started off, a grin on his face. His presence reassured me, and my disjointed thoughts began slowly to coalesce and make sense. It would have been futile to deny that I was afraid. I was afraid, because Zhelko didn't want the truth; he wanted revenge. Balush's revenge.

Clinging to Bada's arms, Rilandri hid under the bushes; who knows what she would say if they suddenly surprised us. I kept following them for a little while longer, but then, fearing for my half-naked body being constantly hit by the rebounding twigs, I sought for spots where the bushes were less dense.

We are fleeing again. *Balush, Balush, you must be favored by the gods. It seems that the vengeance you swore is effective. Whoever gets mixed up with this phumba of a family has to flee from his own shame or they kill him. Running, running away like a coward, because where there are more sticks, there is more truth. What a shame! The progeny of the clan of Peter is on the run to save his skin.*

It's easy to be brave when there is no danger, but if one's back is to the wall, discretion is the better part of valor.

I stepped out of the shadows of the forest. Dilapidated wildlife-feeding sheds were lined up on one side of the sunlit clearing. Bada was already waiting for me there with Rilandri clinging to his arm with unshakable affection. In the world of green grass and trees, her light blue eyes seemed like dull gray sadness next to Bada's grinning face.

"You look like you're in a bad mood, hey!" he rebuked me. "Don't tell me you're scared?"

"Yes," I said honestly.

The grin vanished from his face at my brief statement. He expected something different. He thought I would protest tooth and nail. That's the way it's done. To admit cowardice is as bad as lying. Neither is appreciated.

"Then whadaya say we run," he said, and with that he angrily threw the stick to the ground. One couldn't make out from his words whether he was posing a question or recommending a course of action. What was obvious, though, was that he certainly didn't want to do it. Rilandri stuck to him anxiously, probably sensing something from his shuddering, betrayed by his sternly questioning gaze.

There was no need to introduce Bada to me. I knew his movements, his snuffling, and often also his thoughts. He could play very well, but there was an inner feeling in him that would be hard to define. If it got the upper hand, he would lose his capacity for play. *Run, if nothing else helps; steal, cheat, deceive your father, deceive your mother. Do all this and you increase your prestige; they'll say you're resourceful, that you are a man. But they'll believe you to be clever only if you show yourself to be strong and brave.* He didn't say so now. He stood, staring ahead, a mixture of desire and disdain in his eyes.

Without a word I picked up the stick, spun it around like I had seen it done so often, and swished it into an elderberry bush, where, buzzing and spinning, the leaves flew off. I cut and chopped, until it turned into a bare, erect stake.

"Will there be *maripe*?"[63] Bada asked, overjoyed.

"There will." I gave a parting swish to the remains of the stripped bush. He shook Rilandri off and disappeared behind the rickety feeding sheds.

"I'm afraid," Rilandri said, trembling.

"What are you afraid of?"

"There are many of them, and they can be very cruel."

"We won't be any more lenient, either."

Bada stepped out from behind the sheds with two bay mares.

"This saddled one is yours," he said, and threw the bridle to me. The other, he gave to Rilandri.

"Hold on to it," he said. "I'll go and get myself a strong stick as well."

He was picking and choosing with great expertise from among the split acacia pickets that had been driven into the edge of a shed.

I couldn't stop admiring the horses. Their shiny hair gleamed in the sunlight as they watched our preparations. Bada readied my horse first. He firmly pulled the strap and readjusted the stirrups.

"Try it!" It was my first ride with a saddle. At first sight I was averse to it, but I soon felt comfortable with the small saddle.

"If you stand up in the stirrups it's much easier to rotate the stick." Turning to Rilandri, he instructed her: "And you stay here! Don't move from that spot!" She replied with a consenting nod.

Such setbacks in life always unsettled me. The feeling of not belonging anywhere; the traceless disappearance of hours, of years; the greed for the minute, for the second; the never-ending flight; thinking "never mind, only get away from here"—away to hell, to prison, into

[63] fighting/brawling

oblivion or into that other, timeless, sinking world; just away, because if one has to rot, then at least not here. Not in the never-freshening, rancid-smelling air of this eternal comedy, where the skirts' bright yellow flowers wilt, where blood goes insane from constant obsession, and where revenge is born of love. Out of this world, because nothing is lasting here, only paralyzed time and fear.

"Let's go!" Bada swished his stick in the air, goading his horse to a fast gallop. He then waved it toward Rilandri, but I couldn't tell whether it was in farewell or as a warning. All that I guessed was that Rilandri's eyes accompanied us across the clearing with anxious concern until we disappeared into the bushes.

Had she really fallen in love with Bada? The day before yesterday she seemed okay with her own husband even though she knew full well that he too had slept with the Romungritsa.[64] Yes, she'd made quite a show of being the loving wife, laughing as she boasted about her husband—Yagosh, he was called—and now here she was, worried about Bada.

Barely a hundred yards from the clearing, an arrow-straight trail sliced the forest's shrubbery in half. Its untrodden, thick grass carpet was already covered with yellowed leaves. Outside the woods, all was still stewing in stifling summertime heat, but here, nature was already writing its farewell letters, the grim black extinction of autumn and winter having begun to take hold.

Bada reined in his horse; he too seemed overcome by the pure, overwhelming silence. The interlocking foliage above us formed a ceiling over the narrow corridor, and—where the foliage was sparser—slanting rays reached down, casting a golden sheen upon the grass.

What Bada was thinking, I do not know. I was sorry that I wasn't a tree, one among the many standing here for a century or more—strong, tough, taller and taller, seeing farther and farther. What other goal can there be for a tree or for a man but to look into the obscure distance, defying time, knowing that every fall is followed by a budding spring,

---

[64] Hungarian Romani woman

knowing that there is no death, only rebirth? But what is it that any of us really know in this, our dark, dwarfish world?

I dug my barefoot heels into the horse's flanks. My thoughts ran something like this: *May the whole world perish if it was created to be such a stingy, tight-fisted miser.*

Bada joined me, and we raced each other until we reached the edge of the woods, facing the farm.

"Stay between the trees!" he said. "If they catch sight of us, we'll spoil everything. We need to wait until they leave the forest, so they can't escape."

We waited quietly. We could hear loud arguing from within the woods.

"They probably can't find us," Bada observed. "But when we catch sight of them, you just show me Rilandri's husband. What's his name again?"

"Yagosh. You want to pay for the woman?"

"Yep. I don't want him thinking that a dog took his wife."

It brought a lump to my throat when I looked at the three-pronged acacia stake.

"Get yourself another stick!" I begged. "With this one each of your strokes can be fatal."

"Do you think they're coming with toy swords?"

"I don't, but please throw this one away; it gives me the creeps just to look at it."

"What sort of a man are you?" Bada was annoyed. "As if you couldn't kill a bull with your own stick."

"I'll take care of that."

Reluctantly he went to get another stick. I could hear him grumbling as he began hacking away at a branch.

"This knife is dull!" he cried, half-whispering and yet cursing away, still regretting the stake.

They were coming closer, and I recognized Balush's strident voice as she kept asserting her honesty. We mounted our horses, and my blood ran cold when they emerged from the forest. Eleven robust Gypsies, and all but Grandpa were armed with hoes or pitchforks.

"Hey, what do you think of it? They've sure chosen their weapons. Well, never mind, they'll soon throw them away."

He too began to count.

"Damn them," said Bada, "they can't walk straight. I've been trying to count them for the third time, but one of them always tries taking another one's place." After a while he gave up. "They're moving around like a mob. Now how did that little bird wind up among them? Only a little while ago she was cursing Balush, and look at her now, she's the loudest of them all."

"Don't you take a swipe at her—she's Rilandri's sister—and don't you hurt the old man."

"Which one is he?" asked Bada, narrowing his eyes.

"The one that's lagging behind."

"Isn't he the ringleader? Seems to me I should let him have it. What rabble. We'll have a lot of trouble by the time we can round them up."

Indeed, one or the other was always moving out of the pack; Balush kept stopping, holding up the group by slapping her knees and her rump and pulling at her skirt.

"They're talking about you."

"Could be," I agreed.

"*Now* which one of them is Yagosh?"

"The one waving his pitchfork at the woods."

"That's probably meant for me." I got the shivers from Bada's unfamiliar, strange laughter. A second later I felt the horse trembling under me, so I stood up in the stirrups, firmly gripping his flanks with my knees.

"Are you listening to me?" Bada asked without taking his eyes off the group.

"Yes."

"As soon as we're out of the woods, we've got to go at them from two directions. You from this side, I from the other. Not a single one of them will be able to run away. We'll start with a big circle, so if one of them tries escaping, we can force him back. We'll gallop around them until the circle becomes so tight that they'll be forced into a knot. After that, we'll give 'em what they deserve. We'll talk once they're already lying on the ground. We've got to be really careful—there are lots of them—but out in the open, we're the ones in the saddle."

When they reached the advantageous spot, we sprung out of the woods almost simultaneously. The horses wanted at all costs to run side by side, but then they changed their minds, yielding to our will, and mine turned to the right, Bada's to the left. Now I really valued the raised stirrups. I could stand upright, my knees holding fast to the horse, which seemed to stretch out under me as if flying.

Our foes froze into silence. Khulo was the first who wanted to skedaddle, but when he saw Bada approaching, he suddenly changed course and ran back screaming to the others. They noticed us too late, and by the time they realized what was happening, we closed off every avenue of escape. Grandpa was yelling, crumpling his hat in his hands. The more notorious ones—Zhelko, Yagosh, and even the dumb Muto—tried to flee, and threw away their weapons. The earth shook as we kept galloping round and round, and they turned after us with frightened, giddy-goat eyes.

They woke to the real danger when a young lad rumored to be chasing after Vorzha decided to show his mettle. Raising his pitchfork, he rushed at me. His stroke missed, and Bada felled him from behind.

"Form a circle," shouted Grandpa, "and don't let them close to you!"

They might not even have heard him, but instinctively they surrounded the two women. We lashed out toward them, and they retreated until their backs touched. They became pressed together like figs, and didn't have enough space to defend themselves.

The horses were already prancing in one place as earsplitting howling and wailing replaced the earlier shouting. I didn't look to see where my blows fell; my sole aim was for the mass to grow thinner. I chopped down Yagosh, who desperately jumped toward my horse; I caught him in the neck and, somersaulting far out of the crowd, he fell to the ground. Apart from him, it would have been hard to tell which of us struck down whom. When Bada's huge stick roared past, they fell over like ripe ears of corn.

Wallowing in each other's blood, their pleadings seemed like distant wails. For several minutes, the swishing of the sticks was accompanied by the dull sound of fracturing bones, and the desperate wails changed to painful moans. Their hard, shaggy heads drooped down limply, flashes of astonishment vibrated in their startled looks until rivulets of blood covered their eyes, and then their doubled-over bodies fell staggeringly on top of one another.

They couldn't recover from the surprise caused by the rapid attack, and Grandpa's yelling seemed futile; all of them hid from the blows, practically pushing the others in front.

Zhelko was the first to realize that their mission was not feasible, and he stood in front of the women with outstretched arms. At my first stroke he nearly managed to snatch the stick from my hand; it made a loud clicking sound in his palm; at the next one, blood spurted from his head, and he collapsed like a carpenter's ruler.

Balush burst into ghostly laughter and put her foot on Zhelko's bleeding head.

"Get up, you show-off!"

I couldn't resist the hatred that surpassed even my anger, and I struck her backbone with all my might as, still laughing, she bent over to kick her husband, who was writhing on the ground.

Balush's face didn't get contorted, and she was still laughing when, struggling, she tore at the uncut grass around her.

All the while, Rilandri's sister was screaming like a banshee. She fell silent when she saw Balush struggling. Her large eyes became even larger, and whimpering, doglike sounds burst out of her mouth distorted by her fear of death.

While they wailed, begged, or tried to escape, my only objective was to hit as hard, as pitilessly hard, as I could. I felt not a trace of human compassion in me. Who knew what had become of the concern that had taken hold of me at the sight of Bada's first picket? Perhaps at times I even envied that huge stick of his when I couldn't fell one of them with a single blow.

I was convinced that everything I was doing was for truth, my own truth. The law is the law. If wise old men have decided that truth is on the side of the stronger, then so be it.

The weak are never right. They are either beaten to death or killed by pity. It makes no difference.

Those who must always accept the truth of others have little to be happy about. There is nothing more disgusting than when the truth is spat in one's face. It hurts more than the gory wounds of a cracked skull.

That's what Grandpa was also afraid of. Pointing at his hoary temple, he lurched over his writhing son.

"Hit me here!" he shouted, clapping the top of his head with the open palm of his hand.

"Stop, old man," I called, "or I'll crack your head open!"

"You will, will you?" he asked.

"You'd deserve it. You were after my blood on account of a rotten whore who's been fucked by everyone and his brother, only to cover up your own infamy."

"You're a son of a bitch!" he cried. "Is it not an infamy that you raped your mother-in-law? Your wife's mother? May the blood shed here spoil your luck wherever you go, for you've brought enduring disgrace on us."

"Bater!" the others shouted in unison. Bada silenced the lot by a blow to one of them. They quickly realized that the danger was not over yet.

Moaning, Balush crawled toward the skinny girl. Not for a moment did I have any doubt as to her intentions. If she could lay her hands on the girl, I wouldn't be able to prove a thing. She was capable of scratching her eyes out or strangling her, and then she could say what she wanted.

Rilandri's sister trembled in her coat as Balush kept coming closer to her. The thought of escape was written all over her face, but she was paralyzed by fear either of us or Balush.

Grandpa, misunderstanding my intentions, grabbed the reins with both hands. At first the horse recoiled and then swept the old man away, fortunately causing no harm.

The girl's screams aroused the curiosity of those who, feigning unconsciousness, had dug their heads into the grass. Almost simultaneously we reached for the girl, who had jumped up in fright. Gritting her teeth, Balush clung to her skirt, whose torn-off frills remained in her grip. I raised the girl by the high, upturned collar of her coat; she protested not only with nerve-racking cries but also with long fingernails, until I quieted her down with a couple of slaps.

Riding around in circles definitely appealed to her. The glitter of her eyes, visible between the sides of her collar, showed that she was relenting, and her talons relaxed after one more onslaught against my half-naked upper body. The situation was by far not as tragic as it seemed at first glance. Zhelko and his mob looked positively distraught while fingering their privates on the trampled, bloodied grass. Even though we'd raised our sticks higher than absolutely necessary at times, it was to our credit that we hadn't done so with murderous intent. Compassion took hold of me once again, despite my awareness that those skulls of theirs were used to occasional bloodletting. Even if we hadn't chosen the best method, it was as good as leeching their blood, I suppose.

Meanwhile Grandpa got to his feet, but this time he came only half as close to my horse. It was apparent from the look in his eyes that he was determined to call me to account. Had I not considered his age—so often reinforced by the sad look of that pipe in his mouth—I wouldn't have let that little beast now claw at my upper body.

Among the things I most regret is that my response was simply to lift up Rilandri's sister, that endlessly rattling *kekeraska*,[65] and plop her down on the saddle right up against the pommel.

When she noticed that I didn't want to knock her over the head, she immediately began to negotiate, imposing conditions and demanding eternal fidelity.

It was only out of respect for Grandpa that I tolerated her greasy, chicken-smelling head under my chin.

"Do you see this?" She showed me her wounded forehead. "They're the ones who pulled the pot off it." I thought she was delirious, and realized only later that she knew exactly what she was talking about.

Balush looked at us, puzzled, and the others acted as if this part of the proceedings was none of their business.

As far as Bada and I were concerned, we'd done our best, and only some formalities were left. An *engedelmo mangel* from either side would let bygones be bygones. Proof of the truth seemed desirable only in Grandpa's in eyes; everyone else was convinced that any virtue of Balush's lay not in her capacity for resistance but in obedience.

Romani kris[66] beat only in Grandpa's heart, because by default the great honor with which the years had anointed him demanded satisfaction.

Throwing down my bloodied weapon as a sign of honoring his hollow past, I dismounted.

"What have you got to say in your defense?" he asked as if I were an accused.

"Nothing," I replied.

"You wanted to kill me, you murderer," Balush sobbed, courting sympathy. "You gagged me with this," she said, pulling up her skirt.

---

[65] magpie

[66] Romani law (elsewhere: Romani trial, Romani court)

"Stop your lying!" screeched the skinny girl. "Wasn't it you who lay down beside him in the dark?"

"Me?" she asked in an innocent voice. "May that scooped-out skinny body of yours rot away!"

"You were panting like hell under the young Gypsy boy."

"How do *you* know that?" Grandpa interrupted her.

"I was there behind the tree. I heard everything. Let me eat my mother's flesh in anguish if I'm not telling the truth: when the boy realized it wasn't Vorzha, he kicked your daughter-in-law. Balush just laughed, and said that she had only done it as a revenge, Zhelko's revenge, because you cut out her privates. That she was out to get rid of this phumba of a family and would rape every man who became part of it."

Zhelko tried struggling to his feet, but Grandpa kicked him in the head.

"You were out to defend the honor of this thing here?" Disgusted, Grandpa spat a gob of chewing-tobacco juice between his eyes, then looked up at me.

"*Zha Devlesa!*"[67] he said, extending a hand as an olive branch. "Tell your father I respect him."

I ejected the skinny girl from the saddle, and Bada and I galloped away.

"What an old bitch!" Bada mused as we slowed down in the woods. "It was a shame to leave that girl behind, though."

"No need to worry over the wolves," I replied. "They won't eat each other as long as there's something to fuss over. And it's not like Balush's prestige will suffer, either; if anything, it might even grow. As for Grandpa, he might just realize that it's better to honor the past from a distance rather than bringing it back."

Turning our heads as we rode on, we saw that my prediction seemed already to have been been fulfilled. Grandpa and the skinny girl

---

[67] Go with God!

were nearing the farm, while the others were yelling and pummelling each other. We watched the mayhem for a while, and then turned our backs on everything.

"Seems they're not satisfied with what we gave them," Bada remarked. He was still holding onto his heavy stick, and gave it a good swish in the air.

"Yeah."

"They'll sure remember it for a long time."

I didn't want to exaggerate, but I was convinced that they would hide it among their deepest secrets just like their relationships with Balush. They could make up hundreds of other stories. And knowing my kind, they would always find those stories that most served their purposes.

Our horses trotted wearily along; the noise of the branches crackling under their hooves mingled with the undulating cacophony of birdsong.

The shrill, unrestrained calls of the kestrels circling high above the forest, their brownish underbellies spotted black, only heightened my inner tension. It seemed as if the birds wanted to mimic the desperate wailing of the bloodied Gypsies as they had toppled over one another.

It occurred to me that perhaps I should feel sorry for them. But what good was remorse at such times? Such hindsight, I knew, was worth as much as the number of times I'd lifted the stick and didn't hit with it.

Still, I tried in vain to pity them as their frightened faces swirled before me pleading for remorse. Instead, I felt that, given the chance, I would now hit them even harder.

Again the strident dark multitude in the sky above the trees disrupted my thoughts; even when I managed for a moment to throw together a more or less normal thought, their spiteful gloating knocked it out of my head.

The gnashing teeth hurt. I didn't want to pay attention anymore, but the falcons' incessant cries—*Kii-kii-kiikii*—kept getting on my nerves. I returned to my aggressive thoughts: *those phumbas had brought it upon themselves. Had they not come, nothing would have happened.*

Bada stopped and motioned for silence. He listened, then started off again. I was struck anew by the seemingly frantic-sounding birds hovering like a giant black mark over the forest. All at once Bada dug his heels into his horse and turned swiftly into the bushes; I could barely stay in the saddle in my effort to keep pace. My naked skin was already so scratched up that the branches only tore up old wounds.

As I tried dodging all the many branches that seemed to be rushing toward me, Bada was again galloping in the clearing, stick held high. If I had any doubts at all about what had made him bolt, a thick branch promptly cast them from my mind. Only by a stroke of good fortune did I get away with an undamaged face.

I couldn't hold back my horse. It raced after the other one, fitting under the bushes as best it could.

I wouldn't be able to repeat all the curses that then ran through my mind even if I had a lifetime to do so. The horse shook some of them out of me, but most of them remained between my teeth when I heard Rilandri's wailing. Bada was far ahead of me as I finally exited the woods.

Two farmhands were tormenting Rilandri, who was rolling around in the grass. One of them had pushed his pants down to the tops of his boots, his large white ass betraying his intention even from a distance; he was just struggling to get between the wriggling woman's thighs. The other one—pushing Rilandri's head down—was using his fists to make her obey. He was the first to see us approaching. The naked-assed fellow could only sense the danger and, holding up his pants with one hand, was trying to get a head start. Bada chased the first one; I couldn't follow them with my eyes.

My guy managed to pull his pants on while running, and was heading toward the wildlife-feeding sheds. I beat the horse's flank with my heels because once the guy reached the sheds, the forest would be only a stone's throw away. And I certainly wasn't up to another ride through the bushes. No, not even for a hundred Rilandris.

The guy soon ran out of breath, though, dragging himself along feebly like the wounded rabbit I'd once chased while helping some gentlemen hunt. Just one more leap was all it would take before I earned the reward I had coming to me from the hunters. I will never forget how the rabbit's broken legs dangled behind it, how it didn't give up until all its strength was gone.

How long could this one keep it up?

Wanting to head him off, I galloped along the row of makeshift wooden sheds and would even have had time to pull one of the stakes from the ground. Seeing that I'd cut off his path, he turned around.

Bada was playing a chasing game with the other one, who also managed somehow to change course. By now both of them raced toward the middle of the clearing. *That sure will shake away your lust for a Gypsy gal!* I was sorry I didn't have a weapon with me. Every time I looked back, I saw Bada's guy get a spurt of energy at the sight of the big stick in his pursuer's hand. *Run, run!* I thought, holding back my horse. What good would it do me if I caught up with my prey?

Bada's man seemed to be the younger of the two. He changed direction with annoying dexterity. Again and again it seemed that his pursuer was about to mow him down, but at the last minute the fellow dodged the blow.

He must have lost his shabby soldier's cap somewhere; his disheveled, hemp-hued hair covered both sides of his face, and his mouth—contorted with fear and fatigue—seemed to be frozen into a grin.

The whole thing wasn't so much like a dangerous chase as like an innocent game of tag. By now my guy was just jogging along and, even though I slowed down, I kept getting closer.

I wondered if Rilandri would have been more compliant if she'd met them under different circumstances. In light of what she'd said about the warden I was not quite convinced, even if she had just made it up to mislead the gendarmes. Someone who can paint the Devil so well is not frightened when she meets him on occasion. As far as I was concerned, I would have liked to give up the chase. No longer playing the game, my man was only waiting for me to catch up with him. Pity that Bada didn't pick him; he, at least, would have shattered the guy's horniness in one fell swoop.

I froze as Bada hit the hemp-haired farmhand over the head. The fellow's screams echoed through the woods; he fell, smoothing down the grass, then fell silent. As for my man, he turned to me in fright and began to back away. Meanwhile he kept wailing, "Oh, dear mother!"

The horse let out a groan as I dug my heels in its flank. It snatched the driving rein from my hand and started to gallop. Slipping my ankle into the stirrup as I passed the guy, I kicked him in the face with full force. In silence he sprawled out on the ground; surely he didn't have a tooth left in its proper place.

I didn't turn back to look. I calmed down my horse and trotted toward Rilandri. That evening something made me feel that I got my revenge for the bullwhip. It is interesting how that sound has etched itself into my memory.

They had torn Rilandri's bodice to tatters; her big blue eyes were barely visible, and greenish bruises marred her swollen face. She didn't cry, no, she just pressed her bloodied lips together. It seemed as if all she was interested in was to somehow or other hide her round, brown breasts from prying eyes. We didn't try talking to her. Bada lifted the young woman in front of him, and off we went.

For quite a while we didn't take any notice of each other. Engrossed in our thoughts, we were busy building our futures, each to his own liking. The stormy past few days had accumulated a lot of debris in me, and I didn't quite know how to deal with it. For the time being all had quietened down, I sensed, and my disquiet had abated notwithstanding that the fall foliage, which had once promised such cooling relief, now seemed positively ragged.

Every half hour we changed horses, since one of them now stumbled along under a double burden, but after awhile even that seemed to exhaust them.

"Where do you want to stop for a rest?" I asked Bada.

"In Orosi," he called out cheerfully.

"That's still far; the horses will collapse by the time we get there."

"Don't worry about it," he said reassuringly, "they can do it. We're thirsty, too, and there, at least, we'll find all we need."

I felt sorry for the horses, but I had to admit that Bada was right; the sun was still too hot for them to rest without some shade.

We did need water. The bits formed thick layers of foam around the horses' mouths, and they tried to cool themselves off by constantly shaking their heads.

We stopped by a roadside cross to change horses. Rilandri carefully stepped across the brambles, knelt before the cross, gazed at it at length, and some kind of happiness even seemed to flash over her face. Patiently we waited for her to finish. I wondered what she was praying for—if she was praying. To whom did she owe a debt of gratitude for the past or for the future?

"Whenever I go past a cross, I always spend a few minutes there," she explained, shaking the dust off her skirt. "Do *you* guys ever pray?" You couldn't tell from her face whether she was just curious or really cared. I carefully stepped over the thorns, stopped in front of the cross and, without a trace of piety or repentance, searched the ground with my eyes. The impressions left by Rilandri's knees could still be seen, but so too could a moist little spot that glittered on the trampled grass.

I took a running jump over the brambles.

"Let's go!" I said with a smile.

Rilandri drew her swollen eyes together even more tightly; she either regarded the time spent on devotion insufficient or she became suspicious. She didn't want to take her questioning look off me.

"You didn't have to, not yet," I said to dispel her uncertainty.

"Your brother is a big rascal."

Bada shrugged, as if he had no idea what the woman was talking about. He trotted off with her.

Pulling firmly on the rein, I led the horse after them, pausing once to offer the beast some of the dusty, withered grass at the side of the path. Squeamishly it refused. It was thirsty.

The sun was already sinking, but all the same we tried avoiding places where we might meet up with anyone. The well sweeps rising skyward in the distance were very tempting; perhaps we were too cautious. Still, that seemed preferable than being too rash, for which we might have to pay too high a price.

In any event, I had to get home during the night. If my parents could settle the Kurucho matter within two days, then I hadn't lost anything yet. I hoped we would reach the woods by Orosi as soon as possible. Once night fell, the horses too would be able to stop for a good rest. "Isn't that right, my bay?" I half-whispered. I patted the horse's sweaty neck. After that rest, not even the wind would be able to keep pace with us. It is not likely that the bay could understand my mutterings, but it seemed to appreciate my friendly approach. Little by little it paused to taste the dusty grass, and I let it graze.

Sighing, I roamed around among my thoughts. I couldn't find answers to many questions, and sometimes I even posed the wrong questions.

It's a dog's life and Bada's, I thought. I'd return his horse registration booklets and, if need be, the horse as well. I was quitting this game.

Who would have had more grounds to devote a few genuine minutes to kneeling before that cross, I wondered—Rilandri or I?

Carefully I tucked the money stolen from Balush into my waistband. God is my witness that while I didn't feel much remorse, I wouldn't have begrudged a pengő from St. Anthony had he come to collect it. Who was to say, God might even help in placating Kurucho. And if he didn't, I hoped the money would.

Strange that neither Balush nor Zhelko had mentioned the money. I wasn't surprised about Grandpa seeming so happy. At long last there had been an opportunity for a bona fide *Romani kris*[68]—one that had served, in part, to repay Balush's debt, while at the same time Grandpa had been able to bask in the great honor due to him for applying Gypsy law.

[68] Romani trial (elsewhere Romani law, Romani court)

Bada looked back. He was so preoccupied with the woman that he didn't even notice me lagging behind. He was obviously enjoying himself. By now Rilandri no longer attempted to hide her breasts behind her torn blouse, and they were rolling about on Bada's arm. It definitely wasn't an ugly sight. In fact, it stirred up a certain feeling of envy in me. If her sister had such breasts, I swear I wouldn't have tipped her out of my saddle as I had.

So fascinated was I by Rilandri's bare breasts that I promptly forgot about my resolve once and for all to give up women. We plodded on silently for quite a while; I tried not to be too obvious, and deliberately only cast an occasional furtive glance at her, but Rilandri recognized my thoughts.

Partly fatigue, partly the monotonous beat of the horse's hooves made Bada doze off. Rilandri was visibly pleased with my bold leers, although sometimes they verged on the limits of indecency. An encouraging light shone from her swollen eyes, and occasionally she proudly inventoried her own charms.

"I'm going over to you," she called. "I've got cramps from sitting on the edge of the saddle." Bada nodded, his eyes closed, and his horse kept following right behind us.

I managed to control myself for a while, but soon my willpower left me.

"Don't tug at them so much," she said, trying to calm my lust. "Your brother will see it!"

"So what, do they belong to him?"

"Do you want to marry me?" she asked instead of answering.

"No."

"Then they're his. You didn't think that I would be a wife to both of you?"

"You're right." I sighed, letting go of her breasts.

"You had the chance," she said reproachfully. "If you had said so with a single word, you wouldn't have to sigh now."

"You're right," I repeated.

"What do you mean, I'm right?" she burst out in anger. "It's still not too late, but even the lungs inside you are wicked." With that, she pinched my pursed lips.

"Because I won't take you away from my friend?"

"Your friend?" she looked at me in surprise. "Isn't he your brother?"

"I've already told you I had no brother."

"Well, then, you can hold them." Rilandri put my hand back. She glanced back repeatedly over my shoulder.

"He's asleep," she kept saying, as if to encourage me. After a while the initial fervor, which had begun full steam, waned considerably. I had to search for other reaches of her. Rilandri chuckled and scolded as her mood dictated, and later she was the one who initiated matters. We didn't have to worry; Bada was sleeping the sleep of the just.

Now and then I was filled with apprehension, but the game made us forget everything: changing the horses as well as the passing of time. We held on to each other, covered with goose bumps or perspiration, sometimes clutching extra tight to keep from falling off the horse. As the distance we covered grew, so the off-limit territories fell away. I was already past the hem of her skirt, perhaps even past my common sense, as well as everything that a friend can do to another.

"Did you sleep with Sooki?" she looked at me with burning eyes.

"Who's Sooki?"

"My sister! The one who was lying next to you at dawn." Had she tipped cold water down my neck, she wouldn't have cooled me down more than did her question.

"Are you crazy? Do you think I would sleep with a child?"

"That's good, because if you had, I wouldn't let you touch me!" Who knows what she would have done had I said yes.

She took the drive bar from my hand and led our horse behind Bada's.

"Let's get off!" she whispered.

"What for?" I asked loudly. "I don't want to cut in front of my friend."

Maybe that's not what I wanted to say; only revenge forced me to do so.

"Sssh!" she put her hand on my mouth. "The horse is tired."

I tried in vain to object; wanting her and not wanting her paralyzed me. Bada had fallen asleep holding on to the pommel, and didn't notice that we were far behind him. However, the horse, with its refined animal instinct, sensed that whatever was on its back was unable to steer, and it didn't know the way. It turned and walked back to us.

"Wake up, Gypsy!" I yelled at Bada.

"Damn you!" Rilandri hissed.

Bada awoke and stared at us, wide eyed.

"Where are we?" he asked.

"Not too far away now," I replied. "Take the woman now." Rilandri was not at all overjoyed about this turn of events; I was, though. As Bada dismounted, I lovingly patted my horse; it was if fate had sent it to save me from falling into sin again.

"Don't go to sleep all the time!" I chided Bada. "You're ruining your mare."

"I'm tired," he yawned.

"Why don't you both have a rest then?" I feigned kind-heartedness. The poor woman had no idea what was going on.

"Fuck you!" She meant it wholeheartedly. "Are you always out to trick people? No wonder the Gypsies wanted to kill you."

I winked at her instead of replying. Her eyes were burning with fury, but she just smiled at me.

"Get down on your mother-in-law!" Her palm made a cracking sound on my back, as if giving emphasis to her good wishes.

"I'll see you in the woods." I left them. I didn't look back for a long time, though I was plagued by curiosity.

My emotions jostled one another; I hated and cursed everyone, including myself and, yes, the Creator, who had made us in his own image and then demanded that in gratitude we be better than average.

I wanted to be better, and I defied my own blood in exchanging my coveted roadside idyll for a pot of lentils. Now there was neither salvation nor priority. At least she shouldn't have called me to account about her sister.

Hell, this was all nonsense, anyway. Did Zhelko not know that Tom, Dick, and Harry were drinking from the well he'd dug? Sure he did. Yet he assailed the one who fell into it.

I shuddered to think what trouble I would have been in had Bada not arrived in time. What would they have done had they managed to surround me?

If only this hell would come to an end; if only I didn't need to be constantly running about without knowing what tomorrow would bring.

That said, where there is money every problem can be solved. I kept consoling myself by touching the money in my pocket.

It was mid-afternoon when, having left Rilandri behind with Bada, I finally approached the village of Orosi.

My poor horse's coat was covered by a foul smelling, muddy foam, while thirst and fatigue caused its flanks to huff and puff like a blacksmith's bellows. We left the arid pasture, hacking our way along a road now lined thickly with blackthorn shrubs, and it seemed we were heading right into yet another forest. *Don't you worry, buddy*—so I comforted the bay horse when I caught sight of the first farm—*we'll soon have something to drink*. He pricked up his ears, neighed, and started to gallop.

At the farm, two huge dogs barred my way, and it didn't seem advisable to approach the well—not until a sullen young woman ordered them back.

"Good day!" I greeted her, my voice hoarse from fright. The woman acknowledged me sleepily. She didn't seem suspicious, but rather annoyed at me or the dogs for disturbing her afternoon nap.

"Could you let us have a drink?"

She motioned yes. I timidly led the horse, watching for the dogs that had withdrawn to the end of the farmyard. I never have managed to become friendly with strange dogs; they sniff around me, snarling, and then I have to flee or to beg.

"You shouldn't water that horse just yet," muttered the woman, yawning. "It's still too overheated."

I looked around hesitantly; Papa used to say that, too.

"You can tie it to the manger," she said, pointing to the mulberry tree. "It can have a rest there. At times like these it's easy for a horse to catch pneumonia. It was damn hot today; even the corn gets cooked, right there on the stem."

The horse began to whinny impatiently, so I removed the bridle.

"Go on, rummage around here!" I said, shaking the dry alfalfa at the bottom of the manger. "Hey, don't be so impatient. I'm thirsty too."

"Nice horse," said the woman, waddling closer.

"Yeah," I croaked from my dry throat.

"Well, that won't hurt it," she nodded approvingly as I began to rub the horse's hair with a wad of alfalfa.

My thirst dissipated a bit in the shade of the mulberry tree, but time and again my eyes were drawn to the well.

"There are lots of flies," the woman said with a laugh as I occasionally used the wad on my own sweating back.

"Has there been any rain over there?" she inquired.

"Where?" I asked.

"Well, from wherever you came."

"Only a storm."

"No rain?"

"That too, but more would have been needed."

"Here too."

With wobbly steps she went into the house.

Why the hell are you so nosy? I thought. *Stop asking so many questions.* Forgetting its thirst, the horse was crunching the dry alfalfa with great gusto. *Okay, keep munching, but I for one need a drink.*

I took a huge gulp from the trough, gargled with it for a while, and then spat it out. *Pff.* It tasted like piss.

Only now did I feel how tired I was. As I clutched the well's worn pole and began to pull down, it was as if my bones were creaking in time with it.

I savored the taste of the fresh water, and kept filling myself from the mossy, wooden bucket.

"Come on horsie, it's your turn now." I turned it to the trough, which was full. It gulped and slurped until its thirst was fully quenched.

The woman came out again, having tidied herself up a little.

"You can give it some hay," she said as she walked toward us lazily, carrying an earthernware bowl in her hand. My eyes lit up and my stomach began to croak as if I had swallowed a frog. I hurriedly gathered up some hay in my arms and stuffed it into the manger. The bowl the woman was pressing to herself was playing havoc with my appetite.

I was just about to utter some words of gratitude, when she dipped it into the trough.

"Come on," she said, "I'll wash your back."

My gritted teeth ground the words that were on the tip of my tongue; I looked for a while at the appetizing earthenware bowl, and then spat my thoughts, like chewed cotton wool, into a pile of horse manure.

As I slowly approached her, she kept smiling, and a sort of *it-won't-hurt* consolation seemed to shine from her candid eyes.

Without a word I bent over the trough, and she stood behind my naked back.

"Whip?" she asked while pouring water over my neck.

"Yes," I hissed.

"A reward from your father?"

"No, from a farmhand."

"Hm," she said, fingering the squiggly wound, "he didn't spare the whip."

"No."

"It's already healing," she added, soothing it with a mug of water, "but it won't hurt if we give it a good wash."

Instead of answering, I gasped for air as the water streamed down under my trouser legs.

"There you go," she said each time she poured some more water over me.

I withstood her relentless watering with legs apart, and after a while it no longer felt unpleasant; I got used to it.

Her hard hands kept gliding cautiously along my back, bypassing all the wounds caused by the branches. I hardly understood anything she was muttering; I just hemmed and hawed. Mama's words came to mind: "And when I'm gone," she used to say, "if someone scratches his ass, you'll think he'll feed you." She was right, but I hadn't missed anything yet.

My mouth wasn't sewn up. I had to ask her for something. I did have money on me, after all.

But I couldn't continue my thoughts. Startled, I clutched at my waist. Touching the wet cord that wound around my pants, and then touching my pocket, I stood frozen for a moment. *The bills. Drenched.*

"Oh, Devla, I'm done!" I cried out in fright. Everything became a blur. I felt dizzy as I ran, stumbling, toward the horse.

"I'm done!" I kept repeating. The horse was stomping nervously, and, when it felt the thumping of my naked heels, it began to gallop. My thoughts were perhaps born outside of my mind and died there that very moment. Pain and fear filled my entire body, and I trembled and whimpered like someone being broken on the wheel.

The wild gallop and the desperate wailing that I only felt, but had no strength to voice, shattered all my manhood.

We stopped somewhere on the verge of insanity. At that moment I wouldn't have been able to decide whether at the right or the wrong time. A rattling and hissing iron monster, pulling a long row of clattering flatcars behind it, passed in front of us. Angry, sooty people shook their fists at us from under the black iron umbrella until the ball of smoke spewed from the steam train covered us with its dirty veil.

All that remained in me was the sound of steady chugging, reverberating from my petrified fear somewhere deep down in my soul, its excruciating rhythm pounding my brain. *Curse, curse,* sounded its merciless beat. Yes, Balush's curse. The recognition sobered me, but my strength and my will were still missing. I dismounted and searched long and hard for a suitable place until I finally spread out the sopping wet money beside the railway embankment.

I lay on the grass, remembering scarcely a thing; I sobbed, weeping for the paper money, which had signified my faith in the future-which, to me, had been the future itself. My grand plans now lay side-by-side on the ground before me, hopelessly sodden and worn.

I blamed that farm slut for having bathed me right out of the world; I called her names until my eyelids became heavy. I gathered the now dry pieces of paper with a sigh, and then sleep overcame me.

Some time later, as I still lay there, now half-awake, I struggled with the money, but then everything became muddled. I remember clearly that an impertinent bird was annoying me. It was chuckling and screeching right in front of my nose, its tail constantly teasing my mustache. My tied hands were hanging limply by my side, and I didn't have enough strength to shoo it away. I moaned, and kept turning my head until its sassy chuckling finally woke me.

Sitting beside me was Rilandri, hugely enjoying the facial expressions she was forcing out of me by tickling my nose with the long narrow leaf of some odorous herb. I blinked uncomprehendingly for quite a while and, enraged by the stinging numbness of my hands, which felt as if ants were running over them, I cursed away at Rilandri, who choked with laughter.

The sun had slipped down, standing barely an inch atop the remote forest with a surprisingly friendly mien, as if it hadn't been the very same sun that had tortured me all afternoon. Bad dreams usually give birth to good thoughts. I was carried away by the look of the dying orb, cleansed in its own fire. It stood just above the forest, a black veil speckled with red grief, looking blankly, pleading for forgiveness, as if it had repented all the sins it had committed that day.

Captivated by the sight, I watched as it immersed itself into the infinite nothingness behind Rilandri's head.

"You're lucky," I sighed. "Tomorrow you can start all over again, but what can I do? I can never catch up with what I've missed."

"Serves you right!" Rilandri replied gloatingly to my murmurs. "You're sorry about it now, aren't you? You left me there with the big, strong Gypsy, so what could I do? Let him kill me?"

At first I was perplexed by her complaints, but then I eagerly joined the conversation.

"Didn't you do anything?"

"Of course I did. I wished you to hell."

"You wished me to hell while you were with Bada?" I moved closer to her.

"Sure I did," Rilandri screeched, "because already before that . . ."

I didn't let her continue; I slapped her in the face. She endured my questioning look for a long time before she continued though in a more subdued voice.

"You see, you're like your friend; to hell with both of you!"

"I'm like him?" I asked her with a further slap. "Why didn't you curse *him*?"

"I did curse him, but I was thinking of you."

"You thought of me? At that moment too?"

"I did."

"You've got a good waistcoat." I tore Bada's waistcoat open over Rilandri's breasts.

"I earned it fairly," she said, drawing it together. "If you were as good at other things as you are at fighting, you would be worth a lot."

"What else should I be good at?" I asked, still taunting her.

"Listen, leave me alone," Rilandri burst out angrily, "or I'll rip everything off myself." Now it was she who pulled the waistcoat open.

"Where is Bada?" I asked, changing the subject.

"Over there, with the limping woman." Figuring something was wrong with her, I sought a more comprehensible explanation.

"What limping woman?" I inquired more patiently.

"There, at the farm. All *you* can do with women is slap them around. The limping woman said you ran away when she gave you a bath."

The word "bath" gripped me by the guts, but my curiosity prevailed. Somehow I still didn't understand whom she was talking about.

"How many women are there at the farm?"

"One. How many would you expect?"

"I don't know," I said thoughtfully. "The one I saw was not limping."

"You're right," she reassured me, "only her leg was made of iron. Strip iron," she added.

My world turned over like in those saints who see the fruit of their deeds. Had my curse been effective? *God doesn't strike you, but He listens to heartfelt wishes and punishes everyone in His own way.*

Rilandri's breasts, which she'd spilled out in anger, were heaving between the torn buttons of her violently opened bodice, rousing compassion and desire in me, if despondently so. Once again I touched them, but now with timid awe "Why are you women so dear to God?" I asked.

She didn't comment, no, she just shrugged her shoulders as feminine superiority flared up in her eyes. But those eyes were immediately crushed by the fear of falling into sin.

"We love Him," she said after a long pause.

"I love Him, too, but He listens to you more."

"Ah," she said with a wave of her hand. "If He'd listen to me now, then . . ." She didn't continue.

"Then what?"

"Leave me in peace, Gypsy boy, don't *push mandar*[69] so much.

"Did you curse me?"

"Why would I have cursed you?"

"When I left you with Bada."

---

[69] ask

"Well, yes, I did then. I was furious. I wished then that you should run until your head fell off. You wouldn't have been pleased if *I'd* left *you*."

"You started it."

"Me?" she asked in surprise. "How did I start it?"

"With your precious sister."

"As if I didn't know who she is," Rilandri said despondently. "She has already been with hundreds of men. Yagosh used her like he did me. If she takes aim at a guy, he can't get rid of her. She is like my poor father—may he rest in peace."

"Your father?"

"Yes. Despite being a rich Jew, he was as bad as the worst Gypsy. It didn't matter to him that he had three children. He sold our house when we didn't have anywhere else to live. Do you know how much money two hundred pengős is?"

"I know," I replied, involuntarily clutching at my heart.

"What's up? Is something wrong?"

"Nothing," I said, setting her mind at ease.

Rilandri smiled, folding the outer layer of her skirt over her shoulder, momentarily revealing her naked, bruise-marred thighs.

"Does it hurt?" I asked.

"No, not at all." Rilandri gently took my hand and, as if to hide her pain, slid it across her naked thigh, and then pressed it under her hot belly. I didn't have enough strength to protest.

A current of cool air wafted toward us from the forest, and a number of mosquito groups launched an attack on my uncovered skin, enlisting their armies from the neighboring bushes. Their relentless wild hordes were sprinkling bitter poison over our hopefully sweet moments.

I sought refuge between Rilandri's warm thighs. I hadn't found the right words, yet my fingers circled her black nipples with lazy inertia and passed the time with deep sighs, until she got fed up with it.

"Listen," she snapped, "if you just turn me on again, I'll scratch your face to shreds."

What made me more nervous than Rilandri's threat was that it was still quite light outside. The farm was shrouded in a soft hazy veil, but Bada could gallop out of it at any moment, and being caught in the act is undesirable even between friends. I didn't reply, but kept on striking the spark of her flexible fire tools until its smoke enveloped our brains, and, forgetting about everything, we fell on the apple tree of the lush garden with frantic voraciousness and, sparing neither foliage nor trunk, gorged ourselves on its tart fruit.

Shattered, I fell beside Rilandri. She forced her smooth arm under the nape of my neck and, softly rocking me, tried to shake me back to life.

It took me a long time to make up for my lack of air and, lying motionless, nostrils flaring, I kept staring at the unkempt wisps of cloud in the sky.

"Why do they call you a child?" she asked, mollified.

I was pleased with Rilandri's flattering question, because it reinforced my precocious feelings of manhood. But why did she ask me now, when I was totally wrung out and barely alive?

I didn't say anything yet, waiting to see what she was driving at. I was certain she wasn't inquiring out of sheer curiosity. I shrugged my shoulders.

"You shouldn't go to school any longer; that's why they think of you as a child. If you got yourself a good wife, you'd be better off."

I guessed already what she was getting at.

"A good woman?" I asked, taking a deep breath. "Where can you find a good woman these days? Even if there is one somewhere, she has already been reined in."

"There are still some around, even without reins," Rilandri reassured me "except you won't find them among the hussies like Vorzha and Sooki. They are only good for lying down next to a man."

"How do you know I go to school?"

"I certainly didn't make it up."

I figured Bada had let her into all our secrets.

"You know," she continued, "if you had any brains, even your foot cloth could be made of silk." I was surprised at hearing the familiar phrase.

"How?" I asked, though I knew from the first moment what she had in mind.

"How? You just have to get your mind moving, and then everything goes by itself. You have a good horse, and if you get a bad cart the world is yours. And as for women, you can have as many as you want. You are a young man."

"A guy can get a woman if he has brains, but money is needed for the cart."

"That's exactly it," said Rilandri, grabbing the opportunity.

Her smile seemed suspicious; though it was perhaps because of her swollen face, it put me on guard.

For a moment I was thrown off balance. After all, I wasn't sufficiently familiar with the uniformity of women's thinking. It wasn't only that the wording of Rilandri's confession didn't differ from that of her predecessor, but her actions were also the same. Searching lengthily in her skirt pocket, she pulled out two banknotes, each twenty pengős.

"Do you see this?" she asked, stroking the wrinkled money. "If we elope, it'll be yours. You can buy a top-notch light cart with it."

I can't say the offer didn't appeal to me. The sight of the money lit a glimmer of hope in me again, but the price was too high.

"You know, they have a father and mother as well."

"Where?"

"You'll find out, just listen to me! I'll make such a man out of you that you'll be famous far and wide." Her words seemed so musty and mildewy that I almost felt the breath of her grandmother or great-grandmother on them. What a goddamn good-hearted world this was, where since time immemorial everyone had wanted to make his fellow human being happy while dying of starvation himself.

"But you couldn't whip Yagosh into shape, could you?" I asked, losing my patience.

"That's because the cards ate up his life. Why should I risk myself for a man who wouldn't know how to appreciate it?" She was literally quoting Balush's words.

"How much did you promise to Bada?"

If I made her uncomfortable, I thought, perhaps she would forget her set text.

"Nothing. I don't want to marry him."

"Then why did you come away with us?"

"So you would marry me."

"Me?" I asked indignantly. "I never said anything to you about it. So why want it in the first place?"

"True, you never talked about it, but you always looked at me as if you wanted to marry me."

"That's why you slept with Bada?"

"Would you believe it? I didn't." She looked at me defiantly.

"You said so, didn't you?"

"I said it because I wanted to make you jealous." She ratcheted up the pressure.

"God made you into amazing creatures," I said. "You deceive everyone and don't even spare yourselves. You lie at every turn, and if your calculations don't work out you want people to feel sorry for you. You hadn't even seen Bada yet when you said: 'I'll marry your brother.' Were you already trying to make me jealous?"

Rilandri didn't reply.

"Has Bada told you everything about me?"

She nodded.

"Is that why you fell for me? Because you figured I'm still young enough to do what you tell me? First, you just wanted to escape from Yagosh, and then you acquired a taste for choice tidbits."

"I don't want choice tidbits, but give me half the money you took from Balush! I deserve it." Her crocodile tears dried up in no time. She wanted to add something, but I interrupted her with a huge slap. Then, just to be on the safe side, I added one more to make sure she wouldn't even think of disturbing my train of thought.

"So it was you who was lurking behind that stack of cordwood, not Bada."

I quickly sorted out the conclusions; it seems that my former assumptions had been completely wrong. Conceit usually obscures discernment, and I certainly suffered from severe visual impairment in thinking that this Satan in angel's clothing wanted nothing more from life than choice tidbits. Unfortunately, at my age disappointment isn't restricted to easily tolerated, small adventures.

Rilandri said she also deserved it, that I should give her half. *But why?* I thought. *Just because she managed to eavesdrop? A good beating, that's what I ought to give her—at least then she'd think twice about asking for a portion of the price of someone else's skin. What a cunning plot she's devised! Why, I should ride off with her this instant! But who would I be stealing her away from if she hasn't even slept with Bada? This one sure knows a trick or two! She would take my money, and then feign a sad goodbye.*

I really felt like throwing all the money in Rilandri's face, but she would only have laughed her head off on seeing the now useless pieces of paper.

Disgusted by her craftiness, I spat at her.

"You spat at me, you scoundrel?!" She grabbed my pants. "If you don't give me fifty pengős, I'll light a candle at the cross and curse you so that wherever you wander you'll never have one bit of luck."

I felt that if I didn't give her a sound beating at once, I'd have a seizure.

"Haven't you already put a curse on me?" I asked. "And now you want to light a candle on top of that?" I began kicking away at her sides.

"You can pound me all you want," she whimpered, "but it won't do you any good. I'll curse you even in my coffin until you put the money by my head."

I knew there was no point in beating her; all I wanted was to let off steam. Even if I kept kicking her until daybreak, she would stand her ground until I gave her the money.

"Okay, I'll let you have the money," I said, puffing from exhaustion. "But you won't have much joy from it."

A little while ago Rilandri still pretended to be half-dead, but at the sound of "money" she came to life in no time. Her face bore not the slightest trace of tears.

I wasn't exactly in a good mood, but vengeance encouraged me to play a trick on her.

"Make it up to a hundred, dear brother," she said, showing me the forty pengős. God will bless you for it, and let my earlier curses fall on dogs and cats!"

I deliberately didn't take out the money, but let her grovel instead; at least I enjoyed that. Afterward she'd curse me again. Just let her; I'd leave her high and dry with the bad money. I'd give her what she wanted.

I searched among the horse registrations for a long time, gloating in advance at Rilandri's frustration. Her big blue eyes shone at the sight of the money, and she just kept repeating:

"You'll make it up to a hundred? You will, won't you?"

I wanted to say something that would have suited her question, but I just kept pointing; I couldn't utter a word.

What happened? A miracle? Or was I dreaming? Between my fingers the paper money was crackling with its original vivid colors. I shuffled the banknotes like cards, but they didn't lose their colors. Who could say whether joy or fear caused my remorse?

I knelt beside Rilandri to say a prayer of gratitude, but the only thing that came to mind was a Christmas carol, and even that, only sketchily, so I had to make up for the missing bits with my own words. I kept on with it relentlessly, undisturbed by Rilandri's cackling as she quickly lost patience and resorted to violence. Grasping my hair, she yelled into my ear as if I were deaf.

"So you're praying, are you? Kiss my ass!" I won't continue, because she couldn't continue either; I turned her around with a backhand slap, so that what she wanted me to kiss was now pointing at the sky.

At the same time, I shed my piety and pulled the money out again, put it on the grass and, viewing it from a little further away, tried to discover any faults. They were all perfect, I assured myself. However, this conclusion raised the question of what to give Rilandri, since there wasn't a single faulty note among them. While she was noisily snivelling, I was consumed by rage over the unwary promise I'd made. I didn't have the strength to give her the money, but neither did I have the courage to refuse it.

"Come on, take the sixty pengős!" I said angrily to Rilandri. "And stop whimpering; I know that even the lice on you are unreliable, because they often sting like fleas."

The sight of the money left her unable to decide whether to laugh or to whimper. She just watched it with bulging eyes, wringing her hands in despair to overcome her greed until she couldn't bear it any longer and madly flung herself on it. As she snatched at the part meant for her, her hands still in her skirt pocket, she informed me that she was entitled to half of it, and wouldn't let herself be brushed off with sixty pengős.

I wasn't at all surprised. Anyway, what good would it have done me if I'd started to argue with Rilandri now? I took hold of her curly mass of hair, wrestled her to the ground, and carefully placed the soles of my feet on her throat as one does with a snake, pressing on it for a while until she took the matter seriously. After that, everything went the way it should, and she turned out her pocket without any further ado.

"Well, that's really nice of you," I chided her with a wallop. "With all that money you wanted to take mine, too."

"I did," she said proudly and firmly, spitting out a mouthful of grain she'd sucked up while lying face down next to the railway track. "I deserve it," she said, dishing up the same old story.

"Where did you get that kind of money, you Gypsy woman?"

"Where your mother-in-law, Balush, did."

"I thought so. The phumba boys must have had devilish luck. They gathered the *love*[70] and then split it up among themselves. Too

[70] money (pronounced "low-vay")

bad the other women didn't come; I could have bought the Tisza estate tomorrow."

Rilandri looked down on me mockingly, pretending she wasn't interested in my musings. "How come both of you stole three hundred pengős each from your husbands?" I asked. "Didn't they have any more?" She wanted to take revenge on me by not responding to my words. She kept stubbornly silent until she flew into one of her rages.

"Get a load of you, the filthy one! The more he has, the more he wants. You didn't even have a decent pair of pants and now that you've managed to rob a fortune, you still want more."

"Why, haven't you done the same?"

"I only want my rightful share," she said. "I could have led the Gypsies to you unnoticed."

"Why didn't you?"

"I thought you were an honest man, and I risked my life for you, but you didn't deserve it. Don't you think that if they ever catch me, they won't do the same to me as to Balush?"

"At least you'd suffer unfairly, not guiltily. It would be a pity to take all those curses upon yourself because of the money."

"You're not afraid of being cursed, are you? You think you can always twist what others say? Or that curses don't work on you?"

"Don't you worry about me," I reassured her, laughing. "I'm not interested in curses; I don't care whether they work or not; I want money."

"That's what I want, too," she shrieked, losing her patience. "Give me back my money! I want to get married, or else you've got to marry me. Now that I've left Yagosh for the two of you, it's your duty to marry me! You can't make a mockery of me." Rilandri kept hammering the ground with her open palm. "I swear I'll get you arrested somehow, even if I also have to wither away in jail."

"Why do you keep screeching? Bada will marry you. Don't be choosy. Be glad; you'll get a good man."

"Why should I be glad?" Rilandri snarled, baring her white teeth. "Do you think he doesn't want money, just like you too?"

"What does he need money for?"

"You ask him. He didn't so much as put his pants on next to me."

"Bada?"

"Yes, Bada. Why are you staring at me like dumb Muto? Bada said he needed four hundred pengős to undo the trouble he caused, otherwise you'll remain outlaws."

"So what? He could still have slept with you."

"Of course," she said sarcastically. "You think everyone is like you—you don't mind if it's a dog you sleep with as long as it has a kerchief on its head."

"You're right there, but as you see," and I waved the money before her eyes, "You can't be finicky for such a sum."

"Don't you fear God?" Rilandri asked, shaking her head.

"There's no reason to. I was relatively cheap; Bada asked *you* for four hundred."

"But at least he wanted to marry me honestly."

"Honestly? What did you say? Did you tell him how much money you have?"

"I didn't say a thing, only that I'd find the four hundred somehow."

"Did you count on me?"

"Yes. Help me out, brother, or else he won't want me."

"Why didn't you say so from the start? Now I can believe it or not believe it if I want to. First you go to bed with me, then you threaten me, then you want me to marry you, and in the end you want me to marry you off and pay your dowry. One of us is really nuts, but if you think I'm the one, you're wrong."

She looked at me for a long time, nodding approvingly while searching for the right words for her latest setback.

"They sure taught you at school how to be smart," she said, her entire upper body giving emphasis to her words. "Ten people don't have as much mischief in them as you."

"Will you tell the truth once and for all?" I urged her.

"Yes. I want to buy Bada for myself."

"You've said that already. Stop telling stories!"

"It's true. He looks like such a quiet, prudent man."

I was brooding over what to tell her. A sort of bad conscience was lurking inside me. Should I open Rilandri's eyes, if for nothing else but for the sake of the truth? The wretched woman believed that it was her husband, Yagosh, who invented cards, and that no man besides him knows a thing about gambling. I wondered how she would react if I told her: *You, God's brute beast, where is it that you want to escape from your fate? If Yagosh has gambled away what you had, this one would gamble away even what you don't have.* I was certain she would be offended and laugh in my face, thinking I was jealous.

Rilandri was staring into space, quietly awaiting my decision.

While all this was going on, the horse kept on grazing with gusto, not giving a hoot about our noisy brawling; it was almost lost amid the colorful brush below the railway embankment. It was enjoying the epitome of its dreams in compensation for the afternoon's heat, wading knee-deep in the thin, silky grass. At times its loudly crunching molars stopped; it would suddenly raise its head, let its intelligent gaze wander about, blowing and sniffing the air, making snorting noises.

Rilandri was getting more and more nervous, tearing at the grass, until she finally lost her forced patience.

"Will you give me my money or do I tell Bada?"

I too suspected something from the horse's manner. An animal's instinct and sense of smell are rarely wrong. Rilandri must also have reacted to that. She only figured that Bada would be coming, while I—who was standing, and could feel the descending cool air on my naked skin—was already certain that the air current coming from the farm was carrying the smell of the other horse. And, despite the twilight, the visibility was still quite good.

So that was what you were hiding from me? I can choose whether we split the money into two or three parts. My money, of course.

Frankly, that would be the fair way. After all, not one, not two, but three of us were there. I couldn't keep this a secret from Bada forever; sooner or later he would find out about it from someone—probably from Rilandri. Better to get it over and done with as soon as possible; it had already caused enough complications so far. True, not long ago I'd given up on the money completely, but now, I sensed, if luck was to remain on my side, I would be ill-advised to provoke its anger. You can never tell what money's inscrutable whim might keep in store for me.

The farmhands hadn't hurt Rilandri's eyes sufficiently for her not to notice the change I'd gone through.

"Give me only a hundred pengős—my money!"

I counted out the money without a word, picking the more faded ones, of course, and parting with every piece with a bitter taste in my mouth I threw it down before her.

She watched me with wrinkled eyes, acting as if she hadn't noticed that a fortune had fallen in her lap.

"Why are you looking that way?" I asked, "Every last bit of it there is yours."

"I know," said Rilandri in an insolent tone.

Slowly she gathered it up, stuffed it into her skirt pocket, and then squinted at me again.

"Don't think that it's in God's name!"

"You're looking to haggle again?" I snapped at her.

"No, dear brother, I just want to make Bada believe that I've swindled the money."

"All right, but will you tell me at last why you had to make such a big deal about it when you could have gotten away with it at much less cost?"

"I knew that if I gave him the money, you would immediately realize I stole it from Yagosh."

"So that's how you want to tie him to you? By having something to scare him with in the future?"

Rilandri didn't answer; she just pulled her head sheepishly between her shoulders and blushed.

You miserable thing, I thought, *you'll be happy one day to get rid of him somehow or other.*

Soon our ways parted, hers toward the farm, while I went jogging along in the direction of the forest. Looking back, she made a threatening gesture; my impression was that she meant to say that this should remain our secret.

Rilandri's credibility didn't produce much confidence in me; in less than two hours I'd almost gotten lost in the inscrutable lush thicket of her cunning. To be sure, no matter how she underestimated her ingenuity, God had blessed her with all the mischief that can be ascribed to a Gypsy woman.

I gave the horse a squeeze with my ankles; I would have preferred to gallop after Rilandri, but it was really dark by then. Where to look for her? Every bush offered a hiding place, and if she wanted to make a getaway, she would certainly not go to the farm.

Sighing, I watched the sky, but not a star was to be seen. Where was the forest? At sunset it had seemed barely a stone's throw away, and this road I was on appeared to lead straight to it. I reined in the horse to avoid colliding with something or other. All good thoughts left me, leaving only anger and revenge in their wake. I tried to look around, but I was surrounded by an impenetrable darkness. It felt as if the horse's even gait had become less certain as the clatter of the hooves faded into soft steps.

Dear God, where am I? Rearing on its hind legs, the horse acted as if it also just wanted to look around. It was too late to do a thing; I rolled down somewhere between its hind legs until a thorny bush slowed me down. I panted for a long time, gasping for breath, mentally garbling bits of the Lord's Prayer.

As I groped my way back to the horse, I saw that it was still standing on its hind legs, like a playground slide pegged into the ground.

Cool, humid air hit my face; I could only smell the water of the nearby canal, not see it, and its unpleasant, stale stench made me queasy.

Crawling on all fours, I somehow managed to climb up the bank, but I couldn't see anything due to the fiery circles dancing before my eyes. I waited for them to fade, and in the meantime I tried to get rid of the thorns sticking out of my skin. I stomped around impatiently, a feeling of apprehension growing in me that I had landed in Hell, where prayer would have no effect, because even after the fiery circles had ceased, I still couldn't see a thing.

Having lost all I hope, I led the horse by the reins and we managed to struggle back onto the road. "We're lost, my friend," I said, patting its neck, "and the only things we can rely on in this hell are our ears and noses."

I pondered for a long time, concentrating on working out where we'd come from, but I was out of luck and I started out into the unknown, trusting the horse's instinct. If my sense of smell served me well—of which I was not at all convinced—then the road led somewhere along the banks of the canal. I didn't even dare to rely on which side the cooler air had hit me from; I felt cold all over. My skin was burning from all the abrasions, but they didn't keep me warm.

Slowly I ran out of any soul-warming thoughts as well. Only the promise of dawn held out some bitter solace, but I was still as far from it as an itinerant Gypsy from Heaven. I counted our footsteps apathetically, and although the darkness was disheartening, I wasn't sufficiently fed up with it all to walk out of this world.

The forest must be somewhere on the opposite side of the canal; the only question was how to get across. The thought hadn't even reached my consciousness yet when I felt a pang in my heart. The afternoon's bath had put me off from getting wet again for a long time.

I was counting our steps diligently, or at least that's how I remember it, when I suddenly found myself arguing with Mr. Kapusy, our math teacher, who didn't want to believe me without proof that A squared + B squared = C squared. *Oh, miserable fate,* I thought, *don't you have anything better to do than to amuse yourself at my expense? Here I am, trembling in the dark, my skin perforated like a sieve, and with barely any breath left in me, while you're playing school with me? The theorem can only be proved if I get to the forest, because, although A squared + B squared = Kurucho, I can only reach the proper result if I find Rilandri's square root.*

Once again we arrived at some kind of embankment, but this time I luckily held on in time, avoiding the previous mishap. The horse had tramped up onto a makeshift wooden platform. My unexpected fright was promptly followed by relief. A bridge! We managed to cross the canal without getting wet. We then had to keep on going for quite a distance before I noticed that the clatter of the hooves reverberated more clearly and sharply. The air seemed much milder inside than out, but now I was again faced by a big question: Where should I wait for Bada?

I could hear the prolonged howl of a dog from afar; I'd never been to these parts before, but, according to Bada, the village of Orosi was supposed to be somewhere in the vicinity, just beyond the forest.

I kept listening for a while, unable to decide whether to go or stay. Doubtlessly the safest option would be to wait for them here, at the edge of the woods. *Doubtlessly?* I smiled at my thoughts. *What is doubtless here? Perhaps Rilandri's word? How many priests would have to swear that she would keep it? With so much money . . .*

The solitude and the darkness that had wrapped itself around me also twisted my thoughts. Not a single leaf rustled, and I could hear my own breathing, which seemed abnormally fast. The uneven noise of my chattering teeth was not caused solely by the forest's cooler air.

The only thought that still encouraged me was that, if I couldn't see anything, no one else could see me any better. It was hard to force myself to go any further, but by then I was sick and tired of loafing around at the edge of the forest. It might be safer at the farm. I noticed that the horse was becoming edgy and wanted to go on relentlessly; its nervousness, in turn, stirred up gloomy thoughts in me.

A strange feeling came over me, as if someone was going to hit me over the head any second. I kept rummaging around among the junk in my pocket, but couldn't find anything that could help me protect myself if necessary. And I certainly didn't have enough courage to dismount and look for a club.

And so I turned the reins over to the horse, hugging its neck. *Take me anywhere you like,* I thought, *as far as your eyes can see.* I didn't have to do much prodding. The horse neighed and took off; I dug my face into its mane and let it follow its nose.

It felt good to snuggle up to its warm body, whose acrid sweaty smell mingled with the cool aroma of the forest's leafy litter. It shook me and made me teeter, until its even clattering made my thoughts fall apart.

A yellow-colored world unfolded behind my eyes. From the constantly churning of the tiny, amorphous shadows, smoky human heads billowed out, the seemingly familiar faces once again turned into a vague, shapeless mass. Only the memory of the acrid smoke lingered on; everything else faded into oblivion.

I sensed, rather than heard, that the horse was veering off the road into the forest. Dry leaves were now rustling under its hooves; its soft, cautious steps had wiped the dream from my eyes. Startled, I grasped the rein, but couldn't decide whether to let go of it or turn back. I hadn't dreamt the smell of the smoke. No, a fire was burning on the wooded trail the horse was leading me down.

Hundreds of thoughts ran through my mind. I sat there petrified. Not a soul was in sight anywhere near the fire. That same moment, a figure with a huge cudgel stepped from the trees. I didn't want to waste even a second on questioning him, so I turned around before he could come within striking distance. I spurred the horse to flee.

"Have you gone mad, man?!" Bada called out after me. His voice reverberated through the trees, affecting me more than a punch in the head. This time I'd jumped the gun; I should at least have had the guts to ask him who he was. Ashamed of my failed courage, I sauntered back to him.

"Have I scared you?" he asked with a grin.

"Don't tell me you weren't scared, too!" I said furiously.

"Almost," he said, making fun of my shock, "except that I heard your horse whinnying from miles away."

"Then why didn't you say something? You almost gave me a heart attack."

"A man should be prepared for anything in this darkness, but even I was surprised when I saw you coming on your own."

There was something gloomy in his mood—a futile anticipation that could be felt from his unconcealed sighs. I wasn't depressed by it, though; after all, everything had turned out the way I'd expected. Rilandri had left us high and dry, showing that she could outsmart both of us. There was certainly no doubt about her cunning. I didn't want to dwell any more on that, lest I again make myself into a laughing stock.

"Where is she?" I asked.

"How the hell should I know?" asked Bada thoughtfully. "She told me she was coming back and bringing some money."

"And you believed her?"

"I thought she was telling the truth."

"You're lucky she didn't take your last rags off you! She might as well have done that, too. You sure fell for that big-eyed woman, though you said yourself you can't trust a woman with big eyes."

Bada just waved away my rebuke.

"Never mind; it's worse that it's so damn dark."

"You've been here for long?" I was itching with curiosity.

"The sun was down when I left the farm."

It's possible that the horse had really been whinnying at them, but I didn't dare ask too much, lest I let the cat out of the bag.

"The limping woman mentioned you."

"What limping woman?" I asked, pretending not to know what he was talking about. Although I wouldn't have betrayed any secret, I still preferred to stick to mumbling.

"What are we going to do now?"

"For the time being, we'll wait for morning; we'd only get lost in the dark."

It seemed that Bada was not afraid of the dark, but rather that he was still hoping Rilandri would turn up.

They say that it doesn't show on an apple if it starts rotting from the inside. Bada didn't belong to the choicest of apples, nor was he rotting from the inside, yet something had happened to him that now revealed his state of mind. Usually he didn't stop clowning about, and it could drive a guy right up the wall when he played the philosopher with sayings like, "A woman can only be believed if the goats graze on her grave," "Least said, soonest mended," or "Don't look at the woman, only her bag."

The Bada before me now was not the old Bada. I watched the frozen grin on his face as he talked about the woman with the limp; Bada was in agony like a rootless tree. He spoke only to take his mind off his thoughts. He kept losing the thread, staring into the fire, and it sometimes seemed he was dosing off. Only the unusual wrinkles on his forehead contradicted appearances.

"Are you cold?" Bada asked as I turned my back to the fire.

"I'm keeping the mosquitoes warm."

He didn't reply, just disappeared among the trees. I could hear him crunching the branches for a long time, and then he reappeared with an armful of twigs, trailing his sheepskin coat after him.

"Such a learned Gypsy like you should have at least as much brains as a farmer."

"Aren't you feeling well?" I asked sarcastically.

"I am, but don't stand under a leaky drain when it's raining."

"Well, say thank you on my behalf to whoever gave you this wise advice."

"Would you tell me something?" he asked, wrinkling his eyes.

"I would," I replied hoarsely. *It doesn't make any difference any more,* I thought. *We'll divide it. This damn money has messed up my life anyhow.*

"Why aren't you asking?" I snapped at him.

"I can see you're upset."

"I'm not upset. I know that Rilandri has let you in on everything, except the one thing she ought to have."

"Like what?"

"Let's take first things first."

"Why did you leave your clothes behind? Did you think we'd always travel by night?"

I didn't interrupt him although I had an answer on the tip of my tongue. Relieved, I wrapped the sheepskin coat around me.

"Didn't she say anything else?" I asked.

"Besides all this arguing," Bada replied, "you should at last learn to think like a Gypsy."

"What's that got to do with Rilandri?"

"Nothing," he erupted in anger. "But let me tell you this: If they ask for our papers, don't you think we'll get busted?"

"And if I brought the clothes along?"

"At least they would look at us differently. They wouldn't notice from miles away that a pair of tramps was coming their way. Well-dressed people are always luckier. You'd better learn once and for all that they're always treated better than shabby-looking ones. You've experienced that yourself."

"I'd never have guessed if you hadn't reminded me."

"Am I not right?" asked Bada innocently.

"You're absolutely right. Before you decked yourself out in your stolen outfit, you used to try fading into the background. Now of course you talk to me differently, because I'm a ragged vagrant. And would you please tell me who made me into one?" Bada stared ahead in silence, his eyes wide open, as I continued: "I wasn't concerned about what you were wearing when all you had were rags, you know."

"I'm not concerned about myself, either," he interrupted. "We can't be kids forever."

"Well, well, who would believe you've changed so much?"

"Don't go twisting my words—there's no question of a change, but as long as we've already taken all these chances, anyway, it should at least make sense."

"There's no need for you to worry about me. I'm going home as soon as it's light enough. I'm fed up with this life."

"That's just it, but we'll need money for that. It's not worth our while to take the horses home; it would do us more harm than good."

"So that's it—you want me to go home on foot?"

"There's no talking sense with you," said Bada. With that, he jumped up angrily and set off to gather more twigs.

What an idiot I was! To think I'd been ready to share the money with him. It was just as well I hadn't gotten around to mentioning anything about that. Bada would have been capable of letting me go home on foot.

Not on your life! You'll fall asleep, and then, so long Bada.

I had enough time to get my act together before he returned. Sighing, Bada rekindled the fire, then settled down in front of it. Both of us kept quiet. I watched him from under the sheepskin coat; I'd have given my front teeth to hear his thoughts, to know what was going on inside him.

Bada kept wiping his face with his sleeve as if he was really hot. I'd already noticed earlier that his eyes were shiny but figured the smoke was bothering him. It was the woman who was bothering him. He'd given himself away when he said her eyes were too big, and now he was crazy about her.

"Are you asleep?" he asked.

"Yeah."

"What time could it be?"

"Rilandri won't be coming anymore."

Bada sat up as if something had stung him. It showed on his face that his thoughts were in turmoil behind the tense wrinkles on his forehead. He then relaxed, let out a laugh, and fell back to the ground.

We were sitting, shrouded in silence. Indeed, it would have been nice to know what time it was, because something just didn't let that rascal rest. I didn't think he'd had enough sleep that afternoon unless he'd had a good nap after Rilandri had left him.

"What didn't the woman tell you?" he asked, piping up again.

"That you didn't get laid."

"How do you know?"

"Because you wouldn't be in such a bad mood if you had."

"You're right," he agreed. "But never mind, let's go to sleep and we'll go home first thing at dawn. You're right, I've been worrying too much lately and can't explain myself properly. I too would have been offended in your place, but I swear on my mother's life that I didn't mean any harm. I don't know how you do it; I always try to figure out everything in advance, but I don't know what the hell for. Everything works out in the end, anyway."

"It shows; that why we're here now."

"That's right," said Bada. "I was also toying with the idea this afternoon that we should gallop home tonight. After all, we have the registrations; it's nobody's business where we bought the horses, and we could sell them by tomorrow. And when we have the money in our pockets, we'll be able to straighten everything out."

"But then a young woman turned up," I interrupted sarcastically, "a young woman who said: 'Listen, Bada! If you want to know how shrewd I am, wait for half an hour while I pop out into the plains, and I'll bring you an apronful of paper money. I won't eat or drink or do anything else until I'll have it here for you.'"

"Ahem," muttered Bada, but he was paying attention to some noise. "Listen!" He motioned for silence. "Someone is coming."

"Rilandri."

"No, it's some kind of a cart," he whispered.

I too started to listen and heard a kind of rattling, but if it was a cart, it was approaching slowly indeed.

"It could be some sort of ox cart."

"That would make more noise."

You just keep on watching, I thought. *Who cares?* I retreated into the sheepskin coat but couldn't relax, and I found myself doing the same as he did. We both stared ahead with bated breath.

The fire cast a light along the trail, and the edge of the road loomed like the black mouth of a cave. Whatever it was, it rattled toward us with frustrating sluggishness. Time and again it would stop as if to catch its breath, and then the clatter got a bit louder.

Bada watched both me and the trail. Lying prone, he peered toward the sound like a cat.

"What would come so slowly?" he kept asking.

I shrugged my shoulders. We didn't even dare to think of having a closer look. We weren't in a position to satisfy our curiosity; all we wanted was to be left alone.

I didn't attach great importance to the rumble of the cart, which was clearly audible now; it was mere curiosity that got hold of me. Unfortunately, on my way here I'd been asleep, so I had no idea how far the edge of the forest was from the beginning of the trail. If the cart crossed the illuminated stretch of the trail, I could maybe figure out its speed—not that that would make any difference—but perhaps by then we would see it, anyway.

Something now seemed to appear at the start of the trail, moving without a sound; and then, in contrast to its earlier rattling sound, it continued toward us with an empty clatter.

"Come on!" hissed Bada, rolling between the trees. I followed, wrapped completely in the sheepskin coat, which gave me no end of trouble between the bushes.

Bada crouched next to me, ready to pounce. Looking at it from the haze, the contours of the cart were more visible now, but it seemed that nothing was pulling or pushing it. Nevertheless, we heard the wheels rumbling, and even saw that it was approaching despite its slowness.

I didn't hear Bada's heartbeat, but mine usually gets really loud at times like these. However, when a few last noisy thuds suddenly gave way to a joyful pitter-patter, I almost burst out laughing. Bada looked at me, flashing his white teeth.

"A donkey cart," he whispered.

"That's it," I said, laughing. "Rilandri!" Throwing off the sheepskin coat, I ran to meet her.

"Where have you been bumming around? May worms wiggle inside you and eat out your heart!" she gasped. "Is that cousin of yours here, the one whose face is black as a kettle?"

"Here he is," I gestured with subdued laughter toward the rushing Bada. I took the single tree from her hand as she started off with staggered steps, loudly hissing her blessings at us until Bada picked her up in his lap and echoed his joyful laughter throughout the forest.

Everything changed around us with astounding speed. Even though our mutual suspicion had eased over the past few hours, only now did it finally cease. Our earlier whispered conversations were replaced by Rilandri's chattering; then we all shared our adventures about scuffles with the darkness, sometimes cutting each other short.

"And all the while you were making yourself comfortable here next to the fire," Rilandri chided Bada, "instead of meeting us at the edge of the forest, at least."

There was some truth in her words, but who would have thought about that now? We didn't even ask what we were actually so happy about. Nothing had changed, after all. The darkness, tomorrow's trip, the gendarmes, and even the possibility of arrest all stood before us like a barbed-wire fence. Fortunately, these thoughts didn't embitter us; they slept somewhere in our subconsious, wrapped into the patched blanket of high spirits.

"Bring me my bundle!" Rilandri said, "and don't laugh at the poor people's hardships! Your lips are white from hunger."

Bada was visibly pleased by the woman's scolding. The dance of the bright flames reflected from his smoothed-out face, as if the meaning of the scoldings had changed and their value become equal to praise.

"What's in this, woman? Soil?" he moaned, lifting up the bundle.

“Just bring it here and stop your yacking!”

So far not a single word had been said about where all the stuff she brought had come from. It was highly unlikely she’d met another soul apart from the limping woman and the hungry dogs roaming the countryside. I’d noticed at first glance that, under Bada’s bright-buttoned vest, Rilandri was wearing a wide-sleeved brown blouse that, apart from the odor of sweat, had a pleasant whiff of cleanliness about it.

“That would have been enough to bring on the cart,” said Bada, plunking the luggage on the ground.

“Ahem,” said Rilandri, her eyes lighting up at the sound of praise. “Here, look what I’ve got for you,” she added, pulling a brown shirt from the bundle. Then she undid the tablecloth.

“Eat!” she said.

We didn’t know what to reach for first from among the various kinds of provisions we now saw stacked one on top of the other in the characteristic way Gypsy women arranged food. Rilandri dug out a sizable length of sausage from under a piece of yellow, rancid bacon, some ham, bread, potatoes, and a large variety of vegetables.

“Have that,” she said, breaking the sausage in half. “It’s easier this way.” Not that we ever had to be encouraged to eat, but now we outdid even ourselves.

“We should have brought the pot along,” she grumbled. “At least you could have woken up to a hot meal.”

“I’ve pushed it over your sister’s head,” I said, trying to clear Bada’s name. First Rilandri looked puzzled, then she waved her hand disparagingly.

“Well, let it stay there until the rust eats it away.” She rolled a long cigarette, massaged her legs, which were obviously sore, and waited until we had our fill.

“Come on, you have something too!” Bada kept urging her.

“I’ll have some later,” said Rilandri, picking out a few larger potatoes and throwing them in the fire. Barely had we swallowed the last mouthfuls when we rolled some sizable cigarettes and, free from care and stress, lay down beside the fire. My skin was grateful that I had finally covered it with something whose pleasant smell revealed its civilized background. White bedding, linen tablecloths, and towels were folded into Rilandri's large bag.

"I've brought you something, too, you famous Gypsy!" she said, pinching Bada.

The way she winked at me, I knew that her next step would be to secure the long-term commiment she sought. I wasn't exempt from this ruse, either; after all, I would have had plenty of occasions to let Bada into our secret, but I saw no need for it. He would have committed himself even without the money, and I believe that during Rilandri's absence he had regretted it a hundred times that he'd let her slip out of his hands over such trifles.

I pretended to be interested in her gift to Bada. You could tell from her body language that she knew how to stimulate the interest of money-hungry people. I too was fascinated.

Rilandri pulled out a twenty, smoothed it out carefully, and then placed it on the edge of her skirt, which she had spread out on the ground. She then neatly stacked another two or three bills next to it, and finally threw a haphazard handful on top of them-all the while thoroughly enjoying our frozen gazes. Judging by her motions, it seemed as if she were spooning out an endless amount of cash from her skirt pocket. She made sure the process lasted as long as possible.

"There you go," she said in the end.

All the demons in Bada became unleashed as he picked me up and, with unintelligible whoops of joy, danced around the fire; then, without looking where, he dumped me and raised Rilandri tightly to him.

"I'll never leave you while I'm alive!"

"You'd better not," Rilandri winked at me, "cause you won't find anyone like me in any forest."

While he was cuddling Rilandri, I went in search of the sheepskin coat. I was tormented by shame on account of my earlier, hasty assumptions; I noticed that I was apt to react like that over and over. Without any conviction, merely because of my impatience, I am forever suspicious and tend to believe the worst about everyone.

I didn't begrudge Bada's joy, but somehow I couldn't come to terms with my own world. I disparage everyone, because I'm unable to get to know myself. Days ago I thought that happiness would never cease! And how long did it last? Until I gratified my sexual urges.

Those fleeting hours in the barn on the estate had been just that, only hours, and yet they now felt like a past that had drowned all that might have been. That girl didn't leave anything of her inside me; her mother had shattered my momentary memories. They forced me into becoming a man and deprived me not only of my virginity, but also of anything that I could hang on the wall of time as a keepsake.

All that remained of the piled-up multitude of so many dreams was a bleak sense of satiety, the price of my squandered childhood.

Bada also said that we were no longer kids. There I was, initiated into adulthood, freed from the childish longings of my seventeen years, and I didn't know what to do with myself. I think that force of habit brings old fantasies, although if I were honest with myself, I ought to know that all that is in the past. Other cravings, other thoughts intrude into my life, and I just stick to the old ones, but no longer desire them.

"Hey, where are you?!" Bada cried impatiently. He was waving the bunch of money toward me. "Well, you diabolical Gypsy, can you tell me how much this is?"

"How should I know?" I said indifferently.

"You see," he said, turning to Rilandri. He held it in front of me. "Count it."

"Why should I count it if it won't become any more than it is, anyway?"

"Or do you know how much it is?" Bada looked at me distrustfully.

"How should I know? I'm just not interested in other people's money."

"There you go again."

"No I don't," I protested modestly, "but why should I worry about money that's not my business?"

"Why do you think it's none of your business?" said Rilandri, stepping in. "Do you think that if there'd be any trouble, you'd be left out?"

She snatched the money from Bada's hand and hastily divided it into two piles.

"This is yours, and this is yours," she forced them on us. "You shouldn't only share in the problems but also in the profits. Now, if you think so, you can give him your part or you give him yours," she turned to me. "There can't be any recriminations then."

We both nodded in agreement. Bada was still deliberating, but when he saw that I stuffed the money in my pocket, he handed his part over to Rilandri.

"You see, the dispute between the two of you has been solved. Both of you are equally rich Gypsies, and there is no reason for envying each other. That's what I hated so much about the phumbas. If one of them had two bit coins and the other was dying, he wouldn't part with any of it. They could only yammer but never help. And if one of them ever lent the other a hand, they would rub it in for a lifetime. God save us all from pitying people; they're the most double-tongued people in the world."

Bada smiled when the woman, a tablecloth tucked under her arm, went into the woods.

"When should we start?" he asked, looking lengthily after Rilandri.

"Where to?" she asked.

Bada's face clouded over again and, the way he shrugged his shoulders, it was obvious that he expected me to answer.

"What would happen if you didn't go back to school?"

"I wouldn't miss out on much, but my mother!"

"Yeah, I know, she'd be just devastated." He heaved a big sigh. "But I'm still grateful for this woman; God was gracious to us." He watched Rilandri, as she ambled toward the cart, the tablecloth filled with leaves. "I've never seen that much money in my life."

It seemed that all was settled; that's what comforted Bada too. So far the journey had been successful, even if it was still far from over. In my view, though, the money dealt out to us by the Creator would get me off the hook unless He had other plans for me.

"Hm," laughed Bada, "do you know what I'm thinking? The Gypsies will die of envy when they see us."

"You're thirsting for revenge again."

"That's right. At least now I'll be able to show them that I'm as good as any of them." He got up, helped Rilandri to push the open cart among the trees, and continued: "I told you, they'll follow me one day like puppies," said Bada, gritting his teeth. "They've tricked me often enough; they always took me for a good-hearted fool."

For a while he waited for me to agree, but when I shook my head disapprovingly, he turned on me and exploded.

"Aren't I right?"

"Yes, you are." I said with suppressed fury. "But if they could clean you out of what you didn't have, how much more will they be able to do so if you have a lot?"

"Don't worry, I'll see to that," he said, beating his breasts.

"See to what? Do you think you can shackle the people's tongues? What will Rilandri have to say when she'll hear from everyone that she's living with a fool? Not to mention that she escaped from Yagosh because of his gambling. Haven't you talked about that?"

"I'll never touch a card again. Do you believe me?"

"I don't believe a thing. You've promised it hundreds of times, but unfortunately it didn't depend on you. Neither will it in the future."

"Who does it depend on, then?" Bada asked curiously.

"On the ones who got you into it. They'll always find a way to take advantage of your weakness. It's less than a week since we've left. Do you really believe that they've forgotten who you are? You'll still be 'Crazy Palalo' and 'Dotty' to them, and I think they'll be right."

"Why?"

"Because. You'll figure out why on your own. Did you know how much this woman loved her husband? She was able to forgive Yagosh even when he slept with Sophie Bolygó. But as soon as she realized that, outside of that narrow world, whose boundaries Old Phumba was guarding, there was another world, a wider one where folks are braver and maybe even cleverer, right away she wanted to get away. All the wrongs she hadn't noticed before became a hundred times worse, and she was desperate to flee from things she'd ignored up until then. She has just as many reasons for revenge as you, only that she knows that revenge breeds revenge, that in the end it eats up those who have carried it inside them."

"I love that woman," he sighed.

"She sees a world in you; it would be a shame to crush her dreams just so you can even the score with them."

"I don't only want to go home because of revenge; I want to make amends for what I've screwed up."

"You've done that already, and you can leave the rest to me! As soon as the night lets up, I'll get going at once. The horse has had a good rest and it should be able to cope."

"What will your father say? He ordered me to look after you."

"Don't worry about it; I can take care of myself. If I get home before dawn, everything will be alright."

"Before dawn? Do you know how far we are?"

"No, but I can imagine. I can do fifteen miles an hour, and I should be home in five hours, which won't be too much for the horse.

"It'll be hard to cross the canal."

"Yes, it will," I agreed, "but by then I'll be at home."

"Too bad I didn't go to school," he sighed. "I could think much better. As things stand, I can only figure out things if other folks tell me about them or once things have already happened. You know what I was thinking?" Bada tried to open up to me. "That tomorrow we'll stop in a village, get ourselves some proper clothes, throw a barrel of beer on the cart, and, as fast as the horses can make it, we'll gallop into Gypsy Paris.

"'Drink up, Gypsies!' I'll shout. 'I'll get some more when you're through with this.' Why, they'd crawl over me like flies over honey. 'Give me a pengő, brother,' one of them would say, 'you know I always repaid you, look at my kids, they haven't eaten a thing today.' And I'd say, 'There you go, you don't have to repay it, I'll give as much to a beggar.'

"Then someone else would say, 'Hey, give me some, too. Or do you think he's a better man than me?' I'd say, 'There you go, too.' I'd hand out something like fifty pengős—let the Gypsies have a holiday for once. 'God bless you,' they'd say, full of gratitude. 'We used to tell him he was crazy, and now look at his horse! And his wife is worth more than all these huts of ours. 'God bless him—at least he looked after us, though he could have just boasted and been stingy.'"

Bada paused, and then went on.

"I know it wouldn't really happen that way, but if you daydream it might as well be about nice things." He fixed his eyes on me, more solemnly. "You're right," he said, "where is there enough money in the world to satisfy their thousand years of hunger? I'd only unsettle their appetites, and God save us from the wrath of hungry people."

Bada began reluctantly poking at the fire as he now stared at me with furrowed brows: "Do you know what hurts me most? Even if I did put my heart out to them, they'd say I did it because I'm a fool. They wouldn't even feel sorry for me. . . . You were saying I should run away if I want to really live?"

"If I knew something better, I'd tell you so."

"There is nothing better," said Bada.

Rilandri became suspicious and, having finished getting their lair ready, she ambled over to the fire.

"What are you two whispering about?" she asked.

"The kid is going home; he has to go back to school next week."

"School?" she shook her head. "Hey, you've already had a wife! You'd be better off coming with us. What's the good of school? It's not like you'll become a judge, anyway. And where we're going, you'll find as many girls as you want."

"It's not the way you think," Bada explained to her, although he didn't understand it, either. Nor did I. Actually, I would have preferred to accept Rilandri's advice.

All in all, I knew, I should have felt sorry for myself. Who would benefit from my going to school? How much better was I than Bada or any of the other Gypsy kids? Not only because officials like Kurucho didn't discriminate between one Gypsy and the next, but what would have happened if that sixth grader who got shot years earlier had not been Boncza's son? I'd have been seen as just another nobody and would not have been sent to school to make amends. Yes, everything would have worked out differently or wouldn't have started at all.

"What do you want to become?" asked Rilandri seriously. "An apprentice? Then why did you leave your clothes with Balush? Nothing will become of you like this. No matter where you go, everyone will see that you're a Gypsy and no one would believe you that you went to school."

I knew she was thinking about the affair with the gendarmes. She couldn't resign herself to the way I looked, which is why she had complained to Bada about the clothes. I had to believe they were right; appearances can't be ignored. But what about in the very place where folks knew who I was? Would it make a difference *who* is wearing those clothes? About that, I wasn't so convinced. I felt more and more that I was floundering in the same situation as Bada. He had to leave home, and I had to change my spots if we wanted to be regarded as somebodies. I wish I hadn't invested so many years into it, but by now there was no more turning back.

"I'll pack you some food," said Rilandri, mothering me when she saw that I was getting ready.

"I don't need any," I said, turning her down. "I'll be home by morning."

"Then take these hundred pengős. Once you've taken care of your problem, you can at least buy yourself some clothes. You can't go to school like that." She gave me a wink.

Bada's eyes were gleaming; he couldn't stop himself from embracing the woman.

"Alright, my darling, God has created you for us," he said, patting her back.

"Go on," Rilandri told Bada, freeing herself from his embrace, "Get his horse! He should leave while the world is still asleep, then there's no danger." She looked back at me. "Once you've passed the farm, don't you leave the causeway. The darkness will come in handy. Keep going right.

"God forbid, but in case something really goes wrong at home, we'll be staying here for two more days. I've found a place—the place I got the cart from. I told the lady that tomorrow night I was going to 'visit the spirits,' and if she doesn't have any money to give me, I'll see to it that she never gets married. May trouble and misfortune keep at bay, but if you think you need some help, come back to us. My brothers love smart people. *Zha Devlesa!*"[71] Rilandri kissed me before Bada returned. "And leave your friend's fate in my hands, I'll look after him. I can tell from his eyes what he needs."

"Don't be angry about this afternoon!" I apologized.

"Why should I be?" she smiled. "Life is so rotten, anyway. We just wallow in the sameness of each day—so why leave out anything we'd regret all our lives? Better to have memories, even if they're bad, than endless longings."

"Don't let Bada go home until he's really agreed to stick by your side."

"Leave it to me," said Rilandri, shaking her thick, multilayered skirt. "He won't leave so easily. I think. I've convinced you that I don't shy away from a slap or two; it's just cowards I hate."

"That, you don't have to worry about," I assured her. "Take care he doesn't get you into trouble with his reckless courage. He often gets mixed up in things that could be avoided, and if there isn't anyone to look after him, he'll overstep the mark."

---

[71] Go with God!

With that, I completed my farewells to Rilandri and, like a huckster disposing of his merchandise, added to it a few pieces of useful advice. Then, with the satisfaction of a good bargain, I parted company from Bada with a warm handshake, lest our emotions inflict any harm on our masculine toughness.

The darkness was indeed in my favor. Not a single dog barked for hours on end; all were sleeping the sleep of the just. I didn't have to worry that the horse would get lost. The road, which Rilandri had called a causeway, was flanked by rows of mulberry trees. For a long time I was anxious about whether I was headed in the right direction, but after the first intersection my confidence returned, and after that, the signs showed me the way.

Once my most immediate concerns had passed, I could afford to give free rein to my thoughts. In vain I urged time to pass, though, since darkness followed darkness. My yearning for dawn wrapped itself into a thick mist, and as I looked to the sky for solace it seemed ever more certain that I wouldn't get home dry. The approaching storm was unsettling and yet also comforting. Distant flashes of lightning gave me occasional glimpses of all that lay before me, and that, coupled with the sound of thunder, reassured me that I would see well enough to pass through the nearby villages without having to make a detour.

VII

THE HOURS RAN INTO ONE ANOTHER SLOWLY AND SULLENLY, but long sections of road disappeared behind me.

The thunderstorm was approaching, and I could easily find my bearings by the light of the overlapping bolts of lightning. Strangely, this time I wasn't at all afraid. A few days ago I'd been looking for shelter under the manger and tried to abstain from anything that would provoke the Creator's wrath.

How much had happened since then! Who could now tell a sin apart from a good deed? We've got to live, after all, so we do everything to survive. There will be time to account for our actions when the big gate closes behind us. Until then it's pointless to make promises, because what we regret today we'll go on doing tomorrow anyway. What else can we do? Stop? True, if we stand still and wait, if we don't act, we make fewer mistakes, but who knows when to stop and when to go? Human wisdom will never reach the point where it will be able to calculate the paths of destiny.

Only the previous night I'd thought all was lost, and my thoughts had become completely entangled, yet the horse was now taking me exactly to the place where I had to go.

According to Mama, by thinking ahead you can avoid danger or grab your luck by the scruff of its neck. Papa says just the opposite: things always turn out somehow, but never the way you wanted them to, and you never know if you're pleasing others with it all. Only if you don't do a thing are you doing the right thing. Wise advice indeed, yet it seems useless.

In vain did Mama think ahead; she never did manage to grab her luck, as she remained forever penniless. As for Papa, he'd hammered together sixteen children, and only four of us remained; in his view he hadn't done anything good or bad. He couldn't do a thing when two of his sons were killed in front of him except to cry. There seemed to be no other option than for him to die as well, he said, but few men have the courage for that. Instead his infinite patience saw him grow older. There was no one to go after with the heavy hand of the law, he said, and if there had been, would it have been worth it? Blessings come from one hand, curses from another.

Papa never did believe in justice. He used to tell a tale his grandfather used to tell, having heard it from his grandfather before him:

Once upon a time there were two brothers. One was called Truth, the other Falsehood. Their mother was a widow, with little to live on; so when her sons grew up, she was forced to send them away, so they might earn their bread in the world. Each received a little knapsack with some food in it, and they went their way.

They walked until evening, and then sat down on a fallen tree in the woods. They took off their knapsacks, for they were hungry after walking the whole day and figured that a bit of food would taste good.

"I think that you'll agree with me," said Falsehood to Truth, "that we should eat out of your knapsack as long as there is anything in it, and after that we can eat from mine."

Yes, Truth agreed, so they started to eat, but Falsehood stuffed himself with all the best things, while Truth got only burnt crusts of bread. The next morning they had breakfast, once again from Truth's food, and they ate dinner from it too. Finally there was nothing left in Truth's knapsack.

They walked until late that night, and when they were ready to eat again, Truth wanted to eat out of his brother's knapsack, but Falsehood said no, that food was his, and he had only enough for himself.

"Wait! You ate from my knapsack as long as there was something in it," said Truth.

"That is all well and good," answered Falsehood, "but if you're such a fool as to let others eat up your food right in front of you, then you've got to make the best of it. All you can do now is to sit here and starve."

"Very well," said Truth, "you're Falsehood by name and false by nature. You've always been that way, and so you will be for the rest of your life."

Now, when Falsehood heard this, he flew into a rage, rushed at his brother, and plucked out both of his eyes. "Now try to see whether people are false or not, you blind buzzard!" With that, Falsehood ran off, leaving his brother Truth behind.

"What can you expect from such a blind beggar?" Papa used to ask. "He will always side with the ones who feed him. Those who have nothing to eat themselves can have little hope for justice."

I don't know why I was mulling over this particular story when I could have diverted my attention from the raging storm with hundreds of others. Light filtered through the windows of the roadside farmhouses. It must already have been morning or, at least, dawn. Not that it made any difference what it really was, because in reality all the demons had been unleashed and were thrashing around me with hundreds upon hundreds of fiery whips, fire in one hand and water in the other.

I shouldn't have cheated Bada, I knew; if we'd each taken half the money, I would still have had enough left to fix up all my problems. And I'd thought I had resolved this dilemma in myself for good. Whom did I owe an explanation to? The Truth? . . . When we meet again, I figured, I'd beg forgiveness to him, but until then he'd better leave me alone. After all, everything that happened, had happened on account of him.

I too could have wished for something, but if my destiny depended only on Bada, then there would now be a rosy dawn or a nice, clean daybreak. And then I would be able to see well enough into the distance to know: how far could I get before anyone would catch sight of me?

Glory be to Fate, which sends the night to cover the path of the persecuted, and deters persecutors with lightning.

Who is to say how long I might have praised the divine perfection of my destiny, had I not unexpectedly found myself and my horse sprawled in the mud of the shallows alongside the canal? The horse quickly got to his feet, shaking himself off noisily indeed. He poked me with his nose as if to ask if I was alright. Apart from having had a scare, there was really nothing wrong with me. I kept stretching in the mud for quite a while, poking about for something to grab onto, until I finally got ahold of the reins.

Time and the pouring rain merged into one; I couldn't tell whether it was night or dawn. Now and then it seemed that the storm was about to pass, but again and again it would restart with inexhaustible force.

If only I were on the other side of the canal already, I could be home within an hour.

We dragged each other up the slippery bank and out of the mud with great difficulty. It felt like treading on watery soap, as the saturated, saline soil kept slipping under our feet. I cursed away, yet it was also somehow comforting.

On the far side of the canal I could see a huge fallow field divided by a narrow, timeworn, stone road; if I turned left there, no night could be dark enough for me to lose my way.

But which way to go to reach the other side? There were two options: to go straight into the water or to look for a bridge.

After some thought I realized that I had to give up on the more comfortable possibility—a bridge—because I hadn't a clue as to where I was. If I were to end up at the Okány Bridge, it would mean at least an extra twenty miles of riding.

It wasn't the water that frightened me away. The rain was pouring so relentlessly that I could hardly breathe. At worst, I figured, it would wash the mud off us. I remembered that when the canal was built, it was hard even in dry weather to climb up its sides, which had been cut so steeply. Since then the banks had not been overgrown by grass; everything burns out in this wild, white saline soil. I watched for quite some time, hoping that the lightning would let me at least determine which way the canal was flowing, but to no avail.

To hell with the rice plantation that had been constructed here! The canal used to be just an unassuming, shallow, quiet little waterway, and now I dreaded its roaring surge. Alone I might manage to climb back up its steep banks, but the horse would surely drown.

The horse trembled; he too was cold. We'd galloped a long way and were now hanging around; I didn't know what to do. Whichever way I looked at it, though, there was no other option, and if I kept mulling over it much longer then this one would also be gone.

A nearby strike of lightning ripped apart a cloud with a huge roar; my eyes closed I clung to the horse's flank.

It seemed that everything was beginning all over again. It couldn't have been later than eleven at night when I'd started off, and now it couldn't have been later than three or four. I'd be dead by dawn. Another crack whistled above us, and the horse almost jumped into the canal; frightened, I didn't know whether to curse or to pray.

Suddenly everything turned lighter.

Just five hundred yards or so ahead of us a huge haystack had been struck by lightning, and its flames crackled sky-high. I stood stock-still for a few moments, and then, without thinking, threw myself into the canal. The water was mild, but I had to fight the flow until I managed to struggle to the other side. I dug my nails deep into the canal's slippery side, but no sooner did I move than the water carried me away.

Like a giant candle, the blazing haystack lit up the whole area.

I was fast running out of strength, and I found it increasingly hard to hold on for a breath or two; the current kept dragging me away from the shore, sweeping me toward the middle of the canal.

All the more important elements of my short life flashed swiftly through my mind; there would have been quite a few among them to regret, but at the moment life seemed much more alluring. I gathered what little strength and will that remained in me and thought to myself that if fate wished me to atone, I'd rather do it somewhere on shore.

Eventually I managed to hold onto the hard ground beneath the slick wet surface and, with a huge effort, was able to turn with my back to the edge of the canal.

Even as I was able to hold onto the bank with my fingers, I also dug holes with my heels to be doubly sure not to slip back in. At last I could breathe normally. There was the horse, ambling after me along the canal—on the opposite side—staring, not quite knowing what else to do.

Slowly, mindful of every move, I began to crawl on my back up the side of the canal. The ghastly crackling of the lightning-sparked flames drowned out the roar of the storm; by now no longer one, but three haystacks were ablaze. All around the wind blew pillars of fire into the air until the storm tore them into tiny sparks that vanished like shooting stars.

The awesome beauty of the scene couldn't hold my attention. I dragged myself inch by inch until reaching the top of the embankment, where I stretched out, wheezing. Around me the downpour formed bubbles, and the endless strings of water intermingled into small rivulets running toward the canal.

The storm sent a sustained, sad whinny from the opposite bank. The horse just stood there like a metal statue, watching the water.

"Come on!" I yelled, getting to my knees. "Don't be afraid, Death is only fishing."

He just stood there and looked in the direction of my voice; he didn't believe or comprehend a single word I'd said.

"*Haide!*"[72] I hollered in Romanian, figuring that was the language this horse understood. His head held high, he moved forward; my voice stuck in my throat as the beast, legs outstretched, sliding on his bottom, plopped into the water. *It's over,* I thought.

He approached, nose held high; he tried to swim against the current to keep his bearings.

"*Haide!*" I coaxed him as I started out in his direction.

While I'd been in the water myself, I hadn't regarded death as so disgusting as I did now, from the shore. *Why doesn't the sky burst into flames and annihilate this cruel world that demands everything for itself?*

---

[72] Come!

"Come on, my little horse!" I begged, as if everything were up to him or to me. He swam at an angle to the flow until he approached the shore, and then, standing on his hind legs and curving his spine, he leapt ashore.

I didn't know what to do for joy. I couldn't stop patting and kissing him. Then, holding him by his reins, we ran toward the pasture.

We ran for a long time, looking back now and then. The flames emitted a lurid glow through the curtain of rain, but by the time we reached the rocky path it had faded away.

The day was already dawning, and the purplish bolts of lightning became fainter, but the growling noise of the thunder still sounded the same. The rain pounded me from every side, as if a circular wind was blowing. I lay face down on the horse's back; the wild pealing of a bell swelled the noise—that is, from the church near our settlement, our Gypsy Paris.

The world is burning, I thought. At the last moment I managed to get off the rocky road, carts clattering past me, as did a fire engine rattling in their wake. Opting against getting back up on the road, I instead found myself wading through deep puddles, instinctively holding back the horse as I did so. Only when the municipal council's carriage rolled past right in front of my nose did I realize what was bothering me.

Gendarmes were sitting on it.

I didn't have anything to fear—the storm still hid me—but the mere thought of crossing paths with them was disquieting. My old experiences suggested that, if fate was to bring us face to face, they certainly wouldn't beg forgiveness. But even if that was the entire problem, I thought, they would want much more than I was willing to give.

The horse sank knee-deep into freshly ploughed, muddy furrows of saline soil; trenches and bushes blocked my way forward, finally forcing me to look anew for the rocky road.

The scary tolling of the church bell attracted me; I've never felt such yearning for my home before. While I was far away I was able to put up with it, but as soon as I was caught up in its drawing power, I could no longer get it out of my mind.

A warm tingling sensation ran through my soaking wet body as soon as I caught sight of the first hut. A tense silence lay behind their minuscule windows; surely it was the increasingly muffled thunder that repressed the loud snuffling I assumed was coming from within, which could usually be heard from far away like the even panting of a giant animal.

An anxious foreboding took me in its grip when I saw that our tiny yard looked empty and deserted. Ever since I could remember, the barn stood empty only on hot nights; now, in between the thunderclaps, its chilling silence was filled merely by the buzz of flies.

Timidly I turned the wooden handle of the kitchen door; the swishing rain suppressed its rickety creaking. My feet sank into the wet earthen floor as I groped my way into the room. The hot, airless stench hit me, taking away my breath.

"Who is it?" came Mama's frightened voice.

"Me," I said in faltering voice.

A commotion arose in the hut's bottomless darkness. Mama voiced her happiness with a soft whimper, while my sisters sat sniveling. Kotseh, the youngest, crawled toward me but, startled by the touch of my wet clothes, stumbled back to the others.

"It's pouring outside," I said to allay fears.

"God bless the rain," said Papa, spitting from between his teeth, "but I wish it would stop already!"

His warm, tobacco-smelling saliva spread out sharply between my toes; I wiped my pants in it without a word.

Mama got off her lair and searched for a long time in the drawer, murmuring something that ranged from praying to swearing. Eventually she groped her way toward me with an armful of dry clothes.

"Get changed!" she whispered, stroking my shoulders. "Wipe off your feet on your wet clothes!"

I didn't have to be told twice; I went to the kitchen, where I fiddled around for a while with the dry clothes, trying to determine which was the right or wrong side; in the end I put them on the way they were. Reassured, I took out the money, which was wrapped in rags. I would have liked to spread it all out, but our kitchen ceiling had been like a leaking boat in the autumn rains ever since I could remember. I'd have to wait until morning to scoop out the money. Every fall we intended to fix it, but in the summer, we figured, why bother?

"Don't we have any matches?" I asked.

"There's lightning outside," Mama admonished me. "Don't attract the wrath of an angry God."

It would have been pointless to argue, so I just quietly curled up on top of the oven.

Everyone was shrouded in silence; their subdued breaths erupted into profound sighs each time a sky-shaking thunderclap faded away. My own circumstances had changed only to the extent that I wasn't getting wet. My intense homesickness seemed strange, extraneous; the family had nothing to do with this condemned cell.

I left everything as it was, with the mirror turned to the wall and the darkness simulating the nonexistence by which they tried to deceive God.

How much time and what a distance separated me from them! The years I'd spent at school seemed to grow a hundred-fold; I was here, and yet I didn't belong anywhere.

We could hear the banging of the horse.

"I rode here," I said softly. It looked like Papa was sitting up, his stirring followed by a faint thump, then silence again; he might have just turned over.

"I've also brought some money," I muttered on. "It should be dried, because everything I had on me is soaked."

"Wait, my child, until the storm goes away; don't expose us to the wrath of an angry God. At times like these even small sins are severely punished," Mama pleaded.

"Doesn't he do it at other times as well?"

"Do not sin!" she commanded. "Will you be quiet or . . . ?" She fell silent.

"Alright, I'll keep quiet." I jumped off the oven and groped around on the top of the cupboard until I found the matches. Only then did I continue: "I've spent half the night outside in the storm, and I wasn't afraid of the wrath of an angry God, but I can't bear this silent darkness." I went out to the barn.

There, it was as if the light of the tiny oil lamp conjured up a separate little world around me. The barn was not as warm as at other times, when livestock was in it, but there was light, shadow, the sound of buzzing flies, and the sound of trampling. My horse was merrily feasting on the hay accumulated at the end of the barn. The storm was the least of his worries; he didn't go green from fear although he was a beast guided by sight, hearing, senses, and emotions. We, who have been blessed with such great perfection, are only life's humiliated rags.

In my endless sadness I dug myself into the hay. Papa followed me a few minutes later, blinking bleary-eyed until he caught sight of me. Now it was I who clenched my teeth and didn't reply to his gushing questions until he sat down on the edge of the manger. I was overcome by weeping, and all my suppressed bitterness burst out of me. He too almost broke down at my reproaches, but when I crawled out of the hay and hugged him, he forgot that there had ever been a storm.

The tobacco pouch made an appearance, and we were soon smoking like chimneys.

"A good horse," he said approvingly and took off his saddle. "Pity he's blind."

"Blind? Not on your life!" I said, coming to its defense. "I wish everyone could see as well."

"Don't be so sure," he said, waving me off. "I can tell from the way he's holding his head."

He stepped closer to the horse and waved the oil lamp in front of his eyes; covered it with the palm of his hand, then suddenly took it quite close, but the animal didn't even blink.

"That's amazing; two hours ago he was still searching for me in the water."

"That may be so," Papa admitted "but there has still been a lot of lightning since then. A good horse's eyes have to be bandaged during a storm or not let out at all. They all become the victims of their own good nature."

"Can he be healed?" I asked anxiously.

"We'll see," he said, shrugging his shoulder uncertainly. "For the time being he isn't allowed out in the sunlight."

The horse's injury made me very sad, but eventually we had to get back to our own matter. It seemed that nothing was wrong at home. The little fear that rested on their shoulders would pass with the storm. Looking at Papa, even that didn't bother him any more; he really seemed cheerful. But to add to his happiness, he stuffed the barn's minute window slits with handfuls of hay.

When I shook my head disapprovingly, he started to explain:

"Your mother says brightness attracts lightning at night, which is why she turns the mirror to the wall."

"I know," I muttered gloomily. "But if lightning would be attracted by brightness, then it would strike heaven and not the earth, where all is dark."

"You're the one who goes to school." Papa looked thoughtfully at the flickering lamp; he couldn't decide which of us to believe. Instead he let his emotions loose.

"It might as well strike there, too!" He suddenly changed tack. "Kurucho has destroyed us! He took my horses, my cart; you'll see in the morning that there's not a single pillow left in the hut."

Words failed me; I just swallowed hard, although I'd been so overwhelmed with emotion on arriving home. Papa continued:

"The gendarmes let me go only yesterday afternoon, after your mother paid up."

"How much?"

"Three hundred and fifty pengős," he said, the words stuck in his throat. I became aware only now how much money was tied into the knotted rag. Its dampness was no longer half as frightening as in the afternoon.

"Cheer up," I comforted him. "I've brought a pile of money."

"A pile," he smiled deprecatingly, obviously thinking of the two pengős he had given me days before. "I'd rather he had a registration booklet," he said, caressing the horse.

"He does have one," I sighed. "I tucked it into the hem of my pants before the rain came, but I had to swim across the channel. Who knows what it'll be like once it dries?"

"Never mind," Papa rejoiced, "we'll have it altered." He virtually forgot his so far bottled up fear and sadness, and with his sleeve he wiped his idol, the one and only creature he really believed in and that gave his life true meaning.

Our people's love of horses remained an eternal, unfathomable mystery to me; that endless love with which they idolized them was beyond the limits of my imagination.

The horse either felt he'd found a real master or was gratified that Papa was caressing him. I watched sleepily as both of them shone, one from joy, the other from the coat sleeve. I thought Papa would never stop stroking the beast, as if he were sprucing him up for tomorrow's market. He even stepped away from the animal to take a thorough look.

"It would be worth keeping him for the winter," he said, surveying the horse with squinting eyes.

"Well, then, why don't you?"

"Because we're always cursed with trouble."

"What's wrong?" I inquired.

"The winter. We're all stripped bare."

"I told you already that I've brought money!"

He looked at me with disdain, and went on to clean the horse.

"Only Kurucho has lots of money. He's never seen as much in his life. Why, he's even become a landowner; he's bought up that huge swath of land with all its alkaline soil into the bargain."

"Well, he might as well bury himself in it."

"That's so," Papa growled. "No one has ever harvested enough wheat there for making a loaf of bread. But that's his problem, and it doesn't help us much."

"You shouldn't have been so hasty."

"No? . . . An hour after you left, they took me away, and if your Mama hadn't managed to strike a compromise with them I'd still be locked up. They told me I'd rot there until they found you. What would you have done, smart guy?" Papa looked at me in a huff. "Sooner or later they would have caught you, anyway, but then your skin wouldn't even have been fit for a sieve."

"If it were only a matter of my skin!" I thought out loud.

"See, you agree too? It was the right thing to do! This way at least they'll leave us in peace. To hell with having to be scared all the time. We've been poor before and we still survived. Don't worry, it'll work itself out."

"Why would I worry?" I asked with a laugh. "You haven't seen so much money in a heap than is tied into this rag."

"Me?" Papa looked surprised.

"You." He never could get on with boastful people, and now I'd surely offended his sense of vanity.

"You know," he began, one of his eyes crinkling up, "in the army . . ."

"I know," I interrupted him, "the paper money was stacked high, and you had to guard it. You got a five-day pass, and the others were court martialed; you were the only one who didn't steal anything. I know the story, Papa, but this is even more money."

Like everyone else, he too couldn't suffer being belittled, so he pulled out his accordionlike wallet from the inside pocket of his vest and thumped it angrily.

"You couldn't even count the amount of money that has ever been in this," he boasted, "even though you've gone to school."

I kept quiet; I didn't want to spoil the game. Satisfied, he slipped the wallet back into his vest pocket.

"You don't believe me?" He drew himself up. "All my life I've been a businessman."

"Okay," I said, feigning defeat, "then get this!" Papa froze for a moment on seeing the thick wad of cash now in my upturned hand, and then backed out of the barn with a terrified face.

The storm was passing. Now and then it still rumbled from afar like someone who has been given his walking papers but in the morning rushes to the doorway pale and shivering. Just minutes later Mama appeared, horrified.

"What have you done again?" she wailed.

My answer was, I think, the least thing that bothered her. She turned to Papa, who was virtually clinging to her skirt behind her.

"What did I tell you? I told you so when you entrusted your son to that bandit, whose life has been eaten up by cards! He must have involved him in something again." Mama demanded the whole truth. "What have you done? Robbed or killed someone?"

"Don't shout," I said. "No one has asked you to do business early in the morning while there's still lightning."

"Hey, give me your wallet," I asked Papa, "Let's put it in; at least it'll dry more smoothly."

"In my wallet?" he pressed his hands to his heart. "There has never been any bloodied money in it, my boy."

"See, you never even asked me if I found the horse or stole it. The main thing was that it existed, and a bad, soaking wet registration was all it took to make you feel okay about it. Because it was a horse. But this"—I pointed to the money—"made you shit yourself, even though I didn't get it by murder."

"You found it?" His eyes lit up.

"I was given it."

"So much money?" He sounded skeptical."Who would be such a fool?"

"You've always told me that women are willing to give even their lives if they meet a man of their liking. This is by no means as much as a woman's life. Or did you just say it?"

"Well, it happens."

"Then why do you doubt me?"

"But so much money?"

"That's right. The women who hung around the training camp used to bring you an entire army's pay because you were such a handsome soldier. True or not?"

He looked for help at Mama, who had wrapped her disheveled head in her top skirt and was looking frantically at the huge amount of money curling in my hand.

"Dry it," I said, handing her the money. "Even if I didn't acquire it in the most honorable way, you don't have to be afraid of it. I got it on account of making love."

Papa timidly took out his large, empty wallet. He shook the dust out of its compartments and, regretfully shaking his head, handed it to Mama.

I didn't wait to see how they sorted the money into the compartments, but crept into the hay. Together with me, my thoughts sank into the watery, bottomless abyss of the dream; it was sometime in the afternoon that my impatient friends managed to wake me.

My arrival made a big splash in Gypsy Paris and, although my absence had been quite short, during that time problems had multiplied. First, almost all able-bodied males in the settlement had been drafted.

"You know, if there's a war, they'll take everyone up to the age of eighteen," Lőcs informed me with glee.

"Even then they won't take us," I said, trying to disappoint him.

"That's just it!" he hugged me jubilantly. "Every single *shey*[73] will be left for us."

Seeing that I didn't want to partake in his happiness, he continued in a more subdued manner: "Ever since you left, not once have we even been to the movies; if we dared to leave Paris, we'd be chased down."

"Because I left?"

"No, not at all," he waved disparagingly. "We got into trouble."

"What do you mean by 'trouble,' you bandy-legged Gypsy?" Zolti snapped at him.

"We stole a goose," said Lőcs, turning to me in a more composed way. "We wanted to follow you."

"With a goose?"

"To hell with the goose," he erupted again. "We sold it to get some money."

"And?"

"The one-legged confectioner bought it; we sold him the same goose three times that night, and the fourth time we stole it back for its owner. There wasn't any trouble about the goose; the owner hadn't even noticed it was gone"—he sighed—"but the confectioner set the whole village against us."

"Why didn't you give him his money back?"

"His money?" asked Lőcs with a bitter laugh. "He's demanding the price of six geese."

"Cheer up," I comforted him. "He won't report you."

"Who knows, maybe it would be better if we too disappeared from home. I wouldn't want to fall into the hands of the new gendarme, after all. You'll get to know him," he assured me. "He was scraped out from under his money with a pitchfork."

If my happiness depended on crossing paths with the new gendarme, it was soon fulfilled. While Zolti was telling me about his bad feelings and concern for himself, Papa disturbed our company with quiet equanimity.

[73] girl

"The *porale*[74] are coming, go tidy yourself up!" Moments before, I'd still felt my conscience to be clean, and Zolti's laments triggered only pity in me, while everything else he talked about with chattering teeth failed to touch me. However, a cold shudder ran through me at the news, which Papa spat out dispassionately.

I'd been counting on such a meeting; I wished it would be over and done with, but not so soon. The day of reckoning seemed premature, even if it would only mean a sound beating.

Later I might reproach myself for not heeding my friends' apprehension, but I didn't go with them. There would still have been an opportunity to do so, since in Gypsy Paris the news always preceded events by enough time to avoid those encounters. Instead I waited patiently, changing into a nice set of clothes on Papa's advice; then, at Mama's urging, I gorged myself on a second helping of paprikash potato stew.

"There you are," she said, reassuring me. "It's harder to intimidate a man with a full belly." Since then, I have often had the opportunity to realize the truth of her saying. Then, however, all the stew that wound up in me didn't yield uninhibited cheerfulness; instead it brought on a pleasant, lazy feeling, an overwhelming desire to lie down in the hay. The only thing that held me back was that I didn't want to get my Sunday best dirty.

With jaded equanimity I contemplated the frightened-looking crowd of Gypsies milling about as the gendarmes appeared; everyone wanted to run away or at least hide to be out of striking distance. The din of anxious chattering rising up out of the settlement's residents sounded like the croaking of frogs when a snake appears, but frogs that no longer have either the strength or the will to escape.

Emotions are never triggered by coincidence, it seems to me, but are deeply rooted in our consciousness, which is shaped by practical factors.

The blows could already be heard from the edge of the settlement, and I was still leaning to the side of the hut, yawning impassively.

---

[74] gendarmes (literally "feathered ones")

"Why don't you hide somewhere, young Boncza?" Old Chicken Tony called out to me. "They'll flay you alive when they see you!"

I shrugged my shoulders with negligent nonchalance at his benevolent fury; I felt I had no strength to step out of the magic circle. *Let come, whatever fate decrees.* Anyone who has ever been plagued by fear knows that even if it doesn't show on the outside, it gnaws at you on the inside. Your smile, your haughty brave expression, is meant only for the outsider; you cannot deceive yourself.

In short, putting on a "brave" face is, at times like this, seen by outsiders as requisite to salvation; it is indispensable. True, a vigorous wailing would relieve one's tension far better, but in front of so many Gypsies it would sound worse than blasphemy, although I could have sworn that everyone was murmuring the Lord's Prayer.

So there I was, standing, feigning deadly calm, and spitting long gobs of cheap tobacco-laced saliva as if out of a water pistol clogged with potato peels.

Papa was fussing about in the yard; I've never seen him so intent on tidying up whatever he could. At times, he peered out from behind the corner of the hut, and his movements betrayed where the gendarmes were heading.

"That's how it goes on every day since he's been here," Old Chicken complained, referring to the new gendarme. "He's destroying us," he muttered to Papa.

"Are you scared, Chicken?" I asked, pursing my lips. All I could see was that his face had turned blue with fury; perhaps it was just as well that the gendarmes arrived just then, for otherwise he would have let me have it. Old Chicken tried to pull off his frayed sheepskin cap with a flourish and sported a large smile to gain their benevolence. He was out of luck. Yet it had seemed to me as if a spark of goodwill already flashed on the gendarmes' faces, faces that suddenly froze into looks that could kill. Somehow or other, only the outside of the fur cap had come off Old Chicken's head, while its lining stayed on him, as if to mock the gendarmes.

They looked me up and down impassively. I was all but convinced that they took me for some sort of carved wooden Gypsy saint, not even deigning to pay their respects or ask why I wasn't greeting them. *My time will come too,* I groaned inwardly, as they paced slowly up to Old Chicken Tony.

With a bent back Old Chicken was still sweeping the ground with the outside of his cap.

"Why are you making fun of us?" asked the sergeant, straightening him out with his rifle butt. The poor fellow hadn't noticed yet how enormously he had sinned against God and man.

"I'm asking you!" shouted the gendarme while hitting Chicken's nails with the metal butt.

"I humbly beg forgiveness, worshipful warrant officer," he said, straightening himself up with the aid of his cane. "I didn't say a thing,"

"Well, I'll say it then." The gendarme took the cane away from Old Chicken and with it began whacking away at the lining of the cap that was still on the old man's head. Old Chicken just stood there, bent over like a goat holding its head under the knife in the moment before its butchering, until the lining finally fell off his head. With showman-like dexterity, the gendarme lifted it onto the end of the cane, pressed it against the old man's nose, and then flung it away in disgust.

"You'd better teach respect to your kind," he hissed at me, "or else I'll flay your skin off."

The hut began to wobble behind my back, and I fell limply against the wall, not even worrying about my clothes getting dirty. Papa hurriedly dragged me inside, telling the astonished gendarmes that I was sick. I didn't want to interrupt him, so I went along with the game. Within minutes the hut was full of pitying Gypsies. It hadn't been a bad excuse for escape; all those Gypsies were now acting as if I was the center of the universe. However, instead of inquiring about my ill health, they wanted to know about the gendarmes. To the best of my ability, I played my part—the part of a sick kid—to allay any suspicion. Mama rubbed the area around my heart with vinegar, while Papa kept chiding me with unheard of courage.

"Why are you afraid? I've already paid for everything. I was wounded twice on the battlefield and never got a thing for it, but I had to give a fortune to that pig."

"Yes," one of the other Gypsies shouted amid a chorus of sighs. "And it cost the shirt off your backs, although that gendarme deserved having his face smashed in."

"But at least he's no longer the town crier," someone rejoiced. "With an ugly mug like his they won't keep him at village hall for long."

Old Chicken Tony forced his way to me.

"Does he have navel warts?" he interrogated Mama. "Undo his pants and let me see." He knelt down to me with some effort.

Old Chicken stank of village outhouses. Feeling around my navel, he noisily let out his breath, which oozed forth the odor of methylated spirits. Papa looked at him a little contemptuously, a little pityingly. His capless head was full of contusions.

"*More,*[75] you've sure gotten what you had coming to you."

"Damn it," he said, berating his tattered old cap. "I'll chuck it into a fire. I won't get into trouble on account of it again."

"How come you didn't notice it?" asked one of the others, rebuking him for his carelessness.

"Who the hell knows," replied the old man, shrugging his shoulders ruefully. "An unlucky man can't escape his fate."

Feigning pain, I tugged at my nose; I felt I was also to blame for the knocks the old man got on his head. The others started swarming around me like frightened bees, and everyone began to shout.

"Let him have air, or else he'll suffocate!"

I was beginning to think that perhaps I really was unwell if they were so generous about the air. I was even more stunned when they then started running about the yard, calling for a doctor. Had they gone crazy or had something happened to me?

---

[75] Hey you! (*More*–pronounced "mow-re"–has several meanings depending on the context. Here it also means "Hey Gypsy!")

I soon received an answer: the gendarmes were standing in the doorway. Indifferently they examined the black spots on the rain-soaked ceiling where chips of plaster had fallen off, where piss-colored beads of the storm were still hanging off the rotting reed covering.

"Is he often like that?"

"He's been always like this," said Papa with a sigh. They expressed their sympathy with a fleeting glance and went on their way.

"They're gone," Lőcs called out, jumping off the roof outside. "You can get up now."

I still marveled at Papa's inexplicable courage. What surprised me most was that, completely shedding his usual modesty, he stood before me as if he had never known fear.

"There you go," he said proudly, "that's how it's done."

I was fully convinced that he was praising me, perhaps because I'd feigned illness with such expertise, but he soon disabused me of the notion.

"You sure chickened out pretty fast. What will happen to you when you become a soldier? Will you turn giddy then, too?"

Papa's words expressed more concern than malice, but they wounded my pride nonetheless.

"What do you mean, I turned 'chicken'? Wasn't it you who said I was sick?"

"Me?" he asked, looking puzzled, then shrugged his shoulders and added: "Maybe, but it doesn't make any difference; they wouldn't have hurt you anyway. As of today, you'll have a better reputation at the village council. Just behave properly; I haven't always got a hundred pengős for the village clerk."

"So that's where all that courage of yours comes from?" I asked. Papa nodded.

"Had I known how smoothly it would go, we could have gotten away with a lot less. That gentleman was much easier to deal with than one of our kind—even though the new platoon commander was standing in front of him like a crucifix."

"The village clerk needs the money more than the likes of us."

"He's got plenty," said Papa. "He really does come from a good family."

"Yet he still took the crutch from the beggar," I replied.

"So what? Christ's coffin wasn't guarded for free, either!"

I didn't want to argue about the hundred pengős; that money was gone anyway, and if I only counted today's crop, it had been well worth it.

"You know," said Papa, "it's always good if a man has a little patronage." He took out a brand new horse-registration booklet, lest I thought he was talking through his hat.

"Once you grow up you'll realize how beautifully money can sing."

Papa didn't have to draw my attention to this; I knew anyway. What was unclear me, though, was why Lőcs was running in and out of the yard like a scalded dog. I listened, but didn't hear a thing apart from the general hubbub.

"What's up?" I questioned him when he popped in again.

"The people are calling for you."

I got up and went outside. The older ones were huddled together in the Billat's yard next door arguing about something. It must have been an uncommon topic, because some of them were trying to persuade the others more stridently than usual. Relieved from the earlier terror, the children were squealing around them in a circle, until one of the adults shooed them away. As I walked up to them, the debate abated. Old Bankuli was clearing his throat in advance so his voice would be sharper and clearer.

"After all, I don't want it for free." It appeared that he and Papa were resuming an argument that was interrupted earlier.

"These people," Bankuli turned to me, "say we should send a petition to the emperor demanding that they don't shoot Köszörűs." Köszörűs, Bankuli's nephew, had lately become revered among the Gypsies as a sort of Robin Hood-and, since he'd been apprehended, a martyr-to-be.

"The emperor?" I asked as if I'd misheard him.

"Emperor or king, he's the same person."

"Do you know his title?" I asked.

"His title?" he frowned, thinking hard.

Angrily they asked for an explanation.

"Yes," I continued, "two decades have passed, and the only change here is that you've grown old like bean soup. I don't want to disappoint anyone, but your emperor—Franz Joseph—has been dead for over twenty years."

A slight sense of sadness descended on us as usual on news of a death, and then the others nodded with a forgiving smile.

"He was old, but he wasn't a bad man." Bankuli alone remained indifferent.

"But surely they must have put someone in his place."

"Not so far."

Now their faces really mirrored astonishment.

"With no one in charge," one of them observed, "no wonder the gendarmes have gotten out of hand!"

Tempers didn't calm down for a while, but in the end they just had to be content with the news I delivered: that the country had in fact been led for many years now by His Serene Highness, the Regent of the Kingdom of Hungary, Miklós[76] Horthy. All they knew about him, though, was that his name day was a bit earlier than Christmas; for St. Nicholas Day fell on December 6.

This uncrowned and unknown great lord called Horthy didn't win Bankuli's confidence. On my advice, though, Bankuli did turn to an alcoholic, moonlighting legal clerk to lodge an appeal for clemency to His Serene Highness on his nephew's behalf.

Unfortunately, the appeal was unsuccessful, and a few weeks later a military tribunal in Debrecen, that city on the plains of eastern Hun-

[76] Pronounced "*Meek*loshe," Hungarian for Nicholas

gary some fifty miles north of us, sentenced Köszörűs to death by firing squad.

Old Bankuli then trudged on his own two feet all the way to Debrecen where, thanks to the gracious benevolence of the prison commander, he was permitted to spend a half hour with his nephew in the cell of the condemned. After that, he tied the man's worthless little possessions into a bundle and waited for several days in the cemetery, unsuccessfully hoping to find out where he would be buried.

In Köszörűs the Gypsies had lost an unusual man. The Creator had blessed him with every kind of human emotion; all he seemed to lack was fear. The Gypsies always searched for an adequate term with which to describe his matchless courage, but he proved with his actions that courage had nothing to do with his state of mind. He simply couldn't live with hunger, extreme poverty, and destitution—and, from autumn to spring, all of these lurked in the settlement's hovels, tormenting everyone who lived and breathed.

Now, it is not proper to speak ill of the dead, but it is true that the pantries of an entire village would have fit into his big heart. What Köszörűs had done to earn his ultimate fate was to indiscriminately undo the latches of every smokehouse and chicken coop in the area and allocate some of the pork and poultry to the hungry among his own people. He spent long winter nights stealing honestly, and knew where and what and how much to deliver to pacify the howling hunger of those he served. He never expected any thanks; the smiling faces of his fellow Gypsies meant the greatest happiness to him.

Köszörűs had deserted from the army because summer was gone, taking with it its withered breast that had once been so full of milk. The time had come for him to help the helpless; for the wolf was coming—the huge, hungry, howling wolf called winter—and he had to protect the flock. Who would have thought that he would become its victim before winter even arrived?

Winter was still far away, and autumn had so far dared to flaunt itself only in the early hours of the day. But in the evenings you could already feel the bite of chilling winds sweeping their way toward us from over the plains.

You couldn't do a thing with your days, which became idle and unreliable, for the weather could change from one hour to the next. Those who could did their best to prepare for the coming cold, and tattered sweaters emerged from deep within their beds.

However, the weather proved whimsical: Indian summer came. By day our shirts stuck to us again, and by evening we no longer had to dress up warm to sit beside the fires. It was as if, out of the goodness of his heart, the Creator wished to add another summer to the year. Indian summer lasted long; here and there even the acacia trees started to bloom anew, and fresh green grass shot up among the dead leaves.

The Gypsies were on the one hand pleased; on the other hand they were worried, for the forebodings and predictions of the elders spread from mouth to mouth. What did the old folks say? That we were close to the times when men would gladly change places with their dogs, because even dogs' lives would be worth more.

What compelling argument could I raise to console the desperate people? None. They had evidence, while I straddled the fence between those folks who believed in miracles and those who didn't. I awaited proof. And if the tardy or unwilling winter signified the prophesied time—"when winter can't be told apart from summer, when trees will blossom but bear no fruit, when man will attack man, and when horses will wade in blood up to their breasts"—then what use would consolation be?

For their part, the non-Gypsy Hungarians of the village spent those summery autumn evenings with cheerful weddings and name-day celebrations for which the Gypsies provided the noise. Indeed, more often than not the music they provided would be better characterized as "noise," for their borrowed or makeshift musical instruments were not always played by experts. Some of the Gypsy music-makers, for example, had never used any percussion instrument other than a hammer and an old, leaky pot.

The bountiful, early harvest inspired the villagers to weeks of merrymaking. It now seemed as if, instead of rushing headlong to doom, the world was on the cusp of a wonderful future. And, even if their work was not exactly professional, those Gypsies who did their part to whip up the good cheer by providing the "music" got their share of the pie.

The elders, however, were far from this merry world. Dwelling only within their faith and thoughts, they could not be deceived.

"'The dog also becomes rabid when it is best off,'' they would say, raising their fingers in warning at the skeptics.

Some believed them, for the elders didn't go raising their fingers for nothing, but most, in defiance of the dire predictions, sought to exploit the exceptional weather. That's what Old Shimuy did.

After Michaelmas,[77] most of Gypsies bargained away their nags at the market, and custom dictated that they would buy another horse only after St. George's Day.[78] It didn't make economic sense, after all, to keep a horse during the winter without a barn unless the door of the hut the humans lived in was big enough for the horse to squeeze inside. Besides, gendarmes were invariably suspicious of those who kept their horses for the winter. Not without reason.

Hoping for a good profit and contrary to tradition, Shimuy extracted from the lining of his sweater the money he'd saved for the fol lowing year, and snatched at the chance of making a good deal.

"It's a good horse," said one of the people gathered around him as he galloped into the settlement on his return from the market. The horse experts in the crowd, on the other hand, turned their noses up disapprovingly and promptly pointed out the mare's obvious and hidden faults.

"I bought it really cheap," he answered defensively.

---

[77] September 29

[78] April 23

"It has the heaves," they chided him. "There's no remedy in the world that can cure it. If it were spring, it might be worth something, but who buys a nag in the fall?"

"The weather is good," he said. "She'll graze for a few months, and before long it will be spring, and then she'll be worth a lot of money."

Shimuy's words had some truth to them. After all, there was no complaining about the weather for the time being.

As for me, now in school, it seemed that the curriculum was thought up by some prescient brain specifically with Indian summer in mind. We spent much more time outdoors, and physical education comprised a third of our daily hours.

The school had been transformed with amazing speed into an institution whose main objective was to educate its students to become true patriots.

From one day to the next, the students' appetites increased. And, while up until then the powers that be had been content to have us and our teachers wish each other an insipid "Good Day" in passing, a rip-roaring "Better Future!" now took its place.

The school's debating society was anything but intellectual. It was controlled by a clique of snooty seniors who referred to it as the "altar of the arts." I myself couldn't get near it, because the rules stipulated that it was open only to the initiated. Anyway, I didn't feel any inner compulsion that would have forced me even once to try my hand at it and give up catching the early train home for the night.

Each and every afternoon I could hardly wait for the last class to end, and within minutes I was at the train station, clutching my jam-packed bag.

I pretended that it was by mere coincidence that I always happened to get in the same train car as one of my fellow students, a girl named Kitty Vágó. I sought to allay suspicions by walking as if I had no intention of stopping, eyes fixed straight ahead; only at the last minute would I then seem to discover that there was an empty seat in Kitty's compartment or, if luck was on my side, next to her.

Every time I got up close to her, the world tightened around me, and my thoughts, which hours or minutes before flowed effortlessly, left me without notice. There I sat, teetering silently on my seat, like a hat hung on a nail.

Each day I was seized by renewed anxiety: would there be a free seat next to her in the overcrowded car? Ashamed by my own reproaches, I kept vowing that I would never sit next to her again. But how long did my resolve last? The moment I saw her, I was no longer in control of myself.

On one occasion I somehow managed to break through the wall of silence. Kitty asked the questions, and I replied curtly and confusedly; it happened that I said yes instead of no, or vice-versa.

She said that despite being quiet I was "very funny," and that when I did say something, it was always to the point. Was this a compliment? I didn't think so. Being called funny made me nervous.

Our subsequent commutes passed in each other's company were, however, increasingly pleasurable. Indeed, as the days and weeks passed, we became very close. Kitten—for that is was I now called her—continued to reserve the right to ask the questions. Sometimes she herself answered them in words that spewed out of her mouth and, to me, were most satisfying. I just nodded wisely and relieved, found out everything imaginable about her—even that once she got married she hoped to have a brown-haired little son.

A blond, her restlessly moving blue eyes were fringed by long brown eyelashes. Sometimes she wore her long hair in braids; on other occasions it hung loose, smoothly down to her waist—or she would toss it over her shoulder, its sweet flowery fragrance pervading my senses. Never did I have the courage to stroke it. No, I just cowered beside her in timid silence even when only the two of us were in the compartment. If, at times, I touched her shoulders or, by the gracious whim of fate, her chest, I felt my clothes burning on me, and my blood glowed red-hot on my skin.

Our greetings and farewells were, for me, the nicest part of my daily one-hour trip to and from school. We always shook hands, and Kitten would let her small white hand linger for a moment in my palm. A faint blush would flicker across her face, and then she would fill me in on what was happening with her or else walk away, waving to me from the railway embankment.

I went through wretched nights, falling headlong into feelings that, common sense dictated, could never be reciprocated.

Kitten was very nice, but when the parting moments came I invariably sensed that, should we never meet again, to her it wouldn't be such a tragedy. On other days, there was a certain gleam in her eyes like that of someone who's found gold but, after some scrutiny, soon discovers that it's only copper. Why had this girl accepted me as a friend when, day after day, our ultimate parting seemed all the more inevitable? For a while I let myself go with the flow. What did I have to lose? Why shouldn't I fantasize?

Her mere presence on the train seemed to command respect from everybody, after all. Eventually I found out why, though. At first I didn't understand why the train stopped at the Madarász estate, and why that was where she always got on and off. But I was no longer surprised when I found out that Kitty Vágó was none other than the daughter of Doctor Zoltán Vágó and Hermina Bélmegyeri-Madarász. Everyone around there knew the two wealthy families that had so auspiciously united with their marriage, which had doubled the size of their land holdings.

This information not only surprised me but also saddened me to no end. Unaware of the devastating storm raging within me, Kitten welcomed me every day with unflagging friendliness.

At first these facts couldn't make me resign my secret yearnings, but increasingly I had to accept that I was only deceiving myself by hanging on to such dreams.

On getting home from school every day, I would cast my school things aside and proceeed to spend half the evening outside, dawdling among the settlement's puddles; the overcrowdedness and the smoky, kerosene cacophony of life inside our hut upset me. The yellow moon of those autumn nights conjured the puddles into glistening lakes; from their banks, withered sunflowers and burdocks stared silently and stiffly at their own shadows. In my imagination they grew into spreading willow trees, and soft piano music filtered through their leafless branches from the brightly lit mansion towering high above them. Kitten's blond hair fluttered from behind the lace curtains of one of the open windows as if it were pulling the moonbeam behind it. I stared into space, listening to the lovely music composed by my desires, and I flung such huge sighs into the night that they surprised even me.

Mama wore a worried frown, because from some unconcealed symptom she soon recognized the cause of my illness. She tried to force herself to be patient, though, since she knew that time was the only medicine that guaranteed a safe cure sooner or later.

There were moments when the devil took hold of me, arguing about my condition. He always came at a time when, soaring high, I almost flew beyond the limits of imagination. With his cold breath he forced me back into the real world, where all was rotten and foul-smelling.

"You are a Gypsy!" he said in such a natural voice that it seemed not to be him saying it but me acknowledging it.

"You can't live between two worlds—you must break with one of them!"

In the morning, I woke up tired, with a roaring headache.

"Are you sick?" Mama questioned me.

As a result of my fruitless protest, Papa was also jolted out of his indifference and came to my defense on the basis of his own experiences.

"He has woman problems. I know about these things. At his age I collected women by the dozens. The one that came, I took; and the one that didn't come stayed right there. There were plenty of them in God's stable. I never grieved over a single one of them."

Needing to go back to school so early the next morning came in handy; for I just wasn't up for too many more of Papa's edifying stories, even though he did tell them so simply and naturally.

Judging by his words, he wasn't one to be hiding any lofty human feelings under a bushel; the purpose of love is not only togetherness, he made clear, but also reproduction. And for that, he said, daydreaming was not enough.

"You see?" Papa would surely have said, pointing at Kitten and me had he been with us on the train. "You're not made of daydreams. Take her hand and bring her home. Don't look at whether she's a beggar or made of money. No, everyone gets married; that's the way of the world."

I had plenty of time to think about the way of the world as the train rattled along to town.

I couldn't delude myself for a moment into believing I could hide my amorous thoughts. Only the blind and Kitten couldn't see my secret emotions.

Such thoughts had not tormented me with Vorzha; we'd hurtled into each other, panting passionately, and then we burned up, the smoke and ash carried away by the wind.

But that was not what I was yearning for now. Kitten's proximity was different. It made me shy and speechless and softheaded; feelings and thoughts piled up inside me, and all I could think of was how to get rid of them. And so I took refuge in the world of the imagination, delighting in the game: *For months we've been riding the train together, Kitten always saving the seat next to her for me, waving to me from the window. Sometimes I hold her hand.*

That's all, and yet it was an unhealthy game.

In reality, day after day I planned to open my heart to her, but I didn't even dare risk an encouraging handshake.

I had to smile at what I imagined would have been Papa's proposal: "Take her hand and bring her home; that's the way of the world."

Which world?

In town I got off the train, still sighing, along with a teeming mass of other students. En route to school we inundated the marketplace like a mob; discussions that had begun on the train about so many weighty matters reached their climax here. Huddled in small groups, impromptu student committees decided who was right. Sometimes I too had been asked to weigh in, but no longer was this ever the case, as if I'd had a Medal of Honor withdrawn.

I crossed the town's main square without a word. Mr. Horváth's kiosk gave me an opportunity to avoid the Altmanns' door; it had become common for every student to kick that door at least once every morning. The massive old apartment buildings enclosing the square reverberated the sound of the heavy iron door like roaring thunder.

Those buildings were lined up next to each other in stern grayness, their exteriors emanating the morose silence of centuries-old tax collection offices. In the immediate vicinity of the court building and City Hall, the old Calvinist Church crouched in sleepy idleness, sternly facing the market. From behind its crumbling plaster it preached patience and hope to the silent small town, and then it dozed off again like a brooding hen on hard-boiled eggs.

The changing times were evident also in the fact that previously, any door banger would have received a proper paddling, whereas now the gendarme, looking down from the balcony of the gendarmerie office, smiled at us, enjoying our morning serenade. As shutters now opened and so many residents of the square applauded in approval, he too clapped his hands. Indeed, the students' wake-up ritual had found its way into the hearts of those who lived along our route, who saw in this early morning rampage a patriotic act of the Awakening Hungarian Youth.

Now that the weather had cooled, the students could play their cruel game uninhibitedly; they didn't have to worry about the morose looks the peasants gave them on their way to work: the peasants still frequented the Altmanns' store, because only Mr. Altmann, the Jew, gave them credit.

Some students penned obscene and Jew-mocking lyrics to crisp military marches, and the Turóczi choir, a mob of singing students, terrorized the local Jewish community.

You could feel a new wind blowing from somewhere. A bad joke had grown from tiny seeds sown over the years. Apparently, this too was a game of fate, just as students don't accidentally sit side by side in class.

Miklós Altmann and I had reserved the back bench in class for years, and we got along really well. If the weaker students had been threatened with sitting between us, I dare say the class would have reached a high academic average within a short time. It was to no avail though that Miklós studied and knew a lot; his constant yawning, unrelenting taciturnity, and other negative qualities gradually lost him any standing he might have had. The unbearable garlic odor emanating from his body kept both his teachers and his peers at bay.

Being late for class was the worst of his incurable diseases, however. He lived hardly a stone's throw away from the school, yet day after day he was half an hour late, and even the sternest warnings made no difference. It happened that the school janitor, hoping for a tip, knocked on the door of the Altmanns' apartment to wake Miklós and his parents. However, every cent counted with the Altmanns, and after they happened to forget about etiquette on only one occasion, by neglecting to give a tip, the old janitor—Mister Charlie, we called him—gave their place a wide berth.

Eventually it was our head teacher who solved the problem of Miklós's wake-up call. Accordingly, those students—me included—arriving with the early train knocked on the Altmann's door, which was duly acknowledged by Miklós's old man with a grateful nod of his nightcapped head. This was far cheaper than when Mister Charlie had awakened them; but then nothing lasts forever, and sooner or later one must pay for everything.

Hardly had a month passed, and the lanky Jewish boy was thrown out of school. Suddenly, all of his defects were held against him: he was stooped, taciturn, lazy, forever sleepy, constantly late for school; he smelled of garlic; he couldn't thrust out his chest; and many more of his qualities clashed with the now more stringent school rules.

Miklós was in fact expelled from all secondary schools in the country. His excellent academic record hardly got any mention. Yet the reason for the majority of his failings was that he had to keep up that good academic record at all costs. While others could get away with clicking their heels and answering something or other about the subject, the Jewish boy's answer was expected to be perfect to a tee. As a result, he was left with insufficient time to sleep, much less relax.

Everyone knew that Miklós's constant fatigue was due not to laziness but rather to diligence, yet no one liked him. And if someone doesn't get any respect, his actions aren't appreciated either. Lately he had been publicly mocked, spat at, physically assaulted, and when the school withdrew its gracious protection, he became almost everyone's prey.

Still, it took everyone's breath away when the headmaster read out the faculty's decision. It was only later—when *all* Jews were swept out of the school—that we understood Miklós's shocking indifference. The ostensibly Calvinist high school expelled every Jew. That is to say, each and every student and teacher had to certify that his or her family tree on both sides had been Christian for generations. For once I didn't have a problem proving my origins—in this case, my not being Jewish—despite the fact that the local authorities didn't know a thing about my ancestry further back than my parents.

But one look at me could suggest only that my great-great-great-grandparents must surely have been Gypsies, too. Indeed, Mr. Garabuczi, my favorite teacher, shook his head sadly, indicating that my situation would be more secure if I could come up with at least one distant Hungarian predecessor—meaning a non-Gypsy, fair-skinned Magyar.

His fear proved to be well-founded. During the 10 am break on December 5, I was confronted by Elemér Tarhosy, the scion of a local gentry family and, more specifically, the son of the district judge.

"You're not leaving early today, my little friend," he told me condescendingly. "We're having a celebration to mark the eve of His Serene

Highness, Regent Miklós Horthy's name day. The gym has to be rearranged! Grab yourself some strong lads and join the janitor; make sure the gym is worthy of welcoming the guests." After a brief pause he added, more mildly, "Besides, you too are an interested party."

After a moment's thought I consented with a nod of my head. Why on earth would I be an interested party? I didn't belong to any student group that would normally have seen me accorded such a special role. In any event, the news aroused my interest. At 11 am, Tarhosy again came up to me again, calling over three sixth-graders as well.

"Listen, my little friends, get yourselves over to the Levente youth headquarters. There are two podiums over there we need for this afternoon's ceremony. The principal says it's okay for you to take a bit of time from school for this."

The sixth-graders smiled at one another, beaming with joy. "We're off the hook!" they exclaimed. I figured they'd gotten out of having to answer tough test questions in front of class. But by the time we arrived at the Levente youth building, the sight of the two well-polished, massive podiums wiped the smiles off their faces. We weren't even halfway back, though, when they began cursing Tarhosy, that older kid who had more of a voice in school affairs than did the teachers, even though he was the head of just one "study group" and was always taking off to tend to business at the Levente headquarters. We had to keep stopping after every few steps.

"He just had to pick on me for this bum job," grumbled one of them, a short, scrawny lad.

"Come on," the other two argued, "do you think he doesn't hate us just as much? He'll never forget that our class voted him down to head that study group."

"And where has that gotten us?" complained another. "He became the leader anyway."

School was over by the time we managed to lug over even one of the podiums. Exhausted, the three sixth-graders stretched out on the gym's large trampoline. But then the scrawny little fellow limped away;

he must have had something more important to attend to. The other two went in search of their pal, turning the classrooms upside down, and returned upset and unsuccessful. Their classmate was gone, they reported, bag and coat and all. They were so discouraged by this that they themselves no longer cared about the fate of the other podium; they too then left me in the lurch. Although they promised to return, I figured they wouldn't. As soon as they stepped out the main door of the school, no doubt they themselves didn't believe it, either.

If my train doesn't leave in the meantime, I'll clear out of here too, I resolved. After all, it seemed to me that the mess all around me in the gym wouldn't be tidied up in time even for His Serene Highness the Regent's name day the next day. During the past year, all the school's odds and ends had been collected there. I couldn't even remember when we last did any exercising there.

With bitter thoughts I took in the hideous sight: cobwebs and thick dust covered every exercise bar and rope, every nook and cranny of the gym. As for the heap of broken benches stacked one on top of the other and reinforced as if by prayer, it seemed that a loud profanity would have been enough to collapse it in an avalanche of sorts brought on by God's judgment.

The vaulting horses alone stood out amid the piles of gym equipment, and only because they were off to the side. I'd always believed that creating chaos was the specialty of the gods, but it seems I was wrong; original chaos was likely also the doing of school janitors, because compared to what I now saw all around me, everything else was merely a bit untidy.

Indeed, I had only to think of our janitor, Mister Charlie, and he promptly appeared with his ever-glowing cigarette holder under his nicotine-yellow-gray mustache. Traces of the paprika-stewed potatoes he'd consumed at midday still glistened on his gray, work-issue smock. The large wine-and-soda for which he took a little break from school every day at noon had flushed his otherwise pallid face.

It was rumored that when he was still a road laborer he'd found a car wheel containing a small fortune of coins hidden inside, and that he'd handed it over to the authorities. In exchange for his honesty, the sheriff rewarded him with the janitor's job. Some said the wheel had in fact fallen off the sheriff's car; but most doubted this, for various gentlemen were said to have gotten in touch with Mister Charlie, offering him ample rewards to corroborate in court that the money was theirs. However, when one such gentleman did then press his claim at a hearing in the matter, Mister Charlie denied even knowing who he was.

Later, Mister Charlie could have kicked himself for passing up the rewards. He sought recompense in his work—meaning that he did everything in a slapdash fashion, neglected whatever he could, and appeared at school only to show his face. Even so, his job was as certain as the sheriff's.

I seethed with anger as Mister Charlie looked me over with a dissatisfied glance.

"There won't be much of a celebration here if this is how the work is progressing."

At first I kept quiet and swallowed my anger, respecting his age and gray hair. After a few minutes, though, I was fed up with his insolence, and my respect was replaced by a sort of a ruthless vengefulness. I didn't know how to implement it yet, so I kept waiting for an opportunity.

"How come you didn't have time for the other one?" asked the old janitor, pointing to the podium.

Under school rules, every student was to be addressed as "young master." But Mister Charlie called me that only when others were present. Behind my back he only called me "that Gypsy bastard."

"I couldn't manage both at the same time," I replied.

He frowned and looked at me suspiciously, and then he wiggled his mustache in a grimace.

"If you were anyone else, I'd be surprised, but nothing more can be expected from your kind."

He sneered on saying "your kind."

Okay, I thought, *now I'll pull a fast one on you.*

"Wouldn't you bring the other one?" I pleaded with him in an innocent voice.

"Well, if you can tempt me with something . . ."

"Two wine-and-sodas," I said, jingling the money in my pocket.

"Well, if the young master thinks so," he said in a more respectful tone. "I'll do it."

That's what I wanted to hear!

"You won't regret it," I said, holding out my hand. We quickly negotiated the deal, and he went to get the other podium. I imagined everything, but not that he would really get it. The little old man did only cleaning for the school, yet he had sense enough to have the Levente youth headquarters' caretaker push over the podium in a handcart.

My revenge didn't succeed, but I appreciated his cunning. The caretaker got his fee, and disappeared lest we involve him in other chores, of which there were plenty. As for Mister Charlie, he told me he'd have his drink later; we wanted to get to work at once, but didn't know where to start. Using my increased prestige, I managed to persuade him to get rid of the cobwebs first; at least we could then see the order in which we had to tackle the work. Then we'd just have to carry the damn pile of junk somewhere.

"Carry it away?" Mister Charlie looked at me in surprise with his tiny watery eyes. "The ceremony is this afternoon, young master, not next year."

"That's occurred to me, too, but the gym has to be cleared out," I said. "Otherwise where can we put the audience?"

"To hell with them. Do you think we have to make such a big fuss about a few old bitches?"

"But Mister Charlie, we're celebrating the eve of His Serene Highness's name day, not that of just any old person."

"Come on, young master," he shook his head disapprovingly. "They're not lost for excuses."

I didn't understand what he was talking about; I looked at him as if he had a screw loose.

"Two or three barren cows from the Charitable Society will attend, and they will graciously endow some needy students with junk they've solicited over the year. And they, in turn, should be grateful that His Serene Highness was baptized Nicholas. That's how it's been every year—why should it be any different now?"

I couldn't reply a thing to the old man's words except what Tarhosy had told me.

"Ah, Tarhosy," said Mister Charlie with a dismissive wave of the hand. "He organizes 'worthy celebrations' twice a week, and he'd always like the podiums to reach to the ceiling."

Mister Charlie's words kept coming, and they were still confusing, and yet gloominess took hold of me. Was this what I'd missed the afternoon train for? Only that morning I'd decided to confess my feelings to Kitten. Well, Tarhosy had certainly screwed that up.

"Why would I be an 'interested party' in this ceremony?" I asked Mister Charlie. I was really curious now.

"I thought I told you already," he said. "Gracious St. Nick wishes to give you a present; Miss Elizabeth Tarhosy herself will present the gift bag to you. She will even add a kiss to it."

"Is she related to Tarhosy?"

"She's his aunt on his father's side. He flatters the old spinster, because that's where the inheritance will be coming from. Master Elemér will be rolling in dough once the devil takes Miss Liz, but there will be many 'worthy celebrations' until then."

It wasn't hard to gather from Mister Charlie's words that he wasn't a great admirer of the lady and even less so of the local notables, whose patronage he enjoyed.

"They're all bastards," he said. "They fleece a man and then expect him to be grateful. Well, I say let the maggots be grateful that will eat them up alive."

Sighing, he gave another wave.

"It's okay. Let them live in clover if they want."

The old man's hatred for the upper crust really surprised me. It seemed that not everything was as hunky-dory in that pompous world as it seemed from the perspective of the settlement.

Mister Charlie thoughtfully scratched his ass as he looked around the gym. He clearly wasn't in the mood to rearrange a thing; if only a single piece was moved, the whole dump might collapse.

Crouching atop a vaulting horse, I waited patiently, figuring the janitor would think of something. But he didn't. He only sat there next to me, rolled a cigarette into his cigarette holder, and thoughtfully eyed the place for possibilities. My mind also wandered away, and the rustle of the gym's large, wood-fired tile stove helped me conjure up my favorite thoughts as twilight took a fast hold outside. We sat in silence until the scurrying of mice brought us back to reality.

"We could do with a cat here," I said hoarsely.

"We sure could, but also with doing something. It would be good to stir up all that knowledge of yours, young master." With that, Mister Charlie tried to pass the buck to me.

"I told you already that we should start with the cobwebs."

"To the hell with the cobwebs! Do you think my mother was a mountain goat?" He flicked on the light switch with great élan and pointed to the gymnastic bars on the walls.

"We'll push the podiums there, put one flag each at their sides, hang the picture of His Serene Highness between them, and that's that. Who needs a more dignified background for a 'worthy celebration'?" With that, the janitor drew himself up as if he'd just untied an inscrutable knot.

"You know best," I agreed.

"Well, who else?" he said, panting as we grasped the podium. "Heave-ho, heave-ho." Mister Charlie's studded boots kept a firm grip on the filthy wooden floor, but I fell on my knees at every step and swore under my breath until he ordered a break.

"How the hell did you manage this goddamn podium all by yourself?" he queried, gasping.

"I didn't," I burst out, "four of us dragged it here!" He looked ready to jump at me any second; he glared at me from under his wrinkled forehead, and then suddenly burst out laughing.

"Well, I'll be damned! Young master, aside from what you gave me, which is enough for two drinks, I shelled out some dough of my own to get that rascal caretaker two wine-and-sodas."

"Okay then," I replied, "here's to five small wine-and-sodas! Two big ones! Whatever!" And so we kept encouraging ourselves.

Through the window we saw a small group of students approaching from the other end of Market Square. They were waving flags and singing a rousing, ancient Scythian battle song.

"Where do they think they're going?" Mister Charlie asked facetiously. "Do they think a mountain goat mounted my mom?" Cursing, he beat the cobweb-covered gymnastic bars on the wall with an unfurled Hungarian flag.

"Devil take them and their St. Nick's Day!" he wheezed from behind the full-length curtain of dust. "It'll soon get shitty like Franz Joseph."

"Do you come from Doboz?" I asked, guessing the village on the plains of eastern Hungary.

"What's wrong with that?"

"Nothing. I'm only asking because that's where they always call that dead emperor of ours the 'shitty Franz Joseph.'"

"Do you know why?"

"I don't have a clue," I said, shaking my head.

"Hm." Mister Charlie's face lit up as he shook the dust from the lapels of his coat. "Climb up the ladder," he said, "you're younger."

He rummaged for a long time through the bottom of a lopsided cabinet until he managed to rake up a yellowing, smoky portrait of the regent. He wiped off the glass with the bottom of his coat, spat on it, and smeared it thoughtfully with his fingers until the tiny specks of black so many flies had left behind on it dissolved.

Mister Charlie then walked calmly to the window and watched the students' torchlit procession. Reassured, he then wiped the image again.

"Have you ever heard anything about the Reds?" he asked while ambling up closer to me.

"Of course. The emperor's legendary Red Devils, those Hungarian hussars back in the war."

"Hell, no," said Mister Charlie, beckoning me to lean closer. "Have you heard about the commies?" he whispered in my ear. He could see that I was thinking.

"Well, never mind," he continued, louder. "When the war was over, they took power in our village. First they chased away the village clerk, who'd stolen all the war relief money, and then they gave the Almássy estates to the farm workers. Soldiers returning from the front didn't get rid of their uniforms, but pinned red ribbons to their caps and stood guard with their guns, saying that the old genteel world was now over and done with. Well, some of the peasants were happy about that and others weren't. The better-off ones were not exactly pleased that commies were now in charge, because they still revered the emperor."

I understood little of Mister Charlie's words, but gave a thoughtful nod whenever it seemed appropriate to do so.

"Well," he continued, "the poorer ones soon got used to the new circumstances, and if someone threatened them with the emperor and they could get their hands on him, they gave him a good thrashing. That's how it happened that one such mischievous fellow hung His Imperial and Royal Apostolic Majesty's picture on the door of the village's main outhouse.

"Lots of folks were offended—he'd hung it on the outside of the door, so you could see it from far away—but the young ones who hadn't seen a thing of the good old times grabbed at the opportunity to get a bit of revenge; even five years of a wedding feast would be too long, let alone five years of war, which is what they'd seen. Anyway, not long after this shocking act, most of the village's outhouses were decorated with His Majesty's portrait."

Mister Charlie stopped. His red-blotched drinker's nose became visibly paler as he now handed me the regent's picture, which he'd been absentmindedly wiping all the while; he walked to the window and, after gesturing something to the singers, returned and propped his elbows on the ladder. Neither of us talked. I was searching for the meaning of his words; he, for his cigarettes. Anyway, what he'd told me so far, plus using my imagination, was enough for me to understand His Majesty's nickname.

"Well, where should we hang this?" I asked, dangling the picture in front of Mister Charlie's nose. He looked at it thoughtfully, as if wondering where he'd seen the gentleman before. Pointing at it with his gnarled finger, he then continued with his story.

"Of course his Highness called in the Romanians from the east to give Hungary a helping hand in fighting off the Reds. The Reds were all shot, folks who'd had their land taken away took it back, and the genteel world returned. But, in Doboz, at least, the emperor's portraits stayed right where they were, on the outhouse doors.

"Well, the Romanian troops who passed through our village and saw what in other places would have counted as high treason, saw it instead as a nice Hungarian custom. What else could they have thought when lots of them were seeing outhouses for the first time in their lives? You might even say that those pictures served the Romanians well; at least they could recognize from a distance where they could take a crap.

"Those Romanians love their polenta, you know, and they'd never had as much back home as they did here in Hungary. Their bellies were always full. And so their hands were always on their belts, looking for the picture. Anyone in the village who could do so welcomed their undesirable guests—the foreign troops were quartered in people's homes—with a picture-adorned outhouse.

"As for the village clerk, who'd earlier been booted out of office and now had his old job back, well, he was so damn angry that he had the whole village caned. But as fate would have it, the officers of the Romanian headquarters requisitioned his home for their quarters. He wanted to excel, and not only did he decorate his rooms with heaps of bed linen and fancy trinkets, but also made sure to have a picture of His

Imperial and Royal Apostolic Majesty—who was revered by the Romanians, after all—in a conspicuous spot on his outhouse door.

"But as soon as the officers moved in and saw the portrait of the emperor on the outhouse door, they furiously wrestled the village clerk to the ground as if to castrate him. But before they had their servants give him a good thrashing, they smashed his nose into His Majesty's portrait."

Mister Charlie's story having drawn to a close, we now continued our work with somewhat abated diligence and in a more slapdash fashion. Our keenness could hardly have been rewarded by praise, but we put up what had to be put up and pretty much scooped up the trash. I stuck the drawing of the Hungarian Holy Crown above the regent's portrait, and then, as the celebrating students rushed in, we had just enough time to complete the preparations.

Fortunately, the dignitaries who were expected had yet to arrive, so we still had a chance for some last-minute adjustments. Mister Charlie soon grew tired of the chattering students' romp, though, and quickly moved up one floor. The festive mood was almost at its peak.

When Tarhosy finally appeared with his cortege at the gym door, someone roared, "Atten*tion!*"

The students promptly quietened down, opening a path by which Tarhosy could march to the podium. They welcomed him with a head-splitting "Hurray!"

There I was among all those students standing at attention, without a clue as to what was expected on such occasions. All that I could see was that Tarhosy's head was turning blue, that his eyes were fixed on me, and that he was coming closer with slow, measured steps.

The thought flashed through my mind that, like the others, I should stand at attention and answer his questions in a firm and clear-cut manner; or else I should report that the task entrusted to me had been fully implemented, as Papa had so often taught me to say. Even when I was a little boy, Papa had spoon-fed me the idea that due respect of the leader is compulsory whether you like it or not. "A soldier will always remain a soldier," he used to say, "and a command has to be carried out even if you're sent to catch a squirrel on the front lines." He himself had once been sent to catch such a squirrel, an effort that guaranteed him a lifetime of boasting, for he came back with a bullet—one the enemy rewarded him with, that is—that was still hiding under his skin.

Stopping in front of me, Tarhosy eyed me up and down. The golden braids on his black school-cap, a sign of his superior status, seemed even shinier. My muscles grew taut, and I was just about to stand at attention and report something in a soldierly fashion when Tarhosy snapped at me:

"What *is* this? Are we having a ceremony in a pigsty in honor of His Serene Highness the Regent of the Kingdom of Hungary, Miklós Horthy?"

The silence that followed his question virtually cut into my throat.

"Why would this be a pigsty?" I finally replied. "If I'm not mistaken, it's a gym—correct? Anyway, it was you who assigned it for this occasion."

"I did," he hissed through his teeth. "But I also assigned *you*. I asked for the place to be made worthy of this celebration and not for use as a dunghill."

"Do you think," I said, quoting Mister Charlie, "that my mom was mounted by a mountain goat?"

"Shut your trap!" he yelled. "Anyway, if I'm talking to you, my little friend," he hissed again, "then stand up straight in your rags, so the lice can shriek under them. Otherwise they'll pick them up from the street without you."

While Tarhosy was lecturing me, he kept tapping my nose with elegant strokes of his rolled-up speech, taking care not to damage the paper.

"So that's the thanks I get, my little friend," he rebuked me with paternal rigor. "And yet we wanted to save you for the Fatherland, thinking you'd show more respect for it than all those rotten Jews who are all over the place. Well, let the faculty deal with you—at least the traitors will get their just rewards. And now scram!"

A hushed commotion could be felt in the gym; the group of students who had earlier parted into two long lines moved closer to one another. The well-organized maneuver clearly showed their intention. Neither lengthier discussion nor pleading would have done me any good, I knew.

My fellow students gripped their long, thick, burned-out torches tight enough to crush them, it seemed. My brain raced as never before; I felt like a cat on a hot tin roof. *What now?* I asked myself. No door, no window offered an escape route, and with all those torches around, if I couldn't escape, not even my shoes would get away in one piece.

The tense moments adorned my face with fat beads of sweat that ran down into the corners of my mouth in small rivulets; I felt like someone tasting life for the first time, and I found it salty and bitter.

"Perhaps you didn't understand what I said?" he asked, baring his teeth and once again lifting the roll of paper toward my nose. I felt the color rising in my face as tiny red circles thronged before my eyes. That moment I ceased to think, as blind passion took hold of me. I grabbed the roll out of the gesticulating Tarhosy's hand and threw it among the eagerly waiting students like a bone to hungry dogs. Next I grasped Tarhosy by the collar and gave him a good shake; I felt my fingers going dead as I wrapped the collar of his corded coat around his neck. I then told him in simple and not so simple terms just what he was, gave him a sizable punch to his nose, and sent him on his way.

Lifting his palm to his face, my little friend crashed backward into the stack of benches, which—as soon as his guilty body touched it—collapsed with a huge roar. After that, everything went smoothly. A dark cloud of dust covered the gym, and amid calls of "Help!" and "God, help me!" and, yes, a loud crash, the crowd swept the door away together with its frame. I no longer had any obstacles; all I had to look out for was not to lose my balance by stepping on one of the discarded torches. I just walked out. Mister Charlie was still cocking his ears by the time I got upstairs to the classroom he was in.

"What's going on down there?" he inquired.

"The students are having fun."

"As long as they don't spoil things before the festivities!"

"Don't worry," I reassured him. "Everything is okay."

Down on the street the evening had settled down; the tremulous yellow glow of the tiny light bulbs broke through the darkness. Loudly chattering people swarmed everywhere, and at the end of the square, next to the bubbling artesian well, a large group of women chewed over the local gossip in a leisurely holiday spirit.

Children with canvas school bags, their noses flattened to the glass, stood in front of the ornately lit shop windows, looking wistfully at the orphaned, red-coated Santa Clauses.

I strolled about the street dejectedly; I didn't particularly enjoy my good luck, though it wasn't to be taken lightly that I had gotten away unscathed. Passing by the Altmanns' apartment building, I stopped, consumed by the urge to give the already dented door yet another kick. But so many people had done so already that day that my feeble effort would have been taken as a bad joke.

The pealing of the church bell calling the faithful to service chased me over to the other side of Market Square, where a shabby, drunken figure outside the pub was teetering and tottering with clenched teeth to the rhythm of the bell, staring at the entering guests as he did so.

For a second his eyes rested on me, too; he lifted his finger to his frayed cap, and then went on swaying, making clownish grimaces as if he had just bitten into a bitter lemon.

Gypsy music drifted out of the pub; someone yelled his bitterness into the resonance produced by the violin strings, exhorting a Gypsy to keep up the fervor: "Pull that bow, Zhiga, goddammit!" Then his voice faltered. Surely Zhiga was smiling; if possible, he would lean closer to the patron, right up to his ears, because on such occasions even an otherwise "stinking Gypsy" is allowed to do so, gently, of course, watching for any sign that his proximity might be unwelcome, because if it is and he fails to notice, why, he won't be able to buy bread tomorrow.

How I wanted to run off somewhere-to leave the ringing bells, the music-but where? Out of the world? But how? Life is the strictest of prison guards.

I fixed my eyes on the shabby man at the door, who was swaying like a sign hanging in the wind. *That's how it is,* I thought. *They cringe the way Tarhosy and likeminded sorts require it, because the Fatherland is theirs. If they don't, the faculty will deal with it!* For a second Tarhosy's words echoed in my ears: "At least the traitors will get their just rewards."

Suddenly I got the jitters. Glancing up at the illuminated clock tower, I hoped I had enough time to talk to my teacher, Mr. Garabuczi.

I was about to leave when someone touched my arm.

"Wait!"

Not daring to turn back, I just stood there; I was skeptical even when Kitten took my arm, but as she flooded me with questions, I was no longer worried.

"You were waiting for me, weren't you?" she asked.

"No."

"I'm sorry, I thought you'd be waiting, but this St. Nick's celebration has turned everything upside down. I'm so glad you waited for me. You know that it's on account of my dad that we have met up, after all?"

I didn't interrupt Kitten again. By turns she asked; answered; embraced me; pushed me away; pulled an earnest face; or couldn't stop talking with uninhibited glee. All the while she exuded a pleasant, sweet liqueur aroma.

"But this is serious," she said for the umpteenth time. "If Papa hadn't picked me up, we wouldn't have met. It's lucky he sometimes goes on a binge."

Yet another reveler could be heard calling out a good-natured exclamation to a Gypsy musician inside the pub, and then the same bellwether voice started to bleat the patriotic song: "You're beautiful, you're lovely, dear Hungary!"

"That's him!" Kitten's eyes gleamed in the electric light. "That's him!" By then Zhiga and the band started up another, even brisker, more cheerful song; the pub was quaking, and Dr. Zoltán Vágó clapped and whooped as befits a reveling Hungarian gentleman.

Kitty tapped her tiny shoes to the rhythm. Happily she listened, smiled, and hummed, without a care in the world. And while the music was playing, she didn't want to hear anything else.

"Come on," she said, shaking her blonde head playfully. "I'll introduce you to him." She stood on tiptoes and burrowed her hands under my collar like a child wanting to be picked up. I stood rigidly. My bland past and my bleak future trembled in her large eyes with haughty impatience.

"I'm not going," I said, choking on my words.

"No?" She looked at me, surprised by the unexpected opposition. "Why?"

"Because I'm a Gypsy." I thought it would have been harder to put into words. I'd been covering it up for months, and now that I'd said it, all I felt was relief.

"A Gypsy?" burst out of her involuntarily. The flame that flashed out of her blue eyes was akin to the purple glow that destroys a planet that has veered off course; then everything froze on her face. For a while I kept nodding, witness to the truth of my words, and then left her.

Had I known that I would turn into a pillar of salt, I would have unhesitatingly looked back, but I didn't want to see the humiliating hatred in Kitten's eyes.

I didn't stop until Mr. Garabuczi's place. Soon after I rang the bell, blonde, pigtailed, chubby Klári opened the door.

"Papa's home," she informed me. "He's in the study with Ágnes." Then she ran back into the flat, leaving me to follow; in contrast with other occasions, she didn't take the time to boast about her latest academic achievements.

Mr. Garabuczi looked up at me inquisitively; he'd been making a drawing of his other daughter, Ágnes. The softly hatched pencil drawing portrayed her small, worried-looking face with amazing fidelity. He didn't say a thing, because Ágnes preempted him.

"See," she said, showing me her own piece of paper, "I can draw, too. That's Papa and that's the kitten."

For some reason the kitten was bristling with its prickly pointed mustache at the edge of the page, perhaps because Ágnes had drawn her father's eyes to look sadder than what a playful kitten could handle.

"Beautiful," I said hoarsely, sincerely ashamed that I had questioned Ágnes's drawing ability when her father used to boast about her in class.

Mr. Garabuczi motioned for me to sit down, waiting for Ágnes to finish her story. Satisfied with my brief praise, she continued her unfinished masterpiece.

"Has something happened?" I couldn't tell from his calm voice, friendly as usual, whether he was suspicious about the late visit.

"Yes. I've hit Tarhosy."

As he looked at me, it seemed as if the old confidential smile was flashing from his wide-open eyes. But then he became even gloomier. He bent over his drawing board, squinting, and didn't say a world; he just waited for me to speak. Now I regretted that on the way here I'd thought only about myself, neglecting to plan what I'd say. Finally, with intervals by turns long and short, and at every step correcting my stuttered sentences, I managed to paint a picture of what had happened.

Perhaps due to the nervousness emanating from me, Mr. Garabuczi shaded the corner of his drawing board completely black and looked at me, still squinting, only when I mentioned Tarhosy's threat about the faculty.

"It's a difficult matter," Mr. Garabuczi sighed. "Not that it's been easy so far, but without any proper grounds not much can be done to bring round the most of the faculty."

"Without any proper grounds?" I asked, surprised. "As far as I know, I've never done a thing to deserve a faculty discussion."

"Do you really think, my boy, that the others did?" Mr. Garabuczi replied. "*Their* only sin was to be Jewish. This country of ours is now pretending to do a thorough spring-cleaning, and anyone whose name is susceptible to the adjective 'stinking' is mercilessly swept out of the way."

"But why?" I inquired involuntarily.

He looked at my face for a long time, not knowing whether to let me in on the secret or to put an end to my curiosity with a wave of a hand. He then continued with a sigh:

"The Fatherland is for sale again, and the buyer is fastidious."

How I would have liked to say: *Let them give it away; after all, it's theirs.* But I felt my throat tightening. Six years of hard work in school, crowned by success, had just fallen to my feet like a bird with broken wings. All my aspirations and dreams died with it.

They say that he who has no god doesn't count as a man. What then is a person who has no fatherland and calls the whole world his own, yet has nowhere to rest his head?

The Fatherland is for sale! The words resounded in me as if spoken by a hawker offering shoddy wares for sale at a flea market. Did Köszörűs have to die because he hadn't guarded this Fatherland that was "for sale"? Was that why every house and every doorpost was adorned with the slogan, "No, no, never!" only once again to become prey to merchants' cheap slogans?

"I don't understand this, sir," I sighed. Mr. Garabuczi ran fingers through his curly hair, fumbling to find the part to gain time to come up with some comforting words. Then, shrugging his shoulders, he gave up.

"Perhaps it's for the best," he said, adding, after a pause, "It doesn't do us any good anyway."

"You're in danger, sir." At last I managed to groan out the reason for my coming here. "Tarhosy threatened that when the faculty meets, 'at least the traitors will get their just rewards.' Those were his exact words."

"Not to worry," said Mr. Garabuczi with a dismissive wave. "According to them, anyone who doesn't follow them is a traitor. You could only have dealt with your predicament as you have. It's a consolation to me that beyond your thirst for knowledge and extraordinary diligence you've kept your humanity and haven't abased yourself just to serve them. These people are trying to get rid of everyone. I don't mean it as a solace, but I can reassure you that I don't have to fear Tarhosy's bluster. His thunder has been stolen by this."

Mr. Garabuczi took a draft notice from his desk drawer. "The ministry has rejected my exemption request." He paused. "You see," he added, seemingly recovering his old cheerfulness, "how strange life can be. Both teacher and student fail!"

He stood up and saw me to the door, extending his hand in farewell. "Take care," he said with paternal benevolence. "Everyone is facing very difficult days; don't lose your clean conscience, which you'll need throughout your life. Other than that, everything in life is transient, like the light that dims or blinds or disappears completely.

"I'm not familiar with your world, but I believe that it is more humane and cleaner than this carnival hiding behind masks. Don't be sorry for what was good in it, though; you'll take it home with you, and light is needed where it is dark."

I pressed his outstretched hand as if he had wanted to hand over all his humanity for the rest of his life in one go.

On my way to the train station I managed to acquire a billiard cue, as I expected Tarhosy and his mob to have followed me there. Instead, only two rooster-feathered gendarmes stood among the crowd waiting for the train; I was sure they were waiting for me. Regardless of my intuition, I had to know the gendarmes' intentions if I didn't want to walk all night. But even more so, lest I carelessly walk into the trap. I didn't have to wait for long to find proof. Tarhosy was bustling about among the people there, a white bandage on his head that at a glance gave the impression that he was a woman.

You just wait, I thought, *there's another station too.* Examining the face of the clock tower, I tried to guess how long it would take me to walk there. I might have all the time in the world; if not, I'd run. I'd already been running so much in my life, anyway. I tried to look at things humorously, but something put me on guard.

From a distance I could hear Zhiga and the band still playing. The hooves of the stomping horses in the square clattered, and a quiet, black-clad figure sat on the box of the softly rattling coach. Dr. Vágó's coachman, I figured. I slunk from doorway to doorway; for a long while the sound of the coach clattered in my ears, and when I got out of the more dangerous part of the illuminated area, I accelerated my steps and began to run. However, the loud echo of my shoes soon made me have some sense. *Calm down, calm down. It's dark.*

I tried to fit my thoughts to my remaining courage. With difficulty I overcame my nervousness. No wonder; I was out of practice. These respites had done me no good. He who has to run should run, but so as not to be noticed; if the pack is let loose, that's the end. That is why the hare has learned to creep. A loud ruckus could be heard from the market. Yes, it was them. It would have been good to know what Tarhosy had said. What *could* he have said? I couldn't expect him to lie.

I was overcome by another bout of nerves, but as I reached a poorer district of downtown, it abated. I was reassured by the low, dilapidated fences that I could step over any time if the need arose. I meandered along deserted, dark streets, finding my bearings by the monotonous beat of the power station. I left dark little houses behind me, and met not a soul in the narrow alleys. The dogs were miraculously silent; only rarely would one of them give a yelp, which faded into a solitary, breathless whine. Stopping often to listen, I eventually found myself well away from the town center, in a peaceful, tranquil environment.

I followed my senses, sizing up the distance; my ears told me I was getting closer to the power station. My thoughts wandered.

Mama always called me a doomsayer. True, it eased her soul to knock my dreams. She'd say, "Why don't you dream about bread?" Could I help it if I dreamed of goose? She knew I could sense trouble, though; and that's why she called me a doomsayer. It was a pity to have to tell her about it in the morning. Then she would be nervous, upsetting the whole family's peace.

Had I not stayed after school there wouldn't have been any particular problem. As Mr. Garabuczi said, I would have been expelled anyway. No one can escape his fate. I didn't bash Tarhosy in the nose because I'd been dreaming of goose, but because of his insolence. Of course it was worth it. That had been the only way to deal with the matter. At least he got to know what a "stinking" man's hand was like.

To hell with them. Did I want them thinking that Mama was mounted by a mountain goat? Why had he kept referring to the regent, when it was me he had a problem with?

I stopped. I had to decide which way to go—on the paved road or over the empty lots that lay along the railway embankment? I didn't feel like wandering through the brush, but all the same, my sense of security held me back from cutting across to the road, so I opted for the lots.

It was the right decision. After a little while, the clatter of horseshoes broke the silence, and I glimpsed two gendarmes riding comfortably out of the town. I pulled over instinctively. They wouldn't be able to see me in the dark, but I could see them all the more.

That moment my pride in the glorious deed I'd done that afternoon plummeted. Bayonets also glinted near the gendarme building next to the power station, and slightly farther along two agile youngsters—students from my school—warmed themselves by flapping their arms. The train approached from town with a loud whistle, and I could hear from its puffing that the brakes were biting into its unruly wheels.

There are such things as coincidences, but what were those two students doing here? I could find no better answer to my question than that they were waiting for me. Crouching, I crept closer to the rails. My fast heartbeat began to slow, although I hadn't counted on such a turn of events. My only option was to hop onto the last car.

The engine passed me, braking slowly and steadily, while thin sheaves of reddish light poured from the windows of the rumbling cars, illuminating the billowing smoke and clouds of steam. I crouched, waiting for the right moment; the cars were forced to stop as they bumped into each other. I was ready to jump up when I caught sight of yet more gendarmes, waiting to alight from the steps of the last car.

"To hell with all of you," I almost uttered aloud. What a manhunt! Now it was really time to think clearly. After so much preparation I was not about to fall into their hands.

Indeed, all was not yet lost. You have to wail only when you are beaten, until then there's no cause for lamentation. The train shuffled off with loud whistles. I waited until the gendarmes marched back with hard strides toward town, and then I snuck back into the bushes. I had to sum up the depressing reality: two of them at the market, two at the electricity plant, and two mounted gendarmes waiting for me at the next stop in case I'd managed to elude their net on foot or by train.

There was little chance of escape, I knew, and even that was soon reduced by half. A soggy meadow stinking of oil and tar spread out in all directions behind the plant; the sight and smell filled me with yet more uncertainty. I had to think fast, but hardly had time to do so.

I had to get to the other side of the bridge before the mounted gendarmes turned back, or else every remaining option before me would be closed. I'd already lost fifteen minutes. The darkness and the faint mist that had settled over the Körös River was to my advantage, but the lost time made everything seem hopeless.

These guys were not the types to stomach failure. No, they would soon close off the bridge, and then I'd walk right into their trap. Fear redoubled my remaining strength and, taking deep breaths, on tiptoes I followed the gray, hazy line of the paved road. I looked back from time to time; the town lamps were still faintly visible through the fog and, judging by their weakening light I concluded that I'd made up for some of the lost time.

Weighing up my options, my queasy stomach told me that luck could help at this point only by working wonders. The road was lined on both sides with canals, and only the stout trunks of the old mulberry trees offered some shelter. That was better than nothing, I figured, and while there was even a hair's breadth of hope there was no sense of thinking about anything else.

I took long strides by running softly on tiptoes, taking this risk so the time spent listening shouldn't go to waste. *Keep going, keep going!* These words pulsated within me. If nothing else, there was the river. *You won't humiliate me ever again.* Except that the Körös was still far, and at the same time I thought I heard horseshoes clattering from the direction of the town.

My mind was flooded with the realization that this was the end. Now I truly had my back to the wall. The derisive laughter of a hundred Tarhosys echoed in my mind: *So we're not abasing ourselves, my little friend? You prefer the Körös? Where's the Körös, mountain goat . . . oat . . . oat . . . oat? A trap is waiting, waiting, waiting.* These words repeated themselves within me like the ripples of a stone thrown into my soul.

The approaching clatter of the horseshoes lulled me into a deep sense of resignation. I didn't hear a thing apart from it, and I leaned against a mulberry tree with a yawning fatigue. My steaming clothes were sticking to me, and I would even have liked to hang my treasured winter coat on a branch. At least if I had to run again, it would have been easier, because I hardly think that a gendarme would offer me a seat beside him on his horse.

I nervously untied its braided buttons, and the sharp vapor of the sweat issuing from my shirt made me cough. I no longer cared about keeping quiet and I no longer cared about dying; I needed air, or else I would suffocate or pass out.

I wheezed, gasped; a hundred kinds of noise crowded in my head. The monotonous pulsation quickened into a soft-pitched rattle of a coach with a throaty, ferocious male singing voice, mingled a soft female laughter like a lost pigeon in a storm. I thought I was going crazy! I covered my ears with both my hands. I stood there in the roaring silence, and lifted my hands from my ears when the coach rolled past right in front of me.

I stepped out onto the road elated and ashamed, leaving behind my broken courage under the tree, and started out again much relieved.

After only a few steps I heard the coach stop, turn around, and come toward me. I stepped off the curb while it galloped past me. By the flickering coach light I recognized Kitten wrapped in a fur coat and a blanket as she leaned out from the back seat as if to scrutinize me. The coach passed me yet again, and then turned back once more.

"Whoa!" Zoltán Vágó ordered András, the coachman. The coach halted. "Get on!" he commanded in a gargling voice. "My daughter says she knows you."

"That may be so, sir, but I don't know the young lady."

"I said get on!"

I was still this side of the bridge, and the danger hadn't yet passed. Vanity makes sense only if you can do it in style. I got on. Kitty made room for me next to her, and I wanted to thank her, but the horses ran away with the coach; Kitty nodded and kept looking at the darkness.

The horses furiously trampled the road, red sparkles fluttering in clusters from the touch of their hooves; the coach flew and swam with a melodic sound of cymbals clashing again and again, and the darkness clung to András's hat with crow's nails, flinging its whispering wings into our faces. Zoltán Vágó quietened down and pulled the fur collar of his coat tighter around his neck, letting out a shout only when the horses slackened off.

It all seemed like a dream, and in my heart I was hoping to spend the whole night at home in bed. Dreams can become a reality or come to nothing. I was freezing from the cold grip of my wet, sweaty clothes.

Dr. Vágó offered me his cigar case, and András slowed down the horses while we lit up. We reached a rise, and I involuntarily leaned back, bracing my back to the backrest.

Then, like a young gentleman who has struck it rich, I smoked my cigar.

I lurched in the coach, my head spinning. We reached the bridge, whose iron skeleton reverberated the clatter of the hooves with deep rumblings. The light of the coach lantern flashed dimly below us in the smooth, black mirror of the Körös River. It was a lovely sight, but at the end of the bridge the horses suddenly stopped in their tracks. Two mounted gendarmes blocked our path like two bronze statues.

"Oh, my God," I whispered involuntarily.

"What is this?" yelled Dr. Vágó, "a hijacking?" With that, he snatched the whip from András's hand.

"The Royal Hungarian Gendarmerie, sir. We are looking for a rebel Gypsy youngster."

"In my coach?"

"God forbid, sir, only . . ."

"What the hell, András!" Dr. Zoltán Vágó struck the whip. He left the gendarmes behind with their unfinished message.

"What insolence!" he yelled beside himself. "I'll lodge a complaint with the brigade commander. A rebel Gypsy in my coach! What's going on in this damn world, for God's sake? Giddyup! Giddyup!"

He struck the horses with full force. It took me a long time to come to. András could barely hold on to the harness while I clung tenaciously to the carriage fender, lest I fly out at a bend in the road. *So there are still miracles,* I thought. Dr. Vágó whipped the horses with incessant anger, and the maddening swish of the lashings made them traverse the miles at lightning speed.

Kitten didn't even flinch at the mortal injuries suffered by her father; she sat stiffly, motionless, as if commanding respect and self-abasement. I wondered why she'd given me a lift. She already knew I was a Gypsy.

I hadn't quite finished resolving the riddle in my mind when the answer flashed before me. *Why doesn't God eradicate sinners? Because he needs people who adore him, people he can show his power to, or else his glory goes up in smoke. The purely destructive gods are soon destroyed. The Vágós, the Tarhosys, and the other terrestrial gods—before whom even the formidable gendarmes abase themselves—are aware of this. They want their glory here on earth, and they need us to attain it.*

We were approaching the Rosszeredei farms, and I saw from afar that Mr. Csurka's roadside tavern was still open. The old man knew Papa well, because Papa never went past on his way home from a flea market without stopping in. In bad weather, Mr. Csurka offered not only plum brandy but also his large shed for sleeping in. That's where I'd sack out, I decided suddenly. Papa would pay for it next time.

"Halt, András!" I called out to the coachman. It was quite a job to force the madly rushing horses to stop, but they finally did so quite close to the tavern. I was right about the light being on. It had been market day in town, and on such occasions some peasants always stopped at the tavern on their way home, especially if they had made good bargains at the market. I jumped off the coach in a broad arc, and the honorable Dr. Vágó and his esteemed daughter turned their heads toward me only when I clicked my heels with a loud thud.

"Thank you, sir; thank you, miss." I gave a brief nod to Kitten.

"Only this far?" Dr. Vágó asked, astonished.

"Yes."

I didn't wait for them to start off; I left them. The coach drove away, taking with it my dark and struggling past. Suddenly I saw everything clearly—especially the fact that the problem hadn't begun at school, but somewhere in the realms of the coaches and the debauched nights of the high and mighty.

I felt quite cheerful compared to the previous hours, and the thought of my wasted years of school no longer made me unhappy. In fact, I felt I'd finished school, and that tonight was my graduation ceremony. I hadn't learned as much in all my life as in the last few hours. I had been hoping for a miracle, and a miracle did happen; a devastating and disappointing miracle that destroyed all my childhood dreams.

We believe that fate is evil, that it embitters us and holds us prisoner; therefore we scold and curse it with boundless impatience, although the Master knows what he is doing. He doesn't demand forbearance, suffering, and humiliation from us as propagated by the false gods, but to remain human, adamantly and unyieldingly. Only those who are hard can survive on this large grindstone.

Should I set off into the dark night or ask Mr. Csurka to let me stay? Go! It is childish to shrink from the night when it is your most reliable friend. Yes, get home as soon as possible; for at home, even fear tastes better.

Loud clamor could be heard from the tavern, while horses draped in blankets dozed next to the road. The markets were always bustling before the holidays, with that level of activity returning only the following Christmas. The farm carts, equipped with cages and coops and portable pig pens, stood empty; the pigs and other creatures had all been sold. I examined the signs on the carts warily, lest someone take me for a thief. The light of the oil lamp filtering through from the tavern window was of little help, but I was able to sneak from one cart to the other.

"What on earth is this?!" I said, straightening up jubilantly next to a rickety chaise, then clinging to its side with superstitious joy.

"Is that you?" Mama screamed, tugging her fluffy, frost-coated shawl away from her mouth. "What happened to you?!" Joy lingered behind the wailing, desperate question.

"I missed my train," I said, laughing.

"Thank the dear Lord! We thought something bad had happened."

I could have told her in a nutshell: "I got kicked out of school." I think Mama would have given me a baffled look. *What does that have to do with trouble? The main thing is that you can talk, you can move, you can even laugh; to hell with everything else.*

"Go on, why don't you go in after your father? He's got money!" I sure hadn't heard *that* from her for a long time. Ever since I'd been going to high school, Mama didn't like me to go to the tavern with Papa. I threw the bag stuffed with books into the middle of the cart; I could still hear Mama's chiding as she snatched it out of the hay, and then I entered the door. The interior was like that of any other roadside tavern on market days: a smoke-filled room, flickering lights, and a wood-fueled iron stove in the corner.

Papa stood next to the stove, warming the back of his trousers. As he caught sight of me, the bottle stopped under his floppy mustache, and the brandy almost went down the wrong way, but he managed to splash it back into the bottle in time.

"How did you get here?" He gave me a stern look, his eyes watering from the wayward drink.

"I missed the train." That was all he needed; his unshaven face lit up, and his healthy teeth shone with laughter.

"Did you walk?" Papa posed this question out of habit. It made no difference to him whether I nodded yes or no; the main thing was that I was there. He emptied the rest of the brandy into the spittoon. I don't know why. Perhaps he was offering a sacrifice to some saint or perhaps he was in the habit of spitting his last mouthful into it.

"Mr. Csurka, give us two shots!"

The old bar-owner looked me over with a smile and poured one of the shots into a glass.

"Your son has grown, Boncza."

"He has, Mr. Csurka."

"You've made a gentleman out of him."

"Who knows, maybe that'll be his downfall."

I was surprised, as I expected Papa to take the opportunity to brag about me.

"Well, he certainly has courage," he said, stroking the fur on my coat. "Imagine, Mr. Csurka, he set out on foot in this infernal darkness."

"He doesn't look like a loser; you have to say that for him."

"Indeed." Now Papa did begin to swell with pride. "You know, I wasn't afraid, either, even when all of Hell's devils were carousing on the roads."

"Drink," said Mr. Csurka, pointing to the glass, "it's real plum brandy."

The peasants in their boots and sheepskin coats looked at us with suspicion, but they lost interest when they saw me clinking glasses with Papa.

Mama soon grew tired of the outdoors and snuck in after us. "How long are you staying? The horse will catch cold."

"Give her a bitters," was all that Papa said. Returning to the earlier topic, he continued: "You know, Mr. Csurka, he could become a gentleman if he knew how to use his brains. Because then no one in the world would take him for a Gypsy." Mr. Csurka nodded.

"But he doesn't like horses," Papa added with resignation.

"Does that surprise you, Boncza? My son also spends his time with all sorts of nonsense instead of making use of all the money I've spent on his schooling."

"They'll be sorry one day, Mr. Csurka."

Fortunately a pale young man beckoned Mama to his table, so Papa could keep on chatting.

"He's handsome and brave. What else do you need in life? Brains."

"That's what he's studying for now," said the innkeeper, winking at me.

"Do you think so?" Papa glanced toward Mama and, seeing that she was scrutinizing the young man's palm, he leaned closer to the innkeeper. "You know, I never went to school, but it takes a man and a half to pull a fast one on me."

Mr. Csurka kept quiet, smoothed down his apron, and smiled. "I can assure you of that," he wrinkled his eyes, "though no one believes that a Gypsy sells good merchandise."

The conversation turned more and more to horse trading. Mr. Csurka was as familiar with this subject as any professional, and it seemed he also liked it. Surely he had witnessed many a Gypsy market, as his inn was situated so that even travelers couldn't avoid it; nor was he ever averse to giving credit to people going to the market.

It was getting quite late, and the guests were slowly leaving in groups. Mama left the now sad-looking young man, and kept urging Papa on until we too made our way home. The weather was becoming grim, as if regretting its earlier benevolence.

"There's no winter without cold weather," Papa said minutes later from behind the reins of the cart, wiping his hoar-frosted mustache.

"We thought summer would never end. . . . What did that pale-faced monkey want?"

"He would like to be a soldier."

"Then why the hell doesn't he join the army? Goddamn him!"

"He has tuberculosis." Mama's brief interjection calmed Papa's sudden anger; he fell silent, ashamed of his hasty curse, and didn't say a word until he asked, in a much calmer voice:

"What did you tell him to do?"

"To get married. At least then he won't want to be a soldier."

"Did he pay you?"

"Who wants his money?" Mama replied. "It would only infect us."

Papa chuckled softly, knowing that not a word of this was true.

"You felt sorry him, eh?"

"He's very poor. Do you expect me to take alms away from a beggar?"

"You're right," Papa conceded. "You'll see, the world will perish when they draft the horses into the army; nothing good can come of it."

"Whoa!" Papa called out, suddenly stopping the horse. He got off.

"Go on, take a piss," Mama told him. "We won't get home before morning."

Papa pissed all over the wheel spokes, and then he got back on, sighing. He handed me the reins, stuffed his pipe, and once it was smoking, he asked:

"Well, have they taught you at school how to heal the sick?"

"Why? Who is the patient?"

"Your mother, then you, and perhaps me too."

"Okay, Papa, don't go kidding me; that's a bad joke." I tried to talk seriously to him because I detected something suspicious in his words.

"It's not a joke, son," said Mama, bursting into tears. "We're all sick because of the condition you're in. All we see is that you're gradually shriveling up like a dry weed."

"Me? There's nothing wrong with me at all."

"Keep quiet while your mother is talking," said Papa, putting me in my place. "Do you think that because we didn't go to school, we're fools?"

"Of course not."

"Don't interrupt me, my boy," Mama pleaded. "Sooner or later you'll have to figure out everything, anyway. You wake up at dawn, you leave, you come home at night, you study, and sometimes you don't even know what day it is. But we live among Hungarians, and we hear everything." She was choking back her sobs.

"What have you heard?" I asked nervously.

"We are facing very bad times, son," said Papa, picking up where Mama had left off. "The Hungarians say they're going to put all the Gypsies on paper boats and make them sink in the sea." He too had a lump in his throat, but he restrained himself.

"Spit it out already," I begged. "What on earth are you trying to say?"

"Leave that damn school; it won't do you any good anymore."

Mama wrapped herself in silence.

"Why aren't *you* saying anything now?" I asked. But Mama appeared to have been struck dumb.

"Well, that's okay then," I said, playing my trump card. "I got kicked out of school, anyway."

But Mama didn't seem to have heard what I'd said. Fighting back tears, she turned to me: "Have you heard about that little kid, Nanika, disappearing two days ago?"

"I have. He'll turn up."

"He won't ever again."

"Why not?"

"They drowned him in the school's outhouse; if old Chicken hadn't found him, even his little bones would have rotted there."

I struggled with my words for a long time; I wanted to say something, but I couldn't force a single word out of my numb mouth.

"Beautiful Borshochka went nuts when old Chicken put her only child before her. Here's your son, beautiful Borshochka, I brought him home from school."

"Oh my God, is that why you're performing miracles?"

I could hear Mama's sobs through the rattle of the wheels. Papa was watching the road silently, drawing his sleeve more frequently across his nose. I don't how long this state of affairs lasted.

What is certain, though, is that the quieter it became, the more sharply self-reproach tore at my soul. Little Nanika had died on account of me. Beautiful Borshochka was the only one among all the Gypsies I'd convinced to send her son to school. "He's a really clever kid," I'd said to convince her. "Don't let him rot here among the rest!"

Lord God, never again will a single Gypsy woman in the world allow her child to go to school. You have trampled on those little fireflies that could have carried the light in this concentrated darkness.

I asked Papa for his long-stemmed pipe to help me relieve my gloomy thoughts, but just as with Zoltán Vágó's cigar, all I felt was its bitter, sickening taste.

We must have been passing one of the roadside crosses, because Papa raised his fur hat and nodded his head toward the darkness, muttering under his breath: "Respect for your sufferings!" His words sounded empty, like a creaking gate flapping in the wind.

"Shouldn't you turn one of your skirts inside out, woman? It's around midnight."

"No," said Mama flatly. "I've already put one on with its wrong side out."

Papa sighed with relief; his world was saved because even on dark, deserted highways we can't travel without having to defend ourselves. Fear is a great master; it will soften even the most adamant resolve.

It was around 2 am by the time we got home. Everyone in the settlement was keeping a vigil, and people were noisily milling around behind the dark windows of the huts.

In beautiful Borshochka's hut, violins wept sad, sorrowful melodies, while elsewhere people sang and danced. That is the custom. Sleep must be driven away, for it is dangerous to succumb to it in the presence of death.

On hearing the rattle of our cart, many curious people swarmed outside; some even clambered onto its side, and the lazier and older ones called out after us.

"Hey, Boncza, have you found your son?"

"Yes," said Papa quietly.

"Thank God! Don't let him go to school anymore, so he doesn't end up like little Nanika."

Despite Papa's grumbling, the nosiest folks among those in the crowd flocked into our hut, wanting to know the reason for my being late. "Okay," someone said, "so you missed one train, but why didn't you take the next one?"

"Because we were celebrating the eve of His Serene Highness the Regent of the Kingdom of Hungary, Miklós Horthy's name day," I said like some smart aleck. They listened opened-mouthed to the leader's mile-long title, but the only thing that had registered with them was that I'd been to a party.

"Listen, Boncza, darn that son of yours! He's eating and drinking at a big party while we're dying of worry not knowing what became of him."

During the Gypsies' reproaches, Papa also eyed me with suspicion, but he was wiser than to blame me. All he wanted was to pack me off to bed. But I insisted on seeing the dead Nanika. Mama broke down completely when I then hastily told her about the events of the afternoon and evening, and she had no strength left to keep me back.

At other times, barely four or five persons would have fit into the tiny hut, but now more than ten times as many were packed inside, boiling each other's blood.

Everyone tried to jostle close to whomever he or she would have liked to be with one-on-one. If at other times such secret longings were not fulfilled for some reason, here the opportunity arose to scrounge a few cuddles.

The mourners in the crowded hut parted to let me through. Little Nanika was lying below the low beam, his swollen, defiled body looking like a freshly tanned heap of leather scraps.

For a long time beautiful Borshochka stared at me with a vacant, alien look until the memories became clearer in one of the remaining intact recesses of her consciousness.

"I'll smash your heart out," she cried, pounding my chest with her fists. "Why did you tell me to send him to school?" she asked, drawing me closer to Nanika. "Look what they did to him!"

Mama appeared, her hair undone and a skirt folded up hastily over her shoulders. Someone had promptly informed her about Borshochka's assault, but her eyes, which had been flashing fire, soon softened to pity, and she left, shaking her head. She returned after a little while with a shirt and far less sympathy. The violins began to play. Sick, shivery sounds poured from Taltosh's fingers, and everyone shed tears over the sorrowful, bitter melody.

Slowly folks trickled back, commiserating and trying to help us. They pried beautiful Borshochka off my naked breast, waited until I put my shirt on, and then entrusted me with her consolation.

"Not for nothing did she kill her mother at birth," one of the Gypsies said, pointing to Borshochka as the others nodded. "Sooner or later God will show his power. Any woman who isn't particular about who puts his pants next to her will do penance through her children for her whoring. That's what happened to Borshochka's poor mother—God rest her soul. She'd gone to bed with every Tom, Dick, and Harry, not caring whether he belonged to her kind or whether he was some seedy stranger."

What exactly happened to beautiful Borshochka, who knows? God's ways are unpredictable. Some butcher's apprentice knocked her up in exchange for some beef tripe she had her eyes on, it was said. Borshochka's grandmother, Korri, was set to intervene, but beautiful Borshochka wouldn't hear of an abortion. In her sorrow she hoped to end up like her mother, and she waited for Nanika to be born; then, when she ended up living, after all, she no longer wanted to leave him. She became a serious matron, and devoted all her time to her Nanika.

God is my witness, I often blushed when I was at their place. Examining the child's school notebook, I used to peek into Borshochka's accidentally open blouse, and it seemed that even Nanika's milk teeth couldn't break off the pride of those legendary devil-horned breasts.

Thus it is no wonder that I combined the consolation of poor, lonely, beautiful Borshochka with my own. Trying to ease my conscience, I spent most of my days, and later also my nights, with her.

After the funeral, winter came upon us with such a fury that we couldn't see out of our windows. Huge snowdrifts inundated the settlement, and some of the huts had to be extricated by joint effort because even their chimneys were covered over. No one said so, but everyone thought that the end was near.

Shimuy also lost the hope that the fresh green grass had awakened in him several months ago.

"You can't keep a horse on fodder that you have to buy, brother," he complained to Papa. "I've stuffed everything into it that I could take from my children, so now I'm going to feed it to them. One way or another, its skin belongs already to the dogs."

"Don't do it, Gypsy," Papa implored him. "They'll lock you up for it."

"The big holiday is coming and the Gypsies' pots must not remain empty," Shimuy replied. "This will be their poorest Christmas ever since their skin's been black. They're pale from hunger. Since the first snow has fallen everything has changed; there is no more foraging. They don't even know where to lay their heads; they're happy if they can get an armful of kindling from somewhere."

Papa shook his head disapprovingly.

"But to kill a horse!"

"Believe me, brother, I'm as sorry about it as I would be on account of my own children, seeing how it's lived with us in the hut for the past two months." Shimuy paused, his squinty eyes turning brighter; he gritted his teeth until he managed to overcome his feelings. "Should I let my children go hungry along with it? Which should I feed to the other? There'll be plenty of deaths this winter, so why not let them eat?"

"Do you think they'll be able to survive on it all winter? One horse counts as much for them as one sunfish for a hundred herons," Papa insisted.

"To hell with it, brother, but at least they'll have their fill for Christmas."

You could tell when Papa was moved to pity for someone by his habit of drawing his sleeve constantly across his nose. He motioned to Shimuy, and they entered the warm barn. Two skinny horses were munching impassively beside the manger; Papa pointed to one of them.

"This *bogo*[79] will be yours in spring."

Shimuy was silent; he didn't quite understand what this was all about. He shifted uneasily from one foot to the other.

"I won't swap, brother," he finally blurted out. Sighing, he added, "The Gypsies are hungry."

"I know, that's why I'm giving it to you. At least if we live to see the spring, there'll be something you can start off with. You've already turned the lining of your coat inside out."

"Until spring? Do you think their time won't come? Hunger is a great lord, Boncza." Shimuy shook his thick finger as a warning. "We can't eat up each other."

"Well, no, that's for sure, but all the horses have been drafted." Papa tried to hide his own horses from the law. "I don't feel like going to jail."

"Neither do I, but if you're a Gypsy you have to have a heart as well as a brain."

"Yes, but," Papa fussed, "what if they interrogate folks on account of it?"

"I know there are always some villains. It's not your sin, nor mine, brother. I don't know the taste of horse meat, just as you don't." Shimuy held out his dry, chapped hand to Papa. "And I won't, either, unless they stuff it down my nose."

---

[79] a broken-down, worthless horse; a nag

He waited until Papa shared the tobacco scraped out of his pipe, and then continued, munching. "You know, Boncza, once we used to mourn if one of our horses croaked, hell, we just about called the priest, and now we would dig it out of the earth to fill our children's mouths with it."

"Bad days are coming, Shimuy."

"Bad indeed. We don't even get enough bread. You can have the money in your hand, and then they'll ask you for your coupons. It would be okay if they gave you enough of it, at least you could sell some. Why, I can't even remember when I last had oil or sugar in my hut. What do I need coupons for? I gave them away for half a bag of frozen potatoes. We ate them, as did the horse."

"Oh dear," said Shimuy, sounding exasperated again, "we'll never have enough food for two days in a row. I'll regret it till the day I die that I didn't give that expensive fodder to my children."

"You're talking nonsense, Shimuy."

"Nonsense?" he asked, squinting at Papa. "Do you know how much I used to gather while times were good? It would have been more than enough for your horses."

Papa shook his head skeptically.

"Believe me, because if it isn't true, may I wither away in jail. The children ate all of it." He sighed. "Squash, fodder beets, sugar beets, corn, and whatever the horse ate, they weren't choosey about eating too. Then they would stretch out with their full tummies next to the mare like little lords. Ever since it ran out, they keep touching the horse's rump: 'Daddy, there's plenty of meat here.' Bless their souls, they're drooling over it. What shall I give them? Weeds? It's no good pestering the peasants; they'd ask: 'Where were you in summer?' Well, where were we?"

Shimuy looked at Papa. "We were out grazing our horses. Now we can't even do that any more. To hell with them." He gritted his teeth. "They chased us away when they saw us. Every summer I used to work binding sheaves of wheat, and the little wheat I myself earned doing so lasted us all winter to make pogachas with. But now, if even the small jobs are to be had anywhere, a hundred Hungarians show up for it. So why do they ask where *I* was all summer?"

As word spread of Shimuy's discontent, grubby, unshaven, disheveled Gypsies soon filled up the barn. They listened to his preaching silently, withdrawing into themselves, hoping that one of them would have enough tobacco for a cigarette.

"But they've got enough brains to force the Gypsies to work for nothing!" Shimuy went on.

"One Gypsy is worth a hundred Hungarians," one man in the crowd, Veenchi, interrupted.

"Then why don't the gendarmes force the Hungarians to shovel snow?" Shimuy snapped at him. "Because they're as naked as you are?"

"You're asking me? How should I know?"

"How?" asked Shimuy, annoyed. "On account of Katush's *rinza.*[80] You're always saying one Gypsy is worth a hundred Hungarians. Should that one Gypsy die, then, just because he's a Gypsy?"

"For days now talking sense with this blind Gypsy has been impossible," said Veenchi, looked around seeking support. "What's wrong with you?" Veenchi was strutting in front of Shimuy with his hands thrust in his pockets up to his elbow. "You know, Gypsies," he turned toward the others, "that it's proud folks who make the world stink?"

After searching frantically in his waistcoat pocket, Veenchi pulled out a cigarette butt twisted into piece of newspaper and swallowed it. He looked at Shimuy for a long time and then, like someone who doesn't feel inferior, respectfully repeated his words.

"That's what you are, old man; you're proud because you own a horse."

Shimuy no longer felt like arguing. First he grabbed Veenchi by the collar. Then, all at once, he pinched both ends of the man's floppy mustache and shook them like a donkey's ear, twisting as he did so.

"So I'm proud?" he asked.

---

[80] tripe

Veenchi could only wink a "yes" with his eyes.

"Say it again!" Shimuy forced him to bare his teeth. Veenchi's aching groan didn't satisfy him, so he kept twisting the mustache higher and higher.

"One more time!" Shimuy urged. The unfortunate scrawny man was out of breath from groaning, and only his eyes kept fluttering. His upper lip, twisted out of shape by his now contorted mustache, completely covered his nose.

Reassured by the repeated winks, Shimuy finally let go of Veenchi's mustache.

"You all heard that, Gypsies?"

He opened his wallet, took out a crumpled picture of the Holy Virgin, placed it against the wall, and knelt down before it.

"People," he said, turning solemnly to the others, "if you don't want to see human blood being spilled, you have to do justice here. Or else, and God is my witness"—he said, pointing at the picture—"I'll kill Veenchi."

He got up, brushed off his knees, and with the same ceremony with which he had removed it, tucked the image of the Virgin Mary back into his wallet.

"He's right," more than one voice from the crowd murmured deferentially.

Veenchi just stood there sadly, stroking his mustache, trying to force back its out-of-kilter hairs, but he wasn't very successful; on one side they stood like those of a cat. Eventually he got bored with this and realized he'd better deal with other matters.

"Sit in judgement, then," said Veenchi angrily. "I still say he's full of himself just because he owns a horse. I'm not speaking out of my ass; I said it and I stand by it."

With this statement, Veenchi turned all the Gypsies against him. They knew from experience that they mustn't let such matters out of their control, because tragic consequences could ensue.

Fortunately, Shimuy was marvelously patient; otherwise all the Gypsies would have been brawling with one another already. As far as

Veenchi's *nyamurya*[81] were concerned, God save everyone from them; they were forever looking for a fight.

"Listen," Papa, his nostrils flaring, said to Veenchi. "We all have our own problems—do we really need to add to them with such pettiness? Why don't you just beg forgiveness to the old Gypsy?"

Most in the crowd urged Veenchi to do so, but they soon came to realize that the honorable mandate of seeking justice was not a simple task.

"What punishment can you mete out to that wretched, weedy Gypsy?" one man asked. "He doesn't even have any pants on. *Ahay Devla,*"[82] several of them cried out, looking at one another with dismay. What they had only felt so far now dawned on them almost simultaneously.

Papa passed around his pig bladder bag full of tobacco, figuring that while pipes were smoking, misery would be kept at bay.

"Once it was easy to make law," a voice in the crowd complained. "We paid the penalty from our vest pockets; we meted out the justice our faith and humanity told us to mete out, and not because we were forced to do so. What can we say now?"

They shrugged their shoulders; no one wanted to be the smart one.

The next morning a crowd of Gypsies gathered outside, informing one another about the offender's sins; they did so while hopping about, because the snow was still too cold to stand still on barefoot, which many of them were.

Borshochka and I were still lounging under a big coat in her and Grandma Korri's hut nearby, enjoying the sweet moments of the morning. What we'd missed during the night, we made up for by day.

---

[81] relatives

[82] Oh, my God

Grandma Korri didn't like us fooling around within earshot of her. Her keen sense of hearing allowed her to perceive the restlessness of our blood even from a distance, and she responded by flinging her dissatisfaction at us in words not nearly as chaste as might have been expected.

The frenzied daytime voices of Gypsy Paris were soon forced by winter's icy harpoons back into the gray gloom of the huts. Because of the wind shrieking between the snowbanks of the outside world, only the most necessary things could be taken outside, and even those had to be placed against the wall, where their owners regularly swept the snow away.

The weary, depressing silence plunged the people of the huts into an unnatural sleep. It was Borshochka who first noticed the noise coming from outside.

"Where are the Gypsies running to?" she asked me, startled. "Can you hear them?" She made sure I listened.

"I can. Have a look to see what's going on."

Borshochka quickly breathed on the frosty window to see better.

"They're running," she said.

They are being chased, I thought. *That's when our kind usually runs.*

"Even old Uytuy is being led along, by his grandchild at that," said Borshochka, reporting the newest development. "Go on," she said, turning to me anxiously, "hide at your parent's place!"

I gave in to her pleas. It never hurts to be careful, I figured. Beautiful Borshochka trickled some ice-cold water into my hand; I washed myself and hastily got dressed. She then motheringly rebuttoned my shirt, which I had buttoned up awry. Then, cautiously, I sneaked out of the hut.

"Come along, folks," Petrush, Shimuy's son, yelled from outside, knocking on every window. "Veenchi called my father a shitty guy." I turned back, but Petrush caught up with me. Unshaven downy hairs reared up on his frozen, goosepimpled face. With a chuckle he said, "I was just about to call you, too. I knew you were at Borshochka's." After a pause, he added, "The wise ones are parleying in your home."

"Don't they have anything better to do?"

Petrush pulled his mouth aside; his father must have looked like that as a young man. You could never guess what went on in his head behind his slanting eyes; eyes like that of the fairy king—one crying, the other laughing.

"Who the hell knows what they're bothering about for so long," said Petrush. "If my father doesn't have the guts to do it, because he thinks doing so is a sin, I'll butcher the beast; all they have to do is tell me." He huffed. "Do you think I don't know what Veenchi is up to? Remember, that's what it's all about."

"They're going to kill Veenchi because he told your father he was a shitty guy?"

"God, you're stupid," he said with pity. "It's only an excuse. The holiday is coming, and we have to eat something. You'll have a share of it, too. Don't worry, I'll bring you the choicest bits. Choka told me what her favorite was."

"My sister?"

"Yep," he boasted.

"You know which part to take to her?" I didn't spell it out, but he knew what I meant. He respected me, and I never spoke against his feelings for my sister, yet now he replied angrily.

"I'll take that part to you, because she's a mare."

I didn't move. Petrush saw that I was still waiting for an explanation.

"I'm freezing, brother," he said, his teeth chattering. "You'll find out everything in the nice warm barn, anyway."

"Come on!" I said, grabbing his arm and dragging him back to Borshochka's. "I don't understand a word you said, Petrush."

"Don't do that!" he said, coming along with me reluctantly. "Papa will let me have it when he finds out I've betrayed him."

"Go on, Borshochka, go to my place and ask Choka for some tobacco." She knew why I was sending her away. Petrush's eyes were gleaming.

"Tell her to send me some, too," Petrush called after her. "Her brother and I are having a conversation."

"So, what's the score?" I asked. "Well, buddy, I'm no longer risking my neck for my father's horse; he can do with it what he wants. He has already fed it our heads, not just the fodder. If my poor little brothers and sisters find a pumpkin seed in the horseshit, they fight each other for it.

"Why should I keep on working for that horse while they don't have a thing to eat? If Papa hadn't given the horse all those turnips I've been stealing every night from the estate stables, why, they would have been enough to feed the kids all winter. That's why he can't relax and have a moment's rest. I've put a curse on myself: may my bones be swept out of jail if I make a move while the horse is with us. Let him feed the bones of his children to it; it has already eaten their flesh."

Petrush looked at me for a long time. "You're thinking now that it is my anger speaking. I know, buddy, that you don't like what I'm saying, but if I'm not telling the truth, let me lose your sister forever even though I love her more than life itself."

"Tell me," I said, encouraging him. "Telling the truth doesn't mean you're speaking ill of someone."

"If Papa knew," said Petrush, lowering his voice, "that he could save his horse by doing so, he'd throw any of his kids before it at night even though he loves them, too, very much." Seeing my bewildered look, he added, "You don't know our kind, because for years you've been coming home only to sleep. But I do. Here among us, the horse is worshipped like God."

"But surely he wouldn't do that," I said, trying to defend the old man.

"Why not? Didn't he practically throw me to the wolves each night? What do you think the peasants would have done to me if one of them would have caught me in his barn? Or if I collapsed in the fields? Wouldn't I have frozen there? When someone dies, does it matter if he's eaten by a horse or by worms?"

I had to admit that Petrush was absolutely right.

"You can love horses, brother; I also love them, because I grew up among them, but there is a line that divides them from men. Now my dad has had to find that limit, whether he wanted to or not. The only question now is *who* is going to do the killing." Petrush paused, then smiled. "Not kill Veenchi, but the horse. It's going to croak, anyway, but by then we won't get a thing out of it."

Borshochka returned with a handful of tobacco.

"What's Choka up to?" Petrush asked her.

"She's cooking."

"You see, brother, if your sister wouldn't give me half her food, I would die of hunger. That's why I say that from now on I'll risk my skin only for those I love. For my little sisters and brothers and for ourselves."

"I still don't understand what will become of the horse, and what of Veenchi?"

"What do you think? His punishment will be that *he'll* have to slaughter the horse. Believe me, my father is a mischievous man." He broke into a smile as if he were proud of him. "It's hard to see through his cunning, but I know him inside out. Do you really think that if he'd taken Veenchi's insult seriously he wouldn't have ripped out the guy's tongue right there and then? The whole thing is just theater. The poor wretched Gypsy came in handy. Papa has been taunting him for days to find something to accuse him of.

"Everyone knows Veenchi. Once something slips out of his mouth, he won't take it back for all the world; he'd rather do whatever the law metes out. And that's what Papa wants. He's worked it all out cleverly. And the 'wise ones' tag along with the honorable old Gypsy. Because what would become of this world if we let someone off with impunity? Sure, when the Hungarians call us 'rotten, stinking Gypsies,' Gypsy law can't do a thing about it; it doesn't reach that far."

Seeing that his words saddened me, Petrush tried to give me some comfort. "This has always been true of our world, brother, but it was hidden by some good things. Don't for a minute think though that my father doesn't love us! That's not the case; he would put his head on the chopping block for us any time. But the horse—the horse is a brute creature, and yet it's a sin to kill it. You can see for yourself that all the Gypsies are pale from hunger. But if you asked them, none of them would kill that horse. Yet now is the time to do it, because next week they'd use Holy Week as their excuse not to."

"Would *you* really be willing to kill it?" I asked Petrush point blank. He looked at me, but I didn't repeat my question. I left him to ponder. He kept inhaling the strong, coarse tobacco, and then he spoke at last.

"If you'd asked me in summer, I would have said no. Do you know how much I used to work on some of the nags, even though we never filled our stomachs on the price we got for them? If Papa sold one of them, he bought another. In the fall he sewed the money inside the lining of his jacket, and in spring everything began all over again.

"Poor Mama, with her belly getting big all the time, was working summer and winter to get something to eat for her children, and as we kids grew older we became slaves to the horse. Well, let all the horses croak wherever they are. Yes, I would certainly kill it, buddy. I'd at least do what needs doing to help the kids."

"That will turn out when. . . ." I was incredulous.

"Me?" he looked at me hard. "May my mother die if I wouldn't do it."

"You know what?" I said, "Let's play a joke on the clever elders. Come on!"

"Don't do it. They'll beat us to death. And your father would never let me near his home if we made fools of them now."

"Leave that to me," I reassured him. "It'll be fine." I saw that Petrush liked the idea, and we quickly went over to my place.

The barn was so full that we could hardly squeeze in. The young ones stood outside, some of them barefoot, chilled to the bone, while the older ones sweated inside the humid stuffy stable.

The people had sat old, blind Uytuy on the edge of the crib, and his little grandson, who regularly took him begging, was crouching at his feet.

"He's the apple of my eyes," the mischievous old Gypsy was apt to say of his grandson, but when a young woman walked by he would stare after her.

Papa, Nootsu, Khandi, Old Chicken, Zoga, and Yoka—the smart, respected elders—stood in a semicircle. Veenchi stood quietly before them, leaning against the pillar, fingering his swollen face.

At last we managed to squeeze in among the older Gypsies. Nothing had happened yet. Finally, after lengthy deliberation, they decided that they didn't know how to punish Veenchi, as he owned nothing with which he could compensate Shimuy for the insult to his honor. That's why the courts held at the markets used to be so good. There they promptly made the offender buy that day's round of drinks. Oh, but where had those days gone?

"What is your claim, Shimuy?" the elders asked after drawn-out sighs.

The blind Gypsy had prepared his statement, but he kept stroking his fishbone-colored mustache until there was complete silence.

"Look, brothers, all my life I felt like a man; the name Shimuy was known far and wide. Anywhere I cracked my whip, money flowed, and where other people didn't even drink water"—he looked down his nose at Veenchi—"I drank wine. But I've never been stuck-up. Yet that man"—and now he pointed straight at Veenchi—"has dared to throw it in my face that I was proud because I have a horse. No one has ever said anything like this to me since I've stopped wetting my bed."

Beating his chest with his fists, Shimuy went on: "I would have ripped out such a man's tongue. But, brothers, we barely have our noses above water these days—should we do even more harm to ourselves? The big holiday will soon be upon us, and we can't even give our children a bite of something nice to eat. What can we be proud of, then?"

Shimuy paused, waiting for his words to sink in. "Did the horse make me? Is this my first horse? To hell with the world if we are at each other's throats over such matters."

Petrush nudged me: "Shrewd Gypsy," he whispered. "Just wait; you'll see that I'm right."

"So that's why I've asked you to pronounce justice—you, the elders all the world knows as having been honest all your lives. That's how wise old Gypsies used to do it. God is my witness," he said, fishing the picture of the Holy Virgin out of his wallet again.

"I swear that while I'm alive I'll never again keep a horse over the winter, because to do so only provokes envy. Is a horse worth gouging out each other's eyes like ravens? I have tiny kids, and they're hungry. Your children, too, are hungry. The big holiday is coming, and the pots are empty. What do we have to be proud of?"

Shimuy paused and waited until the sighs died down, then added a long, deep moan. "To hell with the world if we can't fill our bellies even at Christmas, when I have a horse whose bones are still full of fat. We'll slaughter it, Gypsies; at least no one can call me stuck-up after that, and our children will have a treat."

"God bless you, Shimuy," said the people, shouting for joy. Satisfied, Shimuy stroked his mustache with both hands.

Closing one eye, Papa observed Shimuy; their eyes met accidentally, and from the way Papa winked you could tell that he had just realized Shimuy's scheme.

"Long live Shimuy!" the crowd blared persistently. "Hear ye, hear ye!"

Gunchi, short though he was, was able to raise his hands to motion the people to silence. Then he spoke.

"Listen, brothers, and this man dared to tell our Shimuy that he was proud? Would he slaughter his horse if he had one? He wouldn't even push his own dung away if it weren't smelly." Gunchi spat in Veenchi's direction. "All your life you've been eating shit."

"Gunchi is right," someone shouted, "such a man should be beaten to death."

"Hold on," said Shimuy, silencing the people. "Let's leave it to the wise ones. I've said just about all I've had to say. I no longer have a horse; I've given it to the starving children. So Veenchi should kill it. Let *that* be his punishment!"

The erupting joy stuck in everyone's throats. All was quiet; only the crunching of the horses' molars, munching the hay beside the crib, could be heard. The people looked to the elders for guidance. You could even notice a look of sudden compassion for Veenchi on Gunchi's face, although he had as many children as holes in a sieve, and perhaps even a couple more.

I pondered whether we should reveal Shimuy's rascally scheme, because if the elders were to nod, there wasn't a man who could save Veenchi from having to kill the horse. The elders were silent, watching Grandpa Uytuy; none wanted to be the first to take Veenchi's fate into his hands, although they knew there was no way to avoid saying yes; they would shortly come to their senses, and those who had been uncertain at first would be unrelenting on the orders of their bellies.

There had been a time when Bada used to do the slaughtering for all of Gypsy Paris, and that didn't bother a soul, because they considered him to be a simpleton. These people are like wolves. They starve together, they run together, but if one of them stumbles, they promptly devour him even though he is one of them, because hunger is a great master.

All at once Katush burst into the barn with such a big mouth that she barely made it through the door.

"What have you done, Veenchi?!" She stood facing him, arms akimbo, flinging good wishes at his head. "May you spew out that weedy lung of yours for the dogs."

"It's all right," he said, trying to calm her, "don't yell so much."

"Why not? So you've got enough brains to pick a quarrel with old Gypsies whose asses you're not even allowed to drink water from, but not enough to make a child with me."

The silence remained unbroken. No one laughed at Katush's words. Petrush broke the ice.

"I'll make one with you, Katush."

The woman looked around earnestly before turning back to Veenchi and saying, "You sure would deserve it." She gave her husband's mustache a twist. "May our Sándor die by accident, though I don't like to swear on my big brother's life, if I don't let one of the boys knock me up. As for you"—she beat a palm on her pubis—"you'll never get close to this."

When the Creator made poor Katush, he botched the job so badly that the devil wouldn't have been willing to tempt her even for double pay. Still, Old Uytuy formed an umbrella with his hands before his eyes, better to see the woman's naked thighs.

"Can you see, old man," I asked, "what a nice goods Katush has between her legs?"

"*So phenes?*"[83] he asked, pretending to be deaf.

"I asked you whether you could see it."

"I can't see it, my child," he moaned.

"Take it to him, Katush," I said. "Let the poor old Gypsy have a look!"

Katush looked at me and laughed. "Don't fool around, kid; the old man will get angry."

"Go on, take it to him!" I encouraged her. "May your Sándor die if you don't take it, or else someone might say you're proud because you own something nice. Let's avoid any trouble as much as we can."

Katush looked around, pulled up her dress to her armpits, and walked up to Old Uytuy.

"There, old man," she said, pushing out her pelvis, "just take a look—isn't it beautiful? You're the chief judge, after all."

"It's beautiful, my child," he said with sincere appreciation.

"Go on," I said, "show it to the others, too. They don't often get a chance to see something so beautiful."

"Leave me alone, kid," she said, yanking down her skirt angrily, "don't poke fun at me."

---

[83] What are you saying?

"So you're not showing it to everybody, Katush?"

"Look here, Gypsy boy!" First she looked puzzled, then she wanted to say something more, but held it back with a faint smile. "I won't show it; so there!"

"Well, Katush, then you're stuck-up, and I declare it loud and clear so that everybody can hear it."

"Have all of you Gypsies heard it?" She looked around.

"We've heard it," they shouted and laughed.

"You've heard it, too, you wise old Gypsies?" She turned to the judges, fixing her eyes on Papa in particular. "So now you have to make a decision in two cases. I demand, Boncza, that your son should pierce the object for which he called me proud."

The elders didn't know what to do with themselves for shame. Not a word could be heard amid the outbursts of laughter, and all we could see was Papa motioning for everyone to move out of the barn. They departed quickly; only Shimuy and Petrush remained. Papa began to caress his horses nervously. Petrush didn't know what to do, and just stood there looking sad, as if it would be our turn now to be punished for our transgressions. We tried to gather our thoughts and prepare excuses in case we had to account for our actions.

Old Khandi now came back inside, apparently out of fear that Papa would be on my case. He winked at me; he had, it seemed, enjoyed the game.

"Well, friend," Shimuy complained to him, "this Gypsy boy sure made a mockery of us; he acted like some lawyer."

Papa moved away from the horses, brushed off the hairs stuck to his coat sleeve, and stopped thoughtfully before Shimuy.

"In our time, my friend," continued Shimuy, "we were not allowed to meddle in the adults' business until we could twist our mustache around our fingers."

Papa kept silent, letting folks wonder a little longer as to what was going through his head.

"You know, Boncza," Shimuy went on, gathering momentum, "I would never have believed it that it would be your son who'd poke fun at us."

"Why?" Papa finally asked. "Because he wouldn't let a bunch of crazy old Gypsies dance on the conscience of others? You'll remain a scoundrel if you still insist on your dirty trick."

"A scoundrel?" Shimuy looked beseechingly at Petrush.

"Yep," said Petrush, "you've been living a lie. Just admit that you're afraid you yourself will have to kill the horse."

"You're against me, too, Petrush?"

"No, but I'm hungry."

Shimuy slumped feebly onto the empty bucket standing next to the wall. For a while he ran his fingers over the cracked leather of his boots, and then he began to hum a self-composed song of sadness like the one he used to sing long ago as a lullaby to Petrush. He kept rocking his upper body, totally absorbed in his sadness, droplets of water falling on his boots from the tip of his twitching, yellow mustache.

"So," he sighed, "you want me to kill my own horse?" He looked into our eyes, seeking help from one of us and seeking to annoy the other. Our silence made him even angrier.

"I know, Petrush, that this comedy can only be your doing. Well then, if you're so hungry, son, then you kill it!"

"I shall."

Shimuy turned pale; that was the last thing he expected. He lost his composure, grabbing his son by the shoulders.

"You'd kill it?" he yelled into Petrush's mouth. "Don't you consider that it has lived with your little brothers and sisters? It ate with them, it slept with them, as if they shared the same mother, too, and they fed him half their food."

"It was you who did it. You bought fodder for your horse with every penny that turned up in the house. You looked after your children only when you'd already done your duty to the horse. It always came first and we came only after it. We had to look up to it as to a saint; we believed that the sun wouldn't rise without it; we braided our rags into its mane to prevent someone giving it the evil eye. And all the while we ourselves were living in misery. Well, I've had enough of this. I'll kill it or it'll kill us."

"Look!" said Petrush, opening up his shirt. Festering wounds had disfigured both his shoulders. "Your horse did that to me. I've carried the fodder for your horse on these."

Shimuy covered his face with his hands and backed out of the barn. We looked at Petrush aghast, as he hissed when drawing the rags together over his upper body. Papa looked at his horses and then looked at me for a long time, scratching his balding head under his hat.

"So that's how it is," he sighed. "A man doesn't really know why he toils so much for these rotten creatures."

Barely five minutes had passed when little Phuri, one of Petrush's brothers, rushed in breathlessly.

"Come on, Petrush, Papa has stabbed the horse to death." The child's smiling mouth began to tremble at the sight of his brother's face turning pale.

"Papa said we'll make sausages," said Phuri, tugging at Petrush's coat with tears in his eyes, "because there is great hunger among the Gypsies."

By the time we went there, the horse was already lying on the snow in a giant pool of blood. Shimuy was still standing beside it, as if expecting a victory salute; anger and repentance neutralized each other in his eyes, giving them an empty, meaningless look. He came to when we got there.

"Come on, Gypsies!" He raised up the knife. "Or do you want me to take it to you?" As if they had been waiting for this signal, they swarmed out of their huts with sharp knives and set upon the horse.

Not unlike merry harvesters in a vineyard—who, at the sight of the red or golden bunches, can already feel the zest of autumn wine in their mouths, forgetting about the thirst of yesterday in the hope of today—so too the Gypsies forgot all their troubles on seeing and then plunging their knives into the horse's cold, bloodless corpse. Veenchi's grievance was swallowed up by Shimuy's charity, and he left his grief for lonely moments. There was no more anger, and the grim hunger was replaced by the promise of a tasty, gratifying Christmas.

Not much was needed here for happiness; one sunfish was enough for a hundred herons, turning long-forgotten tasty minutes into cheerful days and shaking the people from their winter slumber. They bent over their sooty pots with sweaty faces shrouded in veils of steam, and no longer awaited the wolf.

Had the ravens in the sky landed for but a moment, the people of the settlement would have gouged out their eyes again and again, but instead they flew away, screeching, over snow-choked Gypsy Paris, which promised them nothing good.

VIII

THE LARGER DOGS HAD TO BE KILLED, out of concern that they wouldn't be satisfied with the children's excrement and would instead hunger for a little kid. Any dog that froze during the night was torn apart by the rest of them. Their howling often sent the Gypsies into a frenzy as they then spent half the night chasing what they assumed was a stray wolf. Despite the inevitable letdown, the Gypsies did come away with something, at least, assuming they killed their prey, because the dog's skins could be sold.

The war taught us not to be picky. *Survive, survive!* was the only mantra throbbing in people's minds.

The boundary of Gypsy Paris expanded invisibly, meanwhile. True, the gendarmes with their bayonets stood guard, but misery can't be stopped by force. So too, the drum rolled as the gendarmes went on requisitioning rounds, leaving not a stone unturned; indeed if they found anything that was slightly more than nothing, they confiscated it ruthlessly.

And yet the war spared Gypsy Paris for quite some time. We weren't any the wiser from the meaningless words of the military postcards; all we knew was that the person who wrote them was still alive. Then the postcards stopped coming and were replaced by uniformly worded sympathy messages.

Papa was tormented daily by increasingly serious problems. He evidently wanted to say something important, and he approached every more or less intrepid-looking Gypsy to try on his only pair of good boots. He asked Gunchi to stop by, and they discussed something in the barn. Gunchi tried protesting, but the boots prevailed over his conscience.

Papa sent my younger sister to pick me up from Borshochka's. As soon as her mourning period had passed, I moved in with her; we didn't see any point in late-night frolicking when we could spend our days the same way.

Mama had thought highly of Borshochka even before she noticed that we were attracted to each other, and she was happy about it. In our world, though, parents didn't interfere in such matters. I dropped in sometimes at home when I needed something, but I spent most of my time with the woman.

Papa sat silently in the barn. As I entered, Gunchi tried to force a wry smile onto his face, but he succeeded only when Papa fetched a bottle of corn whiskey from the corner of the manger. "Take a swig!" he said, handing it to me. I didn't play hard to get; modesty had long gone out of fashion. Where were those times when we could afford not to accept something? I coughed for a long time from the strong liquor.

"Sit down!" said Papa, offering me his seat. I kept drinking, at first only sparingly, but when my old man insisted that I pick up my pace, there was no way to resist. As if his tongue had been put in gear, he began to talk about the horrors of the last world war. Every so often he stopped and patted the horses' buttocks to see how their flesh reacted. Even despite the scarcity of feed, the long rest was doing them good.

The liquor soon had its effect. Slow, drowsy numbness permeated every part of me.

"Good liquor," Gunchi chomped. Papa didn't drink, but kept walking from one wall to the other, relating his war experiences. I listened as if interested, though he'd told us these stories over and over again, and sometimes it seemed as if I had also taken part in the assaults and the squirrel hunts. Every now and again he marched a few steps, then stood at attention, and humbly reported that private Boncza had fully carried out his assignment.

"Oh well," he said, quieting down, "it's not good to talk about these things. Today I'd know better, and there would be no god who could drag me to the slaughterhouse."

"Do you know how old I was when they sent me to the front?" he asked.

"I know," I said firmly. He frowned, as if pondering how I knew it. Then he handed the bottle to me again.

"Well, that's why I'm telling you, son. It's better to think ahead; otherwise a man can come off a loser. We'll wake up one day, the drums will be rolling, and everyone from eighteen to sixty will have to join up. Even then, those who are smart don't risk life and limb."

By now I was drunk, and I knew it. Papa's words reached my consciousness incoherently.

"I've told your mother long ago, but she always knows better. A Gypsy has to have brains, my friend, since God hasn't given him anything else. Isn't that so, Gunchi?"

"It sure is, brother."

"Do you think," Papa asked, "that Shimuy was born with that bad eye? No way, that blind Gypsy had enough brains to know better."

"He sure did," Gunchi agreed. "But better late than never."

I didn't understand a word of their conversation, nor was I paying any attention. *I am drunk,* I kept telling myself. My mouth was full of the taste of burnt corn mash.

"Drink up!" they urged me. I couldn't protest; after the first greedy sips I lost all my powers to resist, reaching for the bottle obediently, as they wished.

"It would be a heroic deed if you slaughtered them," I told Papa, pointing at the horses. "You haven't performed a nobler act even during the war. And judging by your stories, you could have won even a lost war. I'm hungry. Everyone is hungry. Do you understand? We are not *chache Roma.* We eat horse meat, because life is short." I started to sing with a stumbling tongue. All of a sudden I had a lot to say. "Fuck everyone who's afraid!" I wanted to stand up, but flopped onto the manger's straw bedding. Ashamed, I tried to get up.

"No worries, son," Papa reassured me. "Here, have a drink!"

"Gimme," I said, grasping the bottle with both hands. "You meant *me?*"

"It's good liquor, brother," Gunchi said, chuckling. My tongue didn't work, and the barn was spinning with me as if I were sitting on a merry-go-round. I was completely drunk.

"Never mind. That's the remedy," one of them said, trying to force more drink into me. My mind was completely numb; what my eyes and ears perceived, my consciousness couldn't grasp. I lay puzzled and motionless, my eyes fixed at the formless curves of the objects around me. Papa pulled out a white cloth from somewhere, held it toward the door, and examined it for a long time.

"Got more brandy?" Gunchi asked nervously. Papa raised the bottle to my mouth, and I had to drink if I wanted to catch my breath; he then poured the residue into himself. The two of them whispered something to each other, then they stepped up to me, and propped me by my back to the manger. Next, they made me hold onto the edge of the manger with my right hand, whose fingers were splayed out.

"Okay," Gunchi whispered. "It'll be alright like this."

I wonder what they want. The thought flashed through my mind, but the strong spirits immediately washed away all thought. They moved silently, not quite knowing what they were doing; Papa turned his face to the wall, squeezing the white cloth in his hands behind his back; his shoulders trembled.

Gunchi picked up a small axe, bent down to me, looked into my expressionless eyes, and nervously wiped the edge of the axe with the sleeve of his coat. He seemed to stiffen for a moment, but then promptly recoiled and threw the small axe into the corner.

"I'm not chopping off his finger, Boncza. He'd kill me when he sobers up. Brother, I wouldn't do it if you gave me a hundred pairs of boots; I've still got little kids at home."

"You're not cutting it off, Gunchi? Do you want my son to rot at the front?"

"I don't have to cut his finger off for that. Look at me! The army will never take me, although I can see well. A little flick of a needle, that's all. Just show me which eye they use for aiming. It doesn't hurt, it'll become bloodshot, and after a month the cataract will appear. He'll never be taken as a soldier.

"Here, I'll cover my good eye, and you hold up some fingers." Papa held up three fingers. "Three," said Gunchi without hesitation. "You all think I'm blind in one eye? Well, you just go ahead and believe it, hehe. Many of the fellows I was with at the front have fallen, God rest their souls, but I'm at home."

Again there was silence, Gunchi knelt next to me and pried open one of my eyelids. He was panting quite close to my face, and my hand fell feebly off the edge of the crib. Gunchi cursed and began to search among the straw.

"All done?" Papa jumped up next to me, gasping.

"Of course not. Aren't you capable of giving a man a hand? You could've at least held his eye open! Now I've lost the needle."

"You sure are one miserable Gypsy." Gunchi didn't answer; he was looking for the needle. Papa stroked my hair. "Bless his dear soul," said Papa. "He's dead drunk and sleeping like a baby."

"Bless his dear soul when he sobers up! He'll give us a thrashing we won't soon forget."

"It's okay. At least I'll know that my only son won't be carried off to the slaughterhouse."

"Call one of your daughters to find the needle or else bring another one," Gunchi snapped at Papa.

"Lizza!" Papa called out to my older big sister. After a while she appeared, scouring a pot.

"Did you call?" she asked.

"Yes. Bring a needle."

"What are you doing to the boy?" Her voice turned shrill.

"Stop yelling," Gunchi said, "or he'll wake up."

"So you want me to bring a needle, Gunchi? Go fuck yourself!" The pot made a loud noise, on Gunchi's head, I think, since he ran out of the barn, bellowing.

"You wanted to have your child blinded," Liza roared at Papa. "I'll cut your head up too with this pot or I'll have you arrested at once. Come on, Gypsies"—she shouted, now from the barn door—"have a look at these killers who wanted to pierce the child's eye!"

Turning back to Papa, Liza added, "Just you wait, Boncza, until Mama comes home; you won't have any skin left on your face."

The last thing I felt was that I was rising up into the air, floating a little, and then plunging into a deep, black nothingness. It was late afternoon when I came to; my head throbbed as if a threshing machine had been rattling inside it.

The images of the morning unfolded in a faltering, vague manner that made it hard for me to decide whether I had dreamt them or whether they had really happened. I secretly covered first one eye and then the other to test them. The whole thing seemed to have been but a dream. Borshochka leaned close to me, looked me in the eye as Gunchi had, and removed the cloth from my forehead.

"Where did you get that from?" I snatched it out of her hand.

"Your father put it on your forehead. There are not enough rags in this house to bandage your finger."

Startled, I looked at my hands for a long time, watching the playful movements of my fingers.

"Poor Gunchi!" I sighed.

"You're sorry for him? He almost blinded you. God bless Liza for hitting him over the head. We would have been in a mess." She mellowed and gently pulled my hand to her belly. "You know what's here?"

"Your tummy."

"And inside it?" I whispered my answer to Borshochka.

"Silly," she said, pushing my hand off her. She looked herself over, and her sudden anger slowly melted off her face; she reached for my hand, but this time she didn't press it to her belly, but to her daringly prominent, heavy breasts. I pulled her taut blouse apart and covered my face with them. If this is all that constitutes paternal joy, then there's no justice in heaven or on earth. Beautiful Borshochka's heart wanted to share her happiness with me, a happiness of which I was the co-creator. I didn't say a word, and searched for the joy and happiness in myself; the counterpart of the feeling that radiated from Borshochka.

"Are you happy?" she asked, caressing the top of my head. I was kissing her breasts, feigning silent happiness, for this is the way of the world; life is a blessing, death is a blessing, and the life lived in between is only an accessory of the great masterpiece that is called creation. The happiness of so many Borshochkas, each one the size of a speck of dust, grows large only if it can be shared with the world, because even the thistle is pretty when it is in bloom.

"I'm happy," I said with a sigh.

"See," she snuggled to me. "I blamed you when my Nanika died; I didn't know then that there could be happiness without him." She looked at me and replaced the wet cloth on my forehead. I could see from her eyes that she was worried.

"Please don't ever take a drink again. That father of yours has some strange ideas. You're still a child." She pulled me back to her breasts.

For a long time I listened to her crooning; the hypnotic rhythm evoked childhood memories, some of which I hardly remembered, as time had covered them with soot. A blonde, pigtailed little girl stood in front of me, her thin, sickly face shining with joy—who knows what had made her happy? Perhaps I'd only dreamed that, too, like the fragrant mist that now slowly engulfed me.

I woke up late in the evening; most of the hut was in darkness. Borshochka was still asleep, quietly, deeply, and we didn't notice that Grandma Korri had come home. She had lit the cob oven, whose doorless opening lit up her face. She watched the blazing play of the fire; she could see that, at least.

"Are you awake, son?" Her myopic eyes kept staring at the fire.

"Yes," I said, yawning.

"You know your wife is pregnant?"

"I know, Grandma."

"You're a smart man, son, so don't kill my orphan child!"

"Alright," I said cheerfully. *Wake up, woman, cook something for your husband; he's hungry.*

Borshochka sat up, looked around puzzled, and searched for the cloth to put it back on my forehead.

"I'm hungry, don't you understand?" I pinched her cheek.

"Look, Korri," she said, turning to her grandmother, "the Gypsy child has gone nuts."

"Come on, get off the lair," Korri too snapped at Borshochka, "don't just lie there next to your man, or else you'll get smelly and he'll leave you."

"What am I supposed to cook for him at night, Gypsy woman?" Borshochka held her hand in front of herself, as I flapped at her with the cloth.

"Meat," I said, "or cook this." I rubbed the cloth to her nose. Grandma Korri's face brightened, and she dismissed our wrestling with feigned anger.

"Eat up or I'll take it out to the dogs."

Borshochka snatched the basket she'd held out to us and snuggled back next to me under the coat; we began to munch the basket's contents as fast as we could. One piece was salty, the other sweet, yet another sour. But who had time to bother with the flavor of each and every scrap of food when it made no difference?

"Try this," said Borshochka, looking for my mouth, "you'll see how divinely bitter it is!"

"It's old." I said, crunching the small piece of hoecake.

"Don't forget to cook the potatoes tomorrow!" Grandma Korri reminded us.

"We've already eaten the potatoes." I searched the bottom of basket.

"No, you haven't; they're next to the oven."

"That's alright, then," I said, and we continued gulping down whatever was left.

"What's the weather like outside?" I asked, stretching out. Grandma Korri had warmed up the hut pretty well.

"Mud. The snow has gone so suddenly, God bless it, that we're drowning in mud."

"Do you hear?" I said to Borshochka, tickling her. "Spring is coming!"

"That'll put an end to us," Grandma Korri sighed. "The Hungarians will all be working in the fields, they'll lock their gates, and it'll be no use for me to go begging for food. We'll all go hungry."

"It doesn't matter, Korri," I said. "We're going to work, too."

"Work? Where are you going to work? The Hungarians are going to the village hall in droves, demanding work. Do you think others aren't hungry too? It's not like it used to be. The Hungarians are also complaining; the war has taken everything. Even so, let us give thanks to the Lord that we haven't died of hunger yet. It's rumored that next year the women will also be called up."

"They won't take you, Korri."

"What good will that do me? I've already lived through two wars. Fortunately, I had no son, but if I had, I would also have pricked his eye. That's not what the women care about. They want a man with brains; that's what's important for them."

Grandma Korri perked her ears; something was stirring at the door. Papa was hitting his boots against the threshold.

"To hell with that mud!" he grumbled instead of a greeting. "Are you asleep?" he asked, groping in the dark.

Borshochka wanted to get up, but I held her back.

"We're not asleep," Grandma Korri answered. "Come in, sit down!"

"And the boy?" he lowered his voice.

"They're relaxing," she reassured him.

"Listen, they're really being mean to poor Kinya," Papa recounted. "They're going to hang her."

"That old woman? Why?" I sat up in surprise.

"Light a candle, young lady," said Papa, chiding Borshochka, "a man can't talk in the dark." I knew he wouldn't let her just sit there. This too belonged to the good old customs: a woman should not rest beside her husband in another man's presence, especially if she belongs to the family.

"We haven't got any lard to make one with," I said, siding with Borshochka. Papa didn't dare provoke me; he sensed that the morning's doings were still seething within me, which is why he put off answering my question.

"Why are they hanging Kinya?" I asked impatiently.

"There is 'marsh' law," he yelled.

"Okay," I said, not correcting him, "but martial law wasn't meant for such old women."

"I told her the same thing, but she just keeps repeating: 'They're going to hang me, they're going to hang me!' I got sick and tired listening to her. I left her, and told her not to come here bothering you, or else I'll kill her before she gets hanged."

"Kinya is home?" I asked, surprised.

"Where the hell would she be?"

"Go on, Borshochka," I said, "tell her to come over. Something isn't right here."

"To be sure," replied Papa, "it isn't, but you're not going to get smarter by talking to them."

As soon as Borshochka left, Grandma Korri found the tallow candle and lit it.

"You said you didn't have any candles!" Papa said reproachfully.

"You've got to economize in wartime. Why should we have the light on when the same words can be heard in the dark? If you'd blinded me, the candle would be burning in vain, anyway."

"Everything is getting worse than it used to be," Papa said sadly.

"This too will be over once," I consoled him.

"It would be nice to live that long," he sighed.

Papa was never one for grinning all the time, but the gloomy expression visible on his face for the past weeks was not like him. He was never sick in all his life, and God save everybody if he had a toothache; he would drive the whole settlement to despair with his roars. Knowing his characteristics and habits, I had to believe that he was worrying about some bad news again.

"What have you heard?"

"Ah, nothing really," he waved disparagingly.

"Come on, tell me," I said, trying to get it out of him.

"They say the Germans have marched in."

"Where to?"

"How should I know? The Hungarians are talking about it." He kept quiet for a while, and then added: "Smart, intelligent people told me, son."

"Isn't it Furkó who is spreading panic? Ever since Köszörűs was executed, he keeps saying that bad times are coming. How can it become worse than it is now? So the Germans have marched in. Does it make any difference to us who is in power if we are hungry?"

"Not really, because they'll leave only the blind and the lame behind."

"So that's why you wanted me blinded?"

"The trouble with you, son," said Papa, trying to avoid answering, "is that you treat everything so lightly."

Borshochka burst in. She had time only to wipe her muddy feet on the doorpost before Kinya and her kin invaded the hut. I felt sorry about the unfinished conversation; even though I protested against Papa's concerns, something made my heart sink, too. But Kinya's wailing made me brush away my thoughts.

"What's happened to you, Gypsy woman?" I asked her point blank.

It was evident that she had already cried as much as she could, and she'd done so moments before only to draw attention to herself.

"They're going to hang me," she told me as matter-of-factly as if the procedure had already been carried out.

"Why?"

At first Kinya just shrugged, but then, like that, she warmed to telling her story.

"Well, you know it all started when"—she began as if it were really a story—"when that mischievous Hungarian told me: 'Kinya! Here's this parcel, take it to the railway station on the cart and have it sent to Budapest. I'll reimburse you when you get back.' Well, I said, 'God bless you, sir, you know I've been honest all my life, although I've already taken two parcels for you to the station.' 'That's why I trust you,' *phendyas.*[84] He's so fat, he is; he's grown out of his pants." She paused, then uttered a prayer: "May his stinking flesh rot from his bones, my dear God!"

"Amen!" the others chimed in.

"You see," she explained reproachfully, "they fined the Hungarian two-hundred pengős, and now they'll take me away from all those hungry mouths. No wonder they say that God shits where he sees a bigger knot," she sighed.

"Tell me, what happened to the parcel?" I asked, guiding her back to the subject at hand.

"Forgive me; I've been stringing one word to another. As soon as I went inside the station, two gendarmes stopped me. 'What are you carrying?' they asked. 'A parcel, sergeant, sir.' 'That I can see,' he asked, giving it a kick, 'but what's in it?' 'How should I know, sergeant, sir?' 'Well, then,' he said, 'push it back to the village hall!' What else could I do? I pushed it back.

"By the time I got there, the Hungarian was already there. He was sweating like a pig. 'Listen, Kinya,' he whispered, 'we're in trouble, be careful what you say!' 'What should I say?' I asked quietly. 'Tell them that this was the only parcel you took for me. We'll take care of it.' He winked. 'Alright,' I said. *Just don't let your hands tremble,* I thought to myself.

[84] he said

Well, they made the Hungarian open the parcel, and guess what was in it? I swear to God's holy precious red blood, it was a scorched pig. Well, Kinya, I told myself, looking at the precious meat, you weren't in your right mind; you could have fed all the kids with all your honesty.'

"'How many parcels did you take for him?' the gendarme asked me. 'One, sergeant, sir. I've never done anything like this before.' 'Then take off one of your sandals.' Ahay Devla, I was overcome with mortal fear. I figured that if I say one more, maybe he wouldn't hurt me. 'Come to think of it, sergeant, sir, I took two.' 'Two?' he scowled at me, and even held up two fingers. 'Alright,' he said, and he took the billy club off the wall. 'Take off your other sandal.' I might as well say three, I thought; I only had two sandals. They'll get the Hungarian to take off one of his boots, and then there'll be three. Do you think they did? No. They flogged the soles of my feet until they were swollen, and all he did was sign the report. That happened in the fall; the big trial was today." It looked as if she'd burst into tears.

"Why did they let you go, Kinya?"

"Who knows the habits of these people, son? Perhaps if I hadn't told off the judge, they wouldn't have. But dear God gave me courage. When he then said, 'Three months, suspended'—those were his exact words—I got really mad. If I'd had a drop of brandy in me, there wouldn't be any skin left on his face. I said, 'You want to lock me up for three months? Me, who's sent five sons to the war? How could I have known what was in the parcel when I'm just a flat-footed woman?'

"The judge was shocked, I'm telling you. 'You're flat-footed?' he said, and hit me over the head with the big book. 'That's me, if you please, flat-footed, because I never went to school for even a minute.' You know me, when the devil gets into me, I wouldn't even mind if they split me in two right there and then. Well, they chased me out. Can a Gypsy get justice anywhere?"

Papa's eyes were filled with tears from laughing.

"You said you were flat-footed, Kinya?"

"What else could I have said when I never went to school?"

"Terrible!" I said disapprovingly. "To say such a thing in court! God has blessed you with great courage."

"You mean me? I don't mind if my head touches the sky; I always say what I want to say." However, Kinya's eyes didn't reveal pride, but suspicion.

"It's your fault," I replied. "There's nothing that can be done about it. You'll be lucky to get away with this much; flat-footed people are usually burned."

"Aren't I miserable enough?" Kinya looked at Papa, who burst out laughing.

"Your father's gone mad," she said, clapping her hands.

"What are you laughing at?" I asked Papa, my face pale with anger.

"This fool," he said, wiping his eyes. "She's frightened the whole world!"

"She's not one to frighten the world," I said. "The world is frightening us."

Kinya wrung her hands in despair. Meanwhile the hut had become jam-packed, and all eyes were on me.

Papa nodded ruefully, his eyes downcast; my words seemed to have struck home. The people waited anxiously for what I was going to say.

"Who remembers the time when the river broke its banks?"

Shedding their tension, they shrugged their shoulders and blinked at each other.

"I remember, son," said Grandma Korri, still staring at the fire.

"And what happened in the days before?"

Korri racked her brains, the wrinkles on her forehead becoming even deeper.

"Something pretty important happened then," I said.

"Your mother was pregnant with you at the time," Papa interjected.

"Yes, but our elders have seen far more interesting things."

"Who the hell remembers, son? They drove us out to the floods. The only thing that comes to mind about our old Paris are the voles."

"That's exactly it."

"Now I know!" said Grandma Korri, her face lighting up. "I remember as if it had happened yesterday." She began stoking the fire to give her time to collect her thoughts. Everyone listened to Grandma Korri. "I'll never forget it; it happened exactly on Christmas, which was on a Saturday. Your father is right: all the able-bodied men were driven out to the water; only the children and women were left at home."

She smiled. "Hmm. . . . The world was different then. We cooked and baked for the holiday. Wherever you went at that time, there was no shortage of food anywhere. But as soon as we brought some food home from the village we had to eat it then and there, because the voles would snatch it right out of our hands. It was a great scourge; if we dared leave the dead alone for a second, the voles chewed off their noses and ears. At night, the women kept their babies under their bellies, and during the day the bigger children kept guard over them with sticks.

"We sure suffered a lot on account of them; the voles made a mess of our huts and chased us out." Grandma Korri clasped her hands in prayer. "But then, suddenly, and I lick God's merciful wounds if it isn't so, they fled in droves, wailing and screaming, toward the pasture, carrying their babies in their mouths. Not a single one remained in any of the huts. The Gypsies fell on their knees and gave thanks to Baby Jesus for having freed us from the voles."

She paused. "But that night, just like the voles, we too left wailing and screaming, wading in knee-deep water and carrying our children on our backs; we left our huts as the flood waters poured in. That's how it was. God feared more for the voles than for us, so he warned them beforehand. It wasn't until spring that we were able to dig out our few belongings from the mud. Most of it had rotted away by then."

"Animals can sense danger ahead, Korri," said Kinya with a sigh, "while we only realize it when it's upon us." Kinya looked at me. "Why is that, Gypsy child?"

"Because, Kinya," I said, "we're flat-footed in our heads. But who knows, maybe you too sense some big disaster like the voles, and that's why you're wailing."

"Look at that Gypsy boy!" she said, her eyes darting around for help. "Do you think I'm wailing for nothing, boy? Or do I sense a flood?"

"Just go on wailing, old Kinya. See how Papa is wailing, as are the other very important Gypsies who are known far and wide for their courage and wisdom?"

"Wailing? He's laughing."

"Only you see it that way, Kinya. He's crying, because he has looked back in time, and from his grandfather's stories he sees the past together with the bleak future. Everyone is crying, because they can clearly see that nowadays there's hardly a difference between being hanged and going to jail-only that in one case you die and in the other you become a living corpse."

Kinya kept staring with uncomprehending eyes.

"I don't understand, son," she said, hitting her head.

"Don't worry, Kinya, nothing will get worse. They're not going to hang you; you were sentenced to three months, and even that was suspended so they don't have to feed you. You'll hang yourself soon enough, anyway, when you can no longer bear to see your grandchildren starving. Beggars are not supported by alms, but by their crutches, and if even those are taken from them, they perish."

I talked a lot, and the others mostly just nodded quietly, sadly. Some of them recalled happy memories, but all of them added, at the end: at least the time when the Hungarians were living well has passed, but what can now be done, now that *everyone* is crying?

Gradually they came to realize that our world was attached to another world, and if the sky above both worlds clouded over, we would be flooded and have to flee like voles. Even God would find it easiest just to say amen to our foreboding, because not even he could change our situation.

Billat hanged himself by the morning; he wasn't able to watch his children go hungry. We were still asleep when his younger son ran over to us.

"Come, my father is dead."

All we could do was to cut the rope. Fortunately, he hadn't taken part in last night's conversation; he was one of those musicians who spent all night in the pub.

Whether out of fear or grief, Papa led one of the horses out of the stable.

"Kill it," he said to me, "don't let us all die of hunger."

Among us, compiling a collection of colorful suicide stories would have been pointless; people were terrified even of natural death, which they always greeted as if they were seeing it for the first time. So Billat's suicide caused as little consternation as did the fact that the horse was beaten to death without a second thought.

The weather shaped people and morals alike. Merry spring evenings stretched into never-ending vigils; death still lurked at every door. It was good that winter was over, but spring had yet to bring enough flowers even for a wreath. Its frosty, biting nights kept the landscape denuded, and if we still harbored the slightest hope of revival, it was blown away by the winds of Lent.

The only days that gave us some relief were the ones when the mailman didn't show up, because all he ever brought were either death notices or draft calls.

What *could* he have brought? Where the letters came from, the men weren't celebrating harvest feasts.

Poor Grandma Korri could barely crawl to the village each morning to beg. Borshochka's pregnancy became more visible by the day, and even if we could otherwise make do with one or two bushes of scurvy grass, we couldn't now feed her only on that. In the early dawns we dug around in the gardens, but where at other times we once found an occasional potato or some edible seeds, this year not even a blade of grass was growing. True, on some fine days that spring we managed to empty the estate's sowing machines of their hemp seeds while the farmhands were on lunch break. Afterward we again resorted to the scurvy grass.

The medical officer and the gendarmes visited us almost daily, the former looking for lice, the latter for culprits. As regards the lice, the authorities shaved our heads with amazing diligence. We were already sick; now we became bald.

There was uncontrollable green excrement all over the place, a consequence of our scurvy-grass diet. Therefore, on the advice of Dr. Bocz, one morning a medical detachment occupied the settlement accompanied by a large number of gendarmes and soldiers. All of us were vaccinated against typhoid. For days we were overcome by high fever, losing what little strength we still had; it made foraging for food almost impossible. One morning, poor Grandma Korri, God rest her soul, beckoned us to her side. She held onto Borshochka's hand for a long time, tears running down her face, which was flushed with fever as she made me promise:

"Look after my Borshochka and yourself too," she said, barely at a whisper. "If it's a girl, that'll be good."

At my solemn assent she closed her eyes with peaceful serenity, as though everything in her life had happened as she had wished. We felt sorry for Grandma Korri, but by then we'd become so used to death that we were sorrier about her no longer going to the village to beg.

Each day Papa berated the Gypsies with renewed fury for not letting him slaughter his horse. However, their pleas mellowed him, and he had to admit that no one should go on foot to his or her own funeral.

After examining a number of people to determine the cause of death, Dr. Bocz came to the conclusion that the mass deaths of the elders were not caused by typhoid. Their completely debilitated bodies couldn't stand up to the sudden high fever, but those who survived came out of it hale and healthy.

Necessity had turned us into a singular species of herbivores, and therefore the color of our feces didn't change. We couldn't shit yellow, after all, if we ate green plants. Despite the authorities' protests, Dr. Bocz lifted the quarantine on the settlement.

Not that we became any happier. No Gypsy could set foot in a single house in the village. The storekeepers touched our money only with paper, since they didn't wish to catch the disease. Rumor among the Hungarian villagers had it that the mad doctor was set on exterminating all of them—that he had in fact inoculated the Gypsies with typhoid fever, and had now set the Gypsies loose on the village.

The gendarmerie assured control of disease in the village. Those of us who still valued our skins steered clear of all the houses. Instead we contented ourselves by plying the craft of fishing, lurking between the reeds. The ancient gods of rivers and meadows were gracious to us, and offered everything they had. All we had to do was find it. We raided birds' nests for their eggs, denuded the region of all edible wild plants, and the fish fell victim to our stomachs before they even had a chance to spawn.

Papa aged at least ten years in a matter of months.

"Leave this place, son," he kept begging me. "The Botoshes will take you across the border to Romania. You'll save your wife's life."

"And you?"

"Not everyone can leave, son, and we can still make do, but your wife is bound to die. Go—at least you'll travel all over the world with Fardi's sons."

"The world?" I replied with a smile. "You know as well as I do that there's a war everywhere in the world. Where can I go when we can leave the settlement only at night, and even then only by escaping?"

Papa burst into tears. Later, he tried once more to persuade me to flee, but then he realized there was no point. The gendarmes registered us and checked on us daily. Dr. Bocz didn't know what to do with us, so he had the settlement quarantined again, and on that basis tried to wheedle some food out of the authorities. All we got was a cartful of lime.

Every ostensible attempt on his part to help us was to our disadvantage; in the end even the priest no longer attended our funerals.

"You see, Boncza," said the people, reproaching Papa for his earlier ravings, "it's just as well we didn't slaughter the horse; our dead would be rotting here among us. Even so, the villagers think we're burying dogs."

Thulo[85]—who no longer looked anything like his name, because all you could see of his now scrawny face was his pointy mustache—approached me on the way to one of the funerals.

"Listen, brother," he whispered mysteriously, "you know, all my life I used to stand next to the priest when the old bastard still came to the funerals."

I never took any notice of who was next to whom on those occasions, so I had to accept Thulo's claim. I waited to hear what he was getting at. For a long time he was silent, though, only kicking at the clods of earth on the road with his hooked stick.

"I want to preach."

At first I scrutinized him suspiciously. Thulo smiled.

"You think I'm crazy?"

"No, not at all," I said by way of begging of forgiveness.

"It wouldn't be surprising even if you did. After all this grief"—he pointed to the rattling cart—"nothing would be a shame. But you know, I thought, to hell with grieving, we'll all end up like this. What's the use of being sad?"

He looked in the direction of the homemade coffin at the particular funeral we were attending. "These folks have gotten rid of all their worries. Then why weep? Or should we envy them?" He paused. "Let them see from up there," he said, holding his shepherd's crook toward the sky, "that we are glad about it."

I didn't understand who he wanted to please with our cheerfulness, but Thulo wasn't bothered about that.

---

[85] fat

"How does it go? 'Our Father or whatever, who art . . .'?" he said.

"My dear Thulo, what on earth were you doing while standing next to the priest all these times? Not paying attention, that's what."

"Listen, Gypsy boy, do you think I understood what he was gabbing about? Just teach me the beginning; I know the ending, it's 'Amen.'"

All the way to the cemetery, Thulo kept parroting the first line of the Lord's Prayer. Meanwhile he was silently doing a voice test, and smiled at my appreciative nods.

"How should I quiet them down if they're making too much noise?" he asked, poking me in the ribs.

"Raise your hand, like the priest does."

"That's not good enough. If they're chattering away you can lift God himself down from the heavens but they won't listen to you."

"You'll put them in their place."

"No, no," said Thulo, shaking his head. "Something is still missing from the beginning, from before the prayer."

"My brethren in the Lord," I guessed.

"That's it! To hell with that bleary-eyed priest," he said, cheering up. "I won't forget it."

Thulo's lips moved at every step we took, and he cleared his throat before we even entered the graveyard. It seemed he would begin his sermon there and then, but he got a hold of himself in time.

In our world, everyone is a relative of the deceased; thus it is fitting for all of us to lament equally, at least until the sound of the clods of earth being thrown on the coffin ceases. Leaning on his crook, Thulo waited patiently at the head of the grave. The creaking rumble of the makeshift wooden crate wiped the stage fright off his face. There was no getting used to this sound. Meanwhile everyone kept wailing, moaning, and crying. But then, in accord with old liturgical rituals, the shower of earth stopped and with that, the lamentations too died down.

"My brethren into the grave!" Thulo cried out. He raised his arms to the sky, together with his shepherd's crook. He looked around at the people. Not all of them were Gypsies. In spite of the typhoid rumors, there were always some curious old ladies from the village who came to gape at our funerals.

"Let us pray!" called Thulo upon the gathering. He waited until they came closer and, lowering his crook, struck up with sublime piety.

"*Amaro Del kon san ando cheri?*"[86] He paused, waiting for a reply to his question, but since all he heard were terrestrial sighs, he continued in the same tone.

"*Sas, kay naysas, zhanel O Del kana, sas yekvar, yek rom, tay yek beng.*"[87]

It would be impossible to understate the surprise reflected in the Gypsies' eyes.

"Holy Christ!" someone whispered. "Listen to this. Thulo is telling a story to God in Romani!" They looked at him and at the bystanders, but when they saw the old ladies from the village-their hands clasped in prayer and not understanding a word he said—they relented and listened to Thulo's story with stifled smiles.

"You see," he asked—having just said "and they lived happily ever after"—"what do we need a priest for? At least you folks understood this story, and they"—he pointed to the old Hungarian ladies—"they're praying for themselves, anyway."

The next time there was a funeral, the priest no longer objected to attending, apparently worried about competition from the pleasant-sounding Gypsy priest.

Episodes such as the one involving Thulo brought us cheer only for a bit. Real pleasure and laughter is possible only if your belly is full or if there is a prospect of filling it.

Every evening, Borshochka pushed her breast into my mouth.

"Go on, suck on it," she said. "You'll see, there'll be some milk. When I had my Nanika, I had as much milk as a cow."

---

[86] Our Father, are you in heaven?

[87] Once upon a time, God knows where, there was a Gypsy and a devil.

I smiled at Borshochka's childish goodwill; if nothing else, I fell asleep while nursing. I often woke up struggling and groaning as she stuffed her bloated bosom back between my lips.

"Did I cry?" I asked.

"No, you just let go of it," she grumbled. I didn't protest; at least this way I could refuse the morsels she would have wanted to give me. I was worried. Most of the Gypsy women miscarried, and the slightest illness brought death.

"Are you alright?" I kept asking her.

"Of course I'm alright, silly," she said, pulling me to herself. I pretended that I was filled with infinite paternal happiness, lest the idea of abortion enter her mind. I embraced Borshochka's lean ribs; the thought of summer gave me some hope that I only lost again minutes later.

Summer was indeed still far away.

Only the sighs welling up from us betrayed our feigned sleep; we hid our anxieties from each other. No longer did anyone presage anything. We were already living in the cruel future whose sufferings stretched into the unforeseeable distance.

The vicious actions of the cursing, threatening gendarmes made everything uncertain that hadn't already disappeared on its own.

We longed for and feared tomorrow; the trepidation of the minutes bound us together, and anyone who slipped out of the pack had no way of returning. Even the most cunning Gypsy stratagems failed. No one wanted to escape, hide, or malinger, and if someone was summoned by the authorities, he showed up, resigning himself to his fate to save the others.

Not that it saved them.

Papa couldn't accept my obstinacy. He pretended that he had given up all attempts, but secretly he was hatching a plan.

"The Botosh family will be here next week," he informed me.

"Have they gone crazy?" I asked, startled. "If they set foot in here, they won't get out alive.

"Don't you worry about them; they know what's what."

I looked suspiciously at Papa. A day earlier, a well-dressed peasant ventured into the settlement to have a look at his horse.

"Who was that man who came by yesterday?" I asked.

"The poundmaster from Szalonta," said Papa, trying to clear up matters. "He came with official papers. Otherwise I wouldn't have talked to him. I don't want any more trouble."

"And?" I looked at him askance. Papa tried to furrow his brows angrily, but gave up.

"The Botoshes have sent him," he confessed. "You have to go, or I'll hang myself."

"Don't cry, Papa, or I'll go crazy," I told him firmly.

"Do you think your mother and I are not going crazy," he erupted with real fury, "when you're being tortured daily in front of my own eyes? Haven't you got the least bit of pity for your pregnant wife? What can you do for her here?" Appealing to my conscience, he added, "Think at least of your own child."

"When are they coming?"

"On Friday," he said, blowing out his anger with a big breath.

"They've chosen a pretty unlucky day."

"They couldn't care less about superstitions when there's trouble. If there was a market earlier, they would come sooner; you'll blend in with the Romanians."

"We'll send Borshochka."

"How about you?" he looked startled. "Do you think she'll go without you?"

"It's easier for me to follow them when she's already safe, but if they catch us together, they won't show her any mercy, either."

Papa mulled over what I had just proposed.

"You're not trying to pull one over on me?" he asked, suspiciously.

"Why would I do that if Borshochka leaves?" It was easier for me to feign anger than for him, so I added, "You'd do better to think about your daughters too."

"My daughters!" he sneered at my concern. "Your mother wouldn't let the little one go, and you needn't worry about the big ones. Each of them has her patron saint. Do you think Petrush is risking his head for himself? He filches food from the soldiers' bread bags so your little sister won't go hungry."

At first Borshochka protested with all her might, crying and threatening, because she figured I'd gotten myself another woman. It took all of Papa's and Mama's powers of persuasion to finally convince her to go.

Not only were the Botoshes careful not to expose themselves to the betrayal of daylight, but they knocked on our door at the crack of dawn two days before the arranged time. We said our goodbyes in haste; they told me where to find them, and then they disappeared just as unobtrusively as they had arrived. Even the Gypsies didn't notice.

We managed to keep Borshochka's absence secret for one day, but that was enough; by then she and the Botoshes had gotten far enough for comfort. We expected far more retribution than the minor scolding we got. I sighed with relief and was happy that Borshochka's fate had been resolved, but without her the nights felt lonely and empty.

It doesn't matter, I thought to myself, *I'll get used to it and, anyway, it can't get any worse.*

On the morning of the Friday we'd originally planned for Borshochka's escape, the gendarmes once again galloped into the settlement. They drove us out of our huts sleepy, unkempt, and unwashed. We examined each other dumbly, numbly; some of us resembled our old selves only by the wrinkles etched into our faces by constant worry.

Dr. Bocz had already given up all his experiments. No longer his yelling, crazy, motorbike-Hussar self, he became taciturn and aloof. "What am I supposed to prescribe?" he would ask if we approached him with some request. "You're hungry, that's what ails you. It'll all be over soon," he comforted us impassively.

As they herded us out to the pasture that morning, it did seem that everything was over. Still, we managed to get away more or less intact from the early wake-up call when compared to previous such encounters. There were hardly any rifle-butt blows on selected bony spines, and the gendarmes even took care to avoid any of us developing a limp or, God forbid, getting bloodied. We didn't know what to make of their behavior.

Perhaps it was the good weather, we speculated. Incongruous, sarcastic grimaces flitted below their gruff, spiked mustaches, and their constant guffawing cheered us up no end. We didn't notice the malevolent way they scrutinized our emaciated bodies from under their rooster-feathered headgear. Long lines of our multicolored, ragged band of Gypsies traversed the pasture.

We stood silently, our thoughts wandering, as the May sun stung our faces with its warm rays. On other such occasions it didn't matter where any of us was standing; the punches and kicks reached everyone. Now we had to line up strictly by family, the father standing to the right, the mother to his left, and next to her, the children in order of age or size.

The yelling didn't alarm us, nor did the regular policemen, who, busying themselves next to the gendarmes, used the flat side of their swords to thrash those falling out of line. We didn't know what we were waiting for; we just stood there patiently.

As time passed, the tension eased. Had they wanted it, we would have been squirming on the ground as usual, and what else could befall us apart from beatings? That was what encouraged some people with weaker bladders to hold up their hands, asking for permission to step aside. No one would have dared to do that earlier in the morning.

Unfortunately, the unanswered calls of nature rapidly became an intolerable burden; everyone was moving and hissing. The gendarmes had fun witnessing the comical scene, pretending not to see the upraised hands, because for us to speak up without being asked would have been cause enough for them to lose their "infinite patience."

All of us tried to hold back the call of nature. We still felt like human beings; parents didn't want to become animals in front of their children, and vice versa. However, there are things you just can't resist or, at least, it takes superhuman strength to do so. In the damp, naked world of the huts kidney problems were rampant, and bladders didn't brook delay.

It seemed that hours had passed by the time the gendarmerie commander deigned to take note of the buzzing, hopping lines. By then, not even the blows of the policemen did any good.

"What's all the commotion about?" he asked in a stentorian voice. "Are you perhaps itching for trouble?"

"We need to piss," the people shouted in unison.

"Well, well, do you have any other wishes? You dirty bunch. Why, you'd be capable of fouling the lawn."

"We *have to,* sergeant, sir," someone hissed as others, likewise shaking, concurred.

"Women and children take two steps back," the commander shouted, "but only number one! I'll make her eat it if someone drops a package! Men, stand at attention! To hell with this impatient mob!"

We stiffened, the commotion died down, and only the children stepped back; the women didn't move, but looked into the distance blushing with shame. Tense silence reigned, and on the commander's signal the gendarmes walked with majestic strides between us, poking the barefoot ankles back into line with their boots. Wherever they sensed any movement, they motioned us to silence with a quiet blow, so that the commander's militant, cracking words could clearly be heard.

"Who has to relieve himself?" he asked ominously. "Out with your tools, and get on with it! Swine!" He didn't mince words.

Stern silence followed. Apparently, our joy was premature.

"None of you?" he said, moderating his voice. "So be it. But if I see anyone with wet pants or if anyone comes forward with such a request again, I'll beat it off together with your flesh."

We had no reason to doubt his threat. Here and there a few faint moans caused by kidney cramps could still be heard, but the quick cracks of rifle butts and swords soon suppressed them.

Time crept slowly, and the rays of the blazing sun shone through our bloodless ears. We supported our cramp-ridden, numb lower bodies by transfixing our eyes to the ground.

It must have been around ten in the morning; we could hear crickets chirping on the pasture. We breathed in unison as if on command. It felt as if our efforts made the air tremble and grow by the minute into a deep rumble. Heavy bombers flew high above us, accompanied by frisky fighters well below them.

"Take cover!" shouted the gendarmerie commander. We ran in all directions, the men away from the women, sprawling on the fresh spring grass and—with the faint rustling of the cause of our cramping pains—we sent our unadulterated gratitude toward the tiny glowing, shiny dots high above us. We lay there with relieved sighs, indifferent to the gendarmes, who had dug themselves into the earth with their bayonets and rooster-feathered hats under their stomachs.

We didn't want to escape, believing that today's lesson was over. However, the receding buzz of the planes slowly shook us out of our dreams, and hearing the crackling commands, we stood in line again with lighter bodies but still with heavy hearts.

Unable to confirm our forbidden acts, the gendarmes could only force our blighted army to go on playing this waiting game. The little joy that had slunk among us after our relief would have found room in a niche of our souls, had not the soft, approaching rattle of the village government carriages scared it away.

Now we understand the reason for us having to wait. Dr. Bocz got off one of the carriages with two bespectacled gentlemen. They must have been some sort of VIPs, because the gendarmes snapped to attention before them. They didn't say a thing, but just looked at us from the distance until the village clerk's carriage also arrived.

"Vaccinations again!" whispered the Gypsies.

Maybe, I thought, though we'd become accustomed to white-coated people performing medical procedures. Then again, what difference did it make what this was all about? We'd die either way. There was no longer a body among us that could survive another typhoid vaccination. The alarm altered our prescribed rows, and the gendarmes wanted to correct, but the civilians stopped them. Next the village clerk arrived with two unidentified gentlemen, followed by all the typists from the bread coupon office.

Ahay Devla,[88] *what's happening here?*

We were full of apprehension. From one moment to the next, our thoughts veered from fear to joy, from one extreme to the other. The gentlemen who'd just arrived were still deliberating or else they were waiting for someone; they weren't pressed for time.

"Perhaps they'll give us extra bread coupons?" someone muttered, and the gossip spread fast. But the next minute we thought of something different, something quite the opposite; namely, that they would revoke the coupons from everyone, because some of us had sold the ones we had? They had done it before.

We comforted ourselves with these and similar words: "To hell with it. So we'll eat a handful of corn flour less. What good are coupons to us anyway? Without money, they won't give us anything for them. It won't make any difference."

But as soon as the district health officer appeared, we dismissed the bread coupon idea. We looked at one another with frightened eyes; there was no doubt now that they would vaccinate us. Terrified, Papa winked at me.

"Let them give it into your arm," he warned me as my sister gave me a reassuring glance, "it's easier to suck it out of there." That was how it was done with snake bites, I knew, except that I didn't know of anyone who was still alive thanks to it.

Wherever I looked, I saw faces contorted by fear. It was enough to set eyes on the obese frame of the district doctor to remember the

---

[88] Oh my God

vaccinations. *Maybe God had sent the planes,* I thought, *because had they not come, nobody's pants would still be dry.*

If only they'd come again! We kept looking in awe at the storks circling high above us.

My poor little Borshochka, I'm so happy you've gone.

Dr. Bocz stepped closer to us.

"Listen to me, everyone," he began in a loud voice. "When someone is called, he'll come and stand here together with his family." He showed us the exact spot. The carriage with the young women in it came closer; one of the policemen climbed up beside the coachman and loudly relayed the message.

Our turn came after the first few families. We stopped in front of the gentlemen; without a word the gendarmerie commander motioned to us to stand up straight. We did. Without being examined, Mama was sent aside, as were the girls, and the two us, Papa and I, were looked over more thoroughly. They did this with all the men. They made us take off our upper garments. *Dear Mother of God.* My heart sank when I saw Papa's skeletal figure. The two doctors seemed to disagree over the two of us. Dr. Bocz insisted that Papa was sickly; in fact, he said, the whole family had tuberculosis, and he pointed at me to prove it.

"I've been treating him since he was a little boy," he said, tapping my back. "It's hereditary."

We couldn't take part in the negotiations, but it was like seeing a horsetrader at work. All that we could manage to gather so far was that the people were being sorted into two groups—the stronger in one, the weaker in the other.

"Show your tongue!" the district doctor shouted at Papa. When he did as he was told, it almost reached his stomach.

"Yuck!" he said, turning in disgust to Dr. Bocz. "He isn't normal." We had to quickly pick up our rags and move on before he could express his revulsion in some other way.

We kept trying to figure out what they wanted, not that we had been doing anything else so far. By now we were more concerned with Dr.

Bocz's behavior, which was decidedly worrying. We saw that the stronger men were made to run around in circles as part of the examination.

"Is this a market or conscription?" asked Papa, as if I knew.

"Which one is better?"

"It's all the same."

I think that's how the other Gypsies perceived it, too. When it was their turn, Shimuy carried Petrush on his back before the committee.

"Please doctors, sirs, I ask you respectfully to give this one here a double shot or I'll kill him myself." And with that he threw Petrush down like a dead dog.

"I'm an old, sick man, yet I have to lug him everywhere; that's no life for him." He threw up his hands in despair.

"Get him away from here, you old swine," the district doctor barked, "or I'll tear out your mustache."

Shimuy pulled Petrush to us by his feet.

"We're in trouble," he gasped. "They're drafting soldiers."

So it seems, I thought.

"Did you see how the gendarmes are standing before those people?" asked Shimuy, pulling up his eyebrows meaningfully. "They're not just anybodies. But I sure am an old fox."

Indeed, Shimuy had played his part perfectly; one could almost say that his performance elicited envy from the other Gypsies. But then, our kind didn't have to look far for cunning. When called upon to make use of their talent, they aimed at perfection with heart and soul. And here it certainly appeared that there was a big need for it. The anxiety of being the pick of the bunch and separated from one's family surpassed anything felt before. Some men in the so-far unexamined rows fainted, and had to be dragged before the committee trembling and soaked in urine, as if they had had a stroke.

The examination slowed down considerably. Making use of the village's carriages, the gendarmerie commander sent half his men on lunch break. Those remaining kept walking between our selected teams, strictly isolating us from each other, lest the two groups mingle.

Eventually it was late afternoon, and it was obvious that the gendarmes were getting truly bored. They nervously shook their rifles, looking for any opportunity to repay us for their lost afternoon rest. And if they were looking for something, they certainly didn't waste time finding it.

As for us, we stood and waited patiently, and it didn't ruffle our feathers even when—despite his perfect playacting—one of the malingerers was sent to the "strong" group. None of us would have been able to guess the better option. No longer did we dare rely on our sixth sense; it had let us down too often lately, after all. Weary from the effort, we let matters take their course. That's what the gentlemen must have concluded as well.

As soon as the two bespectacled civilians left, though, the gendarmes changed their method. They lined up the remaining people, pointed at one or the other, no matter who looked healthy or who was in fact dying, and the young ladies noted their names.

"So there!" said one of the gendarmes, rubbing his hands together. After the long, tiring hours everything now came to order, and the gendarmes quickly subdued the two groups. While the gentlemen discussed the next steps, the gendarmes rid us of the day's languor. The chief clerk, who had so far kept out of the limelight, had himself driven in front of the groups to speak from the carriage.

"Listen to me, please! We have divided you into two groups. We know it's not easy to be separated from your families, but we have to admit that there is a war on, and the country is badly in need of workers. You will be going to two different places to work, but the time will come when you will meet up again."

The last words didn't reach our consciousness. "To work," coming from the mouth of the village clerk, seemed like some fairytale! Colorful, clean, bright images moved into our sooty, smoky minds-pictures of a coveted life. To work, to eat, to be free? Only the Almighty could create such beautiful music. Blessed be his holy name!

Even the little children shouted: "Hurrah, hurrah!" The clerk stopped his speech and watched in amazement as the women fell to their knees and crept closer to the carriage with their infants in their arms.

"Let the highest honors gird you on your exalted seat!" droned one and then others, too, a look of sincere devotion radiating from their eyes.

The village clerk looked around in surprise, not quite sure on whom this great honor was being bestowed. Still, he acknowledged it with a modest nod and continued his speech.

"Tomorrow you will get on a train and you will be taken to your workplaces. You have to realize like everyone else that in the event of a war, military law applies to all, so be aware that it refers to you too. Don't take anything with you apart from clothing; you'll be given everything there. The young ladies will give you three days worth of extra bread coupons, which should last until you reach your destination."

The girls worked very fast, and by the time the chief clerk had finished what he had to say, they were almost finished with everything. Those in the stronger lot received double extra coupons, so everyone was happy. Some of them squealed and danced from joy, and we ambled back to the settlement in cheerful groups. Who cared any more that some of the gendarmes still walked about at the perimeter of the settlement? Let them rot wherever they are; tomorrow we'd be rid of them.

"Slaughter the horse, Boncza!" the Gypsies demanded. "Let's eat and drink; we've had enough of starving. If anyone still wants to die, let him walk to the cemetery on his own two feet."

How little was needed here for happiness! One word was enough for the people to start rebuilding the forever-collapsing sandcastles of their daydreams and will to live. So far only one word had been uttered; an empty, ambiguous word, far from reality, yet their imaginations had already produced sky-high mountains of bacon that they practically tasted amid the thundering beat of wild horses' hooves.

The old high spirits of earlier times moved back, and our Gypsy Paris spewed out lively music that could be heard from far away. The smell of roast and cooked horse meat awakened in the little bees the dormant desire for creation, and they sowed their fertile pollen into the callow as well as fading petals.

Fate, you are incredible! You crush our nothingness into heaps of corpses with your honeyed cruelty; you inundate our world—time-worn from mourning and bitterness—with pain and suffering, only to sweeten the moments with a single word.

"It was a pity to send Borshochka away," Papa sighed with regret. "She could have stayed with the children and at least she would be able to have the baby with the help of your mother."

"There's still time," I consoled him. "We can always send her a message or I can go and pick her up."

"First you have to regain your strength," he lectured me.

You too, I thought with a pang in my heart. We'd been huddling against the cold even since the weather had turned better. Now I understand why Papa never took off his tattered overcoat. He was cold. His good old talkative mood now returned, though he himself hadn't eaten any of the horse meat.

I nodded at Papa's benevolent admonitions. Who would have known better what military law meant? He who had heroically fought in a war and had experienced lots of good and evil. And then there I was, no longer a fancy high school student. With my disheveled, unwashed, ragged looks I too had been sent to the rawboned pack.

A single collective thought kept us going: *Survive!* There was no room for anything else. Here, common sense, desires, daydreams, and humanity had become fossilized. The sullen growl of two stones ground us into animals, and we dripped through its meshed sieve like worms.

Mama packed feverishly, attributing significance to every piece of junk.

"We'll need this, too," she kept repeating, looking angrily at Papa when he objected to something. "You always complain if you're missing something." She too quickly forgot what had never been, even though we hadn't seen anything of the happy future as yet.

"We have to set fire to the straw in the morning," she said, kicking the messy chaff on the floor, "or else the fleas will eat you when you come home."

"Yes, sir, sergeant, sir!" said Papa, standing at attention.

I left them to their light-hearted nagging and walked around the humming settlement. It was only evening; early and late merged as we waited timelessly for tomorrow. Fear was trapped outside the huts' covered windows; inside, in the low glow of candlelight, bronze-colored good cheer showed its white teeth, belching its thoughts, dreaming the future aloud.

"Are we going far?" asked one of the men in a hut I'd stopped in as he and the others picked their teeth.

"Yes," answered another.

"Why," said a third, "even on foot we could go far in three days."

Measuring the distance between their home and the hidden future, they contentedly wiped their greasy fingers in the women's skirts.

"With a full stomach, nothing is far."

"You're right," I conceded. "Then death is just sad, but if you're hungry, even birth is mournful."

"Birth, death?" came a voice. "Who needs them? To live is the only important thing. Because there's nothing more beautiful than life . . . if it is beautiful."

The past had already vanished in the blind alleys of their finite brains. They were roaming the unknown highways of a promising future where horses munched fresh green grass, forgetting that it was they who had eaten grass not that long ago.

Petrush had meanwhile teamed up with my sister. "Why should we postpone it?" they asked. "The Gypsies would only gossip if they saw us lying next to each other."

"And, brother, I am so good at hoeing," Petrush boasted, "that I challenge anyone to do better." I didn't know why he said it, but it didn't hurt to have someone in the family who could hoe well. I was fond of Petrush. His thoughts and actions remained lopsided; and he himself was a mystery who never knew what he was doing, let alone what he wanted; but luck seemed to have stuck to him somehow, or else he would have been lost already.

"Have you eaten, child?" he asked me loudly.

"I have."

"Well, then, I'll tell you a story."

Before Petrush could start, though, my sister dragged him away by the collar. I guessed that the quick wedding had alarmed her; surely it was not her charm that had won him over, no, I'd swear to that. But if happiness is a gift horse, why look at it in the mouth?

The noise died down by dawn. Wherever sleep overcame them, people stretched out on the dusty straw litters; even the ceaseless croaking of their bowels didn't bother them as it used to. The tightly packed grumpy frog of hunger slept with them.

My own thoughts wandered for a while yet, and then they merged wearily into the big, general silence. Once in awhile I woke up with a start at the unfriendly growls of the dogs, but the truncated night flew by relatively fast. Some of the Gypsies were already on stand-by early in the morning, their bundles all tied up; they didn't want the horse meat to run out at home.

The day began quickly. Rubbing their noses and eyes, toddlers demanded breakfast, and if one of them saw another with a bigger piece of bread, they went at each other screaming or threw a tantrum until they somehow got their fair share. The bigger ones kept frolicking around the fire; here and there you could hear a parental slap, elsewhere family squabbles found their rightful place in the settlement's natural order.

The girls were already preening themselves, while the boys were still sleepily scratching themselves, yawning, and gauging the position of the sun. Only the elderly sunned themselves beside the flames of the blazing straw, relating their dreams or desires. Mama was neither happy nor sad that a new member had joined the family; she forced me to eat up just as gruffly and aggressively as she did when there was in fact something to eat.

"Why aren't you offering some to your son-in-law?" I asked, trying to teach Mama manners. "Isn't that the custom?"

"My son-in-law has always found what he's wanted up to now; he shouldn't expect to be served from here on in. He has his wife beside him, but who knows where yours is! Eat!" She had tears in her eyes.

I swallowed the tough, red, horse meat without an appetite, and then hightailed it at a suitable moment. The morning bustle began to subside; all of the journeying men had already fixed up their gear, taken it out of their huts; and then, as the fires began to burn themselves out, idleness forced them to think.

"When are we leaving?" they kept asking. They stared at one another, stunned. It was of no use to wrinkle their foreheads and scratch their heads; they were forced to realize that they knew nothing. Frightened, they searched me out from among the young ones, but I looked at them with the same surprised expression as they did at me.

"What if the train has already left?" they asked, scaring each other. Finally, three men took courage in their hands and approached one of the gendarmes walking on the outskirts of the settlement.

"Stop!" yelled the gendarme. "Where are you going?"

"We would like to ask, please," said one of the men as all three removed their caps, "when the train is leaving?"

"Where to?" That was certainly the question. The gendarmes pulled their necks in and stood motionless, as if planted into the ground.

"Get back at once!" one of them shouted.

The Gypsies didn't wait for any more encouragement, but ambled back, dejected.

"Well," they nodded with a sigh. "That pale-faced chief clerk certainly conned us. We've burned the little straw we had, and now we won't even have anything to sleep on. "How foolish we are," they kept repeating to one another. "We don't ask, we don't listen, all we do is fall for what others say. Is there no justice on this earth?" They looked up to the brightly shining sun. "Perhaps they've regretted it and they're taking others instead of us, letting us starve to death here."

They grumbled for a while longer, but then realized that it wouldn't do any good. In the end they tried to drown their bitterness by ridiculing one another.

"Hey there," they mocked Gigi, "we'll see what sort of bacon you put on the skewer to hold over the fire! Be careful not to burn the skewer, though—losing that big slab of bacon would be a shame."

As for Petrush, he got his share of teasing about his talent for hoeing. I don't know what made them think about hoeing; perhaps spring suggested that idea or seeing the fields drowning in weeds.

A commotion now erupted at the edge of the settlement, and Gigi, who had recently left the group in a huff, came running back out of breath, almost overtaking the scared-looking children.

"A regiment of soldiers is coming!" he said, tugging at his hat. For a second everyone's heart skipped a beat, but then we all cheered up at Gigi's unfounded alarm.

"They're taking you away from your wife now, Gigi!" one of the others said, pulling his leg. Indeed, we surrounded the ten-man army unit with cheerful faces. We became somewhat apprehensive only when their leader announced that we should fall in line with our luggage in accord with yesterday's selection.

Before he even read out the list, he drew our attention to the fact that from then on there would only be commands and obedience. The two must always be consistent; otherwise, well, he said, he'd already experienced a stint in Ukraine, and that had cured him of being a sissy.

"Thank God!" said the Gypsies. The squadron leader looked us over and, seeing that we didn't understand, just shrugged.

"Anyway, I want to take this group to its destination without anyone missing. Do we understand each other?"

"God bless you, sir, you're obviously kindhearted."

Everything was completed considerably faster than had been the case the day before. The troops worked in a soldierly manner: they didn't hurt or kick anyone; they opened our bundles and cast aside the pots and pans, odds and ends, and even a few puppies, and by the time we came to our senses, we were already marching on the road to the station.

The strict, military style felt unusual, but recalling the chief clerk's words, we resigned ourselves to it. There was a war on. And then who the hell knew how much things had changed since we'd been cut off from the outside world? For months we'd been forbidden to even go into the village. The little we'd seen or heard certainly hadn't made us any wiser.

So when they locked us into the freshly whitewashed train cars, even the slight anxiety caused by the presence of the soldiers was dispelled. *We'll get rid of them as we got rid of the gendarmes. Just let us work and eat, that's the main thing; it'll work out somehow.* The women grumbled about their pots, but the war veterans calmed them down.

"What on earth do you need pots for where others are cooking? Or do you want to be the cooks?"

"But what will you eat from if there's any food?" They all rebelled at the same time.

Papa shook his head with pity. "It would be a fine thing if the soldiers would take their sooty pots with them! We'll get a mess tin and that's that. What's important is that it's filled to the brim."

"However much they give," the women sighed, "at least they won't chase us around. Who knows how long we would have been able to bear the beatings and the hunger. But our dear God has looked out for us, blessed be his merciful red blood!" And they pulled their sleeping infants gratefully to their arid breasts.

The train's rattle brought everyone back to the world of happy, hopeful daydreams. Unknown landscapes swept past the barbwired wagon windows, and our smiling gazes got stuck in the showering sparks of the chugging engine. Now and then we emptied the piss-filled buckets, lest their fermenting stench interfere with our lofty imaginations.

A NOTE TO THE READER

Written in the 1970s by a Romani author inspired by his own childhood in rural Hungary decades earlier, *The Color of Smoke* is the story of one boy's journey to manhood in a turbulent era—a boy torn between two cultures and living in a subgroup of settled Roma amid the pressures of increasing poverty and persecution. Hence, while some social norms and behaviors in these pages may be familiar to those of Romani descent wherever they may be from, others will not, as they instead reflect the book's particulars, the perspective of its teenage male protagonist; and, last but not least, the author's singular vision not only of his people but also of the human condition that binds us all.

Romani words and phrases occur occasionally in *The Color of Smoke.* Residents of the protagonist's Roma settlement in rural, World War II–era Hungary would have woven Romani into their conversation even when speaking to one another in Hungarian, the country's majority language. Some of them, especially older people, were fluent in Romani; others were familiar enough with it so using some Romani would have come naturally to them.

A language with many dialects, Romani today has some three million native speakers across Europe and the Americas. The dialect at issue in this book is Hungarian Lovari; its particulars are as remembered by the author in the mid-1970s while setting the story in the rural, World War II–era Hungary of his own youth. Given variations from region to region, and in multiple eras, the connotations of certain words (e.g. see *dulmuta* and *phiripe*) may differ notably from those familiar to most speakers of Romani and those found in dictionaries. All Romani terms are footnoted in the first instance, and again only if subsequent instances occur much later in the book. They are italicized after their first occurrence only if necessary for clarity (e.g., *love*—pronounced "low-veh"—which means "money").

Words and terms of particular significance, and those appearing more than once, are listed below.

bater	so be it
bogo	a broken-down, worthless horse; a nag
chache Roma	true Roma
Devla	God
drabarimos	to read someone's palm; tell a fortune for
dulmuta	old tribe, as used metaphorically in this novel. May derive from *do-multano*, an adjective meaning "a long time ago." The word for tribe is otherwise *tsera* in Lovari (plural *tseri*).
engedelmo mangel	beg forgiveness, begging of forgiveness
gadjo	non-Romani (man)
harniko	capable, industrious
kamzhi	rope-woven bullwhip
kris	trial (i.e. before a Romani court), unwritten Romani law, Romani court
lindralo drab	sleep medicine
love	money (pronounced "low-vay")
Petroeshtyo	Peter's clan

phendom	I said
phendyas	he said
phiripe	place traveled (to), as used metaphorically in this novel. Walking or traveling by its standard definition. More commonly used in other dialects/ variations of Romani are *o than areslo* or just *o areslo,* meaning "the place reached"; and *agorimo* or *agoripe,* meaning "the end (of the journey)."
phumba	pus (literally), used in this novel in the pejorative sense of "slimeball," "slimy"
poralo	the feathered one (literally), meaning "gendarme" (as Hungarian gendarmes were known for their feathered caps)
prekaza	misfortune, bad luck
robiya	prison, slavery
Romungritsa	Hungarian Romani woman
Romungro	Hungarian Romani man
thulo	fat
trastya	sack
zhuklano manush	dogman, dogmen (as used interchangeably in this novel). Literally: people who eat dog meat

ALSO AVAILABLE FROM
NEW EUROPE BOOKS

978-0-9825781-8-6

"[G]enuine imagination and an energetic wit."

—***Publishers Weekly***

"An ode to expatriate living, culture clashes, and the heady days of early 1990s Europe, this novel is a manic, wild ride."

—***Booklist***

"A hilarious hallucinatory satire, built on shots of caffeine."

—Amanda Stern,
author of
The Long Haul

978-0-9900043-2-5

"A master class in how to tell a war story."

—***Kirkus Reviews*** **(starred review)**

"To be savored and relished."

—*Library Journal*

ABOUT THE AUTHOR

Photo © Tamás Székely

Menyhért Lakatos (pronounced *Meñ*hayrt *Luk*utoshe) (1926–2007), Hungary's preeminent twentieth-century Romani writer, was the award-winning author of two novels, a novella, five collections of stories, and one volume of poetry, all of which he wrote in Hungarian. After an early career as an engineer and the manager of a brick factory with a Romani workforce, he became a sociologist and one of Hungary's—and Europe's—most important Romani political leaders. In his forties he began publishing fiction. Lakatos's magnum opus, *Füstös képek* (*The Color of Smoke*), first appeared to critical acclaim in 1975, its fifth edition in 2012. It has been published in more than half a dozen languages; in French it appeared as *Couleur de Fumee* (Actes Sud, 1986, 2000); in German, as *Bitterer Rauch* (Deutsche Verlags Anstalt, 1983).

ABOUT THE TRANSLATOR

Ann Major (1928–), who spent her youth in Hungary, is a prominent translator of Hungarian and German books to English, her credits including Paul Lendvai's *The Hungarians: A Thousand Years of Victory in Defeat* and *One Day That Shook the Communist World* and Eugene Thassy's *Risky Region: Memoirs of a Hungarian Righteous Gentile.* The author of an acclaimed memoir, *A Carpet of Jacaranda* (Sydney Jewish Museum, 2013), she earned an MA from Macquarie University, Sydney, and lives in Lane Cove, Australia.

OTHER TITLES

Ballpoint: *A Tale of Genius and Grit, Perilous Times, and the Invention that Changed the Way We Write*
978-0-9825781-1-7

Eastern Europe!: *Everything You Need to Know About the History (and More) of a Region that Shaped Our World and Still Does*
978-0-9850623-2-3

The Essential Guide to Being Hungarian: *50 Facts & Facets of Nationhood*
978-0-9825781-0-0

The Essential Guide to Being Polish: *50 Facts & Facets of Nationhood*
978-0-9850623-0-9

Illegal Liaisons. "A merciless comedy of modern manners and the politics of desire." —*Publishers Weekly*
978-0-9850623-6-1

Petra K and the Blackhearts
978-0-9850623-8-5

Voyage to Kazohinia. A rediscovered classic of dystopian fiction
"Massively entertaining." —Gregory Maguire, author of *Wicked*
978-0-9825781-2-4

The Wild Cats of Piran
978-0-99000-43-0-1

New Europe Books

Williamstown, Massachusetts

Find our titles wherever books are sold,
or visit www.NewEuropeBooks.com for order information.